OPEN CARRY

Center Point
Large Print

**This Large Print Book carries the
Seal of Approval of N.A.V.H.**

OPEN CARRY

An Arliss Cutter Novel

MARC CAMERON

CENTER POINT LARGE PRINT
THORNDIKE, MAINE

This Center Point Large Print edition
is published in the year 2019 by arrangement with
Kensington Publishing Corp.

The text of this Large Print edition is unabridged.
In other aspects, this book may vary
from the original edition.
Printed in the United States of America
on permanent paper.
Set in 16-point Times New Roman type.

ISBN: 978-1-64358-248-1

Library of Congress Cataloging-in-Publication Data

Names: Cameron, Marc, author.
Title: Open carry / Marc Cameron.
Description: Large Print edition. | Thorndike, Maine :
    Center Point Large Print, 2019.
Identifiers: LCCN 2019017042 | ISBN 9781643582481 (hardcover :
    alk. paper)
Subjects: LCSH: Large type books. | Murder—Investigation—Fiction. |
    GSAFD: Suspense fiction.
Classification: LCC PS3603.A4477 O64 2019 | DDC 813/.6—dc23
LC record available at https://lccn.loc.gov/2019017042

For Annie

PROLOGUE

Prince of Wales Island, Alaska

The maze of deadfall was higher than her head, as if God had walked away from a massive game of pickup sticks.

In the darkness behind her, were the sounds of a predator.

Boots shuffled on dusty ground, stopped abruptly, and then moved closer. Millie pictured the cloud of vapor around a nose, sniffing the chilly air. Her rubber boots made little noise on the carpet of decaying spruce needles. It didn't matter. The scent of fear was enough to give her away.

A branch snapped, somewhere in the shadows, flushing the girl from her hide like a panicked grouse.

Floundering over snot-slick moss and through thorny stalks of devil's club, she fell more than she ran. She thrust herself forward somewhere between a frantic scramble and a scuttling crawl. Blood oozed from gashes on her streaked face, dripping off her chin and onto her T-shirt. Her knees and palms were raw and ravaged. Few of the logs made passable bridges over the rubble, pathways to gain precious ground toward her skiff. Most crumbled at her touch, rotten and soggy, sending her clamoring for a foothold before she impaled herself.

Millie Burkett was Tlingit, people of the tides and forest, and these giant trees had been her friends for all of her sixteen years. Their groans and snaps were normal, and their mottled shadows a perfect place to hide. Her earliest memories were of playing at the mossy feet of the great trees as they watched over her like a kindly grandmother. But now, the Sitka spruce, Western hemlock, and yellow cedar loomed like hateful villains from a movie. An eerie silence pervaded the forest. Rain clouds pressed through the dense canopy, adding a sinister air that chased away the light.

Wheezing and winded, Millie ducked around a massive spruce, at least eight feet across. She yanked a curtain of black hair away from her face and pressed her back against the rough bark. Straining to hear over the thump of her runaway heart, she listened to the sounds of the forest, like her mother had taught her. A branch cracked in the cathedral-like stillness.

Doubling her efforts, Millie crashed through a wicked tangle of leaves and ropy stalks twice her height, oblivious to the scourging. Her camera swung back and forth from a strap around her neck, snagging on the vegetation and threatening to hang her. A spruce hen exploded with a

8

drumbeat of wings to her right. She cut left, into a jagged, half-rotten limb as big as her wrist, that slashed at her belly. Startled, she tried to jump again, but the gnarled branch seemed to reach out and grab her, clawing at the loose tail of her wool shirt, tearing away a strip of plaid cloth and nearly upending her.

She knew these forests. Her people had called them home for thousands of years. The stony silence of Bear, the chiding of Squirrel, or the drumming *whoosh* of Raven's wings—they were to her as the patter of falling rain or the lapping of ocean tides.

But today was different.

She should have known better than to come alone. Tucker had warned her. He ventured out alone all the time with his camera, but he was at least ten years older, probably more—and he knew the risks. She choked back a sob. If only she'd listened.

Head spinning with fear and fatigue, she ducked under, over, and around the towering, tilted trees, many of them two or three meters wide. It was still light enough to pick her way through, but dark enough that there were no shadows.

Millie's lungs felt ready to explode by the time the giant spruces began to give way to thicker undergrowth. There was more light here, and a spit of rain. The odor of rotting bull kelp and low tide swirled on the breeze, filling her with a sudden rush of hope. Her skiff came into view as she ran, at the edge of the water less than two hundred yards below. If she could just make it to the boat, she might have a chance.

Long legs in freewheel down the steep incline, the Tlingit girl was sure she was beating her best cross-country record. Her heart sank when she saw the tide was out. It left the bow of her aluminum skiff on the gravel slope, but the stern still bobbed in the shallows, and the shore fell away quickly into deep water. She prayed her little outboard would be able to pull her off the rocks.

Air chambers in the carpet of bladder kelp popped and snapped beneath the soles of her boots as she hit the tide line. She fell twice between the line of driftwood flotsam and the edge of the water. Broken shells and barnacle-covered rocks tore her shredded knees and hands, but she didn't care.

Sliding to a stop on the slick rocks, she pulled the anchor line off the large stone where she'd looped it and clamored over the side of the little aluminum boat. Her back to the shore, she sat on an overturned five-gallon bucket that made up her seat, and worked to coax the reluctant outboard to life. She pumped the bulb on the gas line, opened the choke, then put her back into the starter rope. The thirty-horse Tohatsu coughed on the first two pulls, as it always did, and she didn't hear the crunch of gravel behind her until it was almost on top of her.

Millie Burkett turned to see a face she knew well, smiling at her.

One hand still on the starter rope, her eyes shot to the dark woods above the beach. "What are you doing here?" Unwilling to take the time to explain the gravity of their situation, she turned back to the motor to give it another pull. "Never mind," she said. "Just get in, we have to—"

Something heavy struck the back of her skull, knocking her off the bucket. Reeling, she flailed out with both hands, trying to catch herself, grasping nothing but air. A second blow, more powerful than the first, drove her to her knees. A shower of lights exploded behind her eyes. Molten blades inside her brain spun with sickening regularity, pulsing with each beat of her heart.

She pitched forward, against the cold deck, vaguely aware of splintered wood and the copper taste of blood. The fleeting image of a rubber boot passed inches from her face, and the heavy ache in her skull dragged her into blackness.

The terrifying realization that she'd been stuffed in some kind of sack hit her all at once. Panicking, she jerked from side to side, finally realizing that only by moving her face away from the rough cloth could she get any air. Her hands

11

were bound in front of her, low, at her waist. The rough cloth was there as well, against her hips. The thump of lapping water on an aluminum hull told her she was on the floor of a boat. Nauseated, she pulled her knees to her chest, trying to keep the world around her from spinning out of control. She wanted to scream but managed little more than a pathetic whimper. The effort was just too painful. The back of her head felt as if it had been opened with an axe. She remembered that there was someone else at the boat when she'd been attacked—a person she knew—but the face escaped her.

The boat rocked heavily to one side and someone grabbed her feet, hauling them up on the metal gunnel. Good. They were getting out. A disembodied voice muttered something she couldn't understand. The boat rocked again as her body was hauled roughly upward. She strained to recall the face.

"Where are you taking me?" Her father had told her stories about what happened to young girls who were kidnapped. "Please . . ." Her chest was racked with sobs. "I don't . . . I don't know anything. Please, just let me go."

Now sitting on the edge of the boat, Millie heard a splash behind her. A line zipped over the aluminum gunnel filling her with deadly dread.

An anchor.

An instant later the rope went taut, yanking

hard at her ankles and dragging her off the edge of the boat. She sucked in a final, desperate breath before she went under, but shock from entering the frigid water drove much of the wind from her lungs. Intense pressure pushed at her eardrums as the anchor pulled her down.

Millie Burkett screamed away her last breath as the anchor slammed into the muddy bottom. She remembered, and the name of her killer rose toward the surface on a stream of silver-green bubbles.

VIAM INVENIAM AUT FACIAM.
I shall find a way—or make one.

CHAPTER 1

Supervisory deputy US Marshal Arliss Cutter knew how to smile—but it took effort and, often, came at great expense. More than once, the flash of his killer dimples had sent him crashing headlong into an ill-advised and short-lived marriage. The dimples were a genetic gift from his mother, but he'd also inherited the resting "mean mug" of his paternal grandfather—whom everyone called Grumpy. The mean mug turned out to be perfectly suited to a man who hunted other men for a living.

Cutter stood beside his government issue Ford Escape—the irony of the name not eluding him as a manhunter. The hood of the small, white SUV was surrounded by the seven other members of his ad hoc arrest team, each of them dressed in the full battle rattle of law enforcement on a mission. The three Anchorage PD officers looked bedraggled, having spent the last six hours of a ten-hour shift shagging back-to-back calls for service. One had a mud stain on the thigh of his dark blue uniform, like he'd slid into home plate. Anchorage could get rough after midnight. The two special agents from the DEA, along with the two deputy US marshals assigned to the Alaska Fugitive Task Force, had the damp hair and scrubbed-pink look of people who'd showered and rushed out the door in order to make it to the 5:00 a.m. briefing. One of the DEA guys still had a bit of tissue paper stuck to a shaving cut on his neck. These two sported neatly trimmed, matching goatees, though one had more salt and pepper than the other.

Counting his time in the army, Cutter had almost twenty years of experience tracking evil men, but this position with the Fugitive Task Force was new. He was a hands-on leader, and would be hands-on during this first op in Alaska.

The chilly breeze teased at his sandy hair, pushing a Superman curl across his forehead. He took a deep breath, drawing in the spring smells of flowing birch sap and new spruce growth. He was a long way from his home state of Florida and its comforting familiarity.

There was a real upside to working fugitive cases in the Last Frontier—at least during the spring and summer. The hours of darkness were few and far between now, so the bandits spent most of their time running around like cockroaches trying to find a place to hide. In Cutter's experience, stomping roaches was easy when they ventured into the light. There had been plenty of cockroaches in Florida and it turned out there were a few in Alaska that needed a boot heel as well.

The roach of the moment, Frederick "Donut"

Woodfield, had a criminal history that said he'd gone peacefully during each of his seventeen previous arrests. There was no reason to believe that today would be any different. Cutter checked the BUG—or backup gun—in any case. It was a small Glock he wore in a holster over his right kidney. On his hip, he carried a stainless steel Colt Python revolver with the Florida Department of Law Enforcement badge engraved over the action.

Arliss Cutter was fresh to the District of Alaska—and as such, the two deputies assigned to his task force were fresh to him. All three were still in what Grumpy Cutter had called the "butt-sniffin' stage." They were untested, getting to know each other's ways, the good, the bad, and the stuff that might get somebody killed. The deputies had yet to see Cutter lead, and he'd not seen either of them in a fight. That too was apt to change. The pursuit of violent fugitives virtually guaranteed it.

Deputy US Marshal Sean Blodgett stood to Cutter's immediate right. Bull strong but thirty pounds on the heavy side, Blodgett's thick forearms rested T. Rex–like on the magazine pouches and personal trauma kit on the front of an OD-green armored plate carrier he wore over a tight navy blue T-shirt. A subdued green and black circle-star badge was affixed over his left breast. A short-barreled Colt M4 carbine hung vertically from a single-point sling around the deputy's neck. Bold letters on the back of the vest said "POLICE: US MARSHAL."

At twenty-six, Deputy Lola Fontaine was what Cutter's grandfather would have called a "healthy" girl. Naturally thick across her hips and shoulders from her Polynesian roots, she took her fitness to the extreme. Decked out in the early morning light, she reminded Cutter of something from an advertisement for tactical gear. Similar to Deputy Blodgett's, her vest identified her as a "US MARSHAL," but her intense countenance and chiseled arms screamed "badass." She kept her dark hair pulled back in a tight bun that highlighted her wide cheekbones and made her look more mature than she actually was. Chestnut eyes issued a challenge to anyone who met them for too long. She was around five and a half feet tall, but Cutter didn't have to guess her weight because she kept a record of it on a piece of printer paper taped to her computer. Yesterday, she'd scrawled, "134 pounds of blue twisted steel." She had proclaimed this her "fighting weight" and no one in the task force offices argued with her. Cutter had heard her tell war stories in the squad room about the fights she'd been involved in, and considering the swagger with which she walked through life, he was inclined to believe her.

Boiled down to its core, manhunting was a

straightforward science. Deputy US marshals cared little for the *what, when,* or *why* of a crime—but focused with a laser-like intensity on *who* and *where.* In theory, now that they had a location on Donut Woodfield, it was a simple matter of closing in and scooping him up. But in practice, few theories survived first contact with a fugitive.

Cutter glanced at the two seasoned agents from the United States Drug Enforcement Administration: Simms and Bradley. Each was dressed in a thin blue raid jacket pulled over an olive-drab tactical vest. Each topped off their extra ammo, personal trauma kits, and other tactical gear with two flash-bang grenades. A little over the top for someone not in a SWAT unit, but it was hard to argue against taking extra gear as long as it didn't weigh you down.

The DEA guys appeared to be capable enough, though Simms, the younger of the two agents, made a lame joke that Lola Fontaine was a stripper's name. Cutter did what any good supervisor would do. He quietly led the man away from the group and threatened to kick his ass if he heard that kind of talk about one of his people again. Although it took a few minutes away from the gathering, it was time well spent. With a six-foot-three, two-hundred-forty-pound supervisory deputy making sure he watched his p's and q's, Special Agent Simms became a picture of decorum. Deputy Blodgett had also made fun of Lola Fontaine's stripper-esque name—but in private and as part of the USMS family, so Cutter had let it slide with nothing more than a raised eyebrow. Even that had the same effect.

As per their standard operating procedure on a raid, both DEA agents wore black balaclavas, ready to roll down over their goateed faces just prior to booting the door. The other five members of the team—the three uniformed APD officers and the two deputy marshals— were young, pitifully so in Cutter's mind, young enough to make his forty-two-year-old bones ache. He was at least a decade older than anyone else there. But young didn't necessarily mean inexperienced, especially for the coppers. Serving a population of three hundred thousand, these APD officers witnessed enough human conflict and unmitigated stupidity every night to mature them at near lightning speed.

Out of habit, Cutter touched the small leather bag tucked into his belt, and then leaned over his Ford to get one last good look at the floor plan drawn there in erasable marker—a mobile whiteboard. It was just before five-thirty in the morning but the other members of the team cast stark shadows across the hood.

He was satisfied that he had a solid mental picture of the apartment complex they were about to hit, but as supervisory deputy, Cutter positioned himself to face the rising sun, making certain everyone else could study the diagram before they went in. He'd seen too many good people die over some piddling mistake—and wasn't about to let it happen on his watch.

The oldest of the APD officers, a sergeant named Evers, was likely in his early thirties. He shot a glance at the sad little set of apartments set among the white birch trees in the quiet neighborhood off Spenard Road, then looked back at the diagram drawn on the hood. "Anybody been inside this place before?"

"I have," one of the APD officers said, raising a black-gloved hand. "It's basically four floors of whores, Sarge." He looked as though he might still be in middle school but spoke with the conviction of a man ten years his senior, and this calmed Cutter a notch.

"The landlord lives in California," Deputy Blodgett added. "He's got a rap sheet as long as your arm for heroin distribution and use. I'm not even sure if he remembers he owns the damn thing."

Lola Fontaine shoved a powder-blue warrant folder across the hood toward the APD officers. It was thick with Woodfield's background information and known associates. She'd folded it open to the criminal-history page.

"Frederick James Woodfield," she said, tapping the photograph with the bright red nail of her index finger. "AKA Donut."

"That's a fit dude for a heroin dealer," Sergeant Evers said. "Doesn't look like someone named Donut."

Fontaine shrugged, wincing a little from the movement. Even in the chill, she was still sweating from her 4 a.m. preraid workout and her arms glistened in the morning light. Both of the younger APD officers were mesmerized by her. It would have made Cutter smile, if he were the smiling sort.

"Whew," she gasped, half under her breath. "It was shoulder day this morning and I am feeling it." She glanced up at Blodgett. "I could barely get into my T-shirt at the gym. Know what I'm sayin'?"

Cutter cleared his throat, keeping her on task. "Donut?"

"Right," she said, rolling her shoulders again. "Not sure why, but that's what everybody calls him. He's got warrants out of California, Washington, and Alaska for distribution. Black male, six-five, two hundred and sixty pounds. He's got ties to the TMHG—Too Many Hoes Gang—one of the Crips affiliates out of LA. Maybe the name comes from them."

The APD officer nearest Cutter dragged his eyes off Fontaine's biceps long enough to study the photograph of their target and whistled under his breath. Officer Trent, a callow string bean who looked fresh out of the academy, tapped the line that showed Woodfield's date of birth and shook his head. "Twenty-eight. Isn't that ancient for a guy in a street gang?"

"True," Cutter said.

"So our guy's on the fourth floor?" Sergeant Evers repeated back information he'd already been given. Cutter didn't blame him. Cops were more terrified of hitting the wrong place than they were of flying bullets.

Cutter looked at Deputy Fontaine, letting her answer. It was a DEA warrant, but they'd turned it over to the Marshals Service. Cutter wanted to make sure everyone here knew this operation was Fontaine's show.

"Correct," the deputy said. "Apartment four oh five. Three down after we top the stairs, on the south side of the hall."

Evers nodded. "I'd still be happy to bring in SWAT," he said. "If you think this guy's going to barricade."

"That's your call," Cutter replied to the sergeant, taking a half step back and crossing his arms. "If it would ease your mind. This is your city." Cutter knew that being able to personally slap the cuffs on a fugitive at the end of a long hunt was a point of pride with those who hunted men. He wasn't immune to the notion, but if there was any indication that Donut Woodfield was going to be a problem he would have stepped in and called SWAT himself.

All the men looked at Lola Fontaine. The two DEA agents shuffled a bit and everyone seemed to be holding their breath at this critical juncture. The whole operational plan could change with her next words.

Fontaine flashed a quick look at Blodgett, then confidently shook her head and pointed to the criminal history. "He's never put up any fight before. I think we're good with what we got." She flashed a grin at the APD officers. Cutter couldn't help but notice that even her face had clearly sculpted muscles. "I appreciate you guys coming along though. A uniform presence keeps the neighbors from going ape shit."

"And anyhow," Deputy Blodgett chimed in, "we got a pile of five more of these mooks around Anchorage that we're going to hit today. SWAT's got no time for that." Blodgett was from Nevada, but used words like "mook" and "perp" as if he'd grown up as a NYPD beat cop.

Evers gave a low groan, still mulling it over. "He's supposed to be alone?"

Fontaine gave a noncommittal shrug. "That's what we understand," she said.

"Okay." The sergeant stepped back from the Ford. "We seven rock stars should be able to handle it. Are you planning to knock and announce first?" He glanced down at the breaching ram resting upright on the pavement at Blodgett's feet. Fifty pounds of steel and painted flat black, it resembled a length of railroad track with two hoop handles and a flat plate welded to the end—because that's exactly what it was.

The older DEA agent coughed, drawing attention in his direction. "There's a good chance this guy's holding a fistful of black tar heroin. If it's all the same to you, we'd like to get inside before he has a chance to run it down the garbage disposal."

"Daisy will make that happen for us." Blodgett smiled and gave the ram an affectionate pat.

The sergeant studied his two officers, looking them up and down the way good field leaders do to make sure their people are squared away. Satisfied, he turned back to Cutter. "No fire escape on that end of the building. We can all go to the front door. You guys will handle the breaching tool, right? If my guys touch it, I gotta call SWAT."

Blodgett hoisted the steel ram to his chest. "Nobody's touching Daisy but me," he said.

Special Agent Simms threw a black nylon backpack over his vest. It held a pair of bolt cutters and a hooked breaching bar that resembled a hammer with one claw called a Halligan tool. It would be invaluable in the event Donut's door happened to open outward, or was too flimsy to make Daisy effective.

"Here we go then," Evers said, waving toward Donut Woodfield's four floors of whores. "We'll follow you."

• • •

Lola Fontaine led the convoy of six law enforcement vehicles off Spenard Road, parking behind the cover of the birch trees on the north side of the building, away from Donut's apartment. With no reason to dally, the team eased their vehicle doors shut, then moved immediately into the main entrance of the apartments. They stacked in the same order they would hit the door. Fontaine was in the lead, Deputy Blodgett behind her with the ram, followed by Cutter, the two DEA agents, and APD acting as over-watch in the rear.

The overwhelming stench of trash and dirty socks hit Cutter full in the face. Deputy Blodgett took a deep breath through his nose as if savoring a favorite meal.

"Hmmm," he whispered. "Yummy . . ."

The building had an elevator, but the team opted for the stairs, moving at a fast trot. They stayed close enough to reach out and touch, but just far enough apart so as not to bump into one another. Her Glock drawn and pointed at the floor, Fontaine indicated 405 with her free hand, confirming that was the apartment as soon as they reached it. Cutter had warned her about spending too much time on target. Rather than ramming the door immediately, she reached to gingerly try the knob. It was not the worst thing in the world to ram an unlocked door, but it was as embarrassing as hell.

It was locked.

Fontaine gave a whispered hiss. "Breacher up!" She stepped to the side, allowing Blodgett room to swing the heavy ram. She would take the lead inside once the door gave way, while everyone else filed in behind her. Blodgett, having dropped the ram and transitioned to his rifle, would follow at the rear of the stack.

The door was metal with a solid core, and from the looks of it, had a deep, reinforced dead bolt. There was a peephole at eye level, so Cutter gave a thumbs-up ordering them to make entry. Blodgett took his stance and swung Daisy back at the same time Cutter saw a camera mounted on the ceiling in the far corner of the hallway. He noticed it a fraction of a second too late.

The heavy door swung open an instant before the steel ram made contact, causing Blodgett to lose his balance and stumble forward. A dark and brawny arm grabbed the deputy and yanked him inside before slamming the door. The dead bolt slid home with a definitive clunk, leaving Cutter and the rest of his team standing flat-footed in the hallway—with no ram.

CHAPTER 2

Arliss Cutter put his boot to the door—getting nothing but a sickeningly solid thud. With the breaching ram and Blodgett in the apartment, Cutter and the rest of the team were effectively locked out.

"What the hell just happened?" one of the DEA agents gasped. They looked up and down the hall in disbelief, guns still drawn, at the ready—one man gone and no bad guy in sight.

It sounded like two elephants battling it out on the other side of the door. Dust streamed down from the ceiling as something heavy shook the wall.

Cutter looked up and saw the hallway had a suspended ceiling and motioned Fontaine over with a quick flick of his wrist. Keeping clear of the door in the event Donut decided to start shooting, he holstered his Colt and interlaced his fingers, stooping to give her a place to stand.

"I'm going to lift you up," he said. "Let me know what you see."

Instantly, she grabbed his shoulders and stepped into his hands, pushing the acoustic tile out of the way as Cutter stood.

"No good," she said when he lowered her back down. "Walls go all the way up to the next floor."

Muffled screams carried through the walls

along with the sound of heavy pounding. Someone was being beaten to death.

Sergeant Evers tried to boot the door again. It did little but scuff the metal facing. Next both APD officers set to kicking the door together. Soon everyone was taking turns with zero results.

The sergeant got on his radio and called for backup—but Cutter knew it would be too little, too late. This would all be over before anyone could arrive with another ram.

Inside Woodfield's apartment, it was all-out war. Glass shattered, furniture crunched as the men engaged in an epic knockdown-drag-out brawl. Donut Woodfield had six inches and sixty pounds on Blodgett. Even if the bandit wasn't armed, Cutter knew there were at least two guns inside—Blodgett's. The deputy was loud and brash, and thankfully, he was built like a small Sherman tank. Cutter just hoped he knew how to fight.

Cutter drew his pistol again and snapped his fingers at the DEA agents. "Use the Halligan," he said.

Simms moved up immediately, drawing the metal tool from his shoulder bag like a sword. He tried to pry the door next to the dead bolt, but it held firm.

"It's reinforced," the DEA agent said through a clenched jaw. He moved the flat edge up and down the jam, beating it against the metal to try and find a sweet spot.

Cutter's heart raced as he listened to the clatter on the other side of the door.

"This is really stuffed," Fontaine whispered, looking much less muscular than she had just moments before. "He's killing Sean in there."

Helpless, Cutter cast his eyes up and down the hallway, hoping to find a fire axe or something with which to make entry and save his deputy. Sean Blodgett had been on his own a full minute—an eternity when you're fighting for your life. Cutter tried not to imagine the scene, focusing instead on a way inside.

The door to 407 opened a crack and a dark eye peered out. The door started to close, but Cutter shoved his foot inside, forcing it open to reveal a bony-kneed brunette with track marks on her arms. She wore a thin T-shirt and loose gym shorts—the easy-on, easy-off uniform of a hooker who worked from home.

"Hey!" she said, glancing backward at the marijuana plants growing by the balcony door. "You can't come in here without a warrant."

"I don't care about your weed," Cutter said, working hard to keep his breathing under control so he could think. "You know your neighbor?"

The battle in the next room was even louder from inside the hooker's apartment.

"He keeps to himself," the woman said. She folded her arms and cocked a bony hip to one side.

Agent Simms stuck his head in from the

hallway. The muscles in his jaw clenched with stress. "Halligan tool's not working for shit," he said. "I can't get through."

A series of ragged grunts came through from Donut's side of the wall. Cutter couldn't tell who made them, but at least there were no shots, and the telltale banging continued unabated. Cutter's eyes fell on the two flash-bangs on the front of his vest before the DEA agent disappeared back into the hallway. An internal clock had started a countdown the moment the door had slammed shut behind Sean Blodgett, with something telling Cutter that if he could get through the door within three minutes, he might have a chance to save his deputy.

He glanced at his watch. Two minutes gone.

"Bring me the Halligan!" Cutter snapped.

Simms stared. "You want it in here?"

"Just bring it," Cutter snapped. "Fast!"

Deputy Fontaine ducked in behind Agent Simms. Sweat plastered strands of dark hair to her forehead from her continued efforts to break down the door.

Panting, she gave Cutter a quizzical look. "Did you find another way in?"

"Maybe." Cutter snatched the metal bar from the DEA agent. "Maybe not."

Using the wingspan of his arms, he measured approximately five feet from the door inside the woman's apartment, then buried the picklike spike on the end of the Halligan tool in the Sheetrock.

The building was decades old and it was easy to see the swell of the wooden studs in the adjoining Sheetrock wall. He punched two holes, six inches apart and at chest level between the swells.

"Hey!" The hooker tried to step forward but Fontaine checked her with a hip. "But this is my house."

Cutter ignored her. He yanked open the Velcro closure of his ballistic vest and slid the entire thing up and over his head, dropping it on the floor. He turned immediately to the DEA agent and held out an open hand. "Give me one of the flash-bangs. You take the other one. Pull the pin and drop it into the wall the same time I do."

Simms nodded, looking like he understood the plan. "This might actually work," he said, dropping his stun grenade into the hollow of the wall in unison with Cutter.

Two seconds later dust shot from each hole with a muffled *whoomf.*

Confined to the bottom of the hollow wall, the relatively small explosions still produced enough force to peel the Sheetrock away from the studs, giving Cutter just enough space to insert the Halligan tool. He ripped upward, frantically tearing away the Sheetrock on his side and exposing Woodfield's inner wall. The studs were set a full two feet apart, but even without his vest, the remaining gear forced Cutter to turn sideways in order to fit.

Heavy bar in hand, he slipped between the studs, sucking in his gut to avoid rusty nails and ancient wiring. Putting a shoulder to the opposing wall, he crashed through the Sheetrock wall, nearly falling over the tangled knot that was deputy and Donut.

Not a stick of furniture in the apartment remained upright. Shattered glass and broken picture frames littered the carpet. A pan of what looked like half-eaten lasagna lay overturned in the middle of the living room floor. Sean Blodgett was on his back, his Glock apparently having been dislodged from the holster. The rifle was nowhere to be seen. Woodfield stood above him with a broken baseball bat high overhead, raining down blows in an effort to brain the deputy. Legs up, Blodgett shielded his face with his forearms and rolled back and forth to avoid the bat. Blood sprayed from Woodfield's nose with each breath. His jaw hung at an odd angle. Blodgett's left eye was swollen shut. Blood dripped from his elbows.

Cutter roared, enraged at seeing his deputy on the receiving end of the beating. Plowing into the startled Donut Woodfield, he knocked the man off his feet and gave Blodgett a few seconds to regroup. Wounded but far from finished, Donut rolled and spun to face the new threat. Cutter lunged forward, oblivious to the bat, swinging the Halligan like a polo mallet. He buried the spike end of the tool in Donut's shoulder as he went past. The fugitive jerked away, shrugging off the wound and raising the bat again. Enraged and intent on braining the fugitive, Cutter rushed him a third time, narrowly missing his head with the Halligan tool but catching the bandit in the right hand as he tried to ward off the blow. The outlaw screamed in pain. Cutter used the spike as a hook and yanked Donut into a left cross that landed on his already shattered jaw.

Woodfield dropped the bat and collapsed screaming to the floor. Momentum from the punch sent Cutter stepping past.

Fontaine had come through the wall right behind Cutter and jumped on top of the dazed fugitive, before Cutter could turn around. Blodgett crawled up beside her, squinting with his good eye while he helped pin one of Woodfield's arms so she could ratchet on the handcuffs.

Nostrils flaring, Cutter came at all of them with the raised Halligan tool.

Fontaine held up her hand to ward him off. "We've got him!"

"What?" Cutter said, blinking, still brandishing the heavy steel bar.

"Arliss!" Fontaine snapped. "It's me, Lola. We're good here. He's cuffed."

Lola Fontaine stared up at her new boss as he held the Halligan tool high above his head, eyeing Donut Woodfield like a piece of meat. A lock of her long hair had worked its way loose from the bun and she blew it out of her face so she wouldn't lose eye contact with Cutter. At length, he let the metal bar clatter to the floor and shook his head as if to clear it. Stepping to the door, he flipped the latch to allow the rest of the team inside the demolished apartment.

Fontaine rolled the now subdued Donut onto his side, patting him down for weapons. She steered clear of his blood-soaked shoulder, but he winced wherever she happened to touch him. Sean had done some damage, and it was clear Cutter had broken a bone or two with the iron bar.

"Did you see that?" She whispered so the thug couldn't hear.

Blodgett chuckled, filled with the euphoria of still being alive. "I can't see shit," he said, squinting at her, a curtain of blood over his face.

"I thought this new supervisor was the picture of calm," she said. "But I'm pretty sure he was about to bury the spike end of that crowbar into this guy's face."

"I told you," Blodgett said, still keeping his voice low. "The new guy's got issues. My friends at headquarters say he did some pretty bad shit in Afghanistan."

"Saw bad shit or did bad shit?"

Blodgett got on all fours and used an overturned chair to push himself to his feet.

"From what I hear, a hell of a lot of both."

CHAPTER 3

Twenty-nine was much too young for Carmen Delgado to contemplate her own death, but gazing out at the cold sea with the frost-covered graves behind her, she could think of little else. The island was beautiful, pristine even, with green mountains, old-growth forests, and more waterfalls per mile than anyplace she'd ever seen. And still, it was impossible to shake the feeling that this place was going to kill her.

She'd never seen a more cinematic location. Even now three fishing boats chugged out in front of her, braving the slap of a cold morning wind to bring back a haul of kelp for the herring roe fishery. Carmen had heard the old "odds were good, but the goods were odd," saw in regards to the male to female ratio in Alaska so many times it wasn't funny. If a girl was into flannel-wearing, hipster guys with well-oiled beards and ear gauges who could make the finest caramel macchiato on the planet but didn't know one end of a chain saw from the other, that was probably true. But so far as Carmen could see, the fishermen and loggers on this island were some of the toughest, most resilient men on earth—which made what she was doing to them even more difficult to stomach.

Hugging her knees to her chest, Carmen pulled her head deeper into her fleece, nibbling on the collar as she often did when she was nervous or thinking. To her left, across the breakwater bridge and up past the boat harbor, the quaint little town of Craig lay nestled alongside a place called Shelter Cove. She couldn't have come up with a better name if the network had sent in a script change.

There were wolves on the island, and bears too, burly black things that were three times her size. A fisherman at JT Brown's General Store tried to calm her fears by reminding her that wolves only ate short people—a small comfort to someone a hair over five feet tall. The same well-meaning guy had gone on to explain that she didn't have to worry about any grizzlies on the island, only the much more timid black bears. As an afterthought, he'd warned her that although black bears were more shy, if one did decide to approach it was because they considered you to be food. Black bears had killed two people in Alaska the year before. But, hey, you got nothin' to worry about, kid.

A Tlingit girl waiting in line at that same general store of horrors began to talk about Native legends of fearsome frogs and shape-shifters who abducted women and forced them into mixed marriages with fanged otter-men.

Carmen had felt out of place from the moment

she'd stepped off the ferry on her first scouting trip months before. She was a city girl, born and raised in East LA. Two of her cousins had been killed in shoot-outs with rival gang members and a third was turning tricks on Atlantic Avenue. Nothing should have fazed her, not wolves or bears or creepy otter dudes. But they did. And what was worse, she had no one to blame for being here but herself.

She'd spent the first seven years after graduating from UCLA film school clawing her way through menial crew jobs on several reality television productions, all the while filling stacks of spiral notebooks with her own ideas. None of them clicked. And then she'd watched a show on Nat Geo about life in the far North. It was an absolutely terrific program, chock-o-block full of interesting characters who not only lived but thrived in the harsh and unforgiving environment. The concept was as incredible as the location and she began to watch everything she could get her hands on about Alaska.

Carmen's brother was an LAPD cop and she spent many evenings talking with her sister-in-law about the close friendships developed by cop-spouses. One night while her brother was at work, she and her sister-in-law binged on pizza and watched a decades-old documentary about fishing in southeast Alaska. The kernel of an idea began to sprout in her mind. She worked through the night, filling up an entire notebook with a draft proposal for a smart new show—one that would inform and entertain. The production company she worked for funded a three-week trip to Craig to shoot a sizzle reel.

She returned to LA fairly giddy with the prospects. Two weeks later, she was ready to pitch.

A network picked up the show right off the bat, but, as par, had their own ideas. They read her treatment, watched her sizzle reel, and showered her with compliments on the fresh approach— then proceeded to change everything. Oh, they named her the executive producer and, in typical network fashion, said she was the one in charge. But she knew how it worked. Unless your title was "signer of the checks," you weren't in charge of anything. In the span of one three-hour meeting with network execs, her baby became unrecognizable.

Now, she and the production crew of her gross monstrosity had descended on this picturesque little village in the middle of nowhere—and she feared the experience would change the place forever. There was something here that was likely to kill her all right, more deadly than any wolf or bear or otter-man, and it wasn't indigenous to the island. No, whatever it was, this had come with her.

CHAPTER 4

Deputy Blodgett needed to go to the hospital, so Cutter drove him. Fontaine and Special Agent Simms followed in her car with Donut Woodfield, who required an Emergency Room visit as well to get his various wounds treated before the jail would accept him.

Blodgett completed his form CA-1 at the hospital, noting his on-the-job injuries in case they caused problems for him in the future. There was no real rush but it would give him something to do while he waited. Cutter assured him he was good to go, despite what looked like a fractured orbital around his eye and a dislocated index finger that was probably broken. He was sure to feel much different once the adrenaline wore off.

Donut Woodfield turned out to have a broken collarbone, three cracked ribs, and a dislocated jaw. The wounds in his shoulder and hand required fifteen stitches combined. None of it was quite enough to keep him out of jail once he was treated. Cutter was pleased when it became clear that Woodfield was hurt worse than his deputy, but he kept that to himself.

Special Agent Simms agreed to transport Blodgett home so Cutter could ride with Fontaine to the jail with the prisoner. He considered himself a "you catch 'em, you clean 'em" supervisor, and if he was in it for the fun of the arrest, he was also in it for the jail-run and ensuing paperwork.

The book-in took forever, with the jail nurse looking over her granny glasses at Woodfield, then the deputies, then the hospital paperwork, and then back to the deputies again. Lola Fontaine bounced with tension by the time she retrieved her handgun from the lockbox in the vehicle sally port and got back into Cutter's Ford. It was the first time they'd been out of earshot of the prisoner.

The deputy snapped on her seat belt and turned to look him in the eye. Her broad, Polynesian face was passive, the kind of mysteriously all-knowing look that used to terrify Cutter when he saw it on his mother. "Is there anything you want to tell me, boss?"

"Nope," he said.

"You sure about that?" she asked. "Because I'm here to tell you, I think you're busting at the seams to talk to me."

"You would be mistaken," Cutter said, putting the car in gear.

"I only asked because things got pretty intense back there."

"Let me ask you something, Lola," Cutter said. "If you had seen Woodfield holding a bat over me, would you have shot him?"

Fontaine shrugged. "Many times, boss."

"Well, there you go," Cutter said. "Deadly

43

force is deadly force. Shoot someone with a Glock or brain 'em with a metal bar—they're the same amount of dead."

"Roger that," Fontaine said, still sounding unconvinced. She stared straight ahead, tapping the infernal pencil on her folder. At length she shrugged, then sat back with a resigned sigh. "I could use a workout."

The Anchorage jail's sally port was long and narrow and Cutter had to drive forward three car lengths in order for the officers in the control center to notice him.

"I was under the impression you worked out early this morning," he said. "Shoulder day . . ."

"So?" Fontaine said, as if that was a supremely ignorant question. "My grandfather was a Cook Island Maori and my grandmother was a robust girl from Nebraska who took up surfing to get off the farm. All my aunties on my father's side are big women—beautiful and strong, but a little too brawny to run very far, if you know what I mean. My mum's this skinny little thing of Japanese ancestry, but I take after my dad and his family. So, I work out . . . a lot." She turned to stare out her side window, looking away from Cutter, and changed the subject. "You ever think about trying out for SOG?"

SOG was the Special Operations Group, the US Marshals Service's answer to SWAT or the FBI's Hostage Rescue Team.

"I have not," Cutter said. "I'm a little long in the tooth to have a cadre of younger deputies scream at me for that entire month of SOG Selection."

"Hmmm." Fontaine settled deeper into her seat. Her constant workouts and apparently clear conscience gave her the uncanny ability to drift off to sleep at a moment's notice. She leaned back and closed her eyes. "Because I've been thinking about putting in for SOG. . . ."

It was nearly one in the afternoon by the time Cutter swiped his proximity card and drove into the underground garage of the James M. Fitzgerald US Courthouse and Federal Building in downtown Anchorage. He took the time to back his little Ford into his assigned spot near the prisoner garage—a habit that allowed for a quick egress. His hands were full of paperwork and the black ballistic nylon "war bag" where he kept his vest and other tactical gear when he wasn't actually wearing it. Lola was also laden down with gear from the raid. Thankfully, the court security officers in the control room noticed their approach on the garage cameras and buzzed open the door without either of them having to put anything down. The prisoner elevator was waiting with doors open by the time he and Lola made it through the steel door from the garage and into the mantrap. It took them up a level to the outer corridors of the cell block and the back hallway of the US Marshals offices.

A uniformed court security officer, or CSO, waited behind a window of bulletproof glass as they came off the elevator. Computers and CCTV camera monitors filled the dark room behind him. Cutter was still learning all the CSOs' names, but he remembered this one as Bill. Like most of the CSOs, Bill was retired law enforcement—in this case, a former Alaska state trooper. He wore a white shirt with a red and blue striped clip-on tie. His work in the control room allowed him to leave the navy blue blazer draped over the back of his chair.

On the other side of the glass, Bill's lips moved in time with the sounds crackling out of the intercom speaker on the wall. He looked directly at Lola Fontaine.

"Your husband's waiting for you out front by the admin desks," he said. The disgusted eye roll was impossible to miss.

As powerful as she was, Fontaine's entire body drooped at the news. She'd been riding a high from the successful arrest, but this seemed to take all the sauce out of her. She took a deep breath, as if to steel herself for what lay ahead.

"Thanks, Bill."

Cutter hadn't met the man, but even in his few weeks in the district, he'd learned it was common knowledge around the squad room that Larry

Fontaine was a highly jealous man. According to the chief, the guy had convinced himself Lola was cheating on him while on a judicial protection assignment in Los Angeles and flew out to try and catch her in the act. Instead, he found her doing dumbbell lunges in the hotel gym. For some inexplicable reason, Lola stuck with the guy. Cutter couldn't help wonder how long that was going to last. There was no doubt she could have gotten someone with a few less hang-ups. Then again, Cutter didn't have room to talk. He'd been involved in his share of toxic relationships.

His hands still full, Cutter shuddered at those memories and pushed open yet another heavy steel door with the toe of his boot. Escape-proof concrete block walls gave way to painted Sheetrock—which was reinforced with metal grating—as they made their way down the final stretch of the secure hallway. Cutter's office was located with the rest of the Fugitive Task Force, on the other side of the federal building, away from the operational squad room and the USMS brass. Cutter had found this layout extremely appetizing when considering the move to the district. Never much of a garrison soldier, he was happiest when working as far from the flagpole as humanly possible. Normally he would have gone straight to his office, but the chief had summoned him with a text, asking him to stop by and fill her in about the raid once they finished at the jail.

Fontaine walked past, rounding the corner at the end of the hall by the administrative staff as Cutter stepped into the chief's office. He paused at the door. Jill Phillips sat pecking away at her computer, her extremely pregnant belly engaged in an ongoing fight with the lap tray that held her keyboard.

Hailing from Kentucky, Phillips had one of the best reputations of anyone—boss or otherwise—in the United States Marshals Service. She'd cut her teeth in the Judicial Security Division, running protective details for threatened members of the federal judiciary—including Supreme Court justices. Alaska was her first foray into the broader duties of management in a regular district office. She'd been off for medical reasons for much of the time he'd been in district, but from what Cutter had seen, she was a natural, generally doing what a good boss should do—staying out of the way.

Phillips pushed her chair back from her desk and rested both hands on the swell of her seven-months pregnant belly. Her brunette hair was cut short in a no-fuss professional bob that suited her slightly round and heavily freckled face.

"What's the news on Blodgett?"

"He'll mend." Cutter nodded. "Donut Wood-field fractured his eye socket and broke his index finger. His hands look like he beat them with a hammer, and he'll be on light duty for a while. But, the bandit has it worse though."

"Glad to hear that," Phillips said. Hands still on her belly, she studied Cutter. "What's buggin' you, Big Iron?" Her eyes fell to the Colt Python on his hip. Every word was dipped in a honeyed Kentucky accent. "We've not really had a chance to talk much since you got here. Remind me why I let you carry that super cool revolver when policy says I have to carry a Glock?"

Cutter turned sideways and displayed the small Glock 27 in a holster over his right kidney. "Don't know what you're talking about, Chief. My policy gun . . . I mean my *duty* gun is right here. The Colt Python is my backup."

"Still . . ."

"The Colt was my grandfather's," Cutter said. "He was with Florida Marine Patrol during my formative years—got me interested in law enforcement."

"Fair enough," Phillips said. "Can't really argue with a tactical grandpa. But do me a favor and make sure you always have the Glock on you somewhere." She waved at the two weathered lavender paisley side chairs and pulled out what was obviously his personnel file, flipping it open.

"Roger that." Cutter sat down, looking around the office. It was decorated with paintings of eventing horses and trophies from shooting contests she'd won. Photos of Phillips with Supreme Court justices and various law enforcement souvenirs also adorned the walls and covered an office-length credenza. Some believed the lavender chairs were the only feminine things in the office—but they were sorely mistaken. To Jill Phillips, doing anything "like a girl" meant doing it better than everyone else.

Cutter sighed, eyeing the file on her desk. "I guess we should discuss the elephant in the room."

Phillips took a long breath. "All right," she said. "You know, talking about my enormous belly that way is wildly inappropriate."

Cutter raised a hand, mouth open, starting to stammer. It would have had less of an effect if she'd thrown a brick at him. "I . . ."

"You know I'm joking," Phillips scoffed. "Seriously, though, what's up with you? I hardly know you, but I know flummoxed when I see it."

"I'm fine," Cutter said, dropping his voice. "I was just listening to Fontaine's husband down the hall."

The chief leaned forward, trying to listen. "What's he saying?"

"He's quizzing her about my four failed marriages. How does that stuff get around the district so fast?"

The chief's desk chair squeaked as she arched her back, tapping a pen on the edge of her walnut desk. "Telephone, telegraph, and tell-a-deputy," she said, still eyeing him. "And anyhow, the way I understand it, one of your marriages didn't end in failure."

"Depends on your point of view," Cutter said, wanting desperately to change the subject. "One divorce and you can blame the ex. Three and the guy I see in the mirror is the only common denominator."

"Well," Phillips said. "Maybe you are just a jerk. Time will tell."

Cutter held up his hand again, craning his head toward the hallway listening to Lola Fontaine's hushed voice and her husband—who was not nearly so muted. A smile spread across his face.

"What?" Phillips said. "It looks weird when you do that."

"Do what?"

"Smile," she said. "I'm not used to it."

Cutter shook his head. "Sounds like Lola's husband is about to come down here and kick my ass."

"Hmmm." Phillips gave Cutter a piercing look, like she was studying the back of his skull for clues. It would have been off-putting had she not been so genuine. "Are you sure you want her on the task force? Don't get me wrong. I like Lola, but she's got a tendency to be a bit of a blue flamer if you ask me. I have requests on my desk for her to get a bomb dog, go to an armorer's school, attend interview training, and take part in a pursuit driving instructor's course in Vegas. On top of that, I have a package requesting consideration for promotion to the Witness Security Division. Kid's like a BB in a boxcar when it comes to applying for jobs."

"There are worse qualities," Cutter said. "She did tell me she's thinking about putting in for SOG."

"Of course she is."

"She handled herself like a champ today," he said.

"Even so," Phillips said. "Her idiot husband could turn into a liability real fast."

"She'll be fine." Cutter closed his eyes and sank further into the soft chair. "I'm not worried about him."

"I'm not either," Phillips said. "I'm worried about you."

Cutter's eyes flicked open. "How's that?" He'd heard Jill Phillips was the kind of chief who didn't hold much back.

"Don't take this the wrong way," she said. "I think every good deputy has to have a little bit of hunter in the blood—but there's something harder about you—a berserk side, if that makes sense."

"Berserk?"

"Like you're a nanosecond from throat punching anyone who gets in your way."

Cutter scoffed, but was a little worried Fontaine had called ahead to discuss his behavior with the Halligan tool. She'd yet to mention it, but he knew the chief was aware of his two shootings. He'd been cleared by the Office of Professional Responsibility in both, but findings of the OPR didn't matter much in the court of deputy opinion. Most in the agency—people with half a brain anyway—chalked the shootings up to the tragic but unavoidable part of the profession. There were more than a few, though, who considered Cutter a trigger-happy psychopath. Some, who'd heard the hushed stories about his time in Afghanistan, stayed completely out of his way.

After the second shooting, a fellow deputy in Florida with one too many Moscow mules under his belt had observed that Cutter only needed one more deadly force incident to tie his divorce record. Cutter hadn't been quite drunk enough to find the comment funny. His buddies had dragged the other deputy away before things got rough.

He gave his second smile of the day to the chief, hoping it looked more genuine than it felt. "I think I've been extremely judicious in dealing out throat punches since I came aboard the Marshals Service."

Phillips patted her belly, as if to soothe the baby. She never took her eyes off Cutter. "Maybe so," she said. "Look, I'm not supposed to ask about Afghanistan . . . but what about Afghanistan?"

Cutter nodded, figuring it would come up. "What do you want to know?"

"What do you want to tell me?"

"Parts of it were fun," Cutter said. "Parts of it sucked."

"Your file says you were awarded a Silver Star."

"Politics," Cutter said. "They could just as easily have ripped the buttons off my uniform and broken my sword."

"What does that even mean?"

"Drummed me out."

"I doubt that," Phillips said. "We'll have to revisit this topic again over a beer one day— when you've learned to trust me and I can drink beer again." She casually flipped through the pages of his record, before folding it closed— apparently satisfied that Cutter wasn't in the mood to reminisce. The most interesting parts weren't in his Marshals Service file anyway.

Phillips returned the folder to her drawer and leaned back again. "Your last chief warned me that you'd always seek out the broken ones— people you think need fixing."

Cutter crossed his legs, studying the toe of his boot. "My older brother called it a Tarzan complex. He was right, I guess. I do have freakishly long arms, a prominent brow, and I'm always looking to save the girl."

Phillips laughed, wincing a little. She put a hand behind the small of her back. Cutter had always thought pregnant women were beautiful, but it wasn't a compliment he felt comfortable giving his chief until he knew her a little better—or maybe never.

"I wish I'd met your brother," Phillips said. "I gotta tell you, this is a good thing you're doing—coming up here to take care of your sister-in-law and her kids."

"Thanks," Cutter said. He tried, and probably failed to hide a grimace, striving to change the subject for the second time. "So, you read my e-mail about the raid?"

He'd sent her a quick note from the hospital. The marshal and chief could forgive almost any sin, so long as they knew about that sin *before* they got calls from the media.

"I did," Phillips said. "Pretty quick thinking to go through the neighboring wall like that. I wonder what walls cost these days. . . . Anyway, I was thinking about Dusty McBride."

"For?" Cutter said, knowing where this was going. McBride was a good kid. A little wet behind the ears, but a solid, nose-to-the-grindstone sort of deputy who did his job and got along with the rest of the squad room.

"The task force," the chief said. "You have a part-time ATF agent, and the trooper, but you need at least two PODs." P-O-D was a plain old deputy, the worker bees and backbone of the service.

Cutter shook his head. "If it's all the same to you, Chief, I'd just as soon wait for Blodgett to get better."

Phillips leaned forward, as if sharing a secret. "I've only been here a month longer than you, but that's been long enough to see Blodgett's kind of an asshole."

Cutter closed his eyes and groaned. Phillips was still in the same position when he looked up. "Chief," he said. "You ever notice how the bad stuff always happens to the good guys?"

Phillips shrugged. "I'd like to think we're all the good guys."

Cutter shook his head and wagged an index finger, wanting to drive home his point. "No, ma'am," he said. "I mean the *very* best ones. In my experience, the decent souls take it in the shorts nine times out of ten, while the ones who might deserve a smack or two walk away unscathed."

"So you'd rather run the Task Force of Misfit Toys?"

"I know it sounds stupid—"

She raised both hands in surrender. "It sounds like you have some unresolved issues from your time in the military," she said. "But I'm not going to push you. You've had enough trauma for one day."

Phillips spun her chair a quarter turn so her belly could resume the fight with the keyboard.

It was a sure sign she was ready to get back to the mountain of budget reports and personnel appraisals that plagued upper management. Her pregnancy forced her to sit farther away from the screen than she was accustomed to, so she put a pair of tortoiseshell readers on the tip of her nose. "You and Fontaine call it a day," she said, wincing. "Damned hemorrhoid . . ." Cutter pretended not to hear as he stood to leave, but she looked up at him, hand back on her belly. "Two pieces of advice, Arliss. Don't ever get pregnant . . ." She nodded toward her door. "And do your best not to throat punch Lola Fontaine's husband on your way out."

CHAPTER 5

Manuel Alvarez-Garza drummed long, manicured fingers against the varnished teak table and stared out the aircraft window at the frothy green water below. Breaking surf and gray gravel beaches set a stark line against the darkness of the rain forest that ran from ravaged coast to the rolling mountains that covered the island. There wasn't much to see, just water and trees, but it gave Garza's mind respite from looking at his boss.

The Gulfstream G-III was a quiet jet, comfortable and well appointed, but the trip from El Paso to Alaska had been a long one, no matter how plush the aircraft. Garza was a tall man, dark where a man should be dark—around the eyes—with a full head of wavy black hair he kept slicked back. On his last trip to Colombia, one of the "prepaids"—the word for a very particular sort of hostess—said he looked like a young Andy Garcia. He'd always liked that particular actor, and tipped the whore well for her compliment. Today Garza wore designer jeans and a gunmetal-gray Brooks Brothers shirt that was unbuttoned far enough to reveal three gold chains across his waxed chest. His knee bounced a little, in time with the drum of his fingers.

"Do not be so jittery, Manolo," Garza's boss

said from the seat across the teak table. He used the nickname "Manolo" as if they were old friends. Of course, being the friend of Ernesto Camacho, old or otherwise, was much preferred to being his enemy. Even friends sometimes found their charred corpses dissolving in a drum of acid—Camacho's second favorite way to dispose of bodies. As the leader of the relatively small but powerful Los Leónes cartel, he found much opportunity to experiment with a variety of killing and disposal methods. Some were private affairs where the bodies were never found. Most of Camacho's murders, however, were of rival cartel members, or politicians and policemen in northern Mexico who dared to cross him. These bodies Camacho preferred to leave out so the public could see them. Others, like his cousin who had dared to skim a few thousand dollars extra for himself, met the acid treatment—but only after the skin had been peeled off his face and sewn to a football so Camacho could kick the traitor around just a little longer after he was dead.

"Seriously, my friend," the boss continued, slapping the table between them with an open hand to get Garza's full attention. "You must learn to relax." Camacho smiled at the woman lying on the sofa that ran lengthwise across the aisle of the airplane. "Is not that right, my love?" The boss breathed a lungful of air through his nose, making a phlegmatic, wheezing rattle. Garza thought he saw a telltale shudder dance across the resting woman's shoulders. Her name was Feliciana Cárdenas, but her pimp in Reynosa called her Flea—a particularly distastful name for a whore, Garza thought. Camacho liked the name Beti, so much so, in fact that he'd called all his girls Beti from the time Garza had first met him, almost ten years before. So Flea became Beti when she'd taken up with the cartel boss.

"Beti" slept most of the way from their refueling stop in Portland and her long, naturally blond hair lay across the plush leather of the sofa as if it had been styled for a glamour shot. This was her second trip to Camacho's mine in Alaska, and she seemed the sort of girl to which the new of things wore off very quickly. An irony, Garza thought, since Camacho had the same propensities about his Betis.

"Relax, Manolo," Beti parroted without looking up. Garza looked at her and shook his head. She would have been much prettier had she not chosen to spend her time with a man like Camacho. Being with Camacho brought out the ugly in people.

"You pay me to keep you safe, Patrón," Garza said. "I only wish you would allow me to do my job."

Camacho leaned across the table and used a thick index finger to grind his point into the teak surface. "What good is it to be filthy rich, if a man cannot go fish in Alaska when it pleases him? I can launder my money in many ways. Why do you think I purchased a mine thousands of miles away from our home? All I ask is to catch one of these halibut as big . . . how do they say it . . . big as a barn door. Or maybe just go for a relaxing walk in the darkness of the ancient forests or explore one of the many caves. Did you know there were caves on this island, Manolo?"

"I did not," Garza said.

"Is it too much to ask that you protect me while I do these simple things that make me a happy man?"

"Of course not, Patrón," Garza said. "But I must remind you that the DEA does not care if you are a happy man or not. Your photographs are very prominent on the Internet and with the reward of half a million US dollars for your capture . . . I am only able to do so much—"

"Then do that!" Camacho slammed the flat of his hand on the table again. The three *sicarios* seated in the rear of the airplane glanced up at the outburst—each a professional killer among their other skills, handpicked for this trip by Garza. After a scant moment, they returned to their card game. Beti Cárdenas yawned. Such outbursts by their boss were not uncommon.

Camacho took another wheezing breath and chuckled, reeling in his apparent anger. "We are at the northern edge of nowhere, Manolo. There will be no one here to see me or attempt to collect the reward. I would be surprised if anyone out here even has the Internet."

The G-III touched down, bouncing once on the mine's private runway. "And if they do, Patrón?" Garza asked.

A wide smile spread across Camacho's jowly face. "As I said, we are at the edge of nowhere. Many things could happen to someone on the edge of nowhere. It would do you well to remember that, my friend."

As per the protocols Garza himself had put in place, he was first to step off the aircraft, followed by one of the *sicarios*, then Camacho. Garza made his way down the folding stairs to meet with Bean, the gaunt man who saw to the day-to-day operations of Camacho's mine—or at least the property where the mine was supposed to be located once it was developed, according to the records of the shell corporation. Unwilling to admit that he was balding, what little fuzz Bean had left on his egg-shaped head stuck out in all directions, like the down on a mangy chick. Standing at the base of the open aircraft door, the man cast furtive looks from side to side. A short-barrel AR-15 hung from a single-point sling around his neck.

"Are you expecting trouble?" Garza asked, eyeing the rifle.

"No, sir," Bean said. "Not especially. I knew you were concerned about security so I thought I'd assist as much as I can."

"Well," Garza sneered, "do not shoot yourself in the foot."

"Yes, sir," Bean said, smiling as if he had a bad case of indigestion.

The fact that the man had a weapon might have alarmed Garza had it been anyone else, but Bean was too jumpy to pose much of a threat. He was harmless, but even if he weren't, Garza and his men would have cut him down before he got his hands wrapped around the rifle. Besides, he was paid well for doing nothing but watch over a property on which nothing ever happened.

Apart from the runway and a few roads—all made from stone crushed on site, the only other improvements to the mine property were the metal building that housed a shop and made the place look official—and a boat dock where Camacho's pride and joy was moored.

Bean stepped to the side and motioned toward the company van that was parked on a gravel pad at the edge of the runway. The air was cooler and cleaner than anything Garza has smelled in years. Garza reminded himself that this was, after all, an island, and he closed his eyes, imagining the nearby sea.

Broomstick thin, Bean had an affected way of scooping at the air with his right shoulder when he walked. This sideways gait brought to mind the writhing of a snake—and made Garza hate him from the moment they'd first met.

"The boat is ready for you, sir," Bean said, bowing his head slightly toward Camacho. His quirky behavior chased away any feelings of tranquility the pristine scene might have otherwise offered.

Garza was not certain how his boss had come to hire the strange man, but whatever it was, it was enough for Camacho to trust him with his life. It was not, however, enough to keep him from growling when Bean was too slow in picking up his luggage. Garza motioned for the *sicarios* to help. He wanted to keep his hands free—and establish his dominance as a gun-carrying drug lord rather than a money-laundering baggage handler.

The two pilots, a German and an Australian, were well aware of the sort of man they worked for. With no ground crew, they set about taking care of the Gulfstream. There was an apartment in the back of the shop, and they would stay there, keeping to themselves until their boss was ready to depart.

"I've arranged for a tour of a nearby cave, sir," Bean said, sliding the last of the suitcases into the back of a white Ford van.

"Later," Camacho barked, glancing at the gold nugget Omega he insisted calling his "Alaska watch." "Take me to *Pilar* before we do anything else." He waved his hand at the rapidly darkening sky. "I wish to be underway and fishing as soon as possible. It looks as though we may be in for some wind and rain very soon." He threw back his head as if to howl and drew in a wheezing breath. "Oh, how I love this air!"

"You are correct in your forecast. I believe we are in for a storm," Bean said. "Probably by tomorrow morning, but I suppose it is good to get away from the heat."

Camacho gave Beti a hard pinch on the bottom, causing her to jump. Garza saw the flash of hatred in the girl's eyes, but it melted into a smile soon enough. Camacho gave her a pat on the rump as if to console her from the injury of the pinch.

"It is good to get away from my wife," he said. "Enough talk. Take me to my boat."

CHAPTER 6

A blue-black raven rose into a slate sky from the top of a giant Sitka spruce two minutes after Camacho had boarded *Pilar*, his fifty-four-foot Nordic Tug. The bird, apparently startled by the sound of Beti's agitated shrieks, settled back into the branches a moment later.

Garza rushed forward, more interested in what had caused the scream than in Beti's well-being.

The blond woman stood at the foot of the queen-size bed, gripping a red silk nightgown in both fists. She held it up, shaking it at the men as they poured into the small cabin.

"What?" Camacho demanded. "Why do you caw this way?"

"Look at it!" Beti howled. "Just look at it! Someone has worn my things."

"Are you certain?" Garza stared at the gown. His mind wandered and he imagined what it would look like hanging off Beti's wide shoulders. She was an attractive woman, so it was a natural reaction. Still, his main concern was of a possible trespasser on the boat.

"Perhaps you are mistaken, my dear," Camacho said.

She thrust the wad of cloth toward him. "Smell

it," she said. "Tell me this is not the scent of someone else."

Camacho sniffed the gown. His face fell into a dark frown as he turned back to Bean, who stood cringing at the cabin door.

"Who cleaned the boat before we arrived?"

The mine manager licked his lips. His eyes flitted back and forth as if looking for a way to escape. "A Native girl," he stammered. "The same one who tidies the boat each time before you get here." His nose twitched, rabbit-like. "She lives in Klawock, a village nearby."

"And does this Native girl make a habit of going through Beti's clothing?"

"Of course not, Mr. Camacho," Bean said. "I mean to say, she does not know who the clothing on the boat belongs to, but she has been instructed not to do anything but air out the vessel, squeegee the windows, and make things presentable for your arrival."

"Bring this woman to me," Camacho said, his eyes growing darker.

Beti sniffed a pair of black panties, then held them up to Camacho. "She has worn these as well," the woman gasped. "Can you imagine? You must teach her a lesson, Ernesto!"

Camacho swatted the panties away, striking Beti's hand hard enough that she cried out.

He drew the Heckler & Koch 9mm. He was seldom without the pistol. "Shut up!" he said.

"I do not care about your precious underwear. It is enough that this woman touched anything on the boat that did not belong to her. For that I will personally—"

"Patrón." Garza raised his hand to interrupt—something that would have earned any other man a bullet. "Perhaps we should wait until you are ready to leave the area before you do anything to this woman that might . . . draw undo attention."

Camacho stared for a long moment, then pointed the H & K directly at Bean's twitching temple, finger on the trigger. One of the *sicarios* chuckled and Camacho spun, pointing the pistol at him and cocking it. "You think this is funny?" he shrieked, spittle flying from his lips.

"No, Patrón," the *sicario* said, eyes downcast.

No one on the boat breathed but Camacho, whose nostrils flared in near apoplectic fury. At length he shook his head, his scowl settling on Bean as he tucked the pistol back into his waistband.

"Patrón," Garza said again, quieter this time. "Please allow me to take care of the matter of this intrusive woman."

Camacho looked away. It was what he did when he knew he had overreacted, which he managed to do several times a day. He dropped the crumpled gown on the cabin floor and stalked out the door. The *sicarios* followed, bumping into one another in the narrow confines of the passageway. Garza sighed and followed them out, leaving Beti with her nose buried in the remainder of the underwear she'd left aboard *Pilar*, sniffing for the scent of unworthy women.

Topside, Camacho stood at the forward rail. He faced away from the island, toward the sea, but his eyes were pinched, focused on nothing. He was thinking—which in Garza's experience was a dangerous thing indeed. The other men in Los Leónes stayed well away when Camacho fell into what they secretly called his "thinking fits." Garza stood at the rail beside him, looking out to sea and doing some thinking of his own.

Camacho turned to him suddenly. "I know she is a whore," he said, his voice soft and steady, as if explaining something to a small child. "But she is *my* whore. When someone disrespects her, they disrespect me. Do you understand? Such behavior must not go unanswered."

"I do not suggest that it should, Patrón," Garza said. "Only that you wait for the proper time. The danger of your being seen is much too great if we act in haste."

Camacho cleared his throat and spat over the side. "I know you believe this trip to be idiocy, Manolo. You have made that perfectly clear."

Garza shook his head, still gazing out to sea. "I only fear for your safety."

"Manolo, look at me." Camacho snapped his fingers. "Do you forget who I am?"

"Of course not," Garza said, turning his head, but keeping his elbows on the rail. "But we are in a different world. Some nosy journalist stuffed in a barrel of acid in Reynosa is one death among hundreds, easy to conceal. Here, the police, the people in general, they do not know to fear you."

"I am beginning to think you do not fear me, my friend." Camacho's face was impassive. He took a cigar from the breast pocket of his wool shirt and a cutter from his slacks. "I am well aware that gutting an enemy here would cause a momentary stir. And, I am intelligent enough to know we do not have sufficient acid, nor barrels of the perfect size for a body." He clicked the cigar cutter in the air for effect.

Garza shut his eyes, but said nothing. Camacho could dream up countless methods to make a grisly point of murder, but ninety-nine times out of a hundred, it was his *segundo*, Garza, who lit the match, flicked the razor—or fit the cigar cutter around a trembling finger.

Camacho lit his cigar, pulling on it thoughtfully while he looked back out at the sea. "Again, I ask you, what is the point of laundering my money in Alaska if I cannot take advantage of the other treasures this place has to offer? Is it too much to wish for a few days of peaceful fishing with a beautiful whore by my side and a trusted companion to see to my safety?"

"As you wish, Patrón," Garza said, smiling to

conceal the fact that he was gritting his teeth.

"Good," Camacho said. "If anyone sees me, that person will simply disappear. The sea is wide and deep, my friend, an easy enough place for someone to become . . . lost." Camacho paused as he took a series of puffs from his cigar, keeping his eyes on the shifting waves. "A reality you would do well to remember before you question me repeatedly in front of the others."

Garza gave his boss a broad smile, not because he was frightened, or ready to fall in line, but because he was smart enough to hide the fact that he would not be threatened—even obliquely, by the likes of Ernesto Camacho.

CHAPTER 7

Cutter threw his Ford into park and watched the twenty-something kid with the neck tattoo go through the front door of the Alaska Club off O'Malley Road. The deputy noticed things like neck tats and gangbangers with bouncing walks that barely kept their low-slung pants on. It was a habit that kept him alive. The kid carried a black gym bag, and had he been walking into a bank, Cutter would have paid even more attention. But tattoos and black bags were not exactly out of the norm in a gym.

Still, instinct made Cutter crane his head to try and locate the kid's vehicle so he could get a plate, but the lot was full so he chalked the feeling up to professional paranoia. He took out his cell phone for one last check of his e-mail before he went inside. Leaning toward Luddite, he hated being chained to any electronic device and made it clear to everyone, including his bosses, that he had to manually check for texts and e-mails. If someone wanted to talk to him right away, they'd have to break down and make a voice call. It had been all of twenty minutes since he'd last checked, and he already had seven new e-mails, three of which were flagged as urgent. The flags didn't fool him. If there was anything Cutter had learned over the course of nearly two decades of military and civilian service, it was that one person's "urgent" was another's "I forgot to buy milk."

He looked at his watch, and then thumb-typed a reply to one, a budget request from some poor minion working late at USMS headquarters in Virginia—four hours ahead and worlds away from Alaska. The rest of the e-mails, he saved for later.

The US Marshals Service maintained a well-appointed gym in the federal building, full of free weights, machines, treadmills, and kettle bells. There were even a couple of heavy bags and a decent mat room. And, it was all located less than ten steps from the door to Cutter's office. They shared it with the US court system so there were, periodically, lawyers who came to work out as well, but even that didn't slow down most deputies. The problem for Cutter was Lola Fontaine.

The three hours of paid FIT time deputy US marshals got each week only scratched the surface for Fontaine's needs. If she couldn't come in early, she stayed late, adding at least another hour each day to what she did in her home gym.

Cutter decided that in order to obey the chief and not throat punch Fontaine's pinhead husband, it would be better if he steered clear of the USMS gym and got a membership at the Alaska Club.

Besides, the Alaska Club had a pool, and like his grandpa, Grumpy, always said, if he didn't get in the water at least three times a week, his gills would dry up.

Cutter was so new to Anchorage he'd yet to meet many people besides fugitives and other cops. The mean mug generally kept anyone who recognized him at bay. The only real downside to working out off-site was that there was no secure place inside the gym for him to lock up his pistols, forcing him to leave them in the Ford's center-console lockbox. This also left him unarmed—but that was all right. He had other skills.

The sound of clattering weight machines and stifled grunts carried out the door on the humid air with the odor of rubber mats and chlorine. Cutter swiped his key fob on the small machine at the reception counter. His name, photo, and the date of his last payment popped up on the computer in front of a muscle-bound kid with a shaved head who sat there. The kid looked up to make sure Cutter was Cutter, and then went back to reading his fitness magazine.

Never one to lift massively heavy weights, Cutter believed in building working muscles. He'd felt in the best shape of his life a high school summer when he and his brother hauled hay for a local cattle ranch. Eighty-pound bales of wire-tied coastal bermuda grass were not particularly heavy for a fifteen-year-old as tall as Arliss Cutter, but bucking them overhead for ten hours a day made for a beach body he'd yet to see again. His fifteen-year-old's hormones had a lot to do with it, but just as Grumpy must have planned, he'd been so tired that summer his beach time to show off his beach body was practically nil. Now, his forty-year joints were more than happy if he stuck to body weight routines, jumped a little rope, and swam a mile every other day. The run-in with Donut Woodfield had turned out all right, but it left his shoulders knotted and cable-tight. The conversation with the chief had only added a twisted gut to the mix. Thankfully, today was a swim day, which would do double duty, working the knots out of his muscles and his brain—insofar as the knots in his brain could be undone at all.

In the locker room, he changed into a plain cotton T-shirt and pair of light blue board shorts, and then slipped into his shower shoes before giving the combination on his locker a good spin to make sure it was secure. He kept the cell phone with him, and would leave it in his shoes while he swam. It was a government phone, with two layers of security, so good riddance if anyone stole it. He took a quick rinse-off shower just inside the exit of the locker room, then made his way onto the echoing pool deck.

It was late enough in the afternoon that school

was out. Families had started to drift in and now lounged in small pockets around the pool deck, chatting away while they braved the stuffy humidity and waited a half hour for the adult lap swim to be over. Two high-school-age girls with chestnut hair falling over narrow shoulders sat with towels over their legs at the end of the bleachers. They looked enough alike to be sisters, and together, they tried to ignore the twenty-something youth with the neck tattoo that Cutter had seen when he came in. The kid was bigger than Cutter had originally thought, built like a swimmer—lean with a broad back and sinewy arms. Cutter was close enough now to identify the tat as a hangman's noose. He wasn't against tattoos on principle. He had one from the 75th Ranger Regiment on his upper arm. His mother hadn't been happy about it, but Grumpy had a couple from his time in the navy, so it was only natural that Cutter would follow suit. It was a declaration of sorts that he wanted to be like his grandpa. Whatever declaration a tattoo of a hangman's noose was meant to make, getting it on the neck was a virtual shout.

Never one to say no to his gut twice in the same hour, Cutter moved in closer to investigate. Near enough to hear snippets of the conversation amid the echoes around the pool, he slid his shower shoes under the bottom bleacher. He stood for a moment and pretended to check his phone. Noose

Neck glanced up and gave him a dismissive eye roll. He was, after all, just another old dude in board shorts and a nondescript T-shirt.

The kid turned back and checked to see if the girls wanted to score some weed, which, he reminded them, was more or less legal in Alaska. It didn't take long for him to make it clear that he had more potent items in his inventory if marijuana wasn't their preference.

Finally sick of Cutter's presence, he turned and stomped his foot, showing off for the girls. He'd left his car keys and shoes on the bleachers next to him and he pushed them away as if to save more space so Cutter wouldn't sit down beside him.

Noose Neck did the little gangbanger dance, bobbing his head as he spoke. "I owe you money or something?" He shot a conspiratorial look at the girls. "Old folks these days, sheeiit!"

The girls looked at their toes.

Cutter wanted to beat the guy down with a ball bat, but he raised his hands instead. "Just here to swim, pal," he said.

"I ain't your pal." Noose Neck turned his attention back to the girls. Cutter backed away, snatching up the kid's keys as he did. The nearest girl noticed and stifled a giggle. Cutter held a finger to his lips and gave her a wink. Noose Neck turned again, but by that time, Cutter was leaving with the keys folded in his fist and out of sight.

Cutter left the pool and padded quickly across the carpeted weight room. Most of the people in the gym were so engrossed in their workouts that they didn't notice he was soaking wet from his preswim shower. At the reception counter he positioned himself so he could get a good look at the computer monitor, then swiped the fob on Noose Neck's keys.

A photo popped up immediately, identifying the owner as Clinton Newberry. His address was, in fact, not five blocks from Donut Woodfield's apartment.

The kid at the desk looked up from his muscle mag at the sound of the scanner blip. Surprisingly, he was on the ball enough to see that Cutter's face didn't match the image on the screen.

He nodded toward a plastic basket on the counter. "Lost stuff goes in the bin."

Cutter pitched the keys in the air and caught them again. "Oh, I know this guy," he said. "He's in the pool. I'll make sure he gets them."

The kid shrugged and buried his face in the magazine. "Whatever," he said.

Cutter stopped near a vacant rowing machine and punched the nonemergency number for Anchorage PD into his cell phone. A female dispatcher with a pleasantly Southern drawl answered on the second ring. Cutter identified himself and gave her a quick rundown of his location and the situation. He asked her to run

Newberry for warrants by name only, without the usual identifiers like date of birth or Social Security number. He figured the odds of previous contact with law enforcement was high for someone with a hangman's noose inked around his neck.

The dispatcher came back almost immediately, going so far as to call him "hon." Definitely from the South.

"The warrant gods have smiled on you, Marshal," she said. "Clinton Newberry is wanted on multiple Failures to Appear for the misconduct involving a controlled substance and misconduct involving a weapon. I have two units heading to you now."

"Thank you," Cutter said, as much to the "warrant gods" as the dispatcher. "Tell your officers they can meet me at the pool."

Cutter pitched Noose Neck Newberry's keys into the air again, playing catch with himself all the way back to the pool deck. The idiot was still working his sales pitch on the chestnut-haired sisters when he got there. The nearest girl shook her head when she saw Cutter was back, scooting farther away from Newberry.

"What," Noose Neck said, "Daddy's little girl too good to talk to me?"

By now Cutter was less than two steps away. "Could be she just doesn't want any of what you're sellin'," he said.

Newberry spun on his heels, glaring daggers. "What?"

Cutter shrugged. "Or, maybe it's just your unpleasant odor," he said.

Newberry's eyes shifted from Cutter to the girls, then back to Cutter again, lingering this time to size him up. Cutter had about four inches on the kid, but Newberry looked to match Cutter pound for pound, all of it youthful muscle.

"This don't concern you, Gramps," he said. "I'm having a word with my ladies."

"Your ladies are leaving," Cutter said, nodding toward the two girls as they hustled to the far end of the bleachers.

A rare smile crept across Cutter's face when he saw the silhouette of a uniformed APD officer appear at the back door to the pool, coming in from the parking lot. He glanced over his shoulder to see another walking in through the main entrance.

Noose Neck loosed a furious growl and rushed forward, driving his shoulder into Cutter's gut. Cutter took the hit, but sidestepped, snaking his arms around the kid's neck, backpedaling across the pool deck. The lifeguard's shrill whistle echoed into the rafters as they both fell into the deep end of the pool—where Cutter was right at home.

Newberry's problem was that he'd never learned to quit cursing before going under. Cutter kept his thoughts to himself and took a deep breath an instant before they hit the water. He'd swum in the army, and was used to instructors administering what was affectionately known as "moderate harassment," which basically meant an underwater wrestling match with a couple of bigger dudes who were trying to drown you.

Cutter drove to the bottom of the pool with a series of powerful kicks, drawing Newberry into a tight bear hug. What little air the man had in his lungs bubbled out pursed lips in a pitiful string. Pinned twelve feet below the surface, Newberry thrashed, attempting to scream, but managed only a burbling groan. Cutter waited for him to relax, then spun him around immediately and towed him back to the surface. Even then, the hapless kid made a halfhearted attempt to fight again, but Cutter, cheek to cheek as they swam to the edge, whispered in his ear, "You seriously wanna have another go?"

One of the officers, a redheaded woman named Fuller, waved. "Hey, Clinton," she said. "How's it going?"

Newberry sputtered, trying to jerk away. "This son of a bitch tried to drown me!"

Officer Fuller smiled. "Looked to us like you pushed him in the water but he saved your ass anyway." She turned to Cutter. "I assume you're the marshal."

Newberry clamored into the shallow end,

coughing. A string of snot hung from the end of his nose. "Marshal? My charges ain't federal."

"I happened to be in the area," Cutter said. "You guys need anything from me?"

Fuller spoke over her shoulder as she directed a sputtering Newberry to kneel on the tiled pool deck while she cuffed him. "Nope."

Cutter took the drowned cell phone from the pocket of his shorts and handed it up to Fuller. "Would you mind putting that on the bench there," he said. "I still have some laps to do."

Fuller took the phone. Water drained from it onto the pale blue tile. "You know this is toast, right?"

Cutter looked at Noose Neck Newberry and shook his head. "I know, right? I'm one lucky SOB. One less bad guy on the street and one less phone I have to worry about. Fifteen minutes in the sauna and this day will be just about perfect."

CHAPTER 8

Carmen Delgado braced herself against the side of the aluminum skiff and set her lips in a tight line. She would have crossed her arms but she had to hold her video camera. The blocky housing of the Canon C300 muffled her voice. "I wasn't happy about this yesterday," she said. "And I absolutely hate it today."

The bottom of the little boat crunched against the gravel, forcing Delgado to grab a handful of gunnel. It ruined her shot, but she had to prepare herself for the approaching jolt that she knew would come when they ran aground. The sea was calm but even the small amount of wave action caused the skiff to rock, scraping against the shoreline.

They'd spent the last two hours scouting locations on their way to this protected bay on the remote southeast side of the island. Greg Conner should have been shooting video. He was a much better cinematographer. But if Carmen had been at the tiller, she would have turned them around at the entrance. This place gave her the creeps.

The prop burbled in the shallow surf like a child blowing bubbles in a milkshake as Greg gunned the thirty-horse motor to drive them farther onto the shore. He was eight years her junior—a mere twenty-one, barely old enough to buy beer for crying out loud. A constant flirt, his eyes held a mischievous sparkle, like Peter Pan with an overactive libido. The thick mop of dirty blond dreadlocks framed his face so that he looked like a young lion. He was cute and talented—a deadly combination in this business.

"You worry too much," he said for the fifth time in as many minutes. "Especially for someone who wears pajamas when we're out on an important shoot." He nodded at the checkered flannel pants Delgado had tucked into the top of her rubber boots.

"Hey." She smiled, flirting back in spite of her misgivings. "I told you, if I'm wearing my bra, these aren't pajamas anymore."

Greg gave a husky chuckle. He was already looking through the viewfinder of a Canon C300 identical to Delgado's, the instrument with which he did his magic. "Wear a bra . . . don't wear a bra," he said. "Those are still flannel jammies— and you still worry too much."

"So says the hardened criminal," Carmen said. "I put my pajama-clad butt on the line to get you on this gig. You know how the network feels about people with felony records."

"That's rich." Conner smirked. "The network couldn't give two shits about my record as long as we give them the footage they want." He panned the Canon toward a tiny log cabin high above the gravel beach. The dark forest of loppy-topped hemlock trees provided a perfect backdrop. A low sun sent a jeweled trail across the surface, bathing the beach grass and the little cabin in glowing light. It was the *golden hour*—the scant few moments each day when otherwise ho-hum footage turned into solid . . . well, gold. And as field producer, Carmen Delgado knew the money people at the network who backed her reality show, *FISHWIVES!*, would love this shot.

FISHWIVES! Carmen still found it difficult to believe this was the show her brainchild had morphed into. She'd pitched a number of ideas over the course of her career—a fish-out-of-water docu-follow about earnest young teachers facing the rigors of bush Alaska, an adventure series about young people working the many harsh and varied jobs the wilds of Alaska offered, and a half dozen other smart concepts. Beginning as *Homeport*, a show about the intertwined drama in the lives of fishing families in Southeast Alaska, the network had turned her idea into the grotesquely popular *FISHWIVES!* The title from the pejorative term for a loud and foul-mouthed woman—and Carmen Delgado was given the task of finding a cast that fit the description.

In order to help her fall into line with their vision of the concept, the network uppity ups gave her creative credit along with the title of executive producer. As much as the particulars disgusted her, a show like this could make her career, so she made it her personal mission to keep things on track—and if not exactly legal, then at least defendable in court.

She got a shot up the bank through the beach grass and brought the sod roof of the cabin into focus. Her camera may have been identical to Greg's but she would get nowhere near the same quality of footage. It was a mystery how this kid˙ who lived on a diet of nothing but alcohol, Red Bull, and Snickers bars—and shot by some sort of gut instinct over technical know-how—hit it out of the park every single time. If Greg Conner hadn't been so hell-bent on flushing his personal life down the toilet, he would have been her boss by the time he was twenty-five.

"Kenny's going to kill us when he finds out we came all the way down here," Delgado said.

"Kenny is otherwise engaged, if you know what I mean." Greg spoke without lowering his camera.

"I have no idea what you're talking about," Delgado said, knowing full well what Kenny was doing, but not wanting to discuss it.

"Never mind." Greg kept his camera rolling but looked sideways at her. "Anyway, he's not going to find out we're here—unless you plan to tell him."

Network insurance required the production have a safety officer on site to guard against the various bugbears and dangers of any rural shoot. For *FISHWIVES!* Carmen had hired Kenny Douglas, an out-of-work commercial fisherman from Ketchikan who had landed a couple of jobs as security on other shows. Kenny wasn't a tall man but he made up for it in rawboned muscle. It was his job to keep them from doing anything stupid—which included boating out to the middle of nowhere without him. He carried a .44 Magnum revolver in a holster across his chest and a knife as big as a sword on his belt. He smiled often, but most of the crew was of the consensus that this was because he'd just eaten a particularly tasty kitten. Delgado was scared to death of him.

She looked through her viewfinder, scanning the perfect layers of gray gravel, green beach grass, and the black line of woods beyond. "I have to admit," she said, "this place does look good in this light. I'm still not happy about us being on CCC property though."

"We're not on mine property," Greg mumbled.

"The map says different," Carmen said, rolling her eyes. This kid just wouldn't stop.

"Private land doesn't start until you get above the tide line," Greg said. He did a slow pan with the Canon. "It's a law. No one can own the ocean. As long as we stay below that line of driftwood and other debris the tide has pushed up, we get the footage the network wants of a quaint little cabin in the woods, and nobody at the mine can say shit to us."

Carmen decided to stop talking and film since they were already here. A network exec had seen some early footage of Fitz and Bright Jonas, arguably the star couple on *FISHWIVES!* Fitz, a professional gillnetter, trawler, and long-liner, had the requisite scruffy foot-of-facial-hair, and crazy eyes to make him a much-loved reality television star. His wife, Bright, possessed the flower-child look and sailor's mouth to make her the quintessential Fishwife. There had been a frightening moment early in the casting process when Carmen discovered that Fitz was actually a gentle soul, despite his looks. Thankfully, Bright knew how to spin him up and they fought all the time on camera, making for just the sort of television the network and viewers craved. To top it off, Bright caused endless small-town drama with her neighbors—a recipe for pure television gold.

There was, however, a very big problem. Fitz and Bright Jonas looked like Alaska fishermen, and they acted like the viewing public believed Alaska fishermen should act—but they lived in a sweet little white frame house in downtown Craig with a picket fence and a basketball hoop at the end of their driveway. The network insisted that they live in a cabin—and not just any cabin. More specifically a tiny, dilapidated log cabin somewhere secluded so that Bright could pitch a fit about her rustic accommodations—all to add to their origin story and give them a better arc. A successful fishing couple that continues to be successful didn't make for good television, no matter how much Bright pissed off her neighbors. She needed to live in a house that looked like it was in the wilds of Alaska, not suburban Omaha.

It was Greg's idea to shoot the exterior of the dinky little cabin that sat on CCC Mine property. He suggested they even get a few shots of Fitz Jonas approaching in a skiff or Bright Jonas standing at the water's edge—below the tide line of course—and cursing at her husband for leaving her home alone in their shack to go off to sea and fish. There was another cabin on the west side of the island, nearer to town, with a killer interior that they could use for the inside shots of Bright Jonas throwing down ultimatums at her poor husband. Once the footage was properly edited, the viewing public would have no idea that the interior and exterior were, in fact, nearly thirty miles apart by boat. By the second episode, the show runner would have Fitz Jonas working hard to appease his warring Fishwife with a new home, the quaint little white house with the picket fence and basketball hoop—where they'd actually lived all along.

Most of the show was shot onboard fishing boats and in town between the arguing Fishwives, who, if the story arcs were to be believed, were a catty bunch of hateful women who were constantly at odds with each other and mistrustful of their husbands. Reality it was not, but it was sickeningly brilliant TV. The pilot episode had garnered a 1 rating. A million viewers was peanuts for the major networks, but for the niche markets of cable, it was enough for the network to order thirteen half-hour episodes.

"This is money right here." Greg set the Canon gently on a padded case in the floor of the boat long enough to step over the side. They were close enough to shore that the water came to midcalf on his brown Xtratuf rubber boots.

Carmen shook her head. "Where do you think you're going?"

He leaned in to retrieve the camera. "Calm down, Miss Jammie Pants. I promise not to go above the tide line." He threw the camera to his eye as he turned toward the ocean. "We just need to get some footage as if Bright is looking out from her shitty cabin at the lonely-ass sea. . . . Dammit!"

Carmen looked up to see Greg fiddling with the zoom on his lens.

"What?"

"I need a shot of the deserted bay from Bright Jonas's lonesome point of view—and now we got another boat in the picture."

Delgado twisted in her seat, rocking the boat

with her sudden movement. She caught herself, terrified for a split second that she would dump the twenty thousand dollars' worth of gear. They were aground enough on the gravel that her movements didn't matter. Calming herself, she used the zoom on her own camera to bring the image of the boat into better view—shooting all the while. It was better to waste a few megabytes of storage than miss something good. The light was right and there were ways they could always rub out the boat if they had to.

"Is it one of ours?" Delgado's voice buzzed against her hands as she watched the gleaming white vessel round the point at the east end of the bay. "Because we could totally make it work if it is." It was less than a quarter mile away. By "one of ours" she meant any of the vessels featured in *FISHWIVES!*

"I don't recognize it," Greg said. "Looks too big."

"Anyone we know?" Carmen zoomed in as close as she could, counting at least three men. "They look dark. Maybe they're Tlingit or Haida."

"Beats me," Greg said. "They don't look very happy for having such a fancy yacht."

A glint of sunlight reflected off something in one of the men's hands as the boat rounded up and put the sun behind it. Carmen steadied herself against the side of the rocking skiff and adjusted the focus until she saw one of the men held a pair of binoculars.

He appeared to be looking directly at her.

Gravel scraped aluminum and Carmen was thrown violently sideways as Greg shoved the little skiff back into deeper water and jumped aboard. She clutched her camera with one hand and the side of the boat with the other.

"What the hell!" she said. "Sink us, why don't you. These cameras are ten grand apiece."

Greg pulled the starter rope and brought the little thirty-horse to burbling life. "It might actually be time for you to worry," he said. "The mine HQ is only a couple of miles around the corner. There's a good chance the guys on the boat are coming from there."

"So?" Carmen said. "I thought you said we're good as long as we stay below the tide line."

"We *are* good," Greg said, using the tiller to steer the skiff toward the western side of the entrance, away from the yacht and back toward town. "I'm just not sure they know the law as well as I do." Silver spray shot past the gunnels and the skiff began to bounce over the waves as they came up on step, gaining speed. Greg threw a nervous glance over his shoulder. "It's something like sixteen miles back to town. I'm not a hundred percent sure we can outrun them."

Carmen tried to steady the camera but her shaking hands combined with the pitching of the skiff to make it almost impossible to get a clear picture. What she did see sent a cold chill down her back. "One of them has a rifle!" She had to shout over the roar of the outboard.

"Hunters maybe." Greg shot another look over his shoulder.

"I don't think so," Carmen said. "Looks like they're getting ready to launch a smaller boat from the back of the yacht." She lowered the camera and turned to look at Greg. "I think they're coming after us."

CHAPTER 9

Aboard *Pilar*, Manuel Alvarez-Garza grabbed the rail with both hands, gripping so hard his knuckles turned white. He could hardly keep his head from shaking. It was even worse than he had predicted. Less than two hours after landing in Alaska his fears had come to fruition. Not only had Camacho, one of the most wanted drug lords in the world, been seen, he'd been captured on video. For all Garza knew the people on the small boat were in the process of uploading this video via satellite at that very moment and streaming it across the World Wide Web.

"Cut them off!" Camacho screamed, standing beside Garza at the rail. The lunatic waved his pistol in every direction, threatening to sink the vessel if it went off. He cursed and screamed at the *sicarios* as they prepared the small aluminum skiff that was tied to the stern of the larger vessel.

"Bring them!" Camacho shouted, spitting as much as he talked. "Bring the sons of bitches to me! I will look into their miserable eyes and watch them die!"

Beti stuck her head out of the wheelhouse door, looking bewildered at all the noise. A smile perked her lips.

"*Mi amor*," she trilled. "Are you sending for the awful woman who wore my things?"

"You stupid whore!" Camacho threw his cigar, narrowly missing her face. "Get your ass back inside!"

Her head vanished like a startled ground squirrel.

"Ernesto," Garza said. "Perhaps—"

"Perhaps what, Manolo?" Camacho wheeled to face him, challenging. His neck was swollen, the veins mapping his crimson forehead pulsing with the anger of a man who'd been undone by his own stupidity. "You are so very smart. Perhaps you think now is the time for one of your lectures?" He thrust his pistol at Garza's face, stabbing the air to make his point. "You would be wise, Manolo, to keep your lectures in your own throat."

He glared for a long moment, then lowered the pistol to his side before turning his wrath back on the *sicarios*.

Garza drew his own pistol and shot Camacho above his left ear before he could say another word.

"And you would be wise not to point a gun at the man you pay to protect you," Garza said.

He glanced up at the wheelhouse and the *sicario* who was driving the boat. Fausto was loyal to him, but even he stared through the window with his mouth agape.

The other two men had already climbed into the skiff. The nearest let his hand drop toward his sidearm at the sound of the shot. None of the three men seemed to be able to make sense of what had just happened.

Garza raised both arms, though he retained the pistol in his right hand. He raised his voice to address all of them. "You men know me," he said above a stiffening breeze. "And you knew our *patrón*, Ernesto Camacho. Now know this: I will never point a gun at you unless I intend to pull the trigger."

The men stared at him, dumbfounded.

Garza shrugged. "Are we good?"

Fausto looked out the wheelhouse window, down at the shattered head of the man who had been his boss just seconds before, then gave Garza a nod. "Yes, Patrón," he said. "We are good."

The other two nodded in quick agreement.

"Camacho killed often and thought seldom," Garza said. "You men know I have no problem with killing. But Los Leónes is larger than Ernesto Camacho. He was wanted by law enforcement officials in countless countries, and the discovery that he has a connection to the mine would have proved devastating. The American DEA has a price of half a million dollars on his head. He has now been seen. This not only endangers us, it endangers the shell company that owns the mine and the entire organization that provides us our livelihoods. Go now and take care of the people who have seen him."

"Should we bring them back to you, Patrón?" Chago, the larger and more sensible of the two men in the skiff, asked.

"No," Garza said. "Patrón," it had a pleasant ring to it. "Bring me their cameras. Put their bodies somewhere where they will never be found." He looked up at the ominous line of black clouds to the west. "But hurry. I want to be off this cursed island as soon as this is resolved."

The men nodded and sped away in the skiff.

"Come, Fausto," Garza said to the man in the wheelhouse as he began to roll up his sleeves. "You will find a spare anchor in the forward locker. I must ask for your help in sinking our former employer."

CHAPTER 10

Alaska State Trooper Sam Benjamin punched in the number to Sergeant Yates in Ketchikan and pushed the bowl of homemade tomato soup across his sparse wooden desk, away from the phone. Yates, his supervisor, was a hard man, prone to bitter conversation that did not go well with soup.

Benjamin had four years on with AST—having come aboard the year after the brass in Juneau pulled the plug on *Alaska State Troopers*, the reality television show that made the agency a household name across the United States. Like many new troopers fresh out of the academy in Sitka, Sam Benjamin had started his life in the blue shirt working as a road-toad in Palmer. He'd done his share of traffic enforcement on the road system north of Anchorage before taking what he felt was a plush assignment to Craig, on Prince of Wales Island. It had been great at first, but then a new sergeant arrived who happened to be a level-ten asshole. Don Yates had transferred in from the bush post of Dillingham and treated it as his sworn duty to, as he put it, "knock the pavement out of any road troopers' mouths" and get them accustomed to working a remote post. But POW Island wasn't exactly remote—and there was plenty of pavement, so Yates couldn't do much but crap all over Sam Benjamin's world with his little nuggets of doom and gloom at every opportunity.

Five months into the posting, during an office visit to Craig, the sergeant had gone so far as to stomp on Trooper Benjamin's Stetson in a fit of rage—over a difference of opinion about what criminal charges should be filed against a local drug dealer. Benjamin had just stood there stupefied while his boss had gone ape shit and flattened the blue felt campaign hat. This guy obviously had some serious anger issues, but the incident had actually worked in Trooper Benjamin's favor. Sergeant Yates remained a hat-stomping bastard, but he seemed to realize that the pancaked Stetson was a serious indictment against him and began to treat his subordinate with a sort of dismayed ambivalence for not reporting his outburst to the lieutenant in Ketchikan. The best thing about it was that Yates more or less left Benjamin alone.

Sam Benjamin was a good-looking young man, a smidge under six feet tall with erect posture and dimpled chin that looked sharp in the blue trooper uniform. Ever since a tall man in a similar uniform had landed a Super Cub on his father's hunting camp when he was ten years old—and let him wear his flight helmet—Benjamin had wanted nothing more in life than to wear the golden bear badge. No shit they could dish out at the academy or any attitude of an angry superior could quell his ambition or stifle the unbridled pride with which he wore that badge.

The television show was a different story. *FISHWIVES!* sucked the life out of him. Not only had he missed his own chance at stardom with the cancellation of *Alaska State Troopers*, but now he had to deal with all the crap that went with a crazy reality show on his island. It included fistfights, frequent drunken parties, and the influx of drugs by the dregs of humanity that hovered around the crew members like flies. And it was, in fact, just one of these sketchy types who was the reason for the young trooper's call to his sergeant. He pulled Hayden Starnes's driver's license photo closer. With a wispy mustache, seventies mullet haircut, and vaporous eyes, he even looked the stereotypical pervert.

"Call the US Marshals," Yates ordered, before Benjamin could even tell him what the federal warrant was for. "They get paid to pick up boneheads like this guy."

Benjamin decided not to point out that he got paid for exactly the same thing. "Will do," he said, knowing it was the only answer Sergeant Yates would accept. "What if they can't make it down? This guy's wanted on sexual assault and kidnapping charges out of Oregon."

"Kidnapping would be the FBI then," Yates said,

an expert at the bureaucratic sidestep. "They'll come down if it gets their name in the paper."

"It says 'US Marshals' on the NCIC hit," the trooper said. "Supervised Release Violation for charges of sexual assault and kidnapping—"

"Now it makes more sense," Yates said, harrumphing like he'd just won some championship debate. "Don't make this a bigger deal than it is. Your bonehead's already been to court on the original charges. He's just skipped town on his probation officer."

I wonder what would make a convicted rapist and kidnapper skip town? Benjamin thought, but he didn't say it.

"You have him located?" Yates asked, sounding for a moment like he might actually relent.

"I did," Benjamin said. "He works as a gopher for the production company that does that show *FISHWIVES!*"

"I love *FISHWIVES!*" Sergeant Yates said.

Of course he did. Trooper Benjamin rolled his eyes.

"Anyway," Benjamin continued. "No one has seen this guy for a day and a half. That's what got me interested in him in the first place. The field producer reported him missing. He was using the name Travis Todd, which happened to be an alias the marshals are aware of, I guess."

"So you've located a federal fugitive and lost him all in the same day?"

"I do not know where he is at this moment," Benjamin said, pushing the soup farther away. "But I'll find him if he's still on the island."

"Call the marshals," Yates repeated. "If you don't have enough to keep you busy . . ."

"Understood, Sergeant," the trooper said. A chime rang outside his office, signifying someone was standing in the lobby outside the front door. He hoped it was Wendy bringing over some extra pizza from Papa's across the strip mall. Sometimes she did that. His soup had gotten cold anyway. "Someone's here," he said. "Gotta go. I'll let you know what the marshals say."

"Whatever," Yates said before hanging up. Benjamin thought he heard ice shift in a whiskey glass. That would explain a lot.

The trooper pushed back from his chair and stood, going through the quick once-over he always did when meeting with members of the public—.40 caliber Glock where it should be in the Sam Browne belt, low across the hips—check; gig-line arrow straight from the top button of his trooper-blue uniform shirt, through his belt buckle and zipper—check; pens in his pocket—check. Unlike many Alaska state troopers, Benjamin often opted for an under the shirt ballistic vest, believing it made him look more squared away and streamlined than the bulkier external vest carrier. A trooper who paid attention to detail had a better chance of surviving when the shit hit the fan—and Sam Benjamin did everything to make certain the details in his life were squared away.

Jenny, the AST clerk, had gone home at five, so visitors had to ring the doorbell. There were two troopers and two Fish and Wildlife troopers—known as brownshirts—assigned to the island. It was a rarity to have more than one working at any given time.

Benjamin stepped out of his office and through the cubicles occupied by the two Fish and Wildlife troopers—who both happened to be off island at the moment—to find Gerald Burkett standing outside the thick glass window.

Burkett was a round man, like a beach ball with legs. His dirty T-shirt had seen better days—and might have actually fit a man seventy pounds lighter. It looked more like a tank top now, revealing a third of Burkett's ponderous belly. He wore a pair of gray sweatpants with one leg stuffed down the top of his black rubber gum boots. An assortment of stains on both thighs showed the sweats did double duty as shop rags in the small engine repair shop where Burkett worked. A full, dirty blond beard bent outward below his chin at a right angle as if he'd fallen asleep with his head resting on a desk. His eyes were bloodshot, but that was usually the case with him by this time of day.

The trooper cocked his head to one side,

catching the sour whiff of cheap alcohol as he opened the door and got nearer to the man. "Hey, Gerald," he said, keeping it professional but friendly. "You didn't drive here, did you?"

Burkett sniffed. He'd been crying. Drunks often sobbed, but not Burkett. He was an oak among soft pine trees—stoic, unbendable, and far more likely to be a mean drunk than a weepy one.

"I did," Burkett said. There was a softness in his gray eyes that Benjamin had never seen before—like he was looking at an injured puppy or something. It was so out of character that it made Benjamin stand up straighter and rest a hand on his Taser.

Burkett continued, oblivious. "I been drivin' around the island trying to find my daughter. Just now had my first drink. You can check me on the PBT if you want." The PBT was a handheld device for administering a Preliminary Breathalyzer Test, and the fact that Burkett called it by name attested to his experience with such things.

The trooper waved Burkett through the door into his office and motioned toward the plastic chair beside his desk. "Your daughter, you say?"

Burkett nodded. He took a long hawking sniff to clear his sinuses, swallowed whatever it was that came up, then looked straight at Benjamin with those pleading eyes. "Millie," he said. "You'd know her, I'm sure. Tall thing, dark hair

104

and skin like her mom. She's Tlingit, ya know."

The trooper took out his notebook and pen. "I've seen her around. When did you see her last?"

Burkett nodded like he heard the question, but answered on his own terms and in his own time.

He sniffed again, using the back of his forearm to wipe his nose. "She's a good girl. And I ain't just sayin' that 'cause I'm her dad. She don't get into trouble much. At least she didn't until those TV guys came into town. They started her carrying that damn video camera everywhere she went, putting ideas into her head that she was some kind of investigative reporter or somethin'. She's just . . . the active sort, you know? Kids like her get bored on an island like this."

"I see," Benjamin said, his pen hovering above the notepad until Gerald Burkett gave him some piece of information he could actually write down besides "tall, dark, and Native female."

"She didn't ever come home last night," Burkett finally said. "That didn't surprise me though. She stays out with friends sometimes, so her mom and me, we just went on to bed. But when I checked, none of her friends had seen her. Come to find out, nobody has, not since yesterday at two when she told Wendy over at Papa's Pizza she was working on a story or some shit."

"Did she tell Wendy what this story was about?"

Burkett shook his head, then buried it in his hands. "Not at all," he said, the words muffled against his palms.

"Where have you looked so far?" the trooper asked. Teenagers hiding out from their parents was not really out of the norm on an island as large as Prince of Wales. There were hundreds of miles of road and countless remote spots to camp and do all the things that teenagers did when they camped.

"I checked all her friends' houses and all the drinkin' places in the woods where I've caught her before. She's been hangin' out with those guys from that show, *FISHWIVES!* I don't like 'em. I just went by their rooms and they're all off somewhere. I don't know, maybe she's gone off with 'em. Her mom's scared shitless she's got herself caught by Kushtaka. . . ." His voice trailed off and he stared at the floor.

"Kushtaka?" Benjamin said, but he didn't write it down. "The otter-man?"

"I'm sure you think my wife is crazy," Burkett said. "But you wait until you get lost in these dark woods. If you're lucky enough to make it out alive, then you come back and tell me you don't believe there's stuff out there honest white men like you and me can't explain."

The trooper read over his notes. At length, he held up the driver's license photo of Hayden Starnes. "You ever see your daughter hanging around this guy?" Word order was important here. If he'd asked if Starnes had been "hanging around" Millie, it might have caused undue worry.

Burkett shook his head. "Looks like a creep. Who is he?"

"Works on the show," the trooper said.

"That figures," Burkett said. "But no, I don't recognize him."

The trooper decided not to go into any more detail. "I need to make a call," he said. "After that, I'll make some rounds and see what I can find out about Millie. Until then, I want you to call your wife and have her pick you up. You can't drive home. "

Burkett coughed a phlegmatic cough. "You're a hardass," he said. "You know that?"

The trooper gave his official grin. "So I've been told."

"I'll wait out in the lobby."

Benjamin showed Burkett out, then sat back down at his desk. He turned to the page in his notebook where he'd written Hayden Starnes's name and date of birth. It was an awfully big coincidence that a convicted sex offender and kidnapper would disappear the same day Millie Burkett went missing. The two had to know each other from the television show. That wasn't proof of anything, but the trooper's instincts told him a shape-shifting Tlingit land otter was the last thing he needed to be worried about.

CHAPTER 11

Anchorage

Cutter sat in his sister-in-law's driveway and stared at the garage door, wondering if she'd made it home. It was nearly seven, but that didn't mean anything. She was an emergency room nurse, and like Cutter's, the length of her shifts often depended on the behaviors of others. Two fights in one day notwithstanding, there were a hell of a lot more minefields in the split-level cedar home than he'd ever had to negotiate at work. Fights he could handle. Emotions, well, they were a different animal altogether.

It had taken him over an hour to get a new phone at the Fifth Avenue Mall, and then he'd stopped to do some shopping on the way home to save his sister-in-law the trouble. He took the time to load all seven plastic grocery bags in one hand so he didn't have to make more than one trip.

Mim's twin seven-year-old boys met him at the front door to the arctic entry, each clinging to a leg in an attempted jujitsu takedown that, thankfully, they had yet to perfect. War bag and ballistic vest in one hand and seven bags of groceries in the other, he tromped across the plywood floor past the coat rack, a line of rubber boots, and white chest freezer, to enter the house proper through a second door. In the summer, such a mantrap at the entrance to the house seemed like overkill, but during the Alaska winters, these arctic entries provided a barrier to frigid air entering the house every time the door was opened. Cutter hoped his Florida blood thickened a little before that.

He paused midstep on the gray slate floor and looked down at the smiling boys.

"I need to take off my boots so your mom doesn't murder me," he said.

Collectively known as the M & Ms, the boys each slid off their respective boot as though dismounting horses. Cutter kicked off his high-shanked Tony Lamas and pushed them back next to the wall with his toe. "What's for dinner?" he asked.

Michael, the elder of the twins by twelve minutes, blinked doe-like brown eyes. He had deep golden hair, like his father had had, and a soft, smiling disposition. He shrugged and opened his eyes even wider. "I dunno."

Matthew, the younger brother, regarded Cutter with narrowed steel-blue eyes. Of the two, he looked the most like their great-grandpa Grumpy—and his uncle Arliss—including the mean mug and flaxen blond hair.

"Mom's not home yet," Matt said, his eyes unwavering—as if he was waiting for Cutter to flinch. "And Constance won't come out of her room to fix us anything to eat."

Cutter set his war bag in the corner and leaned the heavy ballistic vest against the wall.

"Well," he said, nodding toward the granite island in the middle of the kitchen. "You know what men do when no one makes us dinner?"

"Scream?" Matthew said, smiling a crooked smile and only half kidding.

"Of all the things you can do in life," Cutter said, "screaming is rarely the answer." He shooed the twins toward the kitchen. "What men do, is make our own dinner," he said. "Your great-grandpa would have had something to say about this—"

The twins perked up. "Let us be men!" They said it in unison. These were the magic words to get Cutter to reveal one of his grandfather's rules.

Most of these rules described the way Grumpy Cutter believed a man should comport himself— always look sharp, show gratitude, be slow to anger but quick to action. To Arliss, this part of the list had seemed never ending, even constraining at times. It was the many man-skills on the list that he loved. Grumpy made no secret of the fact that before any boy could pass into manhood, he had to know how to do certain things—start a fire, sharpen a knife, saddle a horse, navigate by the stars, and, among other things, cook.

"Grumpy Man-Rule number seven," he said. "A man ought to know how to cook creamy scrambled eggs."

Michael cocked his head to the side, looking unconvinced. "Wait, I thought Grumpy Man-Rule number seven was keep the car waxed and shiny. . . ."

Cutter opened his sister-in-law's fridge and shook his head. He dug behind a net bag of sadly shriveled brussels sprouts to get a carton of eggs from the drawer. "No, keeping a clean vehicle is Grumpy Man-Rule number nine." He set the eggs on the granite island next to the gas burners and grabbed a pan from the rack above. The twins pulled up two chairs from the table and stood on either side of him, elbows on the counter, chins on their hands.

Cutter washed up and threw a towel over his shoulder. "What about Man-Rule number ten?"

Both boys threw back their heads as if to crow.

"When a man cooks a snack," they said in unison, "he makes enough for everyone else in the house."

Matt looked up and patted Cutter on the elbow. "Can I please wear it while we cook?"

Cutter knew exactly what "it" was. He and his brother used to ask Grumpy the same question. He felt like he was looking in the mirror at his seven-year-old self.

"Of course." Cutter pulled a silver coin up from

111

his shirt collar and looped the thin beaded chain over Matt's head. The boy rubbed the medallion between his small thumb and forefinger as if to shine it. A little larger than a quarter, the medallion bore the relief of a navigational compass rose, the heading needle aligned with magnetic north, but the direction-of-travel arrow pointed toward the Big Dipper and the North Star. Both boys studied it with reverent awe.

"Watch your heading," Michael said. "Grumpy Man-Rule number one."

Cutter nodded, thinking how many times he'd heard his grandfather chide him with those same words—nearly as many times as he warned Cutter to "check his windage and elevation" when it looked like he was about to make a sketchy decision.

"Can I please wear it after Matt?" Michael said.

"Roger that," Cutter said. He counted out the eggs so each boy would have an even amount to break. "So, two for each of you, three for me, three for Constance, and two for your—"

As if on cue, the boys' mother, Cutter's widowed sister-in-law, breezed in through the door from the garage. Mim's entrances had always been grand in Cutter's mind. She smiled an honest smile when she saw Arliss and her twins in the kitchen, wrinkling her smallish nose, accenting the blush of her peaches-and-cream complexion. Her dirty blond hair was pulled back in a high ponytail—

no doubt to keep it out of her way during her shift at Alaska Regional, but it suited her. She'd been wearing it in the same way the day they'd first met, twenty-five years and ten months earlier, the summer before they each turned sixteen.

She had been working in a little bait shop on Manasota Key where the Cutter brothers had gone to hunt for shark's teeth—and girls who had peaches-and-cream complexions. Arliss had seen her first, and she had just enough time to tell him that her name was Miriam but everyone called her Mim—before big brother Ethan swooped in. He smiled more, was a year older, and thus more sure of himself. He made the first move. Arliss took Grumpy's Man-Rule number two to heart—"a man does not steal his brother's woman"—so the rest was twenty-five years and ten months of history.

Nursing came naturally to Miriam Cutter. She was empathetic and caring, but more than capable of making someone cry if it was for their own good. Cutter tore his eyes away before she caught him looking. Twenty years of marriage, three kids, and a whole lot of heartbreak had hardly aged her at all. She looked pretty damned sexy in her lavender hospital scrubs. She probably needed to hear it—and the good Lord knew Cutter wanted to tell her—but the "sister" part of sister-in-law, made him keep the thought to himself.

"This looks interesting," Mim said, stepping in to kiss both her boys on top of their blond heads. She touched Cutter on the arm. "What do we have going on here?"

"Uncle Arliss is teaching us how to make creamy scrambled eggs like his grandpa," Michael said. Matt was busy cracking his half of the eggs into a clear glass bowl.

"Grumpy Man-Rules?" She smiled at Cutter.

Both boys raised their hands above their heads and cheered. "Grumpy Man-Rules!"

"Carry on then," Mim said, winking at Cutter. "I'll take two, please. It was a long day at the hospital and I didn't get lunch. Where's Constance?"

"Room," the twins said, again in unison.

"Of course she is," Mim said, heaving a sigh as she looked through a pile of mail on the counter. She took a single envelope—tan and official looking—and left the rest where it was.

"All right, men," Cutter said. "The secret to perfect creamy scrambled eggs is taking them on and off the burner—high heat but slow cooking."

Mim shot an almost imperceptible glance at Cutter. They locked eyes for a brief moment, he nodded, she disappeared down the hallway. There was still a hell of a lot left unsaid between them. He pushed it out of his mind and turned his attention back to the mess the twins were making with the eggs.

"I think we're ready," he said after he'd pinched most of the bits of shell out of the bowl. He poured the yellow slurry in the non-stick pan with a generous gob of melted butter. He held the handle in his left hand and a silicon spatula in his right.

Michael raised a wooden salt grinder over the pan and paused, looking at his uncle. "Salt?"

"Nope," Cutter shook his head.

"Nope," Matt repeated, as if it was common knowledge that salt would start the eggs to curdle a little too quickly at this point in the process.

"We'll salt them when they're almost done," Cutter said. He demonstrated as he talked. "The rest is easy: on the flame until they start to cook, then off the flame and stir with the spatula. Then back on the flame until they start to cook a little more, then off the flame and stir—"

His cell phone began to buzz in the pocket of his jeans. He looked at the boys. "Ready to be men?"

"Let us be men!" they said again.

He passed the handle of the pan off to Matt and the spatula to Michael before turning off the heat on the stove. The eggs were about done anyway. "Don't burn your paws," he said, pulling the towel off his shoulder to dry his hands before picking up the cell.

"Cutter," he said, stepping back to give the twins enough space to mess up, but not ruin the meal.

It was Lola Fontaine. She was the duty deputy

for the month so she'd be triaging calls from the answering service, deciding if they could wait until the next day or were important enough to require a task force call-out.

"Hey, boss," she said. "Got time to chat a minute?"

"What's up?"

"I just got an interesting call from the trooper in Craig, down on Prince of Wales Island."

"Where?"

Alaska was a big state, with nearly ten times the land area of Florida, and Cutter was still learning the layout of his new district.

"Craig is a little town on a big-ass island down near Ketchikan, about eight hundred miles to the southeast."

She went on to brief him about the fugitive Hayden Starnes, an unregistered sex offender who was supposedly hiding on the island. Keeping one eye on the boys, Cutter walked into the living room and grabbed a red paperback Alaska atlas from Mim's bookcase. He sat down on the couch and found Prince of Wales Island in the book while Fontaine talked.

"And the troopers can't grab him?" Cutter put on his budget hat, figuring the taxpayer dollars they'd spend to take a commercial flight to Ketchikan, then the expensive air taxi to make the hour flight west through the mountains to Prince of Wales Island.

"The trooper I talked to says he wants to help," Fontaine said. "But our guy is in the wind—or the woods if you wanna be technical. And get this, boss, Starnes did a hundred and twenty-seven months in Marion for kidnapping and sexual assault—and a teenage girl went missing on the island around the same time he dropped out of sight."

Marion was a US prison, a step up—or down, depending on one's point of view—from the more common federal correctional institution. White-collar criminals were assigned to camps, bad guys did their time at an FCI. Bona fide turds went to a USP.

Cutter looked toward the kitchen in time to see Matthew chastise Michael for twisting the salt grinder over the pan. He stopped them with a look, then gave a thumbs-up to show that the eggs were done before turning back to the call.

"Go ahead and set us up a flight first thing tomorrow morning," he said. "Text me when you know times. I'll call the chief and get her to approve the funding."

"Just you and me?" she asked.

Cutter groaned, wondering if Fontaine's husband was sitting right beside her. He seemed the type that wouldn't let her out of his sight when they were home. But then, she looked like the type to kick him in the teeth for being overbearing.

"With Blodgett on light duty for the foreseeable future . . ."

"True enough," she said. "I'll try to get us a hotel with a good gym."

"Fontaine," Cutter said before she could hang up. "Is this going to be a problem? The two of us going on this trip together?"

There was a long silence on the phone.

"I'm a big girl, Cutter," she snapped. "I don't have to ask Larry's permission to go on assignment, if that's what you mean."

"This is serious," he said. "It's pretty clear Larry has a problem with you and me working together. I'm not going to fight a battle on two fronts."

"Not sure what that even means," she said. The bristles were clear in her voice.

"It means," Cutter said, "that I don't have time to worry about jealous husbands while I'm busy hunting a bandit—and neither do you."

"Roger that," she said, obviously clenching her teeth at the other end of the line. "I'm telling you, it's not a thing."

The line went dead. Cutter sighed, feeling a moment of sympathy for Lola Fontaine. Lord knew he'd married his share of crazies. He pushed the memories out of his mind and turned to the twins, clapping his hands. "Are we good?"

The boys smiled. Both were already helping themselves to the freshly scrambled eggs straight out of the pan.

"Go wash up and get your sister," Cutter said. "I've got an early day tomorrow and I have to pack."

"Pack?" Matt whined, gulping down a spoonful of eggs and throwing back his head. He stuck out his lip in a pout. "Where are you going?"

"Grumpy Man-Rule twenty," Cutter said.

Both boys lit up. "Hunting bad guys?"

Cutter nodded, paraphrasing Isaac Parker, the infamous hanging judge out of Fort Smith, Arkansas—which happened to also be his grandfather's Man-Rule twenty—"Let no guilty man go free."

CHAPTER 12

January Cross lugged the heavy yellow extension cord out of the lazarette at the rear of her homely little boat. Built along the lines of a fishing trawler, but with a semi-displacement hull to gain a hair more speed, *Tide Dancer* was absent the trawling arms of her professional sisters. She had once been a sight to behold. At least forty years old, her bilge worked a little harder now and she squatted lower in the water. A previous owner had done some shoddy fiberglass work to the wheelhouse, leaving the brow over the front windows oddly canted, as if she were scowling. January's father said the crooked aspect put him in mind of a "scandalized" sailing ship. She'd yet to look up the meaning under that context, but liked the sentiment and the word.

A lot of things aboard *Tide Dancer* were scandalized.

Cross plugged the male end of the power cord into the stainless steel shore box, allowing her to run her electronics and charge her batteries during the extremely short time she planned to stay in port. *Tide Dancer* occupied the outer slip on the last float at the farthest end of the dock—across from the drab US Forest Service building that loomed over the entrance to the South Harbor.

She was about as far as she could be from the parking lot and the entrance to the small marina. This gave her some distance between the noisy kids skateboarding or walking past on the Craig-Klawock Highway, but it also put her in the wake of nearly every boat that came in. Given the choice, January Cross would always pick a spot that put her farther from people and closer to the sea. Plus, her position put her closer to *Southern Cross*, the beamy Westsail 32 berthed on the next pier over. She drooled over the double-ender sailboat each time she came to port.

Someday, she thought, every time she saw it. And each time she came away realizing she wasn't quite ready to cut the dock lines completely and sail away.

January was a tall woman, a little broader than she wished she was, but not so broad that anyone would say she was heavy. Her blue-black hair was cut in a style she liked to call short and messy. She had her father's wide shoulders and hazel eyes but the darker skin of her mother, a Tlingit from the village of Hoonah, two hundred miles to the north, nearer to Juneau. Her father was a navy man and the Tlingit were people of the tide, so it was only natural that January would eventually find her way home to the water. It had only taken her thirty-six years to make it happen.

Havoc, her Jack Russell/blue heeler mix, sniffed at the base of the shore-power box and lifted his leg to do his part to add to the mineral quantity of the water below. Leaning more Russell than heeler, he was a small dog with tawny curls but a freakishly wide head that made him look a little prehistoric.

January toed Havoc out of the way and turned the power cord into a neat Flemish coil at the base of the box, so it lay flat and out of the way on the wooden dock. It was the way her father had taught her, so as not to give any of the other live-aboard folks in the harbor a reason to grouse. She was not by nature a particularly neat person, and her father often harangued her with Melvillean sailing words like "ballyhoo of blazes" and "slobgollion" to describe her messy room. The boats beyond and across from hers were in poor repair but their dock lines were shipshape. The power cord of the shabby Hewescraft beside her was turned in a beautiful Flemish coil, a perfect mirror image of hers. January wasn't about to be the only one on the docks setting an example of the "snivelized."

Pleased with the practical neatness of her Flemish coil, she stepped through the transom gate, back aboard *Tide Dancer*, shielding her eyes against the low sun. It cast a soft orange glow over the mirrored harbor, sending up reflections of two-dozen fishing boats—mostly purse seiners but a few trawlers too. There were a handful of sailboats and a couple of other converted fishing vessels—though, in January's opinion, none as handsome as *Tide Dancer*. Another dozen pleasure craft of varying makes and in various stages of repair rounded out the mix.

As pretty as it was, the harbor was still connected to towns—and snivelization just wasn't all it was cracked up to be. Now, thirty minutes after she'd motored *Tide Dancer* into the harbor, she was already longing to cast off and get back out. Uncomfortable or not, there were plenty of reasons to come in. Provisions were low, her laundry smelled like diesel fuel, and then there was that whole doctor visit she had to worry about. A consummate list maker, she had every excruciating minute mapped out and planned to be back on the water by noon the next day. Until then, there was nothing to do but settle in.

Back on board, she opened the portside bench to access the lazarette and the battery switch—which some foolish designer had placed at the far back corner, forcing her to bend completely over and nearly crawl inside the dark locker. Havoc hopped up on the edge of the open seat and peered over her shoulder, as if to make sure she flipped the switch over to shore power correctly.

She heard the tightly wound motor of a boat approaching much too fast, but half in, half out of the locker, found herself unable to brace herself quick enough against the heavy bow wave that slapped the hull as the boat sped past. *Tide*

Dancer lurched violently to starboard, nearly sending January tumbling over the side. She grabbed the rail and straightened up in time to see an aluminum skiff speed past, throwing spray and still on step. She immediately recognized Carmen Delgado and another member of the *FISHWIVES!* crew, heading toward their slip that was located nearer the parking lot at the base of the gangway.

Havoc scampered toward the bow, sensing January's frustration at the skiff, barking his bullish head off all the way.

January yelled above the sound of their whining motor. "No wake zone, genius! Three-hundred-dollar fine!"

Carmen shot a glance over her shoulder but seemed completely unaware of Cross. The twenty-something Rasta dude at the tiller raised a hand over his head to flip her off without even turning around.

"Shit for brains!" January screamed. "You almost knocked me in the water. How about I come over there and see how you like to swim?"

Ten months earlier such an encounter might have reduced her to tears. It was not so much that she'd been weak as she'd been sheltered. No one had ever really yelled at her. Her father was strict but he was also soft-spoken, and if the navy had taught him how to curse, he certainly didn't share that skill with his only daughter. And anyway, recent events had given her a more nuanced view of what it meant to be proper. Her mother was a stately woman who carried herself with a regal air the likes of which January had rarely seen in another human being. January had been raised in a sheltered environment, gone to college with other sheltered girls, married her first crush, and they'd both gone on to become middle school teachers.

But sheltered also meant she missed plenty of signs a woman with more worldly experience might have seen right off, and the marriage hadn't ended well.

Now, she was perfectly happy to act unsheltered as she watched Captain Dreadlocks turn into the *FISHWIVES!* slip and hop out on the dock.

"You're such a dumbass!" January yelled again. "You know that!" Her rant drew a leaning, sideways look from old man Forbush in the twenty-foot runabout one float over. Dreadlocks looked back, but not at her.

"Stupid little punk," January said under her breath. Havoc gave a harrumphing bark to match her grumbles.

January stood there seething and holding a cable backstay as she watched both members of the *FISHWIVES!* production crew unload their skiff and hustle up the gangway to their rented Jeep.

January couldn't remember Dreadlock's name, but she was all too familiar with the Hispanic woman. She'd thought Carmen Delgado was her friend. She'd seemed nice enough when she first came to Craig, before the production's full-scale invasion six weeks earlier.

Being new herself, January had tried to be welcoming and invited Delgado for breakfast down at the Dockside Café. Carmen had repaid the courtesy once the show was up and running by painting January as a man-stealing siren who traveled the waters that surrounded Prince of Wales Island in her converted fishing boat, stealing the hearts of local men when she wasn't pursuing her day job of studying killer whales. Of course the network couldn't actually say it was January. What they could do was show shaky footage of *Tide Dancer* with her name blurred. They blurred January's face as well, but the Fishwives were more than happy to make veiled inferences that led even some of the townspeople who knew her to buy into the sordid stories. Bright Jonas was convinced that January had set her siren song on her husband, Fitz—which was a joke. Any man who would get within fifty feet of a scold like Bright Jonas needed to have his head examined. January had no time for that kind of baggage.

Focused as she was on the departing *FISHWIVES!* idiots, January didn't hear foot-falls until the young Haida girl made it almost all the way down the dock.

"Hey there, Cassandra," January called out when she finally saw her. She stepped back from the rear gate to allow the twelve-year-old girl enough space to board. She knew Cassandra wouldn't answer back. January wasn't sure if she couldn't, or just wouldn't talk, but supposed there had been some sort of terrible trauma in her past.

Cassandra Brown appeared to understand everything going on around her better than most twelve-year-olds. In a culture where parents taught their kids the value of being quiet early in life, she got along fine without talking. A look or pantomime worked plenty well enough to make her intentions known. As she got to know the girl, January couldn't help but think the world might be a better place if everyone kept a few more of their words to themselves.

Cassandra's hair was full and black, hanging well past the collar of a light blue fleece jacket. Like many of the Native families on the island, she was poor. January had seen her house—small and in need of repair, but her mother kept her tattered clothes laundered and well mended. Her patched and faded jeans were tucked into a pair of cheap rubber boots.

Once on the boat, Cassandra put her hands to her face as if she were taking a photograph. Each time January returned from her trips to film and document the pod of eleven resident orcas, the Haida girl stopped by for a visit, studying the photos for hours and making pencil sketches in a worn spiral notebook she carried with her everywhere. She'd taken to carrying her own small video camera—a loaner from the *FISHWIVES!* production crew who were always looking for more footage, even from novices.

January ducked inside the cabin to grab her digital camera and, after Cassandra took a seat well away from the side of the boat, cued up the most recent photos from her trip around the island. Havoc curled up on a deck cushion beside the girl, head on her leg so he could look at the photos along with her. There were hundreds and Cassandra would study each one in detail. She'd be there awhile.

January didn't mind. She liked the kid's company. Her plan was to make dinner and then hitch a ride into town to grab some quick provisions at the AC store—short for Alaska Commercial—while her laundry washed. There was a storm blowing in from the Pacific and the orca were headed up the west side, to the bays where they liked to hang out when the weather kicked up. She'd spend only one night in the harbor doing the tedious but necessary crap people did in harbors, and then head right back out. She wanted to anchor in a protected cove near where she suspected the whales would be, before this low-pressure system pushed in and the seas kicked up. The last thing she wanted to do was get stuck in town with all the *FISHWIVES!* people getting up in her face. There were plenty of great folks in Craig, but January found she preferred the company of wind and ocean to just about anyone anywhere.

As if to prove her wrong, Linda Roundy gave a shrill whistle from the parking lot above the docks. Carrying a bag in each hand, she made her way down the metal gangway grate and along the dock to turn down the last float toward *Tide Dancer*. Linda was a teacher—like January had been in her former life—so they had a lot in common.

"Hey," January said, waving her friend aboard.

"I brought a calzone from Papa's. We can split it if you want."

January put a hand to her chest and batted her lashes in mock emotion—though a calzone from Papa's Pizza didn't require much of an act. "You are the best friend ever, Linda," she said.

January stepped inside the cabin long enough to grab a handful of paper towels, a bottle of wine, and a root beer for Cassandra. The three of them sat and watched the sunset while they ate. The moon was going to be big tonight, but it had yet to rise, leaving nothing but the light from the wheelhouse window to illuminate the deck. January liked it and so did Cassandra. The Haida girl had eaten her piece of calzone and was now working on what was left of January's. Cassandra ate a lot, but the calzones from Papa's were big.

"Can I ask you a question?" Linda asked once she'd run out of all the latest school gossip.

January handed Havoc a piece of pepperoni. She liked Linda, but hated it when people did that. Ask the question or don't. Don't ask to ask.

Linda looked back and forth as if divulging secret launch codes, then glanced at Cassandra and seemed to think better of it. "Walk forward with me a minute," she whispered.

"Okay." January carried the paper towel with her piece of calzone with her, following her friend down the narrow side deck past the wheelhouse to the bow.

Linda stood by the anchor roller, holding on to the top rail with both hands as she gazed across the harbor and up at Mount Sunna Hae—or Sunny Hay, depending on which map you looked at. The mountain wasn't incredibly tall, but a good deal of winter snow still lingered at the bald top.

January knew Linda well enough to see she was gathering up her words. She prodded. "What's the matter?"

Linda turned, still holding the rail. "Can you feel it?"

"What are you talking about?"

"I don't know," Linda said. "It just feels like something awful is happening on this island."

January smirked. "Like that shitty television show?"

"I'm serious." Linda shook her head. "Millie Burkett has gone missing."

"Probably out with some friends," January said. "She'll turn up."

"It's no secret that you don't like her very much," Linda said.

January scoffed. "She's what? Fifteen? Sixteen? I reserve the powers of my wrath for the adults who work on *FISHWIVES!*"

"And they deserve it," Linda said. "But I know Millie's one of the ones helping spread the stories in town about you and Fitz Jonas."

"Like I said, she's just a kid."

"Maybe." Linda nodded. "But I'm worried about her. I'm telling you, Jan, there's something dark going on here. Something . . . evil . . ." Her voice trailed off.

January whistled the theme from *The Twilight Zone*. "Like the Kushtaka . . . ?"

Linda laughed. "More like my ex-husband. I know, I'm starting to sound like a crackpot. But nobody's seen Millie since early yesterday. That's forever on this island. It just feels like something is . . . I don't know . . . broken."

January stared at the black surface of the water, looking at what was left of her reflection in the failing light. "I know broken."

"Well, I gotta tell you," Linda said. "Whatever

it is, it's giving me the creeps. I think I'll drive Cassandra home."

A muffled *woof* drew January's attention to the stern rail and she turned in time to see the Haida girl making her way up the dock toward the darkness of the parking lot.

"Looks like she left without you," January said.

"Dammit," Linda said. "Now I gotta drive home all by myself."

CHAPTER 13

Mim walked barefoot across the concrete floor of the two-car garage. Surrounded by a border of floor to ceiling metal shelves, double rows of blue plastic totes ran the length from door to furnace.

"That's Ethan's hunting stuff along the wall," Mim said. "Sorry it's so cluttered."

Following her lead, Cutter left his shoes in the house. He had plenty of his own outdoor gear, but it was suited for the coastal marshes and beaches of his home state. Insulated rubber boots got about as much use in Florida as his boogie board would get in Alaska.

"It's full," Cutter said. "But it's also crazy organized. Puts any garage I ever had to shame."

Mim laughed. "I know, right? The garage was Ethan's domain—the product of the twisted mind of an engineer. You should have seen the place before the kids and I started to trash it."

Tucked into the far corner was a neat workbench with a well-organized pegboard of hand tools. One of the two overhead lightbulbs was burned out, giving the place a dim and dusty feel. Like many garages in Alaska, this one was packed full of so much outdoor gear, there was little room for a vehicle—not counting the Arctic Cat ATV that sat dusty and forlorn in the corner beside the water heater. This gear, however, was organized and labeled as if by a librarian.

Mim had changed out of her scrubs and into a pair of well-worn jeans and a garnet Florida State sweatshirt. "Virtually everything in here was his," she said, sliding one of many large blue Rubbermaid plastic totes off a metal shelf. She popped open the lid to take a peek at its contents.

"This one has what looks like backpacks and duffel bags," she said. "Ethan was a big lover of backpacks." She held up the lid to show Ethan's slanted, draftsmanlike handwriting in permanent marker. "BAGS," it said. Mim's eyes suddenly lit up.

"Oh, my gosh, Arliss," she said, her voice bordering on giddy. She held up a net bag full of small brown conches and assorted other shells. "Look at this. Remember hunting for these when we were kids?"

"I do," Cutter said, but kept any more thoughts to himself. Mim had to know it was a rough memory for him. They'd talked about it, just before she and Ethan had married—but never since—and especially not now that he was gone.

She dropped the shells back in the tote. "Need any backpacks?"

"I'm good on packs," Cutter said. "What I really need are some rubber boots."

Arms crossed, finger to her lips, Mim perused

the tubs until she found one that was marked "FOOTWEAR."

"Don't forget," she said. "Ethan organized this with his engineer's mind." She held up a pair of black swim fins and grinned. "Footwear . . . I would have put these with scuba gear but, hey, what do I know. Anyway, take whatever you need. I'm sure he would have wanted that. I should have gotten rid of it already, but I keep telling myself the boys might want it someday. That's crazy, right? He always had this dream of taking them both on a big kayaking trip on some river up north. . . ." She stopped, swallowing back the grief. "I'm sorry. You'd think eighteen months would be long enough for me to pull myself together, a little at least, but I still can't seem to make it through a night without crying myself to sleep."

"It's okay," Cutter said. "Nobody's going to blame you for mourning your husband. Least of all me."

"I just . . ." She looked at the ground, as if she was afraid he might see something in her eyes. "Sometimes it all seems so futile. . . ."

"Mim . . ." Cutter was rarely at a loss for words, but he wasn't much good at consolation either.

"Don't worry," Mim said. "I'm not contemplating suicide or anything. I don't have to. The world is already doing a bang-up job of crushing the shit out of me."

"You have an incredible family," Cutter said. "Don't forget that."

"You mean my two beautiful boys and the evil she-wolf who won't come out of her room?"

"Hurt hits us all in different ways," Cutter said.

"Is that a Grumpy-ism?"

"Nope," Cutter said. "Just the way it is. Anyhow, it's good you want the boys to have some of their dad's things. I carry Grumpy's duty gun every day."

"Oh, believe me, I know you do." Mim chuckled and looked at her toes. He followed her eyes there to the startlingly red polish, then looked away before she noticed. "It bugged the heck out of Ethan that you got Grumpy's pistol . . . among other things."

"If our granddad would have been an engineer he'd have given Ethan his . . . whatever it is that engineers use every day. I just happened to follow his footsteps into law enforcement."

"I'm sure that's true," Mim said. She gave Cutter a soft smile. "You're so much alike, you and Grumpy. Ethan knew that. It killed him, but he knew it." Her eyes dropped to her feet again, her naked big toe tracing an invisible line on the concrete floor. "You really do favor him. Your grandpa, I mean."

"Because I don't smile?"

"That's not true," Mim said. "I saw you smile once . . . back in 1998." Her eyes sparkled with a

136

sudden memory. "You know the first time I ever met your grandfather?"

Cutter did, but he found himself wanting to hear her tell the story, really any story, but this one would do. "Tell me," he said. He took a pair of brown Xtratuf rubber boots out of the tote and sat down cross-legged on the concrete floor with the boots in his lap to listen.

She sat beside him, leaning against the stacked totes. "Ethan drove me out to Stump Pass Beach to look for shells," she said. "Remember? Grumpy tied up his patrol boat at the state dock there on the east side of the key. Anyway, up to that point, I'd only heard stories about him from y'all. Ethan warned me we might run into him."

"And you did."

"Oh, yeah," Mim said. "We came up that little path from the beach to the parking lot down by the restrooms—and there was Grumpy. He had your revolver pointed straight at this hippy dude who was lying facedown in the sand. He had another guy bent over the hood of a parked car. I guess he walked up on them while they were doing some smash-and-grabs in the parking lot. The guy bent over the car tried to fight, but you can imagine how that went over."

"I imagine there was a lot of crying," Cutter said, picturing the way his grandfather had taught him to do business with outlaws.

"And some pretty colorful language too,"

Mim said. She smiled and shook her head, remembering. " 'Watch your ass, miss.' Those were the first words Grumpy Cutter ever spoke to me. When he found out I was Ethan's girlfriend, he handcuffed his bandits, gave me the once-over, and then shook my hand. I'll never forget how he had this little tear of that other guy's blood running down his cheek. I thought I'd never met anyone so cool."

"And you never will," Cutter said.

Mim shook her head and looked straight at him. "Maybe so," she sighed. "Can I ask you something?"

"Of course," Cutter said, bracing himself.

"Why did you go away and join the army? Grumpy told me more than once he would've paid for college for both of you boys."

Cutter sighed. He could have said there hadn't been anything left for him in Port Charlotte, but he didn't go there. "Guess I just craved adventure."

"And I hated you for it," Mim said, staring into the corner of the garage. She sniffed back tears as she spoke.

"You did?"

"Not hated, really." She corrected herself. "Resented. Remember that story Grumpy used to tell about the painting of the sailing ship?"

"Nope."

"Well," Mim said, "it seems there was this poor

woman whose husband was lost at sea, so she kept a painting of his ship in her house to remind her three sons of the dangers associated with such things. Of course they looked at the stupid painting every day—and all went to sea when they grew up."

"Of course they did," Cutter said, wondering where this was going.

"I never wanted that to happen to my kids," Mim said. "You went off to find adventure with the military, motorcycles, and gunfights. I married the 'safe' Cutter brother who goes to college and becomes an engineer—probably the most boringly safe job on the planet—and he gets blown to hell. . . ."

Cutter put a hand on her arm.

"I'm not sure what brought that on," Mim said. She ran a finger down the back of his hand, finding a bruise on his knuckle he didn't even know he had.

"Bad day today?" she asked.

"Adventurous day." He left his hand where it was, hoping she might take her time examining it for more bruises. "Even though I left my motorcycle back in Florida."

"Bring it on," Mim said. "If there's one thing I learned, it's that life happens. The boys might as well learn that while they're young. At least one of them is bound to grow up like you—a perfect example that Ethan carried a dormant Grumpy gene. You went through a lot over there, didn't you? In Afghanistan, I mean. I see it every time I look in your eyes."

The question caught him off guard. "I thought we were talking about you."

Mim just stared at him. "Grumpy told Ethan that something must have happened that you weren't telling us. I heard them talking about it right after you came home. He said you were 'war weary.' "

"I was, I suppose."

"Then why do you keep on fighting?"

Cutter sighed. "Different kind of fight."

"Really?"

"No." Cutter pulled his hand away as if she might find one of his secrets there. "Seriously, I came here to take care of you and the kids, not be taken care of."

"We're family," Mim said. "This is what family does."

Cutter closed his eyes, trying to think of something to say. The last thing he wanted to do was talk about Afghanistan. So he didn't.

"Do you still miss Florida?" he asked.

Mim looked at him for a long moment, then gave up on her interrogation. She sighed. "Just about every day. Especially here during the months after Christmas—even when Ethan was alive. The dark can be oppressive, but after the holidays is the worst. Truthfully, Alaska would grow on me if I could ever seem to climb out of this funk. But it really doesn't matter. I can't move until we settle the civil suit. Lord knows how long that'll be."

Cutter sighed. His brother had worked for an engineering company that held contracts for oil companies up on the North Slope. The job had paid for their move to Alaska, gotten them a nice home in the upscale Hillside area overlooking Anchorage—and killed him. Ethan had gone to the Slope to oversee the installation of some piece of equipment involving seals his company, and thus his team, had helped to design. They'd been out at the wellhead near the mouth of the Kuparuk River on the Beaufort Sea that dark and cold morning eighteen months earlier, when the explosion happened. The oil company blamed the engineering company, the engineering company blamed the engineering team—and the team, not wanting to get any of their living members in trouble, blamed Ethan. Witnesses said it had happened fast and that Ethan and the two roustabouts standing next to him were killed instantly. Written reports were more graphic, detailing how the men's bodies had been torn in half. Cutter wondered if his sister-in-law knew the details, but supposed she did since lawyers in civil suits seemed to take great pleasure in using such things to play on the emotions and weaken the resolve of their adversaries. You describe in graphic detail how a woman's husband was torn limb from limb in an explosion, and just maybe she'd stop wanting to bring up the incident.

The engineering firm's insurance company had agreed to pay a claim, but at a reduced rate because they alleged the accident was Ethan's fault. What they hadn't counted on was Ethan being friends with a local attorney. Coop Daniels was a good guy, single, and kind of sweet on Mim. He'd agreed to take the case on a contingency so long as she stayed in Alaska to help him fight it. The boys thought Florida was too hot and were happy to stay in the only place they'd ever lived. Cutter tried for a promotion to supervisory deputy in Alaska and got it, allowing him to move up to help out. It turned out to be a win for everyone—except Ethan—and possibly Constance, the she-wolf who rarely came out of her room.

Mim cleared her throat and stood. She began rifling through more totes. "What else do you need?" she said. "Maybe a fanny pack from 1991?"

"I'll be fine with the boots," he said.

He turned to go back inside but she stopped him, resting her hand on his shoulder.

"I really appreciate what you're doing, Arliss," she said.

"We're family," he said. "This is what family does."

CHAPTER 14

Carmen Delgado felt like an idiot for renting a place so far out of town. The bulk of the crew lived in the same set of apartments in the city of Craig, but in her naive excuse for wisdom, Carmen had decided the main production offices should be located in a five-bedroom cedar house perched on the side of a mountain three miles east of the city. The nearest neighbor was five hundred meters away through a thick stand of red cedar. There were no streetlights and Port St. Nicholas lay like a black inkblot across the road of the same name—which ran along the water to terminate another dozen miles out of town.

The house had a huge picture window that offered a perfect view of the ocean, and the property manager had practically assured Carmen that whales swam right in front of it every day of the week. She'd thought it an idyllic spot for the production offices. The three-mile drive from Craig seemed much farther than you would expect and the extra distance would allow her to step away from the daily grind of dealing with a dysfunctional cast and crew. Maybe, if things worked out, she'd even be able to spend a little alone time with her hunky camera guy, Greg Conner.

But, by the time she finished with her sixteen-hour day and slogged up the steep gravel walk from the driveway, it was too dark to see whales—or anything else, for that matter. The spring had turned out much cooler than she'd expected, and the huge window that had been such a selling point turned out to be poorly insulated, forcing her to split and haul more firewood to heat the house and turning her sixteen-hour days into eighteen-hour days. Worse yet, the window was so large as to make it nearly impossible to cover, even with a king-size sheet, and Carmen could never shake the feeling that there was someone out there, watching her.

The earlier incident at the mine property had left her shaken and wobbly. The guys from the boat had chased them for miles, veering off only when they'd rounded Fish Egg Island and were almost back to Craig Harbor. A lonely house in a dark forest on a darker road overlooking a black ocean was not a place to be when scary dudes were after you for trespassing on their land.

Now, she peered past her own reflection in the same picture window and hugged herself against a sudden chill. Greg sat across the room in front of twin video monitors reviewing the day's footage. The living room had been converted into a production room with aluminum shelving replacing end tables and art along the wood panel walls. Her team of three production assistants had gone crazy with the label makers and everything on the shelves was neatly marked.

Carmen jumped at the sound of a hollow thump somewhere in the darkness. It was either a car door or one of the trees on the hillside behind the house that intermittently toppled over during the night just to scare the pee out of her. She leaned in, pressing her nose against the window, her breath making a little spot of condensation on the chilly glass. The moon was still behind the mountains, but the feeble excuse for a porch light reflected off the hood of the rented Jeep Cherokee that stared up at her on the slanted driveway.

She shot a quick glance over her shoulder at Greg—the only good thing to come out of the damned house. "Did you hear that?"

Greg didn't bother to look up from his spot at the video monitor. "It's just the wind," he said. "I wish you'd forget about those guys. They were only trying to scare us. We're good."

Carmen took one more look out the window at black nothingness and shivered again. She padded across the carpeted living room and warmed her hands over the woodstove. The heat did nothing to chase away the chill in her soul, so she gave up and flopped into the folding chair next to Greg.

He glanced sideways, raising his eyebrows up and down and giving her flannel pants a nod. "Have they morphed back into pajamas yet?"

Delgado reached up and pulled out her shirt, peeking down the collar. "Yep," she said, giving him a wink. "They turned back into pajamas about ten seconds after I walked in the door."

It was a dangerous thing, flirting with your staff, especially one as young and talented as Greg Conner, but being the boss was awfully lonely.

This stupid show made her lonely.

Less than a week after she'd gotten the green light, Delgado, and the other twenty-one members of the production staff, had descended on the island like a conquering army. *FISHWIVES!* followed the lives of four separate couples, necessitating as many as six different field teams. The ins and outs of such a production along with the care and feeding of assistant producers, camera ops, sounds techs, safety personnel, and even lowly production assistants, took a vigilant eye and often required her to be the bad guy— even with Greg. There was no clear rule about sleeping with the help, but it was stupid, and she knew it.

But now Carmen was scared so she cuddled up beside Greg in front of three large computer monitors set atop a long plastic table beside the woodstove, reviewing the day's work. Only Carmen and one of the assistant field producers named Andy stayed at the St. Nicholas Road house. And now Andy, along with the rest of the entire cast and crew, were at a weekly beach party that Carmen was sure only helped to alienate most of the island.

The incident with the other boat had put her on edge, and though Greg was no lightweight, Carmen couldn't help but wish that Kenny was in the house with his pistol and big honking knife.

Footage from each day was downloaded from the cameras onto one of a stack of two dozen hard drives and hand-carried weekly on the Inter-Island Ferry back to Ketchikan, where it was sent by FedEx to the main offices in Los Angeles. The footage remained on the cameras' hard drives as well as stored media cards to create redundant backups until it was downloaded to the main drives in LA. Considering the reception they'd received, Delgado thought it prudent to copy the day's footage as soon as they returned to the office.

Greg gloried in his talent as the footage of the dilapidated little cabin ran on the twin monitors in front of them, the light reflecting off his face and casting the shadow of his dreadlocks on the aluminum shelves behind him.

"I told you this would be gold," he said. "LA's gonna eat it up."

Carmen watched the weather on a small flat-screen television beside the monitors. It was a station out of Juneau.

"Are you seeing this?" she asked. "Looks like

a nasty low pressure system moving in from the west."

"I saw it earlier," Greg said. "Ain't it great? We're supposed to get gale force winds here by tomorrow evening—smack in the middle of the herring roe fishery."

"That kind of a storm will be horrible for the seining fleet."

Greg raised his eyebrows up and down. "Danger is just another word for money in our business. You couldn't have scripted the timing any better."

Carmen knew he was right, but it killed her.

A pounding at the front entry shook the walls and nearly caused her to jump out of her skin.

Greg groaned. "Carmen, bad guys don't knock." He pushed back his chair and got up to answer the door.

"It's your little friend," he said, nodding to her flannel pants. "Sure you don't want to put on something decent?"

"Shut up," Carmen said.

Greg stepped away from the door to allow Cassandra Brown inside. The Native girl walked past him without looking back. Kicking off her shoes, she opened her small backpack and handed Carmen a video camera. The production company used the little prosumer Sonys to scout locations or to give to interns who wanted to try their hand at shooting some footage.

Carmen thanked her and popped out the postage-stamp-sized media cards, grabbing two more from a manila envelope on the shelf. They went through this same routine every few days. Cassandra didn't smile. In fact, the countenance of her face remained as unchanged as a piece of granite, no matter what went on around her. She simply accepted the replacement cards and snapped them back in her camera.

Carmen followed her to the door, expecting to find the car outside that had given her a ride. She saw nothing but the silver-black line of the ocean across Port St. Nicholas Road.

"Are you going to be all right?" Carmen asked. "How does a twelve-year-old girl get all the way out here at this time of night?"

Cassandra just shrugged. She really was a creepy little kid.

Carmen shot a glance over her shoulder at Greg, who was busy reviewing his footage. On a whim, she stepped into the chilly darkness and stood on the weathered front porch with the Native girl.

"I can trust you, right?" Carmen whispered.

Cassandra raised a wary brow. It was slight, but at least it was some show of emotion. A foot shorter, she stared up at Carmen with unblinking brown eyes, before giving a slow and deliberate nod.

"Good," Carmen said, accustomed to doing

all the talking. She reached in the pocket of her jeans and pulled out a flat CFast media card. It was roughly two inches by two inches square and not quite a quarter of an inch thick. "I need you to keep this safe for me. Don't tell anyone you have it. This is important. Okay?"

The corners of the little girl's mouth perked, just a twitch, but for her, it was as good as a full-toothed grin. She seemed genuinely happy to have the extra responsibility.

"Be careful." Carmen said as she watched Cassandra Brown walk down the steep hill toward the road and disappear into the darkness. Back home in LA, she would have called the police had she found a child wandering around on a lonely road at night. As it was, she shut the door and turned the bolt. For all she knew, the creepy little Haida girl had crossed the road and walked straight into the sea.

Greg's face was glued to the computer monitor and the magnificence of his own creativity. "Those Sonys are nearly a thousand bucks a pop," he muttered. "You sure you want to give one to some girl who's probably just going to steal it anyway?"

Carmen slouched down in the chair beside his. "You're a real jerk, you know that. Cassandra's not going to steal it."

"I don't know about that," Greg said. He sounded even more smug than usual. "Tucker gave that other Indian chick a camera and she ran off with it."

Carmen gave him a stiff jab in the arm. "*Native* chick," she said. "And anyway, she didn't run off with it. She's gone missing."

Greg leaned back in his chair to give a long, groaning stretch. "That's what I'm sayin'. She went missing with a thousand-dollar camera, and that's money down the drain. I know the production company's flush with dough now that the show's been green lit, but I'd just as soon you gave that dough to your most talented camera operator in, say, the form of a bonus."

"You're right, as usual," Carmen said. "Tucker does deserve a bonus."

Greg rolled his eyes. "You cut me to the bone, my dear. If you're not going to give me a bonus, how about you make us some coffee. This is a lot of footage we have to go over—and you gave everyone else the night off to party."

Carmen let her head fall to one side. She was severely out of practice with such things, but hoped it looked seductive. "I did give them the night off," she said. "So it's just me and you here looking at footage. . . ."

He coughed, running a hand over the top of his dreadlocks. "I think I'm tracking, Jammie Pants."

"Good," Carmen said.

Greg groaned again, more intensely this time. "Just ten more minutes . . ." His voice trailed off as he looked over his shoulder toward the kitchen.

Carmen's eyes followed his, knowing from the look on his face that she was not going to like what she saw.

There had been no thud, no breaking glass, no telltale creak of the door, but standing in the dark kitchen were the two most terrifying men Carmen Delgado had ever seen. Greg was right—bad guys didn't knock.

CHAPTER 15

The heavy beat of music and the hiss of lapping surf greeted Trooper Sam Benjamin as he stepped out of his patrol car on Cemetery Island outside Craig and situated the flat brim of his blue felt Stetson over his forehead. He loved that hat, and not just because it signified his hold over Sergeant Yates. He never admitted it to anyone, but the Stetson was, in large part, the reason he'd joined the Alaska State Troopers over any other agency. He'd read studies about hats and how they commanded a certain respect. Given a choice between two responding officers, citizens were most likely to turn for guidance to the one wearing a hat. Hard helmets, like motor jocks wore, garnered the most respect, followed closely by the venerable campaign hat—like the Alaska State Troopers Stetson. Ball caps didn't even rate.

Following the music, the trooper passed the Veterans' flagpole and the white stones of the cemetery that gave the island its name and made his way down a wide gravel trail. He caught a glimpse of orange firelight flickering through the thick foliage and heard laughter ahead and to his left, toward the ocean. Huge spruce stood like silent sentinels in the darkness on either side

153

of the footpath. The trooper chuckled to himself as he walked, thinking the big trees weren't very competent guards if they allowed the likes of the *FISHWIVES!* crew into the park.

Following the party noise, he worked his way down the embankment of fiddlehead ferns and across a wide stretch of trampled grass. It was low tide, so the gravel beach was large enough to have a considerable bonfire. Sparks spiraled into the blue-black night, pushed upward on the heat of crackling driftwood. Over thirty people stood out in dark relief to the flames, swaying to a Crosby, Stills and Nash song that poured from someone's iPhone speakers. The night had turned chilly ahead of the approaching storm and the warmth of the fire felt good.

Murmurs of "Hey, Super Trooper!" and "I didn't do it!" rippled through the gathered crowd—not very original for a bunch of creative television folk. Benjamin stifled the urge to pop back and scanned the group until he found Kenny Douglas. Something about the guy rubbed him the wrong way, but as the safety supervisor, Douglas's job was to liaison with law enforcement, and there was little more serious to liaise about than a missing teenage girl. The trooper found him sitting on a large driftwood log tipping back a Heineken, shoulder to shoulder with a doe-eyed girl less than half his age. She was a local with hair pulled back in a fresh ponytail, not long out of high school, and working as a production assistant. Until now, her biggest life adventure had been getting her nose pierced behind her mother's back.

Douglas was in his late thirties with the thick arms and beefy neck you'd expect from a head of safety and security. He'd buzzed his hair into a marine flattop to help beef up his tough persona. He liked to tout his experience using military slang, throwing around terms like "down range" and "battle buddy," but he would never get specific about his experience. If he'd ever actually served, Trooper Benjamin expected it was as some rear echelon pogue.

While the cute, ponytailed brunette sitting beside him was just old enough to make it legal, Douglas was also old enough to know better. Under other circumstances Benjamin might have hassled him a little for being a letch. As it was, he decided to focus on finding Millie Burkett and let creepy old dudes be creepy old dudes.

"You find her yet?" Douglas asked, as if he'd been expecting the trooper's visit.

"You know Millie Burkett?"

Douglas chuckled and toasted the air with his beer. "Everybody on this crew knows Millie Burkett. She's always sniffing around, if you know what I mean."

"I really have no idea," the trooper said.

"She has a little crush on Fitz Jonas. I've

155

handled security on a shitload of these Alaska reality shows and if there's one thing that's a constant, it's that the girls always fall hard for the talent." He smiled in an all-knowing way.

"Was this crush reciprocated by Fitz?" the trooper asked.

Bright Jonas sauntered up from behind the fire. "Not even a little," she said.

Benjamin had known the woman well before FISHWIVES! came along, back when she was just dull old Bright, the busybody checker at the AC store. Full, but not fat, she wore a tight orange tank top that revealed much more flesh than the trooper wanted to see from his local supermarket checker. She was always a close-talker, but the habit became more pronounced when she was drunk. She leaned in to the trooper, each boozy, breathy word hitting him full in the face. "My Fitzy has plenty of full grown women to keep him busy without going for some skinny little kid."

Douglas took another sip of his beer. "It wasn't just Fitzy. Millie had a crush on a lot of people on the set. She was what you might call a groupie—and I gotta tell you, she didn't really discriminate."

A slender man seemed to materialize out of the darkness beyond the fire. He looked to be in his mid-thirties and obviously hadn't gotten the memo about older guys and skinny jeans.

"That's a cheap shot, Kenny," the man said, flipping back dark bangs with a toss of his head. He wore a black turtleneck that perfectly suited his doleful look, like a grown-up trying to be an emo kid. His pout was made even more pronounced by a night of drinking and staring into the fire. "Millie was far more than a groupie."

The trooper held out his hand. "Sam Benjamin," he said.

"Tucker Jackson, camera ops," the other man said. He was certainly too old to be hanging out with a fifteen-year-old girl. "Millie spent time around the crew all right, but she turned out to have a real talent for this." He shook his head, staring into the night. "I've never seen anyone her age with such a natural eye with the camera."

Benjamin took out his pen and notebook. His vision had finally adjusted and the bonfire provided plenty of light to take notes. "So you're saying Millie Burkett wanted to be an actress?"

Jackson pushed away his emo bangs again. "No, nothing like that," he said. "She was a natural *behind* the camera, not in front of one. I showed some of the footage she shot to Carmen, our executive producer, and she let me loan her one of our small scout cameras to shoot B-roll."

"B-roll?" Benjamin glanced up from his notebook.

"Beauty roll," Jackson said. "The images we

use in between the rest of the story. You know, shots of the ocean, misty mountains, that sort of thing. Millie had this way of keying in on the spirit of exactly the footage we needed."

"When was the last time you saw Miss Burkett?"

"Yesterday morning around seven thirty," Jackson said.

"Mind if I ask where you saw her?"

"Not at all," Jackson said. "She dropped the memory cards to her camera by my apartment. She came in for a minute while I gave her replacements."

Trooper Benjamin looked across the top of his notebook to study the man's face while he talked. It was time to turn up the heat a little. Tiny micro expressions often spoke volumes more than any actual spoken words. "Seven thirty? Isn't that a little early for a teenager to be up and about?"

"She wanted to catch the best light, I guess," Jackson said.

"Who brought her?"

"She came by herself." Jackson gave another toss of his head.

"How long did she stay?"

"Five minutes or so."

"Did you talk about anything specific?"

"No," Jackson said. "I mean . . . I don't think so. I really can't remember what we talked about. It was early and I'd worked late the night before."

"Was anyone else there besides the two of you?"

Another flip of his bangs. "No. Just Millie and me."

"Did she mention where she planned to go to catch the best light?"

"Are you telling me she never went home?" Jackson took a shuddering breath, swaying in place.

The trooper didn't say anything, letting the reality of the situation sink in.

"Shit," Jackson said. "Am I the last one to have seen her?"

"We're still working on that," Benjamin said. "She may be over at a friend's house that we just aren't aware of."

"Hell, Trooper," Kenny Douglas said from his perch on the log. "You don't even sound like you believe yourself."

"Hey, Trooper." The young production assistant leaned in, cocking her head. "Do you think something bad has happened to Millie?"

Benjamin gave a noncommittal shrug. "That remains to be seen. How about Hayden Starnes? Did Millie ever hang out with him?"

Jackson looked up from staring at his feet and gave another toss of his head. "Who?"

Looking at Jackson, Benjamin took a momentary deep breath while considering taking out his pocketknife and hacking off that annoying flap

159

of hair. Instead, he flipped back a few pages in his notebook for effect. Everyone around the fire seemed genuinely confused by the fugitive's real name, so he decided to try the alias.

"Sorry," he said. "That was a mistake. I meant to say Travis Todd."

"Travis?" Douglas chimed in. "Sure. That little weirdo was sweet on Millie."

"Why do you say he's a weirdo?"

Douglas crumpled his beer can and started to throw it toward the water but thought better of it. "I don't know," he said. "He's just weird, that's all." The security man looked around the fire. "Carmen was looking for him this morning, but I haven't seen him in a couple of days."

"Where is Carmen?" the trooper asked.

"She and Greg are back at the production house backing up today's footage. She gave everyone else the night to blow off a little steam."

"Was Travis especially close to anyone on the cast or crew?"

Douglas shook his head. "He got along well enough with everyone, I guess. But he did pay a lot of attention to the girls."

The brunette production assistant giggled and elbowed Douglas in the ribs. "Like someone else I know."

A small crowd had drifted over from where they'd been dancing around the fire and were now actively following the conversation.

Benjamin looked at each of them in turn. "Any of you know where Travis might have gone?"

Several looked at the ground. The crowd gave a collective murmur that they had no idea.

"Okay," Benjamin said, deciding a truth bomb for safety's sake outweighed operational security. Sometimes you just had to rattle a few cages. "Travis Todd's real name is Hayden Starnes. He's wanted for sexual assault and kidnapping—so it's important you give me a call if anyone hears from him."

The girl beside Douglas gasped. Her hand shot to her mouth. "I haven't seen him in a couple of days. Millie went missing right after that. Do you think—?"

Benjamin cut her off. "It's best not to jump to any conclusions. But I'm not ruling anything out." He tapped the brim of his Stetson with his pen and said good night. The natural inclination of the cast and crew would be to close ranks and look after one of their own, but they were also television people, so their imaginations about what had happened to Millie Burkett would already be kicking in to overdrive. He'd let them stew on it overnight and question them again in the morning.

CHAPTER 16

Chago Torres shot a glance at the unconscious woman in the passenger seat and gave a forlorn shake of his head. She looked like his little sister, Lucia, which was going to be a real problem, considering what he had to do to her.

The hulking *sicario* gripped the steering wheel with large hands, locking his eyes on the dark road ahead. He'd disappeared dozens of people for his boss, close to a hundred by now. Some of them had been women—but no kids, not yet anyway. Luis had killed a kid, a ten-year-old *halcón* or falcon—a lookout for a rival cartel. He bragged about it every time he was drunk or high—which was at least once a week. Chago hoped he never had to kill a kid. Killing a kid would make him sad. He looked at the woman wearing flannel pants. This would be bad enough.

The woman gave a little moan. He'd never get used to the sounds human beings made when they died. When he went home and watched movies with his mother and grandfather, people just fell over or sometimes even gave long, passionate speeches. He wanted to tell them it wasn't that way but he couldn't. They didn't want to know what he knew. He didn't want to know what he knew.

Chago glanced at the woman again. Her chin hung to her chest and a line of bloody drool dripped from her open mouth. Luis had hit her hard with the leather strap so she'd be unconscious for a long time. Chago hoped Luis hadn't hit her too hard. They needed information, and from the sounds of the guy in the backseat they were going to have to get it from the woman in the flannel pants.

The odor of urine and fear rose up behind Chago. The whimpering was constant, like a burbling buzz. The guy with the nasty hair was awake—and no doubt terrified of Luis. Chago couldn't blame the guy. He didn't even like sitting next to the skinny killer in broad daylight.

The Jeep's headlights played along the white gravel road as he drove, cutting a sharp swath along the dark mountainside. Chago was not sure where he was going, other than away from civilization. On this island that seemed a fairly easy thing to do as the wilderness stretched out in just about any direction. The pressure in his ears told him they were going up, and Chago assumed that the old logging road was taking them over some kind of a pass toward more water. According to the Forest Service map, most roads eventually wound around to end up at the ocean. If he saw any sign of another person, he would just keep driving, or simply turn around.

The logistics of disappearing people on such

a lonely island would not be hard at all. But logistics were never the hard part.

Chago had not become a killer for Los Leónes cartel by choice. Luis had grown up in the world, beginning work as a *halcón* for bosses in his neighborhood when he was just nine years old. It could be argued that Luis hadn't chosen the life of a *sicario* either, but he'd certainly moved in that direction from a very early age. Where Luis was thin, quick, and scrappy, Chago was taller and thickly muscled. His heavy shoulders and long arms made him look stooped when he was not. At first glance people might think him to be slow—but those people would be severely mistaken. Garza always said Luis was the jab and Chago was the hook.

Chago had not even been in a fight until after he was a grown man—when he came to work for Los Leónes. He'd started working full-time for a drywall installer after graduating from the ninth grade. His grandfather said Chago was an artist, the best mudder he had ever seen. It was this same grandfather who suggested he might take his skills to Texas. There he could make a great deal of money and send some of it back to help his family. Maybe he could even marry a girl from El Paso. His grandfather said he had heard of such things happening many times before.

But nothing had happened the way his grand-father had imagined it. Chago had been caught in a border patrol sweep less than an hour after the *pollero*—or chicken herder—had walked them across the river and into the United States. It was his first time, so the process of deportation was swift and relatively painless. The pain did not begin until he was back in Mexico.

Chago had heard rumors that cartels recruited at the *casa migrante*, repatriation centers often run by local churches, offering work to strong or desperate men. In the end, it was his strength that was his undoing. A girl had approached him first, telling him she was staying at a nearby casa for recently deported women. Her cousins were coming up to get her from Mexico City. She was pretty, and hadn't wanted anything but conversation. Naively, Chago had taken her to a nearby cantina and told her his name and where he was from over a bottle of Dos Equis. Her "cousins" had arrived at the repatriation center the next morning with photographs of his mother and sister. Chago was not so naive that he did not recognize the men for what they were.

The *sicarios* made it very clear that he had no choice but to submit to the will of Los Leónes or be disappeared—after he watched his loved ones debased and murdered before his eyes. He hated it still. But what could he do? Manuel Garza was not as volatile a boss as Camacho had been, but he was just as bloody—maybe even bloodier.

Chago had found the cameras and two media

cards in the house when they grabbed the couple, but he suspected they had made copies. If he and Luis did not come back with every piece of footage that showed Camacho on the boat, Garza would not only point a gun at him, he would pull the trigger. Oh, the *patrón* might wait until they returned to Mexico where another *sicario* could catch him unaware and gut him like a pig to demonstrate to others what it meant to fail the *patrón*. No, Garza was not Camacho. He was smarter—and much worse.

Chago drummed thick fingers against the steering wheel. Anyway, the money was good—and he didn't have to kill too many women.

Luis craned his head forward between the seats and pointed out the windshield. "You planning to drive around all night or are we gonna get out and do this thing?"

"The boss said to get them a long way out of town," Chago said.

"Well," Luis said. "You've gone far enough. Pull off at the next wide spot and I'll ask this guy what he needs to be asked."

"I'm going a little further," Chago said.

Luis hit the side of the bucket seat and cursed. "The woods are plenty good for what we need to do!"

Chago ignored him. Luis was like a mosquito when he didn't get his way, all buzz and nonsense.

Luis thumped the seat again, several times in rapid succession as if he'd seen something exciting.

"Is that water up ahead?"

"I think so."

"If that's water you drove us all the way over the mountains."

The guy with the nasty hair carried on with his burbling whimper.

Chago flicked on the high beams. Beyond the gray forest of logged stumps and slender young trees lay a protected arm of the sea. A fat log, treated with creosote to keep it from rotting, lay at the end of the road, presumably to keep people from driving into the ocean. It was breathtakingly beautiful, even in the dark. Chago would have liked to camp here, to play his guitar with his grandfather, and listen to the wind. His grandfather knew the names of many stars and had never killed a woman. Chago put the Jeep in park and looked over at the unconscious woman bleeding from her nose—the nose that looked so much like Lucia's nose.

"This is as good a spot as any," he said.

CHAPTER 17

Carmen Delgado froze when the big Mexican lifted her gently under the shoulders and knees. Carrying her to the front of the Jeep, he set her on the ground at the base of a large stump, just at the edge of the beam cut by the headlights. Her hands and feet were tied with duct tape. Her head and neck were on fire, but she willed herself to relax and let it loll. She prayed he would believe she was still unconscious.

Carmen let her chin fall back against her chest. The left side of her face was swollen—especially around her eye near where she had been hit. Even without touching it she could tell the bone around the socket was badly damaged. She could taste blood in her mouth where her teeth had cut her cheek and more blood was starting to crust under her nose. She tilted her head a little more so as to get a better look at her surroundings with her good eye, trying not to draw attention to herself.

The smaller of the two men had already dragged a screaming Greg from the backseat by the time the big guy got Carmen situated—and this one was not nearly so gentle. The big one—the little guy called him Chago—leaned back against the hood of the Jeep while his partner stood over Greg and put a boot on his neck.

"Hey, *hombre*," the little guy said in accented English. "We don't really gotta talk to you, you know. This is just a . . ." He looked at Chago. "What do you call it?"

"A courtesy," Chago said, sounding tired.

"W-wait, wait!" Greg said, his voice hoarse from the pressure of the boot. With his hands taped behind him, there was little he could do but squirm. "I can help you guys. I know I can. But you gotta let me g—"

The little guy bore down harder, causing Greg to gag. "I got to do nothing, asshole." He looked at Chago, who sighed, and gave a slow nod.

The skinny one stepped back and lit a cigarette while poor Greg sputtered and writhed in the dirt. Carmen watched the ash on the cigarette glow brightly against the blackness. Chago stooped and grabbed Greg by the arms, hoisting him easily to his feet. Already beside the Jeep, Chago spun him so he stood bent over with his belly against the hood. Carmen never would have recognized Greg, his face a swollen mass of bloody bruises. As he was leaning there, the skinny one offered him the cigarette, which he accepted, despite the fact that he didn't smoke. He coughed until spit ran from his cracked and bleeding lips, but miraculously held on to the cigarette.

On cue, Chago secured his arms while the skinny guy came up from behind and slipped a clear plastic bag over Greg's head. The flame from the cigarette burned a hole through the plastic, but Carmen realized at once that the men had planned it that way. The hole in the plastic was much too small to get enough air and only gave Greg false hope. The cigarette fell inside the bag, smoldering against his cheek while he pressed his lips, carp-like, against the tiny hole. He jerked and thrashed against the Jeep's hood, but Chago held him while Luis watched. They looked bored, almost disinterested in this part of their job.

When Carmen felt certain Greg could take no more, the skinny man removed the bag and stepped back.

"Please." Greg hacked and coughed, trying to breathe, but bent on persuading the men not to hurt him again. "Please. I swear . . . I . . . can help. You just have to give me a—"

The skinny one threw the hood over Greg's head again, pulling it tighter this time. He leaned in close so his mouth was directly beside Greg's ear, but screamed his threats as if he were half a block away. "Son of a whore! I told you! I told you already. We don't have to do nothin'!"

The skinny one jerked the bag away, ripping it in the process. Letting loose a string of violent curses, he threw the bag on the ground and grabbed Greg by the hair, yanking his head backward until it looked as though his neck would break. Carmen cringed, wanting to turn away, but was too terrified to move.

"Pleeeease!" Greg pleaded. "Let me go! I'll tell you . . . whatever you want to know."

The skinny one shook his head. "Look at this guy," he said. "Thinkin' a man with a bag over his head has room to negotiate."

"Luis," Chago said, calling the skinny guy by name. "We need—"

But Luis wasn't in the mood to take advice. He slammed Greg's head forward with one hand, and with the other, buried a blade into the base of his skull. Carmen felt as if her soul might dry up and blow away. This couldn't be happening. Only hours before she'd been joking with Greg about pajama pants. Now, his last breath was leaking out of him on some godforsaken gravel road. He gave a slow, raspy groan, and turned his head to look directly at her as he died.

Luis let the body slip off the hood and then stepped back to chuckle at his handiwork. Carmen knew enough Spanish to understand he was talking about the deathblow of a bullfight.

"Did you see that *estocada,* Chago, straight through the neck like a matador, eh?" He nodded at the body, bobbing and weaving, like a boxer proud of a knockout. "You stretch him out. I will see if there is an axe in the car."

Carmen tried to swallow the acid that seared the back of her throat.

Chago shook his head, dumbfounded. "Wait. Luis, why would you look for an axe?"

171

"To cut off his head, you dumb bastard."

"Ai ai ai," Chago said. "But why do you want to cut off his head? We are all the way out here in the middle of nowhere."

Luis raised open hands and shook his head as if it was all so clear. "Because we always cut off their heads."

Carmen pressed her eyes shut with such force it caused her face to cramp. It was impossible to comprehend how a human being could be so cruel. They spoke like they were planning a night out instead of talking about beheading her friend.

"We cut off heads to make a certain point, *pendejo*," Chago said. "Do you see anybody else out here who needs to get the point? And why did you have to kill him so fast anyway? Garza wanted us to question them both."

"It does not matter." Luis shrugged. "We got what we were sent to get anyway."

"Are you sure of that?" Chago cocked his head, staring. "I looked at the cameras and they each hold two cards. These people are professionals. What if they record on both? Are you sure we got them all?"

"We got them," Luis said.

"And you are willing to sit in the same room with Manuel Garza when he happens to see the footage on the Internet—after we assure him it has all been destroyed?"

Luis rubbed a hand through his hair, fuming

now. He looked back and forth from Chago to Greg's lifeless body. At length, he nodded, sneering as if he'd figured it all out. "The girl will know." He stalked to Carmen and gave her a swift kick. The toe of his leather boot took her in the point of the hip, sending waves of nausea. "Wake up, bitch! The time for sleep is over!" Already in shock, it was no act when she fell over and drew herself into a ball, nearly catatonic.

Luis kicked her again and again. Most of the blows landed on her buttocks, but some took her low in the back, directly over her kidneys. She moaned, sure she would vomit. Miraculously, she was able to remain generally limp through the ordeal.

Luis screamed more threats, frustrated that she wasn't waking up, but Chago moved in and dragged him away before he could kick her again.

"You cannot beat her into consciousness, my friend," he said. He waved his hands at the darkness. "We are all alone. That means we have some time. I will start a fire while you find some stones large enough to sink this man you killed. She will wake up soon enough."

"She better," Luis said. "Or we will see if there are other, more enjoyable ways to wake her."

Chago glared at him. "I said, she will wake up soon enough!"

Carmen cringed at the thought that one of her abductors, a terrible man, complicit in the torture and murder of her friend, had now become her protector.

Her face pressed against the cold dirt and, too frightened to move, Carmen watched the scene unfold through the slit of her injured eye. The one called Chago turned off the headlights as soon as he got the fire going. In the flickering light, Luis opened the belly of her friend with the same knife he'd used to kill him, and then stuffed in as many stones as he could fit. He spoke absentmindedly as he worked.

"You know the police found the body of a woman a friend of mine sunk once," Luis said. "They went to inform the husband and said, 'Senor, there is good news and there is bad news. The bad news is that we found your poor wife's body off the end of the jetty and she was covered with blue crabs.' 'Ah, mi,' the husband said. 'But what is the good news?' " Luis looked up from his work grinning maniacally. " 'Oh, this is very good news indeed, senor,' the policeman said. 'We have decided to throw her back in and catch many more blue crab.' "

Chago gave his friend a perfunctory chuckle, then turned back to his fire. Carmen tried to press further into the dirt, anything to put distance between herself and these madmen who thought life so cheap.

Stripping naked, Luis dragged Greg's distended body into the black ocean at the end of the road.

Then wincing and cursing from the frigid water, he used a large log to help him swim the body out into the darkness. One of two copies of the video footage they wanted was stuffed in a plastic baggie in Greg's pocket. Carmen was sure he'd been trying to tell them, but Luis had been too quick to kill him. He'd been so busy stuffing the body with rocks, he'd completely missed it.

"Go further out!" Chago shouted into the blackness. Luis's splashes were becoming quieter. "The tides are big here. You must take him out where it is deep or he will be discovered."

Chago squatted beside the fire, stoking it with more wood he'd dragged up from the shadows. Carmen almost wet herself when he turned to look directly at her.

"We are all very tired," he said. "I will give you until tomorrow morning to rest and think about the things you have seen."

Carmen didn't move.

"Luis has a nickname, you know," Chago said. "*El Guiso.* Do you know what that means?"

Carmen realized the futility of her ruse and opened her good eye. She gave a painful shake of her head. "Soup?"

"Not quite," Chago said. "In my world, we have many ways of disappearing people. Luis has a favorite, taught to him by our old boss. He will stuff the person he wants to disappear into a metal drum. Sometimes, he has to break their legs, but eventually everyone fits." Chago sighed, as if remembering a sad story. "In any case, he then douses this person with gasoline or diesel fuel and sets them on fire. After they have expired, he will fill the drum with acid. We call this *el guiso*—stew. It is also what we call Luis."

CHAPTER 18

Cutter's alarm went off at 4:05 a.m., giving him enough time to shower and go over the gear he'd laid out for the trip before he left to make the ten-minute drive to Lola Fontaine's house. His grandfather's Colt Python occupied the main spot on his war belt, though Cutter had dispensed with the black border patrol holster Grumpy had favored. His basket-weave holster had been custom made by an inmate in the Texas Department of Corrections while Cutter had been on a Witness Security assignment in San Antonio. A few inches behind the revolver on his belt was the Glock 27 .40 caliber that kept him in line with USMS policy. Including the round in the chamber, the little Glock carried four more than Grumpy's .357. An extra nine-round magazine for the Glock on his belt gave him a total load-out of twenty-five rounds—light for most modern deputy marshals, but plenty as far as Cutter was concerned. In addition to the extra mag, there was a Surefire flashlight and a pair of handcuffs on the belt. The cuff case and the belt itself were dark tan basket weave to match the holster—a color Grumpy had called "peanut brittle." Like the holster, these were also made by the TDC inmate.

Along with the items on the war belt, Cutter carried a small jackknife, a Zippo lighter, and a second flashlight in the pocket of his trousers, opposite his cell phone. He eschewed the larger, fighting folders many of his army buddies and fellow lawmen carried, knowing from hard experience that using a knife in a fight was a nasty affair that brought with it a great deal of blood and gore. If, God forbid, he ran out of bullets, he'd much rather fight someone with a rock than a pocketknife.

He packed light, with just a change of underwear, an extra wool shirt, a fleece jacket, and a blue Helly Hansen raincoat. His brother's Xtratuf boots rounded things out, in the event the going got too wet for the Zamberlan hiking boots he normally favored.

Cutter rolled up in front of Lola's condo off Minnesota Drive just after five. Larry Fontaine was waiting in the living room for him to drive up. The goober stepped shirtless between the curtains and the window before Cutter could even put his SUV in park. Unwilling to come outside and actually talk face to face with the man who was about to drive away with his wife, Fontaine did nothing but flex his muscles and glare.

"Chihuahua courage, I shih tzu not," Cutter muttered under his breath. It was something Grumpy used to say to describe dogs or people who barked their heads off as long as they were behind the safety of a screen door.

Not one to shy away from confrontation, Cutter returned the squinty stare and flung open his car door. It had the same effect as stomping his foot at a timid dog and Larry Fontaine vanished like a vapor, leaving nothing but a billowing curtain where he'd once been. Cutter walked to the door and knocked, standing off to the side.

The walls of the condo were thin and it was easy to hear Lola's voice coming through. "Will you get that?"

"I'm not getting it. You get it!" Larry's voice was tight and hushed, but still easy enough to hear. "I don't want to see that guy."

"Holy hell, Larry," Lola said, sounding exasperated. "He's not going to bite—"

Lola flung open the door midsentence. She wore a pair of jeans and a tight black T-shirt that showed off her upper arms and complemented her olive skin tone. Thick, black hair hung past her shoulders, framing a flushed face and a forehead glistening with sweat. "Nearly there," she said. "Just have to pull my hair outta my face and put on my gun." She stepped back and waved Cutter inside. "There's coffee in the kitchen if you want some."

Larry ducked from where he'd been lurking beside the living room sofa and slithered down the back hallway. "For Pete's sake, Lola, don't invite him in—"

Lola grimaced. "Sorry," she whispered.

"I already picked up coffees for us. I'll be in the car when you're ready." Cutter was all business.

Five minutes later, Deputy Fontaine tossed her office-issue duffel in the backseat, and then slid in a black hard case containing a short-barreled AR-15 rifle. Unsure about reinforcements on the island if the manhunt turned nasty, Cutter had asked her to bring the long gun. She had Hayden Starnes's powder-blue warrant folder in her hand when she opened the passenger door and flopped down in the seat.

She shot Cutter an embarrassed smile and then sniffed, pulling the sleeve of her T-shirt up to her nose. "Sorry, boss," she said. "I was afraid I'd miss my workout today so I got up early to get her done. Took a cool shower but I'm still pouring sweat. Afraid I got me a serious case of girl stink."

Cutter ignored the comment. Too much talk of things like girl stink had led to his last marriage—which had failed miserably. As Fontaine's supervisor, there was really no appropriate way to respond.

Fontaine shot him a toothy grin and pulled the sleeve of her T-shirt up even farther, flexing her bicep. "It was an awesome workout, boss. Look at that. Want to feel my pump?"

Cutter leaned away as if she had suddenly caught fire. "No," he said, "I don't want to feel your pump."

She shrugged. "Suit yourself. My point is, you don't get muscles like this by skipping a workout, even if you have to get up at three in the morning to squeeze in said workout."

Cutter hoped they found this Starnes guy quickly. He nodded toward the cup of coffee in the center console and then pulled away, out from under the gaze of Fontaine's jealous husband.

She saw him looking at her house. "I really am sorry about that back there," she said. "I'm only trying to lighten the mood since we'll be working together. Larry just makes me crazy."

"That's what I meant on the phone last night," Cutter said. "You don't have to work the task force if your husband has a problem with me."

She leaned back in her seat and let her head fall to the side, facing him. The normal cockiness was gone from her face. "Larry's not my husband," she said. "Not as of four thirty-seven p.m. yesterday afternoon when Judge Salvatore signed the dissolution paperwork."

This was a surprise. "He sure sounded like your husband at the office yesterday."

Fontaine closed her eyes. "He thinks it's too soon for me to be dating again."

Cutter raised an eyebrow. "You and I aren't dating. We work together."

"And now you see why I got a divorce," Fontaine said.

Cutter gave a low whistle. "I'm not the one to talk about healthy relationships."

"Yeah," Fontaine said. "And I'm not one to talk about my personal problems. But you were just a witness to the Shitty Mornings with Lola and Larry Show, so I thought you deserved an explanation. We've had heaps of problems for a long time. I'm just letting him stay in the condo until he finds something else. It's a two bedroom."

Cutter shook his head, still processing. "And you're not worried about him staying there?"

"Nah," she said. "Larry's jealous, but he's a wuss. I could kick his ass if I had to, but we're both ready to move on. I'll keep using Lola Fontaine until headquarters ships me my new creds."

"Then what?"

"I'll go back to my maiden name, Teariki." She pronounced each vowel separately and the *R* a hard, almost *D* sound. Te-a-ri-ki.

"Lola Teariki," Cutter said. "I like that."

"Yeah," Fontaine said. "It means something like 'the big chief' but it's pretty common where my parents come from. My mum says my family are like coconut palms."

"How's that?" Cutter asked, almost interested.

"I guess palm trees lean slightly uphill. The coconuts that roll down, float to new islands, the others fall a little higher up the mountain with each successive generation. Anyhow, I guess we're known for not being satisfied where we're at."

"Teariki," Cutter said again. "Cool name."

She chuckled. "My mum says Lola Tuakana Teariki sounds a lot less like a stripper than Lola Fontaine." She sniffed again, opening the blue folder on her lap. "You want me to read you more about Hayden Starnes on the way to the airport?"

"That is a good idea," Cutter said, happy to veer off the rickety track of the deputy's personal life.

Fontaine spent the duration of the fifteen-minute drive to Ted Stevens Anchorage International giving him a more complete rundown on their bandit.

Starnes was a thirty-seven-year-old screwup, born and raised in Tigard, Oregon, a suburb of Portland. The lawyer at his original trial for sexual assault when Hayden was just twenty-two insisted his client had been molested as a child. Starnes had no siblings and his parents were both dead, so no one was around to refute the claim. A softhearted judge had sentenced him to two years and counseling to help him deal with his past trauma. The victim of his assault, a college senior his same age, sucked it up and went on to graduate school where she studied marketing.

Just weeks after he was released from prison,

Starnes kidnapped a college freshman by pretending to be security at the University of Oregon and offering her a ride back to her dorm during a rainstorm. He'd held this one in a remote cottage for three days before she'd finally wriggled free from her bonds and run, naked, to a neighboring cabin.

Subsequent interviews with family friends led investigators to believe Starnes's claims of molestation as a child were fabricated. When offered a plea deal of ten years flat if he told the truth, he came clean. He explained that everyone at his first trial, including the prosecutor and the judge, believed that people who did what he did had to have been molested as a child. And besides, he pointed out, he didn't so much as make it up, as he just agreed with everyone when they suggested it.

At his eventual sentencing, Starnes's victim spoke of recurrent nightmares, but went on to lead a campus advocacy group for rape survivors and graduated from the university with honors. Starnes received medication and counseling at taxpayer expense—for the mental issues that his attorney insisted were the root of his predatory nature.

He'd been out a grand total of eight months when he violated supervised release and skipped town, failing to register as a sex offender. This landed him at the top of the US Marshals

Service capture list. Bandits tended to graduate to the crimes a level above their last if they reoffended, so the fact that a young woman had disappeared on the same island where Starnes had been located gave both deputies plenty of cause for worry. The natural progression beyond a kidnapping often turned out to be murder. If the hunt went very long, Cutter planned to call on districts in western Washington and Oregon to send up deputies from the Pacific Northwest Violent Offenders Task Force to assist in the manhunt.

Starnes's background gave Cutter something to chew on during the flight. They were early—which was high on the list of Grumpy's Man-Rules, so he didn't mind waiting while Fontaine ran to the ladies' room. She was a good kid, though she did offer up a little too much information about the effects of her morning protein shake.

An abrupt voice drew his attention to the ticketing line. A bearded man in black and white plaid jabbed his finger at the Alaska Airlines agent, clearly angry about his seating assignment. The guy dressed like a lumberjack, but his smooth hands had likely never been within ten feet of an axe. The agent returned his wrath with an understanding nod.

"I'm sorry, sir. The flight is full," she said. "A middle seat is all I have left."

Lumberjerk leaned across the counter, his finger jabbing accompanied by a string of invectives.

Cutter stepped up to the counter, close enough that his arm brushed the man. He expected to get a nose full of booze, but this guy was stone sober.

The man spun. "I'm not done here."

"Oh," Cutter said. "I think you are."

Fontaine walked up then. "Hey, boss," she said. She'd obviously heard some of the conversation on her approach.

"I have a middle," she said to the ticketing agent. "You can let this guy take my seat if you want."

"What?" Lumberjerk said, incredulous. "I'd still be in the middle."

Fontaine grinned. "Yeah," she said. "But you'd get to sit next to my boss for the whole trip. Believe me, he'd love that."

Cutter nodded, eyes narrow, jaw clenched. "I would."

"That's okay," the agent said, reading a message on her computer screen. "But Mr. Penobscot will not be flying with us today. We'll refund your credit card, sir, but you'll need to find another method of transport to Juneau."

Penobscot's head began to shake. His lips trembled as he looked from the airline agent to Fontaine and then Cutter, before stomping off to talk to a supervisor.

Lola Fontaine chuckled as they watched the man walk away, almost tripping over his own two feet.

"You are in serious need of a Jiminy Cricket, boss," she said. "And I am happy to help you with that."

Cutter sighed, calming down a notch as he turned to the counter.

"Thank you," the agent said. A few years younger than Cutter, she wore a dark blue Alaska Airlines sweater with a gauzy gold scarf.

"My pleasure," he said, meaning it, and informing her that he'd need an armed-boarding pass.

Though not exactly rare, airline passengers with firearms didn't come along all the time. The aftereffects of her confrontation with Lumberjerk had the agent a little addled, and it took her a moment to process what he'd said. He slid his credential case across the counter. She smiled when she saw his badge, then retrieved the form he needed to complete. Marshals Service badges are recessed into the outside of the credentials, so she looked at the silver circle star for a moment, before opening the leather case to peruse the photograph. She glanced up to study Cutter's face before looking back to compare it with his photograph under the hologram on his credential.

"Funny, you don't look like Timothy Olyphant." She slid the case back across the counter.

"Pardon?" Cutter said.

The agent's smile broadened. "Timothy Olyphant. You know, he plays that deputy marshal Raylan Givens on that TV show *Justified*."

Cutter slipped the credentials back in his jacket pocket and gave a slow, contemplative nod. He looked at the agent's name tag and then leaned in across the counter, giving her a wink.

"The thing is, Alexis," he said, "I'm not tryin' to be Tim Olyphant. He's tryin' to be me."

CHAPTER 19

Carmen Delgado spent the coldest, darkest hours of the night slipping in and out of consciousness, curled in a ball where Chago had left her. The rhythmic surf and the cry of a distant loon—sounds that had offered comfort when she'd first come to Alaska—now only compounded her feelings of terror and isolation. The dirt made for a poor bed, but at some point, her body's defense mechanisms kicked in and forced it to shut down, if only for a few moments at a time.

She had no idea what time it was when she awoke, but it was dark, so she suspected it was still the middle of the night. On her side, she opened her eyes and looked around without moving. Chago and Luis snored inside the Jeep a dozen feet away. Their seats were reclined and they'd left the engine running against the chill that blew in from the water. Carmen tried wiggling her ankles in an effort to loosen the tape and get back some degree of circulation. Luis obviously planned to kill her anyway and hadn't cared if her feet fell off. The mere act of straightening out her legs brought tears to her eyes.

Something sharp dug into the side of her face. She raised her head, fighting a searing pain in her neck, and rubbed her cheek against the ground. Whatever it was bit her again when she lowered her head. She jerked away this time, turning to investigate. A bit of shell that had been imbedded in her cheek fell away. It took her a moment to realize it, but she lay next to a large midden. An idea began to worm its way into her fevered brain. Sharp as razors, the broken clamshells left behind by a feeding otter should easily slice through the duct tape around her wrists and ankles. She smiled in spite of her circumstances, thinking that the Kushtaka, the malevolent otter beings so feared by ancient Tlingit and Haida, had provided the mechanism for her escape.

Lack of circulation had destroyed most of the dexterity in her hands, but she was finally able to fumble with a piece of shell long enough to grasp it between her fingers and turn it backward against the tape. Under pressure from being applied so tightly, the tape separated amazingly fast and her hands pulled free after just a few moments of sawing.

The Jeep rocked as one of the men inside stirred. Carmen froze, but neither sat up, so after a short wait, she drew her knees to her chest. Circulation returned, flowing back to her fingers, and she was able to quickly hack away the tape around her ankles. Overwhelmed with hope, she wasn't as quiet as she should have been. Free, or at least more free than she had been, she took one last look at the Jeep. Still unable to walk, she crawled into the buck brush along the side of the road, pulling herself up the hill toward the forest as fast as she could move.

Her knees and hands were raw and bloody by the time enough circulation had returned for her to pull herself to her feet. Even then she had to use a broken spruce limb to help her hobble over the mossy ground. She had no idea where she was, but was content to simply stay in the trees and put as much distance as she could between herself and the wicked men. She could see the stars were winking out through the treetops above, blackness giving way to the blue-gray light of dawn. The certainty that at least one of her captors would be up any moment drove her forward, deeper into the darkness of the forest.

There had to be some cabin ahead or at least a fisherman with a gun. Everyone in Alaska had guns, didn't they? Someone should be able to save her. Then she thought of the hours she and her production staff had spent in these woods and along the surrounding beaches without seeing another soul and her spirits fell.

She was too weak to climb the larger pieces of deadfall, forcing her to skirt around them instead. The trees, the ground, the rocks, the shrubs—everything around her was varying shades of brown or green. She'd been walking for well over an hour when a sudden downslope caused her to lose her footing in the muddy turf. She landed hard on her bottom, her teeth slamming together with such force she was sure she'd broken at least one. The fall knocked the wind out of her and brought tears to her eyes. Then, a familiar odor hit her in the face. She couldn't quite place it, but knew it was something civilized—like a boat or a cabin. A few more steps and she recognized the smell.

A fire.

Thoughts of rescue and survival, when everything had seemed lost, helped to draw her forward. Half running, half falling, she slipped and slid down the scant, almost invisible trail. The hillside grew increasingly steep with each passing step, forcing her to dig in her heels and cling to alder branches to help arrest her descent. Soon, even that didn't help. A mini-avalanche of loose scree skittered down the slope ahead of her. Branches slapped her face. Sharp stones dug into her buttocks. It took everything she had to keep her feet pointed downhill.

She came to a stop in the pile of loose gravel along the edge of the road. Wincing, she reached down to touch her ankle, then took a halting step to make sure nothing was broken. Her stomach heaved when she looked up. Less than a hundred feet away was the Jeep.

The flight through the thick forest had taken her in a tight arc—and brought her right back to where she started.

She'd been so focused on her own misery that she didn't see that Luis had stepped to the edge of the woods to relieve himself. Half asleep, the *sicario* hadn't even checked to see if she was still tied on the other side of the vehicle. He turned now at the clattering racket of her fall, staring directly at her. Luis paused for a moment, tilting his head as if to bring her into focus. Then he shot a glance behind him, no doubt checking to see if Chago was awake. He was not. Smiling, the man they called El Guiso put a finger to his lips and began to walk directly toward her.

Carmen's feet were rooted as surely as if the bloodied soles had dried to the ground. She fought for breath, only able to conjure a shattered scream when Luis was ten feet away.

"Chaaaaago!"

CHAPTER 20

The Alaska Airlines gate agent called Cutter and Fontaine forward early since they were flying armed, allowing them to introduce themselves to the flight crew without the prying eyes of other passengers. Cutter made his way down the aisle and adjusted the Colt under his fleece jacket before folding himself into his seat. Fontaine flopped down across the aisle. Everyone else had yet to board so neither bothered with their seat belts.

"Thought you had a middle seat," Cutter said.

"Like I said, boss," Fontaine said, "I'm here to back your play." She leaned half into the aisle. "Do you have any friends in Witness Security?"

Cutter raised a wary eyebrow.

"Why? Weren't you just talking about SOG yesterday?"

Fontaine shrugged. "I'll have three years on the job in August, so I can start putting in for promotions. Just thinking about all my options, that's all. . . ."

"Hmmm," Cutter said. "Considering the fact that we have a teenage girl missing and a convicted rapist on the run, maybe you should start thinking about how we're going to capture Hayden Starnes."

Fontaine looked at him for a moment, and then nodded. She sat back without another word and stuffed a set of earbuds in her ears. Her head was bouncing to the music on her iPhone by the time passengers began filing onto the plane.

Cutter decided to take his own advice and pushed from his mind worries over task-force overtime, travel budgets, and his last conversation with Mim. He'd gone after sex offenders before, many times. It was at once grueling and rewarding work—like cleaning up all the dog crap from his grandpa's backyard. The job was seriously nasty, but it made the world a lot more pleasant to walk around in after the job was done.

Across the aisle, Lola Fontaine listened to her tunes and read a copy of the *Economist*, marking parts she found particularly interesting with a colored pen. Her outspoken demeanor often crossed the line into crassness, but her intellect was sharp and inquisitive. Judging from her ex-husband, she had sketchy taste in men, but Cutter couldn't help but think she would probably be his boss before the two of them retired.

The Alaska Airlines morning milk-run flight stopped in the southeast cities of Juneau and Sitka before touching down on Gravina Island, across the Tongass Narrows from the city of Ketchikan. A small ferry ran back and forth from the airport to the city at fifteen-minute intervals but Cutter and Fontaine were able to catch their air taxi directly from the airport side of the narrows.

The twentysomething pilot looked much too young to be flying an airplane as large as the de Havilland Beaver. Cutter rode in the right front seat, but the pilot addressed his safety briefing primarily toward Lola Fontaine. He made a lame joke about her using the fire extinguisher to put him out if he happened to catch fire, and turned around often during the forty-five-minute flight to look at her when he spoke, though they were all wearing David Clark headsets. Cutter figured he'd have to get used to this sort of behavior from other men whenever he traveled with Fontaine.

"Hope you brought a change of underwear," the pilot said once he'd crossed Clarence Strait and reached an altitude of five thousand feet over the rolling green forests below. A wall of black clouds loomed ahead of them, beyond Prince of Wales Island and out over the Pacific. "They don't call the Gulf of Alaska a storm factory for nothing," he continued. "There's a monster low out over the gulf that's barreling in with some hellacious winds. Good chance you could end up staying here awhile."

Fontaine pressed her nose to the side window. "I see a lot of boats on the water," she said, asking the question that was on Cutter's mind. "Isn't March a little early for salmon?"

The pilot's voice crackled over the intercom.

"They're after the herring," he said. "Or maybe kelp."

"Kelp?" Cutter asked.

"Yeah." The pilot banked back and forth in a series of slow S shape turns to give them a better view. A dozen fishing vessels dotted the water below. "You're coming to Prince of Wales just in time for the spawn-on-kelp fishery. These guys go out somewhere behind one of the outer islands—I can't remember which one—and harvest thousands of blades of broad-leaf kelp. Then they hang it on racks in pens they've built out of net. When the herring arrive, the same boats go seine them up and dump them in the pens. The fish do their part and lay their eggs on the kelp. Stuff brings good money, especially to the Asian markets. I think it's pretty tasty but it's never really caught on here in the US."

"What happens to all the herring?" Cutter asked.

"They're released to spawn another day," the pilot said.

The plane began to bounce as they flew into the turbulence ahead of the arriving storm.

"Guess I better stop playing tour guide and fly the plane."

"By all means," Cutter said.

The de Havilland Beaver touched down on the paved runway outside the city of Klawock thirty minutes later, bouncing twice and causing the pilot to throw a sheepish grin over his shoulder at Fontaine. Neither deputy had much gear and were able to off-load quickly. The pilot taxied back onto the runway as soon as Cutter and Fontaine were out of his path. He had the plane back in the air by the time a dusty white Chevrolet Tahoe arrived at the edge of the taxiway.

A slender Native man in a long-sleeve blue uniform shirt rolled down his window. "You guys the marshals?"

Cutter nodded. "We are."

"Cool."

He sat looking at them for just long enough to make it uncomfortable, and then added, "I been thinking of applying with you guys."

The officer introduced himself as Jeremy Simeon of Craig Police Department. A sparse black mustache made Cutter guess he was in his early twenties. Thin to the extreme, the uniform shirt looked like it was about to swallow him. His wide smile looked too big for his face.

"Trooper Benjamin asked me to pick you guys up." He motioned toward the truck with a flick of his head. "He's got his hands full with something else."

"Arresting Hayden Starnes, I hope," Cutter said, tossing his duffel in the rear seat and leaving the front to Fontaine.

Officer Simeon threw the Tahoe into gear

and did a quick shoulder check to make sure he wasn't pulling out in front of another aircraft before crossing the taxiway. "Nope," he said. "Somebody's gone missing."

"Millie Burkett," Fontaine nodded. "We heard about her."

"Another somebody," Simeon said. "Two somebodies, if you wanna know the truth. They work for *FISHWIVES!*"

"I love *FISHWIVES!*" Lola said.

Cutter leaned forward, making sure he'd heard correctly. "What's *FISHWIVES!*?"

Officer Simeon shot a glance over his shoulder and gave a long sigh. "Worst thing that ever hit this damned island."

CHAPTER 21

Luis slammed into Carmen hard, taking her down with a flying tackle, riding her all the way to the frozen ground. She slid backward under his momentum, gravel grinding into her spine and shoulders as she bore the brunt of the fall. The tackle did half Luis's job for him and shoved the loose flannel pants halfway down her thighs. Straddling her, the grinning *sicario* must have forgotten she was no longer tied—or else he didn't care. He went straight for her breasts, clawing at them through her T-shirt as if he meant to rip them off her chest.

Past pain, Carmen found her voice, shrieking in earnest now, and clawing at his face, intent on digging out his eyes. Planting numb feet, she bucked her hips. He was surprisingly light and should have been relatively easy to throw, but the flannel pants had formed a hobble around her legs and robbed her of leverage.

He only hooked his heels around her knees, sneering lewdly, and rode her like a horse.

Carmen's thumbnail found purchase in his nostril, digging in and ripping sideways.

Luis screamed and jerked away, rolling to the side, hand to his face. She rolled completely over the top and back under, ending up beneath him again, panting with fear and the effort of trying to escape.

She kept clawing but her strength ebbed quickly and he rained down blows against her face. She finally fell back, stunned, but this only served to infuriate him more. He grabbed her by both shoulders and drove a vicious knee into her groin. Agony surged through her belly. She dry heaved, attempting to draw herself into a ball, but Luis pressed her to the ground. He leaned down, sinking his teeth into her shoulder.

"Bitch!" Spittle flew from his lips. "I am going to cut y—"

Carmen was vaguely aware of a shadow looming above her, then Luis flew away as if launched by a cannon, rolling with a loud *whoomf* into the ditch.

A half hour later Carmen sat on a rock beside the fire. Surprisingly, her hands and feet were still free. Luis stood across from her, soaking up the heat from the fire while he nursed his wounded nostril where she'd cut him with her fingernail. Chago stood back at the hood of the Jeep, looking sad. Neither man spoke of the attempted rape, or of their fight that had stopped it.

"I never been so cold, Chago," Luis said, his teeth chattering, as much from the beating Chago had given him as from the cold. "I think that cold water last night mighta done something to my bones." He looked over his shoulder, staring daggers at Carmen as if his predicament was all her fault. He nodded slowly, unable to keep from giving her a lascivious up and down stare. /

Chago stepped toward the stump, putting himself between Carmen and his foul partner.

"I told you," he said, his voice a gravel whisper, "this one looks like my sister."

"I'd do your sister." Luis shrugged and then backpedaled quickly, nearly tripping over the fire.

Carmen thought for a moment Chago would kill the skinny murderer, but he let the comment pass, turning to her instead.

"Look," Luis said. "I don't want to go back to the boss any more than you do, but I'm tired of this shit. I say we kill her and call it good."

"Shut up," Chago said. He turned back to Carmen. "You have had time to think. Tell us, are there any more copies of the video you took of the boat?"

Carmen sat on the stump, her eyes shifting between the two men. One wanted to rape her, the other thought it would be a mercy to kill her quickly. She was absolutely certain that her life was over as soon as she told them what they wanted to know. Greg had tried to talk to them, and the crazy one had murdered him anyway. They'd made a mistake by backing her against a wall like this. Apart from a quick and merciful death—

which she doubted they'd give her anyway—there was nothing left for them to bargain with.

Her own voice, hoarse and strained, startled her when she spoke.

"Let me understand," she said. "I tell you what you want to know and you will make it quick?"

Chago looked at her with dead black eyes.

"I would do this for you, yes."

Carmen laughed out loud, rocking back and forth with both hands on top of her head. "Holy shit, Chago! I don't know if you realize this, but that's the worst incentive on the entire planet." Too exhausted to think clearly, the smile bled from her face. "I saw what you bastards did to Greg. You won't believe me no matter what I say. Even when I tell you, you'll only torture me to make sure." She pointed at Luis, wagging her head though pain from the movement made her nauseous. "That one will say he has to rape me to be sure that I'm telling the truth, but *the truth* is it makes him feel good to hurt people."

Luis drew the knife from his belt. "I don't have to listen to this!"

Chago stopped him with an open palm to the chest. "Idiot! She is trying to make us kill her."

"Good Lord, Chago." Carmen rolled her eyes. "I don't want to die."

Chago cocked his head to one side, looking at her. "Then why do you hide the footage?" he asked. "It is not as if you are protecting your national security. Your silence does not make you a martyr. This video means nothing to you."

Carmen wanted to scream. "You never even told me what you wanted until after I saw you stab Greg! Now I'm just trying to stay alive."

Luis snorted. "That is never going to happen."

Chago held up his hand. "Please," he said. "What do you propose?"

She took a deep breath, knowing it might well be her last. "There are two copies."

Chago slammed a fist into his open palm. "I knew it!"

"Shit!" Luis said. "Where?"

"You killed Greg because he tried to negotiate," she said. "But what do you expect people to do?"

Luis grabbed her by the hair and jerked her head backward over the top of the stump. Chago watched him do it and made no move to stop him. It exposed her throat to his blade.

"I expect you to tell me what I want to know," Luis hissed. "You got no room to bargain."

Carmen thought her heart might stop until Chago stepped in and loomed above them. Luis backed away, nicking her neck with the blade in the process.

She spoke directly to Chago, feeling a flimsy glimmer of hope. "Each camera was set to record on two cards simultaneously. You have two of them, but there are two more. I'll tell you where one of them is as a sign of good faith. Then we'll have to figure out a way for you to let me go—or I promise you that the second card will be found and the video will come to light."

Luis spat into the fire.

"Chica," he said. "I once cut out a woman's rib and beat her to death with the bone. So don't think you can threaten me."

Carmen gulped, then decided to press on, even if it killed her—which it was very likely to do. Her voice began to tremble so badly she could hardly speak. "This is not a threat," she said. "But this *is* the way things are. If you kill me, there will still be a card out there—and I won't be around to tell you—"

A stiff wind blew in from the water and kicked up the fire. Chago's voice rose with the flames. "Both of you shut up!" he said. "I need to think." At length, he glared down at Carmen. "Okay. Tell us about the first one then."

Carmen felt hope grow into a painful lump in her throat. "Greg said we had something important as soon as you started chasing us," she said. "We had no idea what it was, but he said we should each hold on to one of the cards, just in case. He hid his in a plastic baggie in his pants pocket."

Luis's knuckles clenched white around his knife. "What did you say? I swam that guy's dead ass all the way out there and he had it on him the whole time?" He shot a look at Chago, speaking in rapid-fire Spanish. Her nerves were on edge, but Carmen had no trouble following the meaning. "We're good then, right?" Luis said. "I mean, the guy's sunk."

Chago turned to Carmen, studying her. "Would not the water kill the media card?"

She shook her head. "The baggie should protect it," she said. "Salt won't do it any good, but it's solid state, so even if the water gets in it might still be all right. Put it in a bag of rice and it could be dried out enough to retrieve the data."

Chago turned to Luis. "Will he stay down?"

"Shit!" Luis pounded the top of his head with an open hand. "I think so. . . ."

Chago's face grew dark. His breath came faster. "Tell me now. Where is this second media card?"

Carmen swallowed her fears. "Chago, I . . . I can't," she said. "That wasn't the deal. Maybe I should talk about this next part with your boss."

Chago stooped down to look at her nose to nose. She could feel the heat coming off his body. "You want to talk to my boss?"

Carmen fully expected him to stab her to death at any moment. "I . . . do," she said.

Luis looked skyward and broke into a fit of nervous laughter.

Chago wiped his hands together, as if washing them of any responsibility. "You think El Guiso is cruel," he said. "But when we deliver you into the hands of Manuel Alvarez-Garza, remember, chica, you asked for it."

CHAPTER 22

Officer Simeon parked on a gravel apron on the ocean side of the pavement. Across the narrow road was a two-story cedar home with a white Alaska State Troopers Tahoe and another half dozen assorted island vehicles parked haphazardly along a semicircular driveway. As much as Cutter loved his home state, he had to admit that the AST golden bear on the Tahoe's door was a little cooler than the Florida Highway Patrol's orange.

The house perched on a lot that was cut out of the mountain, against a wall of black rock and dense evergreens. Wood smoke poured from the chimney, curling through the moss-covered branches in a hazy cloud. Behind the house were several freshly cut cedar stumps, their tops bright orange against the prevailing blacks and greens. Apart from the house itself there was nothing level about the place. At least twenty people milled in the small front yard, some leaning against trees, others huddled around a weathered picnic table that looked like it might come careening down the mountain at any moment.

A fleshy redhead with twin braids draped over the shoulders of a purple fleece jacket studied Fontaine's approach. Her patched denim skirt looked as if it was sewn from a pair of faded blue jeans. Alternately bawling as if she'd just been beaten and screaming in fits of red-faced rage, she was attended by two younger women as if she were royalty. One young woman held a box of tissues within easy reach. The other, a mousy thing, appeared too frightened to get within striking distance of the seething monster. A few feet away, a brunette wearing extremely tight yoga pants and a cowl neck sweater stood sobbing with a tissue to her nose. A young man with a long beard, braided like something straight out of a Viking movie, tried to console her. The place looked like some kind of beard convention with more than half the men in the yard sporting similar facial hair. Several men and at least two of the women wore dreadlocks of varying lengths. Half of them, including the men, were crying. Most looked like they'd walked out of an REI catalog photo shoot.

Officer Simeon shot a glance at Cutter. "And that," he said, "is *FISHWIVES!*"

A squat but thickly built man stepped out of the open front door, blocking their way with folded arms. He was a head shorter than Cutter, with a buzzed flattop. Somehow, he'd poured himself into a black T-shirt that was two sizes too small. The sleeves were rolled up making it impossible for anyone to miss his sculpted biceps.

"The trooper's busy with a crime scene," the man said, not yielding.

"This is Kenny Douglas," Officer Simeon said. "He thinks because he's a security guard for a television show he outranks me."

Douglas wagged his head, his grin dripping with derision toward the Native man. "Firstly," he said. "I am a security consultant, not a security guard. The difference being about eighty K a year. Secondly, the trooper told me I should stand here and watch the door. And, lastly, this isn't the city of Craig, so technically, I do outrank you."

Fontaine was slightly ahead, so Cutter held back to see how she handled this. She fished her badge out of her jacket pocket and flashed it, nodding toward the door. "US Marshals."

"So?" Douglas said. "Missing persons aren't a federal matter."

The deputy studied Douglas for a long moment, sizing him up. "You're right," she said at length, stepping forward to invade the man's body space. She stood so close her lead foot was directly between his feet, her knee a fraction of an inch from his groin. "But we often assist locals, sometimes just by jerking a knot in the ass of some smart guy who's hampering the investigation."

Douglas backpedaled enough that Fontaine was able to push her way through the door without actually getting physical.

"Pity," Cutter said as he went by. "That would have been fun to watch."

Officer Simeon leaned in to Cutter as he followed them in. "I really like your partner," he said.

The living room was in shambles. Flat-screen monitors, tens of thousands of dollars in cameras, and a variety of video equipment lay strewn around the floor. Across the room, where it connected to the kitchen, the trooper stooped beside the open back door, examining the leading edge. He stood and peeled off a black nitrile glove to shake Cutter's and then Fontaine's hands in turn. "Sam Benjamin," he said. "You must be the marshals."

"We are." Cutter nodded. "Officer Simeon says you've had two more go missing?"

"Looks that way," Benjamin said. "No witnesses so far, but as you can see, these two didn't exactly just wander off."

Cutter stepped around the trooper to have a look at the back door. There were no tool or pry marks. "You think someone picked the lock?"

Benjamin shrugged. "That's my guess. Her reality show's a pitiful excuse for entertainment, but Carmen Delgado's a smart woman. I don't see her leaving a door unlocked with all this equipment in here."

Fontaine moved closer to the door, having a look for herself. "Delgado works on the reality show?"

"She's the big cheese," Benjamin said. "The

producer. From what I hear, the entire thing was her idea. And I gotta tell you, that doesn't exactly endear her to some of the folks on the island."

Cutter stepped out to look at the ground around the back door. The trooper had already poured dental stone, taking casts of three possible tracks.

"So she has some enemies?" Fontaine asked.

The trooper looked around the room. "I wouldn't have said anyone hated her bad enough to trash the place . . . and yet, here we are. Carmen's gone, along with one of her cameramen, a guy named Greg Conner. I've already dusted for prints, but I'm not hopeful. If someone's enough of a pro to pick the lock, I doubt they're going to leave fingerprints."

"Looks like they were after something," Cutter said. "Do you know what's missing yet? It's none of my business, just curious."

"Another couple sets of eyes don't offend me," the trooper said. "You're not hurting my feelings at all. My partner's working a sexual assault up at Port Protection near the north end of the island. Our only Forest Service officer's down in Seattle visiting his new granddaughter. Craig PD's down one, and one is off island. The officer from Klawock is at the academy and the brownshirt came down with food poisoning last night. Simeon's the only one around now, besides me."

Cutter toed through the pile of video gear on the floor. "What's a brownshirt?"

"Fish and Wildlife trooper," Benjamin said. "Same training we have, just different uniform and duties. I can usually rely on him to back me up."

"Sounds like a perfect storm," Fontaine said.

"An everyday occurrence around here," the trooper said. "They cover for me as much or more than I do for them. So, I'm happy for all the help I can get. Anyway, as you can see, it's tough to tell if anything was taken without knowing what was here before the break-in. One of the field producers is supposed to come in and get me an inventory as soon as I'm done grabbing any prints and photos."

Cutter nodded at some media cards on the floor. "These are all numbered," he said.

"They are," Benjamin said. "And from the looks of it, eight of them are missing. According to the cameraman I talked to, that really doesn't mean anything. They're probably with all the other field cameras at their apartments in Craig. He's going to check and get me a list."

Fontaine picked up a small plastic vial. "Blood?"

"Good eye," Benjamin said. "You guys keep me on my toes. I got it off the table there by the video monitors. We can hope it belongs to an aggressor. It's more likely one of the victims put up a fight."

Cutter gave a somber nod. "You think this might be related to Hayden Starnes?"

The trooper gave a long sigh. "Could be. Carmen was his boss. It's possible he came back and wanted his last paycheck and she told him to get lost."

"That's not what happened!" A shrill voice carried in through the front door. Cutter turned to see the emotional Fishwife queen standing there beside Douglas, the security specialist. She was a large but well-proportioned woman. The fiery braids and her tremendous size made her look like a Wagnerian opera singer missing her horned helmet.

"That's Bright Jonas," the trooper said, nodding at the woman.

"It was that nosy bitch, January Cross. She did this," Bright said. "Anyone with half a brain can see it."

Trooper Benjamin cocked his head to one side and looked at the deputies. "News to me," he said under his breath. "Why do you suspect her?"

"Because," Bright said, "she had a fight with Carmen and Greg last night when they came back in from an evening shoot. It's not enough that she sneaks around trying to seduce our husbands. Now she's gone and hurt Carmen."

Simeon shook his head in disbelief. "Bright, you know that's just a made-up thing for the show's story line, right?"

"Where there's smoke, Jeremy," Bright fumed. "*She* did this. I'm sure of it."

"Thanks, Bright," Benjamin said. "Officer Simeon, would you mind showing Mrs. Jonas outside?"

"There's no way January Cross kidnapped two healthy people," Benjamin said as soon as the Craig officer had taken the talent outside and shut the door behind him. "More likely it was Millie Burkett's father in a fit of drunken rage. Millie was doing some work for the production company and Burkett felt that work was responsible for his daughter's disappearance."

"Three missing people," Deputy Fontaine mused. "And a wanted sex offender with a record for kidnapping. That doesn't sound good to me."

"You got that right," the trooper said.

"Can we help out with anything?" Cutter asked.

Benjamin raised an eyebrow. "I'm about finished here," he said. "But I need to talk with Gerald Burkett. You guys mind going over to have a chat with January Cross so I can tell Bright we checked her off the list? January's relatively new on the island, but she's all over the place with her boat. Everyone knows everyone around here, so there's a good chance she'll have a lead on Starnes anyway."

"I'm happy to go talk to her," Cutter said, "just as long as she's nothing like that Bright Jonas gal."

"Not even close," Benjamin said. He looked at Lola Fontaine, then back at Cutter, thinking.

"Mind if I take your partner with me? Gerald Burkett might calm down a notch or two if he thinks I brought the Marshals Service in to help me look for his daughter. Simeon can drop you off at my office. The receptionist will give you the keys to the extra truck the sergeant drives when he comes to visit. Feel free to wreck the hell out of it."

CHAPTER 23

"I don't care if we get in trouble," Dillon Sweeny said. He maneuvered his rod over the side of the fourteen-foot aluminum skiff and flipped the lever on his reel. A cloud of herring oil shimmered upward and left a rainbow sheen on the surface as his bait sank into the water, dragged toward the bottom by a four-ounce lead sinker.

Max George sat at the bow of the boat glancing along the forested bank as he attempted to bait his own hook.

"You're gonna shove that hook through your finger," Dillon said.

The Haida boy shot a defensive glance at his friend. "Shut up," he said, though he didn't act like he meant it. Max was tall and big-boned, looking much older than his thirteen years. Sweeny found him overly superstitious but chalked it up to his young age and the fact that he was Native. Sweeny had to admit though, this place had great fishing—but it gave him the creeps almost as bad as it did Max.

The boys had no GPS or fish finder, but Sweeny knew exactly where he was. The bay itself was about the size of a city block, relatively shallow at around sixty feet. A large monolith of stone rose up from the bottom, two-thirds of the way out toward the mouth. The stone became visible if the tide was low enough, with a good two feet jutting above the surface. Local legend was that many generations before, the daughter of a local chief wanted to marry a boy from a rival clan from the other side of the island. Her father forbade it, as did the boy's. Undeterred, the star-crossed couple ran away into the forest but were eventually captured by the girl's brothers. The boy was killed, and the distraught girl swam to the rock at low tide and waited for the water to fill the cove. The frigid water had sapped her strength—as she had known it would. Heartbroken and completely exhausted, she sat on the rock and waited for the tide to rise and the cold sea to engulf her. The villagers didn't hear her wistful cries until after it was dark—and too late to save her. From that night, they'd called the place Wailing Rock Bay. Even now, locals said they often saw the dead girl's face staring up at them from the deep.

Max said he didn't believe the story. But Sweeny found him awfully jumpy for a nonbeliever.

"You see that?" Max George said. He turned his head to look at the water from his spot near the bow. He'd been in the middle of weaving a hook through the eye of a herring.

"What?" Dillon said. He felt the weight on his line hit bottom.

"There it is," Max said, pointing to a piece of white paper a few feet beneath the surface. A bank of heavy clouds had rolled in from the west, turning the water dark and brooding. "Give me the net so I can check it out."

Dillon ignored him, bouncing the tip of his fishing rod to cause the herring on the end of his line to dance at the bottom and hopefully catch the attention of a halibut or rockfish. It was still a little early for lingcod—not that he really cared about the fishing regulations.

The current caught the paper—or whatever it was, causing it to swirl and twist as if alive without coming to the surface.

"Don't you want to see what it is?" Max asked. "It could be a note or something."

"You're always seeing boogeymen and Kushtaka." Sweeny scoffed. "More likely some tourist boat came into the bay and pumped out their shitter. I'm not gonna let you net some piece of toilet paper and bring it on my skiff."

"I guess it could be that," Max said. "But if it is, you want to eat the fish we catch from here?"

"Shut up," Sweeny said. "It's a piece of paper. Don't make a big federal case out of it."

"And besides that," Max George said, "you shouldn't make fun of the Kushtaka. Not while we're all the way out here by the Wailing Rock." George was serious about his boogeymen.

"I thought you said that Wailing Rock story wasn't true."

"It's not," Max said. "But it's still not wise to make fun of the old stories and traditions."

A stiff breeze riffled the surface, rocking the boat and sending a chill down Dillon Sweeny's spine. The wind hadn't really kicked up yet, but it was just a matter of time. Dillon had spent all his seventeen years on this island. He knew the secrets of Wailing Rock Bay. It was his favorite fishing spot, even with the weather and bad juju. The tide was huge, providing a gigantic flush a couple of times a day that cleared out the bay and brought in new water from the ocean—even if some charter boat had dumped their holding tanks here.

Dillon came here to fish as often as he could sneak away. The school had probably already called his mom at work and told her he hadn't shown up. His mom would have tried to call his cell—which he'd left in the truck because it didn't work all the way out here anyhow. Then she would have called his dad, who would have pretended to share her anger that their oldest son was skipping school so near the end of the semester. But Dillon's dad was cool. He understood that sometimes a guy needed a mental health day—and there was no better way to do that than go fishing. Later, his dad would assign him some chore he'd been going to make him do anyway and then privately confide that he was glad Dillon was fishing instead of frying his brain on computer games.

The tip of his rod dipped sharply, bringing a familiar surge of adrenaline down both arms. No matter how many times he put a line in the water, when a fish hit, it was like Christmas morning, waiting to see what was on the other end. Sweeny flicked the rod to set the hook. He kept the tip up and began to reel. Whatever it was, this was a monster.

"Got it," Max George said, leaning over the bow with the landing net. His hook and the piece of herring lay in the floor of the skiff. He held up a piece of lined paper that looked like it had been ripped from a notebook. "Told you it was some kind of note."

"Forget the stupid note and get the net ready." Sweeny reeled fast to stay ahead of the fish on the other end. He yanked backward, horsing the rod to bring the fish to the surface. The line suddenly went taut as if he'd snagged on the bottom. "Dammit!" he said, an instant before it snapped.

Sweeny glared at the Native boy.

"It's not my fault," Max said. He craned his head to one side and pointed. "Look. It's another piece of paper."

Sweeny turned to look at the water. "Would you shut up about—"

A shadowed movement caught his eye, deep in the water—well below the new piece of paper. At first he thought it was the fish that had broken his line. They swam to the surface sometimes when they were dazed. But this was bigger.

"You think it's a halibut?" George said. "Maybe a harbor seal."

"That's no seal," Dillon said, bending over the side to get a closer look. "Maybe a halibut though. Hand me the net in case it gets close enough."

An instant later he shoved away from the gunnel, nearly falling over the other side of the boat. Max saw it at the same time and screamed, a full octave higher than his normal voice.

It was no halibut or seal floating up from the depths to meet them, but the face of a young woman. Her lips had been eaten away by sea lice and shrimp, causing her to look like she was snarling. Her neck arched backward and lidless eyes stared heavenward as she rose up from the depths.

Max vomited over the side when the body broke the surface. She was wrapped mummy-like in heavy burlap cloth with only the head exposed. Her hands and feet looked like they were tied, but the boys didn't stick around to make sure.

CHAPTER 24

Jenny, the clerk at the Alaska State Troopers office, drew Cutter a map, but there was no need. Craig Harbor was almost close enough to the AST post he could have hit it with a rock. The parking lot was located on the north side of the Craig-Klawock Highway, overlooking the larger harbor normally occupied by dozens of fishing boats. According to the trooper, the forty-two-foot vessel January Cross used for her orca studies was moored at the very end of the smaller South Harbor. Jenny said he'd be able to recognize it by the US Forest Service enforcement boat in the slip two boats down.

The deputies hadn't yet had the opportunity to check into their rooms, but the small rental apartments Fontaine had booked for them supposedly overlooked the harbor. Cutter decided to go see January Cross first, and drop off his gear after he finished.

Gray clouds hung from a low sky as Cutter turned the trooper pickup into a parking lot on the north side of the highway, then crossed the road to make his way down to the docks. The sound of his boots on the wooden docks alerted a tawny little dog to his presence. The dog barked once, then stood with its front paws on the gunnel of a boat named *Tide Dancer* and growled as Cutter approached.

Cutter's grandfather had spent a lot of time on his Boston Whaler and Arliss had spent a lot of time with his grandfather. Grumpy would say things like, "Only a fool fights the ocean." He told him to treat the sea like a woman. "Watch for the little signs and tells that will let you know when she's sweet and inviting or in a devilish, sour mood." Like a woman, a boat could take you places you could never get to otherwise, but only if you knew how to take care of her. Arliss couldn't help but think that if he'd been able to apply Grumpy's techniques to human women, his life would have been much smoother sailing.

Cutter himself had endured a not too secret love affair with boats his entire life. At least two of his ex-wives had made it clear early in their doomed marriages that they derived no pleasure from walking up and down the docks looking at other people's boats. Cutter, on the other hand, could walk the docks and stare at other people's boats for hours. It was just a matter of imagining what you would do and where you would go if the boat were yours. There'd been many times over the years when he'd seen a particular boat and dreamed of what it would be like to take her out. Some boats beckoned you aboard.

Tide Dancer was not such a boat.

Cross's converted trawler was moored stern

to the dock, among boats of much less frequent upkeep. A dismasted sailboat sat forlornly on the other side of the float. Below the waterline, her nameless fiberglass hull had become home to many years' worth of trailing kelp and blossoming anemones. To *Tide Dancer*'s port side, a lopsided aluminum runabout with a weathered blue ragtop wallowed low in the water. Grumpy would have certainly stopped such a vessel on suspicion of carrying a load of contraband. *Tide Dancer* was neat and shipshape if not handsome. In sharp contrast to her neighboring boats, she was clean and uncluttered, older but in good repair. Cutter couldn't help but notice she'd had some work done, and by someone who didn't possess the sure hand of a master boat builder. There was a crookedness to the vessel that while not ugly, was just not quite right.

The dog stopped growling and opened its freakishly wide face in a long yawn—as if Cutter wasn't worth the trouble.

A tall woman with mussed black hair nearly as short as Cutter's looked up from wrestling a five-gallon propane tank into a lazarette along the starboard side of the vessel. She wore a gray hoodie with the sleeves pulled up to her elbows against the relative warmth of midday. Faded jeans, snug where the hoodie was conspicuously loose, were tucked neatly into a pair of chocolate-brown Xtratuf boots like the ones Cutter had borrowed from Mim. It wasn't politically correct, but men looked at women's figures—and January Cross was pleasantly curvaceous, even in the baggy hoodie. She carried herself with a regal and upright air, as if she knew she was the captain of not only her vessel, but of a great deal of everything else going on around her as well.

"Can I help you with that?" Cutter said, stopping beside the boat's transom and giving the unwieldy propane tank a nod. "I'm in no way saying you're not strong enough to do it," he added. "But if I was trying to get a full bottle of propane down in that little locker, I'd accept your help if you happened by."

"Put that way," the woman said, "I'd be most grateful."

The little dog jumped down off the transom bench and scampered over to sniff Cutter's pant legs as he swung open the gate and stepped onto the aft deck.

"Havoc's usually a little less trusting." The woman shoved a pile of wrenches and shop rags into a canvas tool bag and then glanced up at Cutter, hazel eyes smiling, thanking him for the help.

Cutter stepped back when they were done, wiping his hands together. The woman peeled off a pair of leather work gloves and extended a petite but strong hand. It was calloused, but not overly so. Her calluses were pink and, Cutter suspected, newly acquired.

225

"January Cross." She gave his hand a firm shake.

"Arliss Cutter," he said. "I should have introduced myself before I came on your boat."

Cross shook her head. "I knew who you were as soon as you stepped onto the float. Everybody on this island knows everybody—and their business. And anyway, I had no doubt I'd be on someone's list when I heard Carmen and her cameraman had gone missing. I'm just glad you're not that Sergeant Yates. There's a first-class jerk if there ever was one."

"I'm not with the state troopers," Cutter said. "United States Marshals."

"I heard that too," she said, looking neutral and unimpressed.

A string of cursing erupted from the next slip, under the ragtop. Cutter glanced down to see a balding man bend over the dock working to retrieve two hard plastic rifle cases similar to the one Fontaine had brought to the island. Adrenaline shot down Cutter's arm when he noticed the AR-15 carbine hanging from a sling around the man's neck. Cutter's gun hand brushed the front of his jacket, putting the Colt Python within easy reach.

January noticed and gave an imperceptible shake of her head. She waved at the man.

"Hey, Bean," she said.

"Jan," the man said. He hustled brusquely

toward the parking lot with his armload of rifle cases.

"That's Bean," Cross said once the man was out of earshot. "He's a weirdo, but he's basically harmless."

"Likes his rifles, I see," Cutter said.

"I think he must sell them or something," January said. "He told me once he builds them himself. His day job is doing something for the Triple C Mine. He lives in town but I guess they have a nice shop out there."

"Interesting," Cutter said. Unwilling to turn his back on an armed man, he watched Mr. Bean exit the parking lot above in a newer Ford pickup.

"In any case," he said once the man was gone, "I'm down here from Anchorage looking for a federal fugitive named Hayden Starnes."

Cross shook her head. "Don't know anyone by that name."

"He was going under the name Travis Todd," he said. "Did odd jobs for the production company. Trooper Benjamin said you travel all around the island. He thought you might have noticed Mr. Todd camping out on one of the beaches." Cutter gave her Starnes's description.

Cross took a water hose from the same lazarette where they'd stowed the propane and dragged it toward the faucet on the dock. "Wish I could help," she said. "I haven't seen anybody like that."

Cutter stepped up and helped feed the hose out of the locker, making certain it didn't kink before she had it screwed into the faucet.

"Okay," he said. "The trooper also asked that I talk to you about the argument you had with the production crew last night."

Cross laughed. Finished with the hose, she stepped back aboard. "Who said it was an argument? They sped past in their boat without paying any attention to the no-wake zone. It just about knocked me into the drink, so I told them to slow down. Admittedly, I did use my eighth-grade teacher voice."

Cutter raised a brow. "From what I remember about my eighth-grade teachers, that could be considered a deadly weapon in some jurisdictions."

"You got that right," she said. "Anyway, they were in too big a hurry to argue. Carmen didn't even acknowledge me. The kid with the dreads—I can't remember his name—he just flipped me off as he shot by without slowing down."

"You're a teacher?" he asked.

"I was," she said. "Biology. At present, I'm working on an orca study for the state of Alaska."

"Nice," Cutter said. "So what time did Carmen and this guy with dreads speed by you?"

January shrugged. Her eyes looked upward, the way someone did when they remembered rather than fabricated. "I don't know, around seven thirty or eight maybe. It was just beginning to get dark."

Cutter pretended to be writing.

"I see what you're doing here," she said at length.

Cutter looked up from his notebook. "And what's that?"

"Most people dislike a vacuum in the conversation," she said. "The guilty ones fill it up with incriminating stuff without your even having to ask."

"So," Cutter said. "Is there any incriminating stuff you want to add?"

January chuckled. "It's no secret that I've been pissed at Carmen Delgado. Most people think it was because of the husband-stealing siren thing on her stupid show."

"Seems like a good enough reason to be upset," Cutter said.

"I suppose," January said. "But that's not it, really. Have you seen the totem poles and carvings on this island? Prince of Wales is brimming with Native Tlingit and Haida culture. These are incredible people and even more incredible stories. Carmen promised me when she first came here she'd include those stories in her television show." Cross shook her head, disgusted. "I haven't seen a single Native person in any of the episodes."

"I've never understood why people watch what they do on television."

"I suppose," January said. "But she did make me a promise."

"Can anyone else corroborate your version of the events?"

She shrugged again. "Let's see," she said. "Linda hadn't gotten here yet. Cassandra Brown was here."

"Cassandra Brown," Cutter repeated, writing the name down to pass along to Trooper Benjamin.

"She's a twelve-year-old Haida girl who's sort of befriended me," January said. "But she doesn't speak, so she's not going to be much help."

"Was the balding guy on his boat here when this went down?"

"Bean?" January said. "No. He must have been out at the Triple C." She brightened. "Havoc was here."

"You're not trying very hard."

"Hey, the dog's more trustworthy than Bean. He's half heeler."

"Did you run into either of them again after the incident?" Cutter asked. "Later that night maybe?"

"Nope." She shook her head. "My friend Linda Roundy dropped by shortly afterward to bring me a calzone. I went and did some laundry at her house. After that, I bought some groceries and came back here and went to sleep."

Cutter made a few notes in his book. "Okay then," he said.

"Can I ask you a question now?"

"Go for it," Cutter said.

"What's with the medicine bag? I haven't seen many white people going against the fashion police with a leather bag tucked into their belts."

"Stuff from my grandpa," he said, reaching to pat it as was his habit from time to time.

"Was he Native?"

"Nope," Cutter said. "Just a cool grandpa. He passed on some things that mean a lot to me so I prefer to keep them with me. That's all."

January studied him with eyes as unwavering as a CT scan, but said nothing.

"So," Cutter said, closing his notebook, "I'll pass this on to Trooper Benjamin. You probably shouldn't leave town though."

"Why?" January asked. "Because you might call me?"

Cutter couldn't be sure if she was flirting or just wanted to know if he'd follow up.

"Maybe," he said.

"Well," January said, "leaving town is exactly what I plan to do, about as quick as you get off my boat. I'm not trying to run away from anything though, and I'll tell you exactly where I'm going." She held out her hand, snapping her fingers. "Let me see your notebook?"

He let her take it.

"There could be a bunch of double top secret marshal things in there," he said.

She flipped through the book, stopping to look up at him with a grin. "Like this top-secret recipe for cheeseburger soup?"

"Exactly," he said. "You would not believe what I had to do to get that."

She fished a pen from the kangaroo pocket of her hoodie and sketched him a map. "The pod of whales I follow hangs out up near Tuxekan Passage during a storm like the one that's about to hit us. I plan to drop my anchor and ride out the night in a cove near there so I can get a jump on them after this low pressure blows through." She flipped the notebook around so Cutter could see her hand-drawn map. "No cell service, and the mountain blocks the radio unless you come up on the sea side. But if you need to talk to me, it's out Forest Service Road 2051, a place called Kaguk Cove."

CHAPTER 25

Footsteps clomped down the wooden float behind Cutter, and he looked up to find Deputy Fontaine and Trooper Benjamin coming toward *Tide Dancer*.

"Well, crap," January said. "I scared you so bad you had to call for backup."

"You need to turn your phone on, boss," Fontaine said. She raised a wary brow toward Cross.

Cutter reached in his jacket pocket for his phone. He'd been so caught up in his conversation with January, he hadn't felt it vibrating. "What's up? Did you nab our bandit?"

"Afraid not," the trooper said. "But I could use some help if you're done here."

January nodded. "We're done."

"For now," Cutter said. He looked at Benjamin. "What's up?"

"A couple of boys say they had a body float up on them while they were fishing in a small cove down toward Soda Bay."

"The Burkett girl or one of the others?"

"Still unknown," the trooper said, looking grim. "It could be someone else. Seems like someone trips over a hunter's bleached bones every couple of years on this island. I had a lady call on a deer

233

skeleton she saw underwater last week. So listen, Lola said you're a diver?"

Cutter glanced at Fontaine. She must have made some calls on him to find that out. "I am," he said.

"Still current?"

Cutter nodded. It was an understandable question. A lot of people took a diving course on vacation, then didn't put on a tank for decades— but still identified themselves as scuba divers. It looked cool on a Facebook bio. "I did quite a bit of diving with the Florida Department of Law Enforcement team. My last dive was a couple of months ago, as a matter of fact, just before I moved to Alaska."

"Outstanding," Benjamin said. "I hate to ask, but I might need some help with an underwater search of the bay. It'd keep me from having to drag the bay with hooks."

January scooped up her dog and scratched him behind the ears. "Do you think it's Carmen?"

The trooper shook his head. "I just don't know, Jan. The boys seem to think the body is a female, but Greg Conner had long dreadlocks, so who knows."

The pink left January's cheeks. "This is horrible. I have some tanks and a couple of dry suits onboard if you need them. I need to get the zipper fixed on mine, but there's one that should fit the marshal."

Fontaine all but growled. "That won't be necessary. The trooper has a dry suit we can use."

January winced as if she'd been slapped. "Okay then. Just thought I'd offer."

"And I do appreciate it," the trooper said. "Weren't you just down near Soda Bay?"

"I was," January said. "Following the whales wherever they take me."

"Going back?"

"Other direction," January said. "That low is sending big winds and rain our way. The orca are out with the herring and I hear there's a pretty good run up near Kaguk Cove. I'd like to get up there before this storm hits—if I'm allowed to leave."

"You're fine," Benjamin said. "Get on with your life. We know where to find you." He looked up at the mountain above the harbor, nodding in thought, then turned to Cutter. "I'll call you on your partner's phone if we need to dive. I still have a lot of interviews but I've got to go see what these boys found. Officer Simeon's chief has cut him loose to help out. My partner's back from Port Protection and they're interviewing some more of the *FISHWIVES!* crew as we speak. We've had a couple of Hayden Starnes sightings that could be checked out. He's a prime suspect, so you'd be doing double duty if you were able to find him."

"Of course," Cutter said. "Just point us in the right direction."

Benjamin tore a page out of his notepad and handed it to Fontaine. "You should talk to Blind Bob first. He's got a camp with four or five other vagrants out on the point past the Craig cemetery. It's about a mile or so in through the timber. This map should get you there."

It was Fontaine's turn to look suspicious. "How good a witness could a guy named Blind Bob be?"

The trooper laughed. "I'm not sure why people call him that. To tell you the truth I don't know much about him. I understand he disappears during the winter but shows up every spring like clockwork and throws up his camp out there on the point. Strange dude though, I'll tell you that."

"Strange dudes are my specialty," Fontaine said. "Isn't that right, boss?"

CHAPTER 26

It took longer to walk up the dock to the borrowed trooper pickup than it did for Cutter and Fontaine to drive down Hamilton Street, past the docks again, and across the breakwater of granite riprap to Cemetery Island.

Old-growth forest enveloped them quickly. Clouds ahead of the approaching storm obscured the spring sun, and towering stands of spruce and cedar defused the remaining light, giving the place an otherworldly feel. The baseball diamond was surrounded on three sides by thick undergrowth and tucked in behind an acre of white crosses and gray headstones. It felt like they'd stumbled onto some ancient Mayan ruins instead of a sports venue on the edge of town.

Lola broke off a cedar frond as they walked past, crushing the aromatic needles absentmindedly and holding them to her nose for a sniff. "You seemed to be pretty cozy with that chick on the boat," she said.

Cutter turned to look at her as they walked. The trail was wide and fairly level at this point. "Cozy?"

"You know what I mean," she said. "A little informal for a simple interview."

Cutter nodded. "It's good to listen to people

once in a while when we're not booting doors—and she had some interesting things to say. Anyway, you and Trooper Benjamin look to be getting along well enough. So you gave him your phone number already?"

"He has interesting things to say." Fontaine smiled.

Following the trooper's instructions, they took a fork to the right. The gravel trail rose steeply, moving away from the ocean and up over the backbone of the small island. The sound of breaking surf gave way to the hiss of wind through the trees and the intermittent chirp of birds. The island was less than a mile across and the trail soon began to slope down again toward the windward side.

Cutter smelled the camp before he saw it.

Armies, Boy Scout troops, mountaineering camps—any group of people who stayed in a place for more than a few hours had to deal with the disposal of their own human waste. To Cutter, the odor of Afghanistan would always be one of wood smoke, rotting garbage, and an overabundance of uncontained crap. It was a smell pervasive in every Third World country he'd ever visited, clinging to his clothes and hair so strongly that the odor was the first thing anyone mentioned when he got off the plane in Miami. The closest thing he'd experienced back in the States was the smell of a homeless camp on the edge of the Everglades—and now the windward side of Cemetery Island.

It was a small place, as homeless camps go. Cutter counted five shacks of varying size and design nestled back in trees, all easily spotted because of their bright blue tarp roofs and walls. Some were nothing more than simple lean-tos, but a couple were the Taj Mahal of blue tarp construction with anterooms and awnings strung out with guy lines made from scavenged net and fishing line. Driftwood and deadfall poles made up the bulk of the construction as the camp occupants apparently didn't want to run afoul of the Craig city fathers by cutting live timber in their protected park.

A woman of indeterminate age sat in a folding camp chair under the nearest awning. She was at least forty, perhaps much older . . . or younger; Cutter couldn't be sure. Her face shone with the shellac of someone who spent a life exposed to the weather and rarely bathed in anything but the wind, giving her an ageless, almost mummified appearance. Her faded jeans consisted of more patch than original garment. A few strands of silver hair slipped out of a loose top bun that had run amuck.

The woman took a swig of something from a metal coffee thermos with a bent top. "The ocean's that way, if you're lost." She had a few more teeth on the bottom than she did on top—which wasn't saying much—making her lower jaw appear to jut in a sort of gummy under bite.

"We're looking for Blind Bob," Fontaine said.

"You guys cops?"

"We are," Cutter said, figuring there was nowhere to run anyway. "US Marshals."

The woman chuckled, her round belly bouncing in time with her laugh. She took another swig from her mug. "So Blind Bob's went and got hisself in trouble with the *federales*, huh?"

"Not at all," Fontaine said. "We just need to ask him some questions."

There was a rustling inside the tarp house and a bony man wearing nothing but a pair of briefs emerged from the blue shadows. Thinning gray hair stuck out in all directions as if he'd just crawled out of bed. His skin was startlingly pale, especially when contrasted to the dingy briefs, which were no longer whitie or tighty. The underwear sagged so badly he might as well have worn nothing at all but, thankfully, he stepped into a pair of blue running shorts that he snatched from one of the guy lines. Shirtless, he flopped down in the camp chair next to the woman, apparently unfazed by the chilly wind that blew off the ocean.

"Blind Bob at your service," he said. "Step into my castle."

Cutter tipped his head toward the tarp-and-driftwood structure. "I thought this was her castle."

"Who, Meg?" Blind Bob shook his head, then turned to the woman. "She's just visiting. As a matter of fact, why don't you give us some space, my dear. In case the marshals have something sensitive to discuss."

"It's okay with me if she stays," Cutter said.

"That's all right," Meg said, wallowing to her feet with a grunt, careful not to spill whatever she was drinking. "I need to visit the little Meg's room anyhow." She raised the bent thermos as if to toast, and then threw Blind Bob a conspiratorial wink before she waddled off into the forest, vanishing quickly among the ferns and shadows.

"Come on in and sit," Blind Bob said, motioning to Meg's chair and a seat someone had carved out of a cedar stump. Cutter let Fontaine choose, and to his relief she let him have the stump, taking Meg's seat for herself.

Blind Bob grinned, showing a near perfect set of teeth. Upon closer inspection, Cutter saw that he was relatively clean, and his body absent the unwashed gloss and the odor that went along with it. A pyramid of toilet paper rolls was visible just inside the flap of the tarp house, as was a washbasin and a neatly made cot.

"Let me guess," Blind Bob said, patting his bare thighs with both hands as if singing a camp song. "You thought I'd at least be wearing Mr. Magoo glasses."

"Well," Cutter said, "they do call you Blind Bob."

"They do," Bob said, nodding as if contemplating the answer to a great mystery. "So, you met Meg."

Cutter and Fontaine nodded in unison.

"The other guys here, they call her Megladon on account of her caboose being so large . . . and whatnot."

"Kinda mean hearted," Fontaine said.

"That's what I thought," Bob said, slapping his legs harder. "Anyhow, let's be honest. Meg doesn't have much in the way of classic beauty, but she's a hell of a gentle soul."

Cutter was beginning to see where this was going.

"You should have seen my first wife." Bob spoke quickly, as if afraid his guests might leave if he stopped talking. "Or maybe not, I suppose. Next to her, Meg looks like Miss America. My friends all tell me I must have been blind to have married that woman, but I told them I saw beauty there—at least I did until she tried to drown me for the insurance money. I didn't see that coming. Everyone at the university started calling me Blind Bob."

Fontaine shot a sideways look at Cutter. "University?"

"I know, right. Guess it's surprising to find a professor of psychology turned hobo on an island in Southeast Alaska . . . or anywhere, for that matter." Bob gave a sheepish shrug. "Everyone processes their wife trying to murder them in different ways, I suppose. A man sails off to a desert island and lives in a grass hut and people call him adventurous. I come out to an island in Alaska to live in a hut and folks think I'm the third M."

"What's that?" Fontaine asked.

"They say people come to rural Alaska for good paying jobs, because they want to save the downtrodden Natives, or because they just aren't cut out for normal society—money, missionaries, and misfits."

Cutter gave a solemn nod. It was impossible not to like Blind Bob; he was so forthright. Out of habit, Cutter searched the ground for a likely piece of wood, and when he found a chunk of cedar that would suit his purposes, picked it up and took out his pocketknife. He held up the wood and a Barlow pocketknife. "Do you mind?" he asked.

"Be my guest," Bob said. "My dad always said you could trust a man who whittled."

Cutter eyed the length of cedar, then went to work as he spoke. "We wanted to ask you about a man named Hayden Starnes. You might know him as Travis Todd."

"Sure, I'm familiar with Travis." Bob smoothed the wayward hairs back over his head with the palm of his hand, getting down to business. "He came here a couple of days ago, looking to hide out. An odd duck, if you want my professional opinion."

"You have good instincts," Cutter said. "He was working on a television show in town—"

"*FISHWIVES!*?" Bob said, leaning forward and eyes sparkling with animation. "I love *FISHWIVES!* You know, there's a never-ending litany of reality shows about Alaska every year, but every last one of them is as fake as a glass engagement ring—except for that one. It's the best show on TV by a mile."

"I'm with you there, Bob," Fontaine said. "My husb—" She caught herself, shot a glance at Cutter, then continued. "I watch it all the time."

Cutter looked up from his carving. "How do you watch television clear out here?"

Bob hooked a thumb over his shoulder toward the tarp. "We aren't all savages," he said. "I have a little knockoff generator that I picked up at the Costco in Ketchikan. It's overkill, but I use it to charge my iPad so I can stream *FISHWIVES!* and check in on Facebook every few days."

"Good to keep up with the news, I guess," Cutter said.

"I'll skip the news, thank you very much," Bob said. "It's nothing but a pack of lies now anyway." He craned his head up and looked past Cutter, down the gravel beach and out to sea. "The fleet's going out," he said. "Herring must have arrived."

Fontaine nodded toward the thick bank of black clouds marching in from the Gulf of Alaska. "They'll still take their boats out in that?"

Bob shrugged. "I'm a professor of psychology, not marine biology, but it could well be that the storm is what pushed the fish in," he said. "I don't know. But what I do know is that the herring won't wait on the weather. If the fleet doesn't get them netted and put in the kelp pens, the fish'll find their own beds to spawn in."

"Speaking of the herring fleet," Fontaine said. "Who's your favorite Fishwife?"

"Bright Jonas," Bob said without hesitation. "No question about it. I've not had the pleasure of meeting the buxom lass but, to put it in *FISHWIVES!* terms, I'd say she's quite a catch. That damn fool Fitz doesn't seem to realize what he has."

Blind Bob indeed, Cutter thought, still whittling.

Bob put his hands together as if in prayer, eyes sparkling. "What about you, miss? Who's your favorite Fishwife?"

"I'm squarely in the Svetlana camp," Fontaine said.

"There's one named Svetlana?" Cutter asked.

"She was the weepy one wearing black leggings at the break-in where we met Trooper Benjamin."

"I see," Cutter said. There'd been a lot of leggings and a lot of tears, but he thought he knew who Fontaine meant.

245

"Wait a minute," Bob said. "There was a break-in? Bright wasn't harmed, was she?"

"No, sir." Cutter shook his head. "She's fine. But the show's producer and one of the camera operators are missing. As is a Tlingit girl named Millie Burkett."

"Millie's gone missing?" Bob's mouth hung open, genuinely surprised. "When?"

"For a couple of days," Cutter said, staying vague on purpose. "You know Millie?"

"Good kid. Real inquisitive. She started coming out to the camp a couple of weeks ago, right after I got here this year," Bob said. "At first she wanted to make a documentary about everyone in the camp, but you can imagine how that went over with a bunch of wrecks just trying to be lost to the rest of the world."

Cutter lowered the knife and looked up.

"Did her project make anyone upset enough to hurt her?"

Blind Bob shook his head. "Nah," he said. "Poor kid felt so bad about her misguided attempt she brought us a couple boxes of donuts to apologize. . . ." He looked at Cutter with sad eyes, thinking. "A couple of days would put her disappearance about the same time that Travis Todd pervert was here."

"Why would you say he's a pervert?" Fontaine asked.

"You don't spend a lifetime with your head

246

buried in the *Diagnostic and Statistical Manual of Mental Disorders* without learning to spot a psychopath." Blind Bob gave a sheepish grin. "Though the females of that ilk are a little harder to identify."

Cutter chuckled, still carving. "On that we can agree," he said. "Did Todd say where he was going?"

"Afraid not," Bob said. "He did seem like he was in sort of a hurry though, now that you mention it." The homeless man brightened. "I don't have a phone, but if you're on Facebook I can send you a message if he comes back."

"That would be grand, Bob," Fontaine said. "I'm under Lola Teariki."

Fontaine's cell began to chirp. "Sorry," she said, standing to excuse herself. She walked toward the beach to get a better signal.

"You're a lucky man," Bob said to Cutter after she'd gone.

"She and I aren't an item," Cutter said. "We just work together."

Bob scoffed. "Don't you be blind. You could be working with the likes of Meg. Count your blessings, man."

Fontaine came back a moment later. "That was Sam," she said.

"Who?" Cutter said.

"Trooper Benjamin," she said. Glaring, knowing that he'd just made her spell it out when he knew exactly who Sam was. "He's going to need you to do that underwater search after all." She gave a sad shake of her head and mouthed the words "Millie Burkett," so Bob couldn't hear.

Cutter stood to leave, returning the Barlow to his pocket and extending his hand. "Thank you for your candor, Bob," he said. "I never did catch your last name."

"Do you really need it?"

"I guess not," Cutter said, shaking Blind Bob's hand and wondering if he'd ever meet another hobo with an iPad and a Facebook account. It suddenly struck him that he was indeed a lucky man. Thankfully, none of his previous wives had tried to kill him for the insurance, at least not so far as he knew.

CHAPTER 27

Cassandra Brown awoke on her belly. she was nestled into a pile of quilts that Miss January stored in the quarter berth, a narrow tube of a bunk down the stairs from the wheelhouse. The rear deck was directly above her. To her right was the fish locker—if Miss January would have ever used the thing. The little compartment was below the waterline, and beads of condensation ran down *Tide Dancer*'s fiberglass hull, dampening the blankets if they brushed the wall to her left.

Cassandra rubbed her eyes, trying to figure out what had roused her. The grinding *whir* of a boat starter. The motor stopped and Miss January filled the silence with her curses. The starter *whirred* again, and the motor chugged to life, urged on, no doubt, by the cursing. Sometimes, when Cassandra wanted something to happen very badly, she thought curse words in her mind—not the really bad ones like Miss Cross used, but bad enough they should have gotten the job done. But they rarely did. Things either happened or they didn't. Thinking curse words in your mind just didn't work as well as saying them. Or maybe grown-up words carried more power than those of a kid like her.

The motor struggled as they chugged out of the harbor and along the breakwater past Cemetery Island. Cassandra couldn't see it, but she could picture in her mind exactly where they were. Two minutes later, Miss January added power, easing the strain and picking up speed. Havoc scampered down the companionway, whining when he saw Cassandra. He licked her face as if to try and tell her something, and then scampered back up the stairs. Miss January said something to the dog, but Cassandra couldn't quite hear it. It didn't matter. Havoc talked no more than she did. There was no way he would tell Miss Cross that she had a stowaway. By the time she found out, they'd be too far out to turn back and everything would be fine.

The boat rocked once, then pitched violently, shoving Cassandra against the clammy hull. They must have been rounding Fish Egg Island, moving into the storm chop of the wide fetch between Fish Egg and San Fernando Island, a mile away.

At the wheel above, Miss January began to curse in earnest now, helping the boat through the storm with her words.

Cassandra snuggled down in the quilts and closed her eyes. This was going to be a bad one. But Cassandra's uncle was home—and no matter the storm, and no matter how much Miss January cursed, nothing could possibly be as bad as that.

January Cross reached above the wheel and touched the varnished teak plaque her father had made for her when she was fifteen. It was a quote by Isak Dinesen.

"The cure for anything is salt water—sweat, tears, or the sea."

Boats were sparse in both the North and South Harbors by the time she motored out past Fish Egg Island and turned back to the northwest toward San Christoval Channel. Many of the inlets, islands, and passages around Prince of Wales had been named by two Spanish explorers, both named Francisco, who arrived a few years before Captain George Vancouver and his ship HMS *Discovery*. Prince of Wales was so large, the Spaniards hadn't realized they were looking at an island, so left that to the British explorer.

The herring fleet was up ahead, beyond Christoval. They'd yet to come into sight, but January heard their excited chatter on the marine radio. It was a party out there, and though she'd been invited, she'd decided not to attend. The *FISHWIVES!* cameras would be there, and her presence would just give them fodder for their sick conspiracy theory. She'd let the guys have their fun.

In some areas of Southeast Alaska, the spawn-on-kelp herring roe harvest was a winner-take-all fishery. But crews here on POW worked together toward a common goal. The chatter on the radio was convivial and far from the cutthroat attitudes portrayed on *FISHWIVES!*—no matter how Carmen Delgado tried to spin it.

Even so, Cross felt more pity for the woman than any kind of animosity—and not just because she'd gone missing. Carmen Delgado was a smart, if morally corrupt woman. January was pretty sure Delgado had enough of a conscience to get a little nauseated when she looked in the mirror every morning. It was sad really. And anyway, she would probably stagger into town any minute with a good story to tell about how their car ran off the road. She was probably already there. That thought made January happy she'd already taken *Tide Dancer* out.

She took a wave on the beam, cursed, and adjusted course to make the ride a little less like a rodeo. There were a hell of a lot of reasons to be gone from town, even in the storm.

It sounded like the troopers had found Millie Burkett's body near Soda Bay. Poor kid. That was a tragic deal. But everyone, including Cross, had warned the girl not to go turning over stones and filming what was underneath. The darkest secrets on this island were buried for a reason.

January had chased her pod of orca around the south end of the island for the past week. This Marshal Cutter was a smart dude. He was sure to suspect her, at least a little.

It did no good to worry. She really couldn't help what he thought. She had to admit though, the marshal was worth mulling over. January cursed herself for not being a little more persuasive during their conversation. There was a serenity in the man's face that at once relaxed her and put her on edge. She wondered what kind of sailor he was. Her father always said you could tell a lot about a man by the way he handled a boat.

Anyway, nothing to be done about it now. Nothing to be done about any of it.

A rising wind brought larger waves, shoving the bow around, pushing thoughts of the deputy to the back of her mind. She quartered into the waves as much as possible, maneuvering *Tide Dancer* between the clutter of the tiny Hermanos Islands, and favoring the south side of San Christoval as she headed into the Gulf of Esquibel. She would be relatively protected there, from the infinitely larger Gulf of Alaska. Still, Esquibel was wide enough to turn up some serious chop and she poured on the power, hoping to make a quick run north to the lee of Heceta Island. The teeth of the storm would be on them soon, and she would bite down hard enough to hurt.

January kept her course generally north/ northwest, taking breaking five-foot seas off the bow. The ocean was angry, and the waves would be twice that in an hour—perhaps even bigger. Even fighting the waves, January found it impossible to stop thinking about Cutter. It was stupid to get wrapped around the axle over a man who considered her a kidnapping suspect. For all she knew, he suspected her of murder as well. Even if he did decide to brave the drive over the logging road and come question her some more, he was likely to bring his Polynesian lady partner. He wasn't on this island to play. He had a job to do and it looked like he was good at it.

January couldn't help but wonder how good.

This island had been idyllic when she'd arrived four months before. Isolation and frequent rain seemed to wash away the hang-ups so common in the rest of the modern world. Friendly chats over shopping carts at the AC store were common. Everyone on the island knew if so and so's kid got accepted to the nursing program in Anchorage or joined the army or was down in Seattle working as a barista with a new boyfriend who had ear gauges.

January hadn't known a soul when she'd arrived in midwinter to get the boat ready. It was hard work, and many times she'd found herself unequal to the task. She'd never asked for help, but people from Craig and nearby Klawock had dropped by to help—men, women, and kids alike. That's how she'd met Cassandra. Even Bright Jonas had baked a plate of brownies to celebrate the completion of the work—a "boat-warming" gift. That's just what folks did on an island where family was often thousands of miles away.

And then the *FISHWIVES!* people arrived.

The change had been a slow burn, sneaking up on everyone involved. Carmen Delgado had invited January to lunch early on. She was full of smiles and promises about showcasing Tlingit and Haida culture, even vowing to highlight strong Native women to her television audience as an example to younger indigenous women around the country. She and her production company made a litany of promises and burned up several days of January's time shooting video, camouflaging questions about local "characters" with lengthy discussions of Tlingit values and traditions. They ended up with hours of footage that they could cut and edit into all sorts of slanted crap. Thankfully, January never signed a release.

The eclectic—and just plain weird—film crew flooded onto the island like an irresistible tide. *FISHWIVES!* was as quirky as it was unstoppable. Delgado was swept up in the wave and, embarrassed to meet January's eye, stopped talking to her altogether. January retreated to the safety of the hidden coves around the island during the first two weeks of filming, spending time instead following her pod of killer whales.

When she returned to Craig, she found that Delgado's betrayal was even worse than she'd imagined. Not only had *FISHWIVES!* completely ignored any promised Native connection, they'd written January in as some sort of boat-borne succubus, a lusty siren who skulked around the harbors stealing the hearts of married men.

Even so, it was worrisome that Delgado had disappeared. January wouldn't put it past her to do this as some sort of publicity stunt—but that was probably over the top, even for the producer of such a bizarre television show.

She climbed a face of a wave, then surfed down the other side, taking green water over the bow. It was time to get out of this.

She gave the Yanmar diesel more throttle, feeling the hardy little boat shudder as she passed the Culebras, longish, snakelike islands along the coast. January often wondered about those brave Franciscos—and Vancouver and his crew—who navigated by sextant and took soundings with a lead line to negotiate treacherous shoals. Their ships were larger than *Tide Dancer*, but they were older too, with no engine but wind and sail. A storm like this must have been horrific.

Honest seven-footers began to break over the port rail, throwing spray onto her windshield. She cheated into the wind, attempting to abate the roll, planning to cut back north when she was closer to the protection of Heceta Island. The Lowrance satellite display above her wheel showed her already sailing into the edges of the bright orange blob that was the storm.

A navy father and Tlingit mother had taught her from childhood to look for signs of coming weather. Satellite images and the falling barometers only confirmed the observations she'd already made of the natural world around her.

Just this morning, she'd watched kids fishing from the docks get strike after strike, taking home heavy stringers of fish. The moon had been particularly bright last night, and such a clear and dustless sky, her mother said, was a good forecast of a storm. Even the harbormaster's gray tabby cat felt the storm's approach and spent all morning sitting on the docks, grooming its sensitive ears in advance of the approaching low pressure system.

This was going to be a bad one.

January didn't care. She wasn't about to spend another night near town. Intermittent raindrops spattered against the windshield. Now and then, the bow hit a larger than average swell, plowing in and driving green water up and over the gunnels to splash against the glass and drain out through the scuppers. She slid the side window open enough to let in some of the breeze, licking her lips to taste the air.

Kaguk Cove ran north and south, paralleling the narrows in the lee of not only Heceta Island, but a sizable peninsula of Prince of Wales Island itself. The protected waters offered the perfect anchorage to wait out a storm. She just had to make the sixteen-mile trip before the squall hit. Her little boat chugged along at a hair over nine knots in good weather. She was doing half that now, bashing against the wind and waves.

Three hours in this crap was going to be ugly.

CHAPTER 28

Carmen Delgado found it impossible to control her shaking hands as she took the neatly folded stack of clean clothing. Manuel Alvarez-Garza had seen to everything. Or, at least, his men had. There was clean underwear, socks, a black cashmere sweater, and a pair of linen slacks that were surely more expensive than anything Carmen had ever tried on, even as a lark. An attractive woman wearing an equally expensive pantsuit sat on the white, tufted leather settee at the other end of the boat's spacious salon. She glared as if Carmen had just stolen her boyfriend. Carmen guessed her to be from somewhere in Colombia, judging from her propensity to drop her *S*'s and speak Spanish at a blistering, almost unintelligible pace. Chago and Luis stood well back from their boss as if fearful of being backhanded for just being there. Luis held a moist cloth to the wound on his nose, the hateful fire still burning in his eyes.

"I must apologize for the behavior of my men," Garza said. "Of course, I am well aware that as a prisoner, it is your duty to try and escape. But you must also understand that it is the duty of those I employ to punish you for this attempt."

Garza was what Carmen's mother called a

close-talker. He loomed over her when he spoke, consoling and intimidating at the same time, near enough to smell his cologne—which for a madman, was not overbearing.

"But you are here now," he said, with a smile that was almost genuine. "All having done their respective duty. You must be starving, *pobrecita*." He flicked manicured fingers, gesturing down the passageway. "Please, have a hot shower and get dressed. We will discuss the course that lies before us when you are clean and we are eating a hot meal."

Carmen managed a trembling nod. Garza seemed to accept that in lieu of actual words and nodded toward the cabin door.

"You may lie down and have a rest after your shower if you wish," he said. "Beti will retrieve you when the meal is ready. I think you'll find Luis is quite talented in the galley, despite his poor manners."

Carmen shut the door. She heard the click of a dead bolt sliding home from the outside. Being locked into a room on a boat should have terrified her, but she didn't care. It felt good to have a lock between her and these evil men, even if that lock was on their side.

The cabin was cramped, but luxuriously appointed, with varnished teak lockers and crystal lamps. A small flat-screen television was fixed to the bulkhead at the foot of the queen-size bed. Two long portholes allowed in plenty of natural light. A padded slide-out bench sat beneath a spotless vanity mirror. There was just enough room to walk up one side of the bed and reach the door to the bathroom.

Astounded to be alive though her nerves were shot, Carmen set the stack of new clothes on the edge of the bed. She stood there for a long moment, eyes fixed on her injured knuckles. Taking off her clothes for a shower was unthinkable, but something in Garza's eyes made her believe his simple requests were far more important to him than the large ones—or at least equally so. She glanced around the room, and seeing no obvious cameras, struggled to unbutton her blouse with wooden fingers. Too filthy to sit on such a nice bed, she stepped out of her flannel pants standing up, and pulled her T-shirt up over her head. Her body seemed much bonier than it had been even a day before, the treatment from Luis reducing it to a mass of black bruises. She put a hand to her swollen breast and, overwhelmed with pain and fear, collapsed naked onto the bed. A bloody scrape on her hip blotted the crisp cotton of the duvet. These were the sort of people who might murder her for soiling their boat with her blood—though they had been the ones to give her the wounds.

She sighed, trying in vain to pull herself together. It couldn't be helped now.

The small shower compartment was even more cramped than the cabin, but Carmen found herself grateful for the hot water. She stood under the spigot for as long as she dared. Blood and filth ran down her skin and swirled in the drain at her feet—but there was plenty more blood to be shed.

Beti stood on the back deck of the boat, her hip cocked to one side, her bottom lip sticking out. Her blond hair was pulled back in a thick ponytail, her arms folded across her ample chest in a heaving sulk. "You gave her my finest blouse, *mi amor*," she said. Her eyes shone with the rage of a spoiled child who'd been made to share her favorite toy.

"I let her borrow *a* blouse," Garza said, sounding and feeling fatigued. "I am sure it was not your finest."

"Well, I am certain it was," Beti said in rapid-fire Spanish. "It was my favorite as well."

Fausto was at the helm, working to keep the bow pointed toward their destination, a bay located on the northwest side of the island where Luis and Chago had sunk the dead cameraman. It was a wonder that the girl hadn't escaped completely. These two imbeciles had taken the time to sink a man on an island with a forest that was so thick a person might wander ten meters off the roadway and never be heard from again.

They were heading west for the moment, along the southern end of the island, near the little cabin where this mess had all begun. The boat porpoised up and down in the rolling waves, fighting the wind and bashing against the approaching storm. Soon they would cut back to the north. Chago stood by, opposite Beti, waiting for orders. Luis was busy in the galley.

Garza took a long breath through his nose, considering how best to proceed. He nodded at Beti.

"Your favorite blouse?"

"It was," she spat. "And I do not know what you mean when you say you let that woman borrow it. I will not be able to wear it again after you kill her in it."

Garza shot a look toward the door, then put a finger to his lips. "Shhh," he said. "We will discuss this later."

"But, Manolo, I—"

Garza took two steps across the pitching deck and slapped her across the face. She staggered backward, but he caught her by the tiny throat, fighting the urge to crush it in his hand.

"I . . . said . . . later!"

Beti attempted to nod, but his hand kept her chin from moving. Her lips parted, allowing a pitiful gurgle to escape. She began to shake all over, like a little dog. Garza found himself wondering if this sort of reaction had worked on

Camacho. He shoved her away and she caught herself on the rail of the boat. Her ponytail had come loose and the wind whipped her hair across her face. She put a hand to her neck, but said nothing.

Stepping back, he tugged at the cuffs of his fleece jacket. Then he smiled and helped Beti back to her feet, swatting her on the buttock, more for her benefit than his. It was the behavior she was accustomed to, and he needed her to remain calm, for the moment at least.

Carmen sat on the bed, damp hair mopping her shoulders, and thought how foolish her swollen feet looked poking out the end of the expensive slacks. She almost laughed. It was idiotic to worry about her feet when her chances of survival were close to nil.

She nearly fainted when someone pounded on the door. Whoever it was, they didn't speak, but left no doubt that the knock was a summons to come topside.

Garza was sitting at the dining table when Carmen stepped up from the lower level into the main salon. He pushed himself to his feet at her approach. Had she not known him for what he was, she would have thought him a gentleman. Chago stood by the door that led out to the deck. Beti lay back on the settee across from the dining table. Knees up, she glared over the top of a German fashion magazine called *TUSH*. The smell of garlic and onions hung heavy in the close confines of the boat, but it only made Carmen's stomach slither deeper into her gut. Thankfully, instead of food, a nautical chart was spread out on the dining table. Garza tapped it with his index finger.

"Chago tells me the bay where your friend was sunk is here," he said, tapping again on a spot on the northwest side of the island. He spoke as if he were talking about a favorite camping spot, rather than Greg's mutilated body. "We are going there now."

Carmen nodded. "Okay."

"I want to be certain I understand," Garza continued. "There were only two copies made of the footage?"

Carmen gulped back her fear, trying to be brave—and more than that, smart. Bravery alone wouldn't keep her alive. "Other than what you have now, that is correct."

"And one of the remaining two is in a plastic bag in the pocket of your friend," he said.

She nodded again, afraid her voice would shatter if she spoke.

Garza took a long breath through his nose, looking down at the chart. "I thought I might simply forget about that one," he said. "Unfortunately, the bay where my witless men left your friend's body is less than fifteen meters deep.

The combination of a low tide and this storm could possibly drive the body onto the shore—and lead to the discovery of the media card." He looked at her, narrowing his eyes. "And so I find myself with an immediate problem. We have two sets of dive gear aboard this vessel, for examining the propeller and through-hulls, but only one of my men knows how to dive. I do not suppose—"

Carmen shook her head. "I can barely even swim."

She felt stupid the moment the words left her lips.

"I see," Garza said. He drummed his fingers on the table, glancing at Chago. "It looks as though one of you will have to learn."

"Of course, Patrón," the larger man said.

Carmen looked at the chart, racking her exhausted brain for some kind of plan. In order to reach Kaguk Cove they would motor past Craig and Klawock—the most populous areas of the island. If she could get outside, there was a chance she could get attention. She could jump in, but the odds against her drowning or dying of hypothermia were only slightly better than being murdered on the boat.

Garza put a hand on her shoulder, sending her recoiling as if she'd been shocked. He smiled widely, relishing the power he had over her.

"Come," he said. "Luis is almost finished

preparing our pasta. Let us all go out for some fresh air while we wait."

Chago opened the door and stepped to one side, allowing his boss to exit first. Stopping just outside, Garza turned to flick his fingers at Beti, who was still on the couch. "Come with us, my dear," he said. "The air is incredibly fresh."

Beti let her magazine fall to the floor and gave Carmen another hateful glare. She slipped on a pair of low rubber deck shoes and trudged toward the door like a child on her way to do a chore. She took up a spot beside the stern rail at the far aft of the boat, out of the wind, putting distance between herself and Carmen—as if she knew what was coming.

Garza put his hands together and brought them up to his mouth, toying with his top teeth with the tip of his index fingers. At length, he let his hands fall, clapping them together in a loud pop.

"Miss Delgado," he said. "It is very important that you tell me the location of the second media card."

Carmen gasped. "I want to," she said, her gut churning. "I really do. But please understand—"

Garza raised his hand. "I do," he said. The wind blew a strand of black hair across his eyes. He pushed it back into place. "You sincerely believe that by withholding this information, your life will be prolonged." He shrugged. "And while in theory, this will obviously be the case, those remaining hours of your life will be more unpleasant than anything you could possible imagine."

"I don't have to imagine," Carmen said, hit by a sudden flash of anger. "I watched the way your men treated my friend when he was trying to tell them he had one of the cards. I saw—"

Garza drew a black pistol from under his jacket. Chago stood by passively. A wide smile spread across Beti's face.

"So," he said. "You judge me a man with whom you might bargain?"

Carmen stood still, her mouth open.

"I assure you," he said, pointing the gun at Beti. "I am not such a man."

He shot the Colombian woman in the belly.

Beti dropped one hand to the wound. The other clutched at the rail as she struggled to keep her feet. A tremulous pink tongue touched her upper lip as she slid to the deck.

"*Mi amor . . .*" she whispered. Her words were torn away by the wind.

Garza shook his head. "Oh, my dear," he said. "Just because you were Camacho's whore does not mean that you are mine."

Carmen sank to her knees and began to vomit on the deck.

Garza stood in the wind for some time, studying her. At length he looked up at Chago and flicked his hand at Beti.

"Tie her to one of the spare anchors and sink her so we can be on our way." He turned to walk inside, then wheeled back after one step, holding up a hand. "But please, Chago, be certain we are over deep water."

Beti cowered at the stern rail, blinking, trying to swallow. Black blood pressed between tiny fingers at her trembling belly.

"Of course, Patrón," Chago said. The big man raised a thick brow. "She has not yet expired. Shall I finish—"

"Do not bother," Garza sighed. "The sea will take care of what the Beretta did not." He returned the gun to his belt and ducked inside without another word.

Carmen wiped her mouth and locked eyes with Chago. She shook her head in disgust, in spite of the danger. Spray from the breaking waves washed across the deck and she sat in the wet with her arms wrapped around her knees. Survival was impossible among these people. Life was not merely cheap with them; it was worthless.

Chago walked by, muttering to himself.

"Very soon," he said, "we are going to run out of spare anchors."

CHAPTER 29

Wailing Rock Cove had taken on a macabre, carnival-like atmosphere with the discovery of Millie Burkett's body. The line of cars and trucks wedged into the alders on either side of the gravel logging road stretched inland a quarter mile from the beach. Children, unaware of the terrible circumstances that caused the party, ran and played in the dark woods that surrounded the bay. Cloud bunches rolled overhead. Virtually everyone on the island had heard about the Burkett girl's disappearance—and those who could spare the time made the drive south to see what they could see.

Trooper Sam Benjamin stood at the tailgate of his Tahoe. A black DUI dry suit and the corresponding quilted undergarment were folded down around his waist so he didn't overheat. He fiddled with the regulator on his scuba tank while he talked with Officer Simeon and a second trooper, who'd just returned from the investigation in Port Protection. This one was a decade older and carried a little paunch to go with his experience. Benjamin introduced him as Trooper Allen, a recent lateral transfer from a police department in Idaho. Burkett's body was already bagged and loaded in the back of a trooper pickup parked inside a ring they'd cordoned off with yellow crime-scene tape.

A handful of reporters had gotten wind of the body recovery, one from the public radio station having already flown in from Ketchikan, even with the approaching storm. All but one of the reporters respected the barrier tape—not to mention the fact that there was the body of a dead teenager in the truck just a few feet from where they stood. The lone idiot of the bunch was a twenty-something kid with a Jedi braid festooned with beads. He strained against the tape, leaning in with his camera to try and get footage of the body bag.

Simeon looked up from where he was attaching the regulator to a second steel tank identical to Benjamin's. "That *FISHWIVES!* asshole is getting on my last nerve," he said.

"I thought I recognized him," Fontaine said.

"He was at the house when we went by," Simeon said. "One of the camera operators. But he makes a little side money working for some online feed, regurgitating news. You know, the kind that puts up a Tweet, then repeats exactly what the Tweet above already said to fill up space, and then calls it news. He thinks he can break in to the big leagues if he elbows enough people out of the way."

Cutter shook his head. He'd met plenty of good reporters over the course of his career, but

271

asshats like Jedi-braid made him suspicious of all of them. He watched as a young woman holding a toddler walked up to the tape and waved.

"Excuse me, Trooper," she said. "We found the remains of a campfire over here. Just wanted to let you kno—"

Jedi-braid had the camera pointed at himself. Angered that the woman had interrupted what he surely considered an eloquent line of reporting, he shrugged violently, as if to rid himself of someone on his back. The motion struck the woman with his shoulder and then his elbow. She tried to sidestep, but holding the toddler, lost her balance and fell, knees first into the gravel.

"I was here first," Jedi-braid growled.

Cutter looked at Officer Simeon and the troopers and took a long breath.

"Excuse me a second," he said, striding toward the crime-scene tape.

Behind him, he heard Simeon say, "You guys watch. This should be good."

Cutter flashed his badge. "You okay, miss?"

She nodded, still on her knees, clutching the child to her chest.

Cutter glared at Jedi-braid. "Are you filming?"

"I sure am," the kid said, hiding behind the camera. "I have the right as a journalist!"

"First Amendment all the way," Cutter said. "But be sure and get it all. You won't want to miss this." He leaned down to help the lady up.

"US Marshals, ma'am. I saw what happened. Would you like to press charges?"

Jedi-braid peeked from behind the camera. "Press charges for what?"

"How about you do a little pan down here," Cutter said. "Let's get a record of the damage you did to this poor woman's knees." He scoffed. "You should be ashamed of yourself. Every other journalist here is getting the footage they need without shoving innocent civilians to the ground."

The reporter from public radio and the guy from the local newspaper shook their heads in disgust, distancing themselves.

"She snuck up behind me," the kid said. "I just—"

Cutter leaned in, looking directly at the camera. "I told you I saw what happened—as did a dozen other honest people."

Jedi-braid kept filming, then without warning, kicked a bunch of gravel at Cutter. The action was off camera. He surely hoped it would incite some kind of fight that he could catch on video, even if it cost him a bloody nose.

Cutter would have let even that pass, but for the wind that blew a cloud of dust and grit from the gravel into the toddler's eyes.

"Tell you what," Cutter said.

He swatted the camera out of the way, then pulled the handcuffs from his belt, spinning Jedi-braid by pushing on one shoulder while he gave the other a quick yank.

Thankfully, the kid had a temper and decided to fight back. Jerking free of Cutter's grasp, he turned to square off. One hand held the camera, the other doubled into a fist. Cutter advanced quickly, stomping on the kid's lead foot. Cutter had him by six inches and at least fifty pounds. Unable to retreat because of the weight of Cutter's boot, the kid fell backward after a single open-handed slap to the side of his head. The camera landed in the gravel beside him.

"You bastard!" the kid screamed, voice quavering like he might break in to tears. "This is police brutality!"

Cutter reached down and grabbed Jedi-braid by his elbow. "Stand up, kid," he said. "You're embarrassing yourself."

Officer Simeon skidded to a stop in the gravel, eager to grab the other elbow.

"I don't have to stand for this!" the kid screamed. A crowd of onlookers pressed closer. He looked to the other reporters for help. "Call the attorney for *FISHWIVES!* Call the ACLU!"

The other journalists turned away.

"I don't think they want to be associated with you," Cutter said, ratcheting on the handcuffs. He leaned close, next to Jedi-braid's ear. "You should be glad they're here though, because if they weren't, I'd rip off your arms and beat you to death with them for that kind of behavior."

The kid glared at Simeon. "Hey, you heard that!"

The officer ignored him.

"I said hey, Indian Joe," the kid said. "You heard exactly what he said."

"I heard the wind," Officer Simeon said, and he frog-marched Jedi-braid to his patrol car.

Cutter ducked in behind Sam Benjamin's Tahoe and stepped into the quilted nylon undergarment before pulling on the black DUI dry suit, identical to the one worn by the trooper. Unlike neoprene wet suits, which warmed a thin layer of water next to the diver's body, dry suits kept out all the water, relying on a layer of air and an insulating undergarment.

His feet were enclosed in the waterproof material and would eventually go into a pair of rock boots, essentially black high-top sneakers. He stretched the silicon rubber seals over his head and wrists, but left the neoprene hood off until just before he actually got into the water.

Benjamin stuck his head around the corner of the Tahoe. "I forgot to tell you. I have an external catheter for you here if you want it."

Cutter pulled the zipper up across his chest. "Not sure I like the sound of that."

The trooper laughed. "It's like an extra strong condom that connects to the P-valve inside your thigh. "You can't piss in a dry suit like you can in a neoprene." He gave a conspiratorial nod. "Not that you would ever pee in your wet suit . . . Believe me, it's worth rolling the suit back down to put this thing on so you can just let it flow when we're at depth." He handed Cutter a piece of tan rubber that looked like one of the thumb covers accountants wore when they worked with reams of paper.

"How does it stay on?"

"Glue," the trooper said.

Cutter grimaced. "Adventures in diving," he said, but rolled down the suit anyway.

Cutter's first experience scuba diving was when he was thirteen years old. He'd logged hundreds of dives since in Florida, but his only dry suit time had been with his second wife, diving for abalone in California. His wife at the time had absolutely hated it, and he'd spent most of the afternoon swimming through the kelp forests, praying a shark would eat him so he wouldn't have to surface and deal with the fuming woman.

Sam Benjamin looked to be a more than capable diver. The gear was neat and well-kept, allowing Cutter to feel streamlined. Grumpy had many rules for general character and behavior, but he piled on to the Do It Right cave diver's mantra of never diving with a "stroke"—basically anyone who looked like they didn't know what they were doing. It sounded glib, but there was something to be said about a diver who dove with gear that was in place and squared away. A lot could go wrong sixty feet down, and you couldn't just pop back to the surface if it did.

Trooper Benjamin had quizzed the addled boys who'd discovered the body, and then studied tides and nautical charts to make an educated guess of where to begin the search. If they were dealing with a serial killer, the bay might very well be a graveyard of discarded bodies, but that only made a systematic search all the more important.

Cutter checked the pressure in his tank and shrugged on the buoyancy control vest. He walked to the water's edge where he donned black jet fins over the rock boots.

The divers held on to the sides of an aluminum skiff while Officer Simeon towed them out to the dive site. He dropped a five-gallon plastic bucket filled with concrete over the side, playing out a length of heavy line, and clipping the surface end to a bright orange buoy when the bucket hit bottom. Fontaine waited on the bank, looking envious. Cutter was sure he'd have a request for dive school on his desk the moment she got back into the office. He gave her an okay sign, making an O with his thumb and forefinger, and then turned to give the trooper a nod. The waves had a little chop, but the cove was protected and it was nothing the boat couldn't handle. The divers oriented themselves with the bank and the orange buoy, checked their watches, and took one last look at their air pressure before pressing the valve on their BCs to descend into the darkness.

The two men kicked downward, trailing strings of silver bubbles through shafts of muted green light. Cutter listened to the on and off click of his regulator as he took slow, even breaths. He pinched his nose every few feet, feeling his ears clear with a telltale squeal as the pressure built at depth. He followed Benjamin down to the submerged five-gallon bucket that lay at sixty feet. Broad blades of kelp rose up here and there, waving in the tidal current—but the bottom was otherwise barren of plant life. The beam of Cutter's dive light passed over a halibut the size and thickness of a trash can lid gliding across the bottom hunting for food. He was accustomed to flounder. Both fish had eyes that migrated around to one side of a flat body, but this halibut looked like a flounder on steroids.

The trooper clipped a yellow line to a ring on the lip of the bucket, then swam away a distance of approximately twenty meters. Taking the line in his left hand, he played the wrist-mounted light back and forth with his right. Cutter held the trooper's tank strap with his left hand and played his own light back and forth with his right. Both accomplished divers, they propelled themselves forward with gentle kicks, a scant three feet off the bottom—searching without stirring up a cloud of sediment.

The attached line wrapped around the bucket as they swam, decreasing the scope of their search by a few feet on each complete revolution. It was slow but efficient and the trooper's light played across a galvanized anchor less than fifteen minutes into the dive. Benjamin filled a cylindrical orange tube with air from his regulator and deployed this surface-marker buoy on a spool of line to mark the spot.

Another twenty minutes yielded nothing else and the trooper called an end to the dive, pointing upward with his thumb. Trooper Benjamin retrieved the anchor and both men kicked to the surface water.

Cutter pushed a button to inflate his buoyancy control vest, and then slipped the mask down so it hung around his neck. A mask on top of the head looked good in the movies, but was a sign of distress that accomplished divers avoided. They'd been at sixty feet long enough to require a rest interval before going down again in order to off-gas the buildup of nitrogen in their blood.

"A short break?" Cutter asked as they worked together to lift the anchor over the side of Officer Simeon's boat.

The trooper wiped a hand across his face. "If there's another body down there," he said, "it's not near this one. I say we focus on Millie and see what we can learn from what we have."

The men opted to swim to shore on the surface rather than try to wallow up the flimsy boarding ladder Simeon hung over the side of the skiff. Cutter removed his black jet fins at the water's edge and carried them up the gravel where Fontaine stood waiting with Trooper Allen.

"This diver thing is a good look on you, boss," Fontaine said, giving him an up and down once-over. "Can you believe my ancestors are from the South Pacific Islands and I don't know how to dive?"

Simeon dragged the skiff up on the beach. Jedibraid saw him and began to beat his head against the side window of the patrol car. Simeon ignored him.

"Hey, Will," the trooper yelled as he sloshed up from the water, fin straps over his forearm.

"Afternoon, Sam." A slender man standing beside the state trooper's pickup gave a little wave, his hand covered in a latex glove. He wore faded jeans and a buffalo plaid shirt with the sleeves rolled up to midforearm. A blue Seattle Seahawks ball cap was pushed back to reveal straw-colored hair. Millie Burkett lay on the tailgate of the pickup in two body bags, one inside the other so that no evidence was lost. The bags were partially unzipped to reveal her head and shoulders.

"The medical examiner already got here from Ketchikan?" Cutter said.

"Don't laugh," Benjamin said. "But that's my dentist."

Cutter looked at him, raising an eyebrow. "Your dentist?"

"Yep." The trooper gave a long sigh. "Don't tell Sergeant Yates. He'd crap angry little bricks if he found out what I do on a daily basis just to get the job done. We do what we have to out here. ABI investigators won't even try to make it out of Ketchikan today with this storm blowing in off the Pacific."

"But journalists did," Fontaine said.

"I know, right?" Trooper Allen said. "News won't keep. Dead bodies will still be dead tomorrow."

"Anyway," Benjamin said. "Doc Gelman's got enough medical training he can take a cursory look. It helps me move forward without screwing anything up. I'll be able to put the body in a silver bullet and send her back to Anchorage for a full autopsy and they'll be none the wiser."

A silver bullet was the aluminum coffin used to transport bodies on aircraft, and a mainstay in rural Alaska. Cutter had seen far too many during his time in Afghanistan.

"Sam," Dr. Gelman said, leaning over Millie Burkett's head to snap close-up photos with his cell phone. "You're going to want to see this."

Trooper Benjamin motioned Cutter and Fontaine to follow, but a commotion behind the

281

crime-scene tape drew their attention away from Gelman's discovery at the body.

The crowd of onlookers parted as someone shoved to the rear of the trooper pickup.

"Is that her? Is that my baby girl?"

"Gerald Burkett," Fontaine said under her breath.

Trooper Benjamin groaned and gave her a sideways glance. "I was hoping we could avoid this."

The trooper stepped forward, meeting Burkett just as he reached the fluttering yellow tape. "I need you to stay back," he said.

Burkett's eyes were bloodshot and swollen. The smell of alcohol and body odor blew in ahead of him on the breeze. "I got the right to see her," he bellowed.

"No, Gerald, you don't," Benjamin said, keeping his voice low and consoling. "Not yet. This is awful. I get that. But you have to stay back there and take care of Lin."

Lin Burkett, tall and slender like her daughter, grabbed her husband by the shoulder. "Let 'em do their job." She teetered on her feet, nearly falling in the process. She'd been drinking as well. But who could blame her?

Gerald Burkett stood at the crime-scene tape and seethed. He leaned against the side of the pickup for support. His wife, in turn, leaned on him, still clutching the sleeve of his oil-stained hoodie. Cutter and Benjamin returned to the body while Fontaine and Simeon waited with the Burketts, attempting the impossible in trying to console the grieving parents.

Still in his dry suit, Cutter opened the zipper across his chest, venting some of the heat that had built up as soon as he'd exited the water. Even in the cool air of an approaching storm he was already sweating heavily inside the airtight suit. He thought about stepping around the Tahoe and changing clothes—even if only to retrieve his pistols—but decided that could wait until he saw what the dentist had found so interesting.

He happened to glance up, past the crowd, to see a lone man standing in the shadows at the edge of the tree line. Concentrating in an effort to keep from staring, Cutter's hand dropped reflexively to his side, searching for the gun that was still in the truck. His cuffs were already in use on the reporter. Watching the man with the corner of his eye, he gave the trooper a tap on the elbow.

"Don't look up," he said, "but I just got an eyeball on Hayden Starnes."

CHAPTER 30

Arliss Cutter had chased enough outlaws over the course of his career to learn that human beings were particularly attuned to the white space around another person's eye. It was the reason lecherous guys wore sunglasses in the gym. Even from hundreds of feet away it was a simple matter to tell if you were the object of another person's focus. If that person happened to be a six-foot-three deputy US marshal, the impulse to flee kicked in pretty quickly.

And flee Hayden Starnes did. With any pretense of surprise blown, Cutter pushed his way through the crowd of onlookers to find his quarry was no longer in sight. He didn't slow down though, yelling as he ran, ordering Starnes to stop. He had no real notion that the tactic would actually stop the fugitive in his tracks. In fact, the contrary was true. Cutter wanted him to speed up, to expend his energy and run without thinking.

Cutter darted left when he reached the trees, following a gouge in the mossy earth where Starnes had turned to get away, scrambling over a decaying log as big around as an oil drum. Cutter vaulted over the log, tearing a gash in the thousand-dollar dry suit, and jumping headlong into the shadowy tangle of roots and shrubs and decay. The lightweight rock shoes offered surprisingly good traction, but the dry suit was suffocating. Cutter could feel his body temperature rising with each bounding step. Thankfully, he had a longer stride than Starnes and, though he didn't have a visual, felt certain he was closing the gap. There was a better than average chance that Starnes had some kind of weapon. Cutter had no idea how far behind him Fontaine and the others were, but heard the crash of brush and the telltale wheeze of other runners, so he was confident they were back there somewhere.

Cutter identified himself as a US marshal again, shouting for Starnes to stop. Grumpy had taught him that most human beings would generally take the same route between two points. "Similar flow" he called it. Some trackers knew it as taking the "natural line of drift." Whatever you called it, the phenomenon became more pronounced when a quarry was given no time to think. Cutter could probably have run through the woods with his eyes shut and ended up within feet of where Hayden Starnes ran out of steam. But that wouldn't keep him from getting shot if Starnes was armed.

Cutter pulled up when he reached a clearing, skidding to a stop on the decaying forest floor. The palpable scent of fear hung heavy in the air. That was good. It meant Starnes wasn't thinking clearly.

Cutter opened the zipper across his chest

another few inches, then reached inside to do the same on the zipper of the quilted undergarment. Still too hot, he tugged at the latex collar that fit tight around his neck, pulling at the seal until it opened like a Ziploc bag, and tore it from the rest of the suit. Moist, superheated air bellowed out through the larger opening.

A branch snapped in the stillness to his left, sending Cutter running again, ducking under and around widow-maker logs that leaned like enormous deadfall traps against living trees. A chunk of moss, kicked loose by a passing foot, caught his attention as he rounded a granite boulder the size of a small car.

A low whooshing sound greeted him the moment he stepped past. He ducked a fraction of a second too late and caught the branch in Hayden Starnes's hands straight across the chest. It had surely been meant for his face, but Starnes was shorter, and was standing in a hollow, making him shorter still and foiling his aim.

Inside the swing now, Cutter pressed forward rather than attempting to block the blow. He drove Starnes back, pushing him against the trunk of a thick Sitka spruce. Cutter shoved the offending club out of the way and followed up with an openhanded slap against the other man's ear. He brought his elbow back across, smashing Starnes in the nose. The outlaw slumped, the back of his jacket snagged on the tree. Cutter rained a flurry of blows to his ribs and face. Starnes threw his arms, screaming, blood pouring from his nose. Nearly blind with rage at the thought of Millie Burkett's lifeless body, Cutter struck the rough bark of the spruce almost as much as he hit Starnes. His knuckles were raw and bloody by the time Fontaine and the trooper ran up and dragged him away.

"Help me!" Starnes screamed. "This crazy son of a bitch is trying to murder me!"

Cutter was gratified to hear the nasal drone from the elbow he'd given the man. He noticed for the first time that Starnes was missing the thumb and forefinger on his right hand. That little bit of information wasn't in the warrant file. The skin was healed but still pink, leading Cutter to believe the wound was relatively new.

Starnes put on his tough-guy face once he was safely handcuffed and there were enough witnesses present to keep Cutter from jumping on him again. "You all saw him," he said. "I want to file charges."

Cutter bent over, wheezing, resting his hands on his knees. He looked up at Starnes. "Come to admire your work?"

"My work?" Starnes said. "I don't even know what that means."

"It means, smartass," Fontaine said, "that murderers often come back to the scene of the crime to gawk at what they did."

"These guys are out of their minds," Starnes said, looking at the trooper. "You know me. I work for *FISHWIVES!*"

"That's right," the trooper said. "You do. When's the last time you saw Carmen and Greg?"

Starnes looked up, sneering. "What the hell are you talking about? And what did he mean by admire my work? I don't even know who it is you pulled out of the water."

"We'll see about that, Hayden," Cutter said.

Starnes deflated at the use of his real name.

A raindrop hit Cutter directly on the top of the head. Another followed, blown through the thick forest canopy on a fierce wind. The storm had finally arrived.

"Come on," Benjamin said, hooking a thumb back toward the road. "We can sort this out back at the trooper post. I want to make sure and keep Millie's body out of this rain."

Starnes's head snapped around at the name. "Millie?" he said. "Millie Burkett's the one who's dead?"

"That's right, Einstein," Fontaine said.

"Shit!" Starnes whined. The rain fell harder now, and water dripped off the end of his nose. "With my background . . . nobody's gonna believe I didn't have something to do with this. . . ."

"You got that right," Cutter said, grabbing him by the arm to lead him back the way they'd come.

Starnes was on the verge of weeping by the

time they'd gone a dozen steps. "Can we take off these cuffs?"

"Nope," Cutter said.

"But I can't hold myself up. I'm liable fall and break something."

"Fancy that," Cutter said.

CHAPTER 31

Incessant rain battered the roof of the Alaska State Troopers post like a kid beating on a metal trash can.

Trooper Allen had gone to check on a three-vehicle accident north of Klawock—everyday law enforcement duties didn't stop because there had been a murder. Lola accompanied Officer Simeon and Doctor Gelman to take Millie Burkett's body to the human-sized cooler in the locked storage room at the back of the trooper post. It would remain there until the weather cleared enough to put the silver bullet on a flight back to Anchorage.

Hayden Starnes had wailed all the way from Wailing Rock Cove, not stopping until Benjamin got him settled in the interview room. Even now, his chest heaved periodically, post tantrum. Trooper Benjamin sat on one side of the metal table with his notebook open. On the other side, Starnes was chained to an eyebolt in the floor and his hands cuffed in front of him. The prisoner slumped in a forlorn posture, wads of TP stuck up both nostrils.

Cutter sat in the corner of the interview room, his chair tipped back against the wall. He appeared disinterested in the conversation going on between the trooper and Starnes, focusing instead on carving the piece of driftwood he'd picked up in Blind Bob's camp. Both the trooper and the deputy had left their sidearms in the lockboxes outside, but if Benjamin had a problem with Cutter bringing a knife into the interview room he didn't mention it.

Starnes beat his forehead slowly against the table in despair. "What was I supposed to do? I know I shoulda never run like that. Now nobody's gonna believe I'm innocent."

"Oh, you're miles away from innocent," Cutter observed, looking up just long enough to see Trooper Benjamin give him a pointed glare.

"So you knew Millie?" the trooper asked.

"Of course I do," Starnes said. "Everybody on the production crew knows . . . knew Millie. She was a good kid."

Sam Benjamin tapped his notebook with a pen. "You have to admit how this looks," he said. "From our point of view, I mean. Millie Burkett disappears a few hours after you do. She's about the same age as the girl you're convicted of kidnapping and sexually assaulting in Oregon—"

Starnes looked up, his chest still flat on the table. "Hey, I did my time for that."

The trooper ignored him. "Maybe Carmen and Greg knew something about it, so you had to take care of them too. You should have stayed hidden, but the body recovery was just too much for you.

291

You just had to come back and take a look. I think *you* would probably arrest you."

"That's not how it is." Starnes sniffed. "I heard Carmen and Greg were missing. But I didn't have anything to do with that either."

"How'd you hurt your hand?" Cutter asked.

"Table saw," Starnes said, his voice quivering. "Look, my probation officer's gonna revoke my supervised release just for coming up to Alaska and trying to get a good job. Do you know how many people will hire a sex offender? What am I supposed to do?"

Cutter wasn't having any of the man's sob story. "My granddad always said Tryactin helped."

The trooper raised an eyebrow.

Starnes sniffed. "What the hell is Tryactin?"

Cutter stood, letting the chair fall forward with a loud bang against the floor. He pointed to the chunk of wood for effect. "You could *try actin'* like a man for once in your miserable life."

CHAPTER 32

Sam Benjamin wheeled on Cutter as soon as they made it out of the interview room. "Are you okay?"

"What?"

The trooper shook his head. "Oh, I don't know. First you about rip that reporter's head off back at the dive site and now I'm thinking you would have used that knife to cut Hayden Starnes's nuts off if I hadn't been in there with you."

Cutter waved him off. "I'm fine," he said. "Just thought I'd play 'bad cop' for a while."

"Well," Benjamin scoffed. "You're pretty damned good at it." He calmed a notch. "Seriously though, I like that *Tryactin* thing."

"So, what do you think?" Officer Simeon asked when they made it back to the office. "Is Starnes good for Millie Burkett's murder?"

Cutter shook his head. "He's a piece of trash, but I'm not sure he's the specific piece of trash you're looking for."

Dr. Gelman was waiting in Benjamin's office poring over a series of eight-by-ten photographs with Fontaine and Officer Simeon. He looked up when he saw the trooper.

"Whatcha got for me, Will?" Benjamin said. He had to raise his voice over the pounding rain on the roof.

"Not a whole lot, I'm afraid," Dr. Gelman said. "But what little I do have is interesting enough. The victim's gut appears to be full of water so I'm guessing the autopsy will reveal the lungs are as well."

"So she drowned," Cutter said.

"I believe so," Gelman said, passing across the photographs. "It's common for a drowning victim to swallow water while fighting the reflexive desire to breathe. But, this young woman was struck on the back of the head before she died. There are deep lacerations on the left side of the back of her head."

Cutter thought about that. "So if she was facing away, the killer likely used his left hand."

"That's my guess," Gelman said. "I didn't want to screw with the wound site, but I'd guess the killer fractured her skull before he tied her to that anchor and dropped her in. The drowning finished the job."

Trooper Benjamin studied the top photograph for a moment, then passed it to Cutter. "Starnes uses his messed-up hand more than his left, so I'd guess him to be a rightie—but that doesn't mean he wouldn't use his left hand to wield a weapon."

"Somebody really went to town on her," Cutter said. "I count six separate wounds."

"I don't think so." Gelman shook his head. "That's what I thought at first. But look here." He held the edge of a piece of paper along the image in the photograph. "I believe she was only struck twice. It's difficult to tell without removing her hair, but see how the wounds line up perfectly in two groups of three? There are three here—a quarter-inch wound, three-quarter-inch gap, one-inch wound, one-inch gap, quarter-inch wound—and another three here with identical spacing."

Cutter and Benjamin both nodded. Fontaine and Simeon stood by, listening. They'd already heard the theory and were obviously onboard.

"The ME might say something different," Gelman continued. "But I'm guessing she was struck two times by a long object that is relatively thin. Something with vacant spaces along its leading edge that would account for the spaces between the wounds."

"Any ideas?" the trooper asked.

"Unfortunately, no," Gelman said. "I was hoping one of you might be able to think of something."

"Maybe we should ask Hayden Starnes," Simeon said.

Fontaine leaned in to study the photos again. "An axe with bits of the blade chipped away?"

"Right idea, wrong tool," Gelman said. "Whatever did this was thin, but not sharp enough to embed itself in the skull like an axe would. I'd say you're looking for something about a quarter inch wide. Judging from the depth of the wounds, it will be relatively flat along the leading edge, and likely made of metal. The wounds damage the skull, but are relatively shallow. I'd guess the weapon was not incredibly heavy—at least not as heavy as an axe or a hammer. Think crescent-wrench—leverage, but not too much."

"That's good work, Will," Benjamin said.

"This pattern looks familiar," Cutter said. "I just can't put my finger on it." He flipped through the rest of the photos, stopping on one that showed the rope wound around Millie Burkett's feet. The coils lay neatly alongside one another, ending with a simple timber hitch. Cutter thumbed through the remaining photographs, then shot a glance at Dr. Gelman. "Did you happen to get a shot of the trailing end of the rope?"

"Where it came loose from the anchor?" The dentist nodded. "I did. I must not have printed it if it's not in the stack there." He scrolled through the album on his phone, then passed it to Cutter, who zoomed in on the photo with his thumb and forefinger.

Officer Simeon crowded closer. "What do you see?"

"Maybe nothing," Cutter said. He passed the phone back to Gelman, then sat down to carve while he thought. Something was beginning to take shape very nicely on the chunk of driftwood, though he couldn't tell what it was. He nodded at Simeon. "Take a look at the photo of the end of the rope and tell me what you see."

"It came untied rather than wearing loose," the officer said. "I'm guessing that's what you white guys call a clue."

Cutter nodded. "Can you tell what kind of knot?"

The trooper held the phone closer, then shook his head. "No idea," he said. "I'm not sure how anyone could tell from this."

Cutter folded his knife and shoved the piece of driftwood in his pocket. "Got a piece of rope?"

Benjamin looked around the office until he found a scrap of parachute cord about four feet long. Cutter threw a quick bowline in the end, and then stood on the loop. When he felt reasonably sure he'd put enough pressure on the knot, he untied it and then compared the crooked end to the photo. The bend patterns matched almost perfectly.

"A bowline then," Dr. Gelman said.

"And a timber hitch around the girl's legs," Cutter added. "I could be mistaken, but Hayden Starnes is missing two digits. Maybe he could have bashed that poor girl's head in with his left hand, but I think he'd be hard-pressed to tie either one of those knots if you held a gun to his head."

"Which you are, no doubt, happy to do," the trooper said.

"Hold a gun to his head?" Cutter said. "I am at that. But I mean it more literally. Given time, he'd be able to use his left hand and tie the knots fine. But you see how he acts under the stress of interrogation. Look how the wraps on this hitch lay perfectly alongside one another."

"Dammit," Benjamin said. "So he didn't do it."

"I didn't say that," Cutter said. "I just said he doesn't seem likely."

The trooper gave the photographs another long look before tossing them on his desk.

Gelman's phone chimed. "Damn," he said. "Looks like one of my paying customers broke a molar."

"Thanks for your help, Will," the trooper said. "We've gone about as far as we can go here." He looked around the office. "Anybody besides Deputy Cutter want to ride with me when I take Starnes to the jail?"

Cutter raised an eyebrow, feigning concern. "What's that supposed to mean? You could hurt a guy's feelings."

He took the driftwood out and started carving again. It helped him think.

"No offense intended," Benjamin said. "I'm just sure the sight of you would make him pee down his leg, and I don't want to stink up my Tahoe."

"Listen," Cutter said, gesturing to the sound of beating rain with his pocketknife. "Starnes is in custody, so our mission here is done, but there's no way we're getting off the island tonight. Is there anything we can do to help you look for the two missing film crew?"

"Good question," Benjamin said. "According to one of the other camera operators, Greg Conner said he was going to the south end of the island to shoot footage of some cabin. Supposedly he and Carmen Delgado made several trips."

"Do you know of any cabins on the south end of the island?"

Simeon shrugged. "Only about a couple of hundred," he said.

Cutter glared up from his carving, pointing at the young officer with his pocketknife. "Giving me lip's not apt to get you hired."

The Craig officer grimaced. "Sorry."

"He's pulling your chain," Fontaine said. "Have you heard me talk? I give him all kinds of lip."

Benjamin rolled his eyes. "I wouldn't worry, Sim," he said. "I think giving people lip is mandatory if you're a deputy marshal."

"Anywayyyy," Cutter coaxed, rolling his knife in get-on-with-it circles. "They were shooting footage at some cabin. . . ."

"Right," the trooper said. "None of the other *FISHWIVES!* crew had any idea where Carmen and Greg were heading, but they should all be interviewed again anyway."

"That's a lot of interviews," Lola said. "We could help out with that."

"We could," Cutter said, tapping his knife against the driftwood.

"We need to talk to Jan Cross again as well,"

Benjamin said. "She spent all last week on the south end following her pod of killer whales. There's a chance she ran across them at some point."

"Can we call and ask her?" Fontaine said.

"Nope." Cutter folded his knife and returned the driftwood to his jacket pocket, trading it for his notebook. "But I know exactly where she's anchored for the evening."

"Kaguk Cove," Benjamin said. He walked to a laminated topographic map fixed to the wall of his office and traced his finger along the route. "It's up north, across the mountains on some logging roads, but not incredibly far. I should have asked her about it before she left, but I got sidetracked with this body recovery. And I have plenty to keep me busy here. That would be great if you guys want to go out and talk to her."

"I can handle a few questions on my own." Cutter glanced at the trooper. "Mind if I borrow your truck?"

"Boss?" Fontaine grinned. "Are you actually showing interest in a woman?"

Cutter let the comment slide. "You stay here and lend these guys a hand."

"My shift is over in an hour," Officer Simeon said, looking at Cutter. "I can tag along and keep you company if you want."

"Now you're just talking crazy," Fontaine said. "He just turned me down. Does he look like a man who wants you for company?"

And Fontaine was exactly right. Cutter wanted to do this alone. Not because he had developed any sudden feelings for January Cross. He did, however, have a hunch. The television crew had spread too many rumors about her already. If he was wrong, he'd leave quietly with no one the wiser. If he was right, he'd arrest her and a few rumors would be the least of her problems.

CHAPTER 33

A tear fell from Gerald Burkett's eye and landed on the dusty glass of his daughter's school picture. He sniffed, shuddering with grief, then set the framed photo back on the kitchen table. He was unworthy to even hold it. There can be little else on earth as soul-crushing as losing a child to violent death, especially when it was so apparent that she had suffered. The Burketts attempted to cope with the loss of their daughter separately and in different ways—Lin through meditation, prayer, and alcohol—Gerald through alcohol alone. He didn't know where the hell his wife was, most likely out in the trees behind their house, bathing in smoke and talking to the same God that let their little girl die. She'd walked off as soon as they'd gotten back home.

Gerald dragged himself past the kitchen and into Millie's room, a new bottle of nine-dollar R & R whiskey in his hand. His eyes were nearly swollen shut from draining the rest of the bottle he'd started the day before, but he was a pro. Another bottle wouldn't be a problem. He stood in the doorway for a long time, using the frame for support. She'd been a real neat freak, his daughter. An "I STAND WITH STANDING ROCK" poster was tacked to the wall above a neatly made bed. Her wafer-wood chest of drawers had fallen apart when the pipes burst last winter, but she kept all her clothes folded in two sets of laundry hampers along the wall by the baseboard heater. Gerald stepped into the room and fell back on the sagging bed, cursing himself for not giving his daughter a better life.

That trooper had seemed surprised that his little girl was so neat. Burkett scoffed thinking about it. Damned cop probably thought that with a father like him she'd be living in squalor. To be fair, this was the cleanest room in the house by a long shot.

Gerald took a long pull of R & R, wiped his lips with the back of his forearm, and straightened the pile of books on the rickety table beside the bed. Groaning, he leaned forward to grab one of his little girl's shirts from the laundry hamper, then pressed it to his nose. It was clean, but it still smelled like her. Shirt in one hand, bottle in the other, he sat and sobbed for the better part of ten minutes.

His head began to hurt from all the tears, and the dull ache of despair grew into a white-hot anger. He wadded the shirt in his fist and flung it against the wall, screaming at nothing until his head hurt even worse. Sadness came back with a vengeance when he was all screamed out, and he reached for another of Millie's shirts to console himself. When he did, he saw the corner of a red notebook in the bottom of the hamper. He quickly figured out it was Millie's diary.

It took him fifteen minutes of staggering around the house and cursing to find his reading glasses. When he finally found them by the toilet, he took the journal and collapsed in his beat-up recliner. His rheumy eyes followed the flow and curve of her pen across the pages, marveling that he could hear his little girl's voice as he read the words.

Customarily quiet in life, Millie turned out to be a prolific writer. She noted her favorite teachers, boys she was sweet on, and her thoughts on the long talks she often had with her mother. She wrote of her first experience with alcohol—which oddly enough, considering who her parents were—hadn't come until she was fifteen years old. She hated the stuff, vowing never to touch anything stronger than a Red Bull. Gerald sniffed back tears and ironically, toasted her decision with another slug of R & R.

He'd drunk past the bottom of the label on his bottle by the time Millie started writing about *FISHWIVES!* The producers had come to her school to talk about careers and had offered some of the kids internships. His little girl must have shown promise because some of the crew had even started to mentor her. He took another drink, and then turned the page.

He read the next part twice, gritting his teeth harder with every word. He forced himself to read it a third time, then slammed the book shut and flung it across the room. Pushing himself to his feet, he staggered down the hall to his bedroom. Still clutching the bottle of R & R, he grabbed his pistol and headed for the truck.

CHAPTER 34

In the relative solitude of the borrowed trooper pickup, Cutter admitted to himself that he would have written up any one of his deputies for doing what he was about to do.

He made the short drive into Craig from the trooper post to check into his room at the Blue Heron Inn, which, interestingly, would have almost overlooked January Cross's boat had it still been moored in the South Harbor. Fontaine had the room above, yielding the larger room with the deck to him. It was a nice place, with a full kitchen and comfortable furniture, the kind of place where he wished he could spend more time. There was even a fireplace for crying out loud. The deck was covered, but with the rain blowing in sideways, that didn't make much of a difference.

Cutter stopped by the AC store for a couple of things on the way out of town, getting drenched even wearing his Helly Hansen raincoat. He found himself glad he'd opted to put on his brother's Xtratufs at the trooper post since the grocery store's uneven parking lot had long since become a lake of uncertain depth.

From the AC store, he followed the directions January had put in his notebook, driving north out of Klawock on Big Salt Lake Road. He'd been warned that one of Prince of Wales Island's abundant blacktail deer might dart across his path, but the driving rain kept them hunkered down in the heavy timber, solving that problem while it created another.

He turned off the pavement to follow a Forest Service logging road to the north for a few miles before cutting back to the west. Rain combined with mud and loose gravel to form a treacherous soup threatening to send Cutter sliding down the mountains into oblivion. It wasn't quite dark, but blue-black clouds were quickly closing in on the last feeble hopes of light. A runaway creek had jumped its banks ahead of him and now rushed across the road in a slurry of white foam and floating debris. He barely had time to bring the truck to a stop and keep from sliding into the swollen mess.

Snugging his rain gear around his neck, he got out of the truck to search for a stick so he could test the depth before he crossed. Wind ripped his hood. He had to lean forward just to walk forward. He found a likely piece of alder and with a few tentative tests, discovered the roadway was still intact for the moment. The water was only halfway up the shaft of his rubber boots but appeared to be rising. Not one to let being stranded in the Alaska wilderness stop him, Cutter threw the stick in the back of the pickup in case he needed it later, then like Caesar crossing the Rubicon, drove slowly into the rising torrent. Gravel crunched beneath his tires. Water shoved the truck sideways, but he made it across. Coming back might be a little trickier, but he'd worry about that when the time came.

The wipers were working overtime by the time he slogged over the top of the last mountain before he reached the ocean. He slowed to a crawl in a modified and not quite controlled slide down the backside of the incline. Gullies turned into waterfalls, gutting the roadway as they tore their way across. Movement at the corner of his headlights caused Cutter to tap the brakes. At first he thought it was a deer, but on further inspection he realized it was a stump, riding on a gigantic mudflow off the clear-cut above him.

A quick glance in the rearview confirmed that Cutter was abeam the slide. He stomped the gas to keep from being hit broadside and swallowed up in the mud. Fishtailing through the muck, he didn't stop until he was well into the flat. Even then, it took a five-point turn on the narrow road so he could use the headlights to get a good look behind him. A monster mud slide with broken trees the size of his waist completely covered the road. There was no way the pickup could make it out until a road crew came out for cleanup.

Cutter leaned against the wheel, thinking, making a plan. The rain kept falling, and he had no idea what lay ahead, so he turned the truck back around before some other portion of this road tried to kill him. The mud slide was certainly going to complicate matters with January Cross.

The old logging road cut back to the south less than five minutes later, then ended abruptly at a soggy gravel apron and a thick stand of alder bushes. A barrier of logs at the end kept people from driving into the water. The white light from a lone boat at anchor burned brightly less than seventy-five meters away. Shrieking williwaws blew across the surface with every gust, turning the boat stern-to the shore, but the bay was absent the rollers and chop in the less protected waters just outside. It was not, however, absent the driving rain.

Cutter turned off his lights. He watched the squat vessel weather vane with the shifting wind while he mulled over his suspicions about January Cross.

Never a man to think for too long when he had the opportunity to act, Cutter flashed his headlights on and off several times, signaling *Tide Dancer* that someone was on shore. He'd told January he might need to talk to her again. If he was any judge of human nature, he thought she half expected him to drop by.

There was movement in the boat, then the flash of light as she signaled him back. Cutter watched through a pair of binoculars from the dry cab of the pickup as she looked back at him with her own pair of binoculars from the dry wheelhouse. It was too dark to get a read on her face, but he thought he might have seen her frown. Unhappy or not, she donned her foul weather gear. The door swung open a moment later. Cutter looked on guiltily as she left the comfort of her warm boat and made her way through the rain to a skiff that was tied off the stern rail. It took her a moment to get the engine started in the cold air of the storm.

He turned on his lights again so she could see to navigate but moved the truck at an angle so as not to shine them full in her eyes. Raindrops peppered the surface of the bay, throwing up a layer of back-splash spray a foot above the surface. The little outboard screamed above the wind as Cross approached the shore. One hand clutched the tiller, the other clamped an orange nor'easter rain hat on top of her head against the wind. Cutter backed the pickup into a hollow in the alders, getting it off the main roadway, and then stood on the shore in the downpour, waiting. He stepped up as soon as he heard the skiff's bow scrape gravel.

"I'm surprised you made the trip!" January shouted above the hiss of rain and howling wind.

"I know," Cutter said, sloshing in to push the boat back into deep water before he climbed over the side. "Mud slide has the road completely blocked!"

"That sounds good!" she yelled, throwing the boat into reverse. "I've been too busy to eat!"

Cutter tried again, holding on to his own hat now. "I said the road is blocked!"

She gave him a thumbs-up. "Great! I'm starving."

Cutter gave up and returned the thumbs-up, deciding to wait until they were on the boat. He'd either just made a poor woman venture out in the driving rain so he could ask her a few questions— or he was about to explain to a murderer that he needed to spend the night.

CHAPTER 35

Garza grabbed a wooden handrail beside the dining table and braced himself. They were in the teeth of the storm now and *Pilar* skidded down the face of another wave, plowing into the trough at the bottom. The incredible headwind sent monstrous waves breaking over the bow, slowing the boat to a wallowing crawl.

It was late, but no one could go down below without getting sick. The storm made the pitching boat feel much smaller than it was. Fausto wrestled the wheel, peering back and forth from the rain-streaked windscreen to the glow of the GPS, working hard to keep from running aground. He'd suggested they stop, but Garza forced him to press on, determined to retrieve the media card before the body washed up on shore. This island was far from uninhabited. A body would bring an investigation and it was only a matter of time before someone doing the investigating recognized the fool Camacho on the footage.

Another wave broke, shoving the bow downward and holding it there for an agonizing moment. Garza released a penned-up breath when they bobbed back up again. Fausto cursed and readjusted his seat. According to his last report, if they didn't all drown, they would round the bottom of the island sometime close to midnight. At that point they would stop beating against the storm and move into the lee of the islands that formed a barrier between the fetch of the open ocean and Prince of Wales Island, bringing welcome relief from the monstrous waves.

Garza looked across the table at the pitiful prisoner and forced a smile. She looked away, obviously terrified to be living on the same earth with him. It had been a mistake to force her to the brink by killing Beti before her eyes. He should have let the poor girl hold on to some small possibility that she might survive this encounter. Of course, her survival had become impossible from the moment she'd lifted the camera to her eye and filmed the face of Ernesto Camacho. And now she was a witness to Beti's killing. Perhaps that had been a mistake. No, he thought, he needed to make a point. That was all there was to it.

Luis had asked to be the one to kill Beti, but she'd been standing there talking incessantly, making such demands—and it had just happened. Garza looked at this trembling woman sitting across from him. Perhaps he would let Luis kill her.

Luis, he was not very smart, but he was loyal and deserved to be rewarded once in a while. The skinny man with the rat-mustache now sat across the salon next to the aft exit, his face bent over a five-gallon bucket, sallow and green. Garza had warned him about throwing up on the carpet. Chago slouched at the navigation station across from the dinette. He leaned forward, elbows on the small desk, head in his hands. He wasn't seasick, but he was broody. It didn't really matter to Garza. Chago was always glum about something. He did his job. That's what mattered.

And Beti, well, if Chago knew how to tie a knot and the nautical chart was correct, Beti Cárdenas would remain strapped to a twenty-kilo Lewmar anchor, thirty fathoms below the surface.

Carmen had seen violence before. She'd been walking out of the Costco in Commerce with her grandmother when a gangbanger had dragged a girl out of his car and stomped her to death right there in the parking lot. He had looked like a monster, with sagging pants, a shaved head, and a face covered with tattoos.

Manuel Alvarez-Garza, on the other hand, was a good-looking guy, the kind she would have talked to in a club. He was probably ten years older than her, but not old enough to be gross—and he had money, which made the age gap even less. He wore pressed khaki slacks and an expensive cotton shirt rolled up with one turn at the cuffs. His Brooks Brothers alligator belt alone was likely worth more than her first car. He had no visible tattoos and his hair and nails were neat and well groomed. When he spoke, his voice was soft and even.

And that made him all the more terrifying.

"The devil will not be dressed as a monster, my child," Carmen Delgado's grandmother would often say. "Oh, no. The devil will be handsome. He will come to you like a lover and he will smile and offer you a sweet."

Carmen had never felt so trapped. Garza had shot his girlfriend as if she were a stray dog. His men had dutifully dumped her overboard without so much as a shrug. Luis looked like he wanted to kill everyone on the boat. And Chago, who had seemed a tenuous ally, would no longer even meet her eye. Even the boat seemed bent on killing her, on the verge of sinking with each crashing wave.

She racked her brain on what to do when they reached the cove. If they were able to find Greg's body, she still owed Garza another media card. She could tell him where it was but she might as well put a gun to Cassandra's head herself if she did that. There had to be a way to get these men the second copy of the footage without getting anyone else murdered. She just had to figure it out before they reached the cove.

Across the table, Garza smiled benignly.

"I am afraid this storm is making you ill, my dear," he said. "Eat this. It will settle your stomach." He pressed a piece of ginger candy into her hand like the devil that he was.

315

CHAPTER 36

"You want a piece of cake?" January Cross asked while Cutter hung his dripping raincoat on the wet locker just inside the door next to hers. "It's store-bought but it might take the edge off your chill. Easy to get hypothermia out there in the rain."

"I'm fine," Cutter said. "Not much of a cake guy." Havoc came up to sniff his leg, then, clearly not impressed, turned and went below.

Cross was still dressed in the same clothes from earlier that day, but both hoodie and jeans had dark blotches where rain had worked its way past her foul-weather gear. She crossed her arms and stood back to look him up and down in the harsh yellow glow of her cabin lights. A large video camera with clear plastic housing sat on the dinette table to the port side of the salon, along with a half dozen smaller GoPro units. A pile of red shop rags and various tools said she'd been working on the cameras before Cutter signaled her.

"Likely story about the mud slide," she said. "I've never had a guy use that one on me before."

"Sorry," he said. "It's the only story I have." He wiped rainwater out of his eyes with the back of his hand, and, out of habit, he scanned the room for weapons. If she noticed, she didn't say anything.

"There's plenty of room on the boat," she said. "But you're bound to ask me a lot of questions since you're staying the night. Do you need to read me my rights or something?"

Cutter nodded, feeling a familiar flutter of adrenaline in his chest. Was she testing the water? "Maybe I should," he said. "If you have something to hide."

"Oh, Deputy Cutter," she sighed as if she were completely exhausted. "The sum total of the things I have to hide would mortify you."

"So, it sounds like you're hungry?" Cutter changed the subject.

"Don't know where you got that idea." January grinned. "Did it have anything to do with the incoherent begging for you to cook me dinner when I picked you up in the skiff?"

Cutter raised an eyebrow.

"Yeah," she said. "I could hear you fine about the mud slide. I just hoped you'd whip up one of those cool recipes I saw written down in your notebook."

"I told you," he said, smiling for the third time that day. "Those recipes are double top secret." He glanced at his watch. "It is dinnertime, but mind if I borrow your satellite phone? I'll cover the cost."

"Knock yourself out," January said. "But you'll

have to stand there with the door open in order to get a signal."

On January's advice, Cutter stood half in, half out so he could get a signal and not get completely drenched. He braced the aft door against the wind with his foot. Even in the protected bay, the storm made it impossible to hear over the phone.

Fontaine seemed unimpressed that he'd just about been pushed off the mountain by a mud slide. She gave the information to Trooper Benjamin, who promised to pass it along to highway maintenance so they could get the road cleared once the storm abated.

Cutter's next call was to Mim. His heart sank a little when Matthew answered.

"It's Uncle Arliss!" he shouted, calling over his brother. They had a habit of holding the phone between them so talking to one always meant talking to them both.

He asked if they were being good and obeying Grumpy's rules. They laughed their seven-year-old belly laughs and said they were obeying the fun ones. They asked when he was coming home. It had been a long time since anyone had asked Cutter that question. For some reason, it filled him with immeasurable loneliness.

"I'll be home before too long," he said. "Is your mom there?"

Mim must have been standing beside them because she came on the line immediately.

"Hey," she said.

"Just thought I'd check in," he said. "Let you know I made it safe."

"I'm glad," she said. "Did you catch your bandit?"

"We did," Cutter said. "Chased him into the woods. Big fun."

"I'm sure the boys will want to hear all the gory details." She paused. "Not that I don't. I just mean—"

"It's okay," Cutter said. "I get it. Gory details have never been your thing. Listen, this is a satellite phone so it's costing a bajillion bucks a minute. I gotta go."

"I'm glad you called," she said.

"Me too," he said. He ended the call and stepped back inside feeling flushed.

"Checking in with the wife and kids?" January looked up from the dinette where she sat with a cloth cleaning the lenses on her pile of cameras.

"My sister-in-law and her kids," he corrected.

"Okay," she said. "If that's the way you want to play it."

Cutter stood at the door looking at her. "Why would you doubt my story?"

"Because *you* sound like you doubt your story," she said.

"Touché," Cutter said. "Doubtful or not, the story's a long one." He picked up one of the GoPros. "Trooper Benjamin says you spend a lot of time around the south end of the island."

"Getting right down to business, huh?"

"I did ask to borrow your phone first," Cutter said. "Didn't mean to be rude."

"No worries," January said. "Tlingit people have a figure at potlatches and feasts called Naa Kaani. He's the guy on the totem poles wearing the button blanket and holding the speaking staff. He keeps the meeting in order." She passed him a wooden spoon that was sitting on the table. "Here is your speaking staff. You have the floor."

"The south side of the island," Cutter reminded her.

"Yes," January said. "I go where the orcas go. This pod liked the fishing down there. Now that the herring are in, they'll be up here."

"Carmen Delgado and Greg Conner had supposedly gone to shoot some footage on the south end the day they disappeared."

"You mean the day I threatened them?" January said.

"Yep. That's the day."

"Footage of what?"

"That's one of the things we're trying to figure out," Cutter said.

January went back to cleaning the lenses. He noticed she used her left hand a great deal in her work.

"I didn't notice before," Cutter said. "Are you left-handed?"

"Depends," she said. "Is your killer left-handed?"

He shrugged.

"No," she said, going back to work on the lens. "I'm sort of ambidextrous. I'm predominately right-handed when I commit any nefarious deeds though."

"I'll make a note of that," Cutter said.

"Anyway," January said. "I rarely see anyone out there besides a few fishing boats. The production crews use small skiffs though, so they'd be near shore. I might never notice them. Carmen may have had one extra fuel tank onboard when they zipped by me yesterday, but I think I would have noticed a bunch of spare cans. That limits their range out of Craig Harbor to a few dozen miles."

"True."

"I wish I had seen them," January said. "I really do."

"What do *you* think happened to Carmen Delgado?" Cutter asked.

January leaned back in her seat and sighed. "I have no idea," she said. "But like I said, I really wish I did. Absent that stupid television show, Carmen can be a nice enough person."

"People on this island don't seem overly fond of her show."

"They either love it or they hate it," January said. "It's making some people rich, some people famous, and some people pissed—but I think it's making everybody crazy."

"Sounds like it," Cutter said. He picked up the

large video camera and turned it over in his hand. "Do you get a lot of underwater footage of the whales?"

"Some," January said. "They've gotten accustomed to the boat so they stop by for visits once in a while. They have a habit of spy hopping off the aft rail and scaring the crap out of me while I'm on deck having my morning coffee."

"Spy hopping?"

"Kind of like treading water," she said. "You've seen it before if you've been to a commercial-type whale show. It's when a whale or porpoise sticks its head out of the water so it can look around."

"I'd like to see that out here in the wild," Cutter mused.

January shot him a smile. It didn't seem like the smile of a killer. She picked up the clear plastic housing. "As a matter of fact though, I need to get this back on the brackets next to the keel. Problem is, the zipper on my dry suit separated on me the last time I went down."

Cutter shuddered. "That had to be uncomfortable."

"Like a full-body ice cream headache," she said. "Nearly broke my own back writhing around under the boat. I have another suit onboard that I was going to try. It's way too big for me so I'm sure it would leak. It would probably fit you. Maybe you'd consider hooking this up for me tomorrow, after the storm passes I mean."

Cutter shrugged. "It's the least I could do."

"That would be super-duper cool." She began to rummage through the pile of shop towels on the table. "A guy in Craig designed the bracket for me and fixed some bolts to the hull near the keel so I can mount it. It's a Frankenstein's monster type of deal so there are about three different sizes of bolt." January found what she was looking for. Cutter's stomach tightened when she held it up in her left hand, her right still under the table and out of sight. "He made this special tool to put on the bracket," she said. "See, it's pretty ingenious—a flat wrench with cutouts for the bolts all along this one side."

CHAPTER 37

Sam Benjamin tapped his pen against the black basket-weave leather cover of his trooper notebook. The only thing enjoyable about interviewing Bright Jonas was watching Deputy Fontaine dish it right back to the obnoxious woman.

Bright sat across her living room, lounging with one leg draped over the arm of her overstuffed chair, swirling a glass full of ice and something else. She wore a loose T-shirt with a silkscreen of her own photograph from the show, and a pair of gray yoga pants that made the trooper happy her shirt hung all the way to midthigh. She wasn't really a heavy woman, more full-figured, like Marilyn Monroe, but the overabundance of guile and self-importance added to her weight. Her husband, Fitz, sat beside her in a shabby recliner, leaning slightly away as if he didn't want to catch anything she might have. A big man, his full beard did little to hide the clenched jaw and sickened look of a man who wanted to cut his own throat.

Sam Benjamin couldn't blame him. He could easily have listened to Deputy Lola Fontaine talk for hours, but he had all he could stomach of Bright Jonas after a minute and a half. The trooper had known Bright since he'd come to this island, and she'd never been particularly easy to get along with. But now, as a preeminent member of the *FISHWIVES!* cast, her nose was so high in the air she would have drowned had she stepped outside in this rain. Benjamin forced himself to slow down and ask the questions that needed to be asked, though he'd rather be at the production company's apartments interviewing some slightly less dysfunctional souls.

He took a long, focusing breath and decided to gut it out and get through this if it killed him. He reviewed his notebook for the questions he'd already asked, then looked up at Fitz.

"Did Carmen or Greg say anything to either of you about going with them on a remote shoot?"

Fitz shook his head and opened his mouth to speak but Bright cut him off.

"I've already told you, dear," she said, affecting a mid-Atlantic whine. "We have no idea where they went."

Benjamin nodded and asked Fitz again. "How about you?"

Bright wallowed herself up straighter in her chair. "I just told you we do not know."

"I'm asking your husband," the trooper said.

"I said 'we.' "

"I get it now," Fontaine said, nodding as if she'd finally caught on to something important "I thought you were using the royal 'we.' "

Fitz Jonas looked at the floor, stifling a chuckle. Bright shot him a withering stare before wheeling on Fontaine. "My husband and I have a good enough relationship that we can speak for each other. We are like one person."

"You must do that a lot," Fontaine said. "Since I've not heard him speak at all."

Bright Jonas leaned forward, staring daggers now. "I can see what you're doing, Deputy Fontaine. It's obvious from your tight clothes and über-fit body that you think you're some kind of God's gift to men."

Benjamin shut his notebook and got to his feet. "We should go."

"A little word to the wise, sweetie," Bright said, turning up the heat. "A real man enjoys a woman with a little meat on her bones, not some gym rat with muscles as hard as a metal road grate."

"Maybe so, Meaty Bones." Fontaine chuckled. "But I can do a handstand and the splits at the same time. The men I know don't seem to mind that at all."

Trooper Benjamin herded Fontaine to the door, standing strategically between her and Bright Jonas as they left.

He turned to face her when they were both in his Tahoe and buckling their seat belts. "It's none of my business," he said. "But can you really do the splits while you do a handstand?"

Fontaine batted her eyes, doing a poor job of

looking innocent. "All damned day, Sam. All damn day."

The radio on the console squelched, rescuing him from saying something he would surely regret. It was the swing-shift dispatcher at the Craig Police Department.

"You on the radio, Sam?"

The trooper put the Tahoe in gear and pulled away from the Jonas house, just in case Bright decided to shoot the person she saw as her bony competition. He scooped up the microphone when they made it down the street a ways. "Go ahead, Shirley," he said.

"Sam, call the station please," the dispatcher said.

Benjamin fished his cell phone from the pocket of his vest carrier and punched in the speed dial number for the PD. "What's up?" he said.

"I didn't want to put it out over the radio," the dispatcher said, "but I got Lin Burkett standing outside in my lobby. She's in pretty bad shape, but who can blame her, ya know? I'm pretty sure she's intoxicated but no one deserves to get arrested on the day their kid's body is recovered."

"I agree," Benjamin said. "Is there someone she can call?"

"She wants to talk to you personally," Shirley said. "Says it's something really important about Gerald. Life or death type of deal."

Should have led with that, Shirley, the trooper

thought, ending the call and returning the phone to his pocket.

Lin Burkett sat with her face buried in her hands in the Craig Police Department lobby. She rose unsteadily to her feet when Benjamin and Fontaine came in through the door. Both stood for a moment, letting the rain drip off their jackets onto a large rug left there for that purpose.

Burkett shook her head. Her bloodshot eyes pleaded for help. "You gotta stop him, Trooper," she said. "Before he does somethin' stupid. He found her book. I'm sure he read it, and now there's no telling what he'll do." Her nose was stuffed from crying and she sounded like she had a bad cold.

"Slow down, Lin," Benjamin said. "We can get you a safe place to stay if you're afraid for your safety."

She looked at him, blinking and shaking her head. "What are you talking about?"

"You and Gerald have to be under a lot of stress," Benjamin said. "Did he threaten you?"

"Not me," she said.

"Who then?"

She shoved a well-worn spiral notebook at the trooper.

Benjamin opened the book and gave it a quick glance before passing it to Fontaine and turning back to Mrs. Burkett. "Millie's journal? I looked through her room. Where did you find it?"

"It was layin' there in the living room when I got home," she said, her face stricken. "Right next to Gerald's recliner. I don't know where he got it from."

"And you think he read something in Millie's diary that's going to make him do something stupid?"

"He's gone," Lin sobbed. "I checked the drawer and his gun is gone too. You gotta help me, Trooper. I want that son of a bitch dead as bad as he does, but I can't lose Millie and Gerald too. Please stop him."

"What son of a bitch?" the trooper asked.

"The one on that show!" Lin spat.

Benjamin thought of the *FISHWIVES!* camera operator he'd interviewed at the bonfire the night before. Something about the guy had seemed off—and he'd admitted to having a working relationship with Millie Burkett. "Are you talking about Tucker Jackson?"

Lin shook her head, sniffing back tears. "Who?"

"It's not Jackson," Fontaine said, holding up the notebook so Benjamin could see the entry. She gave a slow shake of her head. This made sense. "Millie Burkett was having an affair with Kenny Douglas."

"That's right." Lin Burkett nodded. "And I'm positive Gerald's out drinking up enough courage to kill the bastard while we're here talking about it."

CHAPTER 38

January stared at Cutter, then looked back and forth around the cabin. "Did I say something that offended you? You look as though you just saw a ghost."

Cutter's hand hovered near, but not on, his sidearm. He gave a nod toward the flat "Frankenstein" wrench. "Can I take a look at that?"

"Sure." January handed the thing over, and then lifted her right hand out from under the table. It held only the microfiber cloth she'd been using to clean her camera lenses. "I always get the weird ones," she said under her breath.

Cutter held the wrench by the end, letting it hang while he looked it over. Where the weapon used to strike Millie Burkett had to have had two cutouts to leave its distinct pattern, this one had three. Cutter gave an audible sigh. "Do you have any other wrenches like this one?"

January shook her head. "Nope," she said. "I think one's enough. Like I said, my friend made it so it's all I'll need."

"I'd be happy to mount the housing for tomorrow," he said. He gave her back the wrench. "Seems like I remember you saying you were hungry before I borrowed your phone."

"I'm starving," January said. She slid out from between the dinette and the padded bench and went to the small galley where she began to look through the various lockers there. At length, she held up an onion. "I bought a bunch of groceries yesterday, but I swear, I can't find anything that goes together to make a meal."

"How many onions?" Cutter asked.

She turned to look at the bin over her shoulder. "Four."

Cutter gave a thoughtful nod. "You have butter?"

"I do," she said.

"Beef stock?"

"Boullion," she said.

"That works. How about bread?"

"Yep."

"Wine?"

"I have that too."

Cutter rubbed his hands together. "It just so happens that you have all the ingredients for one of the ten recipes my granddad taught me."

"I'd like to hear more about this grandfather of yours," she said. "We Tlingit revere our elders. It's nice to hear of someone who feels the same way—especially in this day and age when everyone seems to shove their grandparents in a home. Did I hear you call him 'Grumpy' earlier."

"I couldn't say 'Grandpa' when I was young," Cutter said. "So I called him Grumpy. It stuck,

I guess, and by the time I was in high school everyone I knew called him that. It suited him since he didn't smile much."

"Like someone else I know," January said.

"Sorry."

"Don't be," she said. "I think most people smile too much. Makes them look silly."

"Grumpy would have liked you," Cutter said. "So, back to our meal. According to Grumpy, King Louis the Fifteenth wanted something to eat after a long day of hunting but could find nothing in his chalet but some onions, bread, and champagne." Cutter held up the onion. "You have more than King Louis did to make a French onion soup. Grumpy used to make it for my grandmother."

"Was she a good cook too?"

"She died before I was born. Could be why the name Grumpy stuck so well." Cutter sighed. "Anyway, I could make us some soup if you'd like."

"That would be most cool," January said. "I'd help, but *Tide Dancer* has what my navy father would have called a 'one-butt' galley."

"No worries," Cutter said. "It's kind of a one-butt meal."

The rich smell of butter and frying onions soon filled the cabin. The boat's gentle rocking combined with the steady drum of the rainstorm seemed to stimulate deep conversation. The pair were soon talking about things they would have never dreamed of touching in less heady circumstances. January went into great detail about her job, getting out thick albums packed with photos of each orca in the pod. She spoke of their individual personalities and idiosyncrasies as though they were her own children. But when Cutter asked about her time teaching and why she'd quit, she fell silent.

He decided to cook and let her be quiet. He was, after all, her guest.

"You know," she finally said. "It takes a brave man to stay on board a boat with a murder suspect."

He looked up from the loaf of bread he was in the process of slicing. "What makes you think you're a suspect?"

"Come on," she said. "I saw your face. There was something about that wrench that made you nearly shoot me."

"You don't have much faith in me as a copper," Cutter said. He found a bottle of poultry seasoning and gave it a generous shake over the sautéed onions, and then stirred the pot before pouring a cup of red wine over the mixture. He let this simmer a minute, then followed up with several cups of beef stock.

"I'm right though," she said. "Aren't I?"

"You are," he said. "But your wrench is the wrong kind of wrench. I go where the evidence takes me, but I'm a pretty good judge of character. You don't seem like you're hiding something as big as a murder."

January cocked her head to one side. "But you do think I'm hiding something?"

"Like you said, we're all hiding something." Cutter went back to slicing the bread. He made the pieces thick so they wouldn't dissolve when he floated them in the soup. "But yes, I think you in particular are hiding something. It might not be any of my business or have any bearing on the case, but you're hiding it nonetheless."

"It's not, you know," she said. "Any of your business, I mean."

"Okay," Cutter said. He put the bread on a cookie sheet and slid it into the oven to toast. "I'll take your word for it."

"Is that what Grumpy would have done?"

"Have you got any cheese?"

"What?"

"Cheese," Cutter said. "Swiss if you have it. Gruyère would be best, but mozzarella will do in a pinch."

She nodded toward the small refrigerator in the corner. "I don't think I've ever even tasted Gruyère, but there's some Swiss in the door."

Cutter looked through the shelves and found the cheese behind a bottle of mustard. "Got it," he said. "And no, Grumpy would have resorted to bright lights and thumbscrews to find out what your secret is."

"Really?"

"Nope," Cutter admitted. "Despite his gruff demeanor, Grumpy was mostly a 'live and let live' kind of guy."

"Like you?"

"I'm not half the man my grandfather was."

"You know what I think?" January said. "I think you already know my secret, but you're too much of a gentleman to say it."

Cutter gave a contemplative nod. Instead of speaking, he took the toasted bread out of the oven, putting one slice in each ceramic bowl before he ladled the rich soup. He crowned each bowl with a second piece of toasted bread, sprinkled this with cheese.

"Two pieces of bread?"

"Grumpy's secret," Cutter said. "He liked a little soup with his toast and cheese."

"That smells incredible," she said.

"It's the poultry seasoning."

"And the butter," January said. "And the onions, and the wine . . ."

Cutter put both bowls on a cookie sheet and slid them into the hot oven to melt the cheese. It really did smell amazing.

He threw the hand towel over his shoulder and leaned against the counter. "So," he said. "You want to talk about it?"

"What?"

"I only ask because it seems like you want to talk about it."

January put her elbow on the table and rested her chin on her hand. She gave a little shrug. "I . . . guess I kind of do."

"How long have you been sick?"

"You're awfully intuitive," she said. "Was it my lopsided chest or the freakishly short haircut?"

Cutter leaned back against the counter and shook his head. "I've been through it before," he said. "My wife."

"Did she . . . ?"

He nodded. "Five years ago."

"I'm so sorry," she said.

"Thanks," Cutter said. "But you're out here so you must have beaten it."

"It was a mutual beating," January said. "I was diagnosed with cancer the same day I discovered my husband was having an affair with the choir teacher at the school where we both taught. He bawled his head off and begged me to take him back, but I couldn't stomach him any more than I could the chemo. I lost a C-cup breast and a six-foot boob all in the same month." She gave a sad chuckle. "I got sick of everyone telling me what my new normal was going to be like. The fact is, I just got sick of everyone, period. After my last round of chemo finished up, I was up late one night crying into my keyboard and surfing singles sites looking for guys who might be interested in a bald woman with one semibodacious ta-ta . . . or, semibodacious ta, I guess—"

"Stop that," Cutter chided gently.

"Anyway, I came across this job doing whale studies for the state of Alaska. It was remote and I'm used to remote. I grew up in a village near Juneau but didn't want to go back there right away. The interview was over the phone, so the cancer never even came up. By the time I showed up, my hair had grown just enough to look edgy on purpose, so no one around here suspected. I don't want my identity to be the sad woman recovering from breast cancer." January leaned her head back against the dinette seat and stared at the ceiling. "I really don't know why I'm telling you all this."

Cutter turned and used the hand towel to take the soup out of the oven and place it carefully on the stove top. He nodded to himself when he saw the cheese had bubbled over and run down the sides—just like Grumpy liked it.

"I'm a stranger," he said. "It's easy to talk to someone you're not likely to see again."

"There is that," January said. "But what if—"

A hoarse cough pulled their attention to the forward stairs beyond the galley. Cutter turned to find a sleepy-eyed Native girl with mussed hair holding an equally mussed dog in her arms. The girl scratched her cheek and blinked at the cabin

337

lights as she sniffed the air, presumably smelling the soup. Havoc did the same as she plunked him down by the table.

"Cassandra!" January gasped. "How did you get here?"

The girl pointed over her shoulder and leaned her head sideways, closing her eyes.

January looked at her with narrow eyes. "You were sleeping in the quarter berth, weren't you?"

Cassandra nodded, moving toward the soup.

"Careful!" Cutter said. "That's hot."

January stood and smoothed the girl's messy bed head. It was easy to see the air of mutual trust. "This is my friend, Deputy Cutter," she said.

"Arliss," Cutter said, stooping to eye level as he shook her hand. "Are you hungry?"

Cassandra nodded.

Cutter winked. "Powerful stuff, this soup. It will make a person friends for life."

January gave a soft smile, looking genuinely happy to have the company during the downpour. "I'll try to be careful."

Cutter passed the bowls one at a time, careful not to spill the near-boiling soup. "Cassandra can have mine," he said. "There's enough for me to make another. Won't take me a minute."

January gave Cassandra a spoon. "Don't burn your tongue," she said. "I'll get some extra sleeping bags out of the locker below. Lucky I have enough for a slumber party. I think I even have popcorn so we can stay up all night talking and painting each other's toenails." She looked at Cutter. "Bet they don't cover that in the fugitive-hunting handbook."

Cutter gave a somber nod. "They do not."

"Better than sleeping on a boat with a murder suspect," she said.

"That's the truth."

She leaned in close enough Cutter could feel the warmth of her breath. "You think she heard us talking about my boob?"

Cutter shook his head.

January stood there, close.

Cutter eyed the rain hitting the windows. "Mind if I make one more call?"

She nodded at the satellite phone. It was right where he left it, on the edge of the dinette. "You know I didn't kill Millie Burkett, don't you?"

Cutter walked toward the door, turning before he went out to brave the rain. "Grumpy wasn't just a cook," he said. "He was an incredibly gifted cop, and he had a saying when it came to homicides—'Everybody's a suspect but me, and sometimes, I'm not so sure about me.' "

CHAPTER 39

Sam Benjamin left Trooper Allen to take Lin Burkett home, while he and Fontaine headed over to the *FISHWIVES!* crew housing. Pounding rain pelted Benjamin's Tahoe with such intensity he may as well have been driving through a car wash. Pavement blended with forest, wrapping him in a black sheet and forcing him to make an educated guess as to the whereabouts of the road as he drove. Even so, he tore his eyes away from the thumping windshield wipers long enough to steal a quick, sideways glance at Lola Fontaine. The subdued glow of the dash lights added angles to her high cheekbones. The line of her jaw . . . well, the line of her jaw gave him a stomachache. She was the only woman he'd ever seen who looked good bathed in ghostly green light. He caught her throwing him a couple of glances as well, at least he thought he had. But, she'd let it slip about a husband a couple of times—often enough that he knew the guy's name was Larry. Odd, though, that she didn't wear a ring.

He cleared his throat, half afraid she might hear his thoughts in the silence. "What's the story with your boss? I mean, does that guy ever smile?"

Fontaine turned slightly to meet his gaze. She laughed, showing incredibly white teeth, looking even prettier in the light. "I know," she said. "He's a piece of work. . . ."

"Don't get me wrong," Benjamin said. "I'd bet he's a good guy to have around in a fight."

"True enough." She gave a qualified nod. "But there seems to be an awful lot of fights when he's around."

"I can imagine," Benjamin said. "He seems pretty old-school—the 'you can beat the rap but you can't beat the ride' kind of cop. There's still a place for that, I suppose, but old-school will get you put in a new prison these days."

Fontaine started to answer, but her cell phone began to play "Let the Bodies Hit the Floor" by Drowning Pool.

The trooper took his eyes off the road again long enough to shoot her a look at the choice of songs.

She blessed him with another toothy grin. "Cutter's ringtone."

"Appropriate," he said.

Fontaine answered the call, making little grunts to show she was listening while he presumably briefed her about something. "He's driving," she said at length. "Get this, boss. Millie Burkett kept a diary. You'll never guess who she was having an affair with. . . . How did you know? . . . That's friggin' weird. You know that? Yeah . . . Hello . . . You there?"

Fontaine held the phone away from her ear,

looking at the face of it to see if she still had a connection. She turned to the trooper, concerned. "He got cut off."

"Not surprised," Benjamin said, pulling the Tahoe up in front of the *FISHWIVES!* apartments at the edge of town. He killed the engine, listening to the rain, wishing he could forget about murders and missing people and just sit there with the deputy for a while. "He had to be calling from Jan's satellite phone. They're great tools, but in this weather, the clouds can do a number on the connection. There's nothing to worry about."

Rain fell down, up, and sideways, drenching them by the time they reached the outer door that led into the apartment building. The overpowering smell of new carpeting hit Benjamin full in the face when he pulled it open. Prior to *FISHWIVES!* the apartments were rented mainly to hunters and fishermen who visited the island. The production staff had balked at the 1970s shag that smelled like deer musk and fish blood. Carmen Delgado paid for new carpet and paint. The owner didn't care. Once these people left, the hunters and fishermen who returned would be happy with the refurbished digs—so long as the idiots in the crew didn't burn the place down first.

Once inside, Trooper Benjamin consulted a note written on the palm of his left hand, and then moved down the dimly lit hallway until he found number 3, Kenny Douglas's apartment. He pounded on the door with his fist. Fontaine stood on the other side of the frame. Guilty people did crazy things when they were cornered, so both the trooper and the deputy made certain they didn't park themselves in the fatal funnel just in case Kenny's crazy involved a .44 Magnum and the wooden door.

The door directly across the hall opened a crack. An African American girl with cornrows braided with colorful beads peeked out. When she saw the trooper, she opened the door all the way and smiled. She turned and hissed over her shoulder, "It's okay, Sarah. It's just the cops." Leaning casually into the hall, she said, "We had a drunk fisherman the other night who thought he lived here. Sarah just about peed herself thinking you were him."

"We're not," Fontaine said, giving the young woman a humorless look. "Kenny Douglas around?"

"He's in number three," the girl said.

Benjamin nodded. "Doesn't appear to be home."

The girl pointed to number 5 as her roommate Sarah peaked over her shoulder in curiosity. "He might be over in Tucker's room. I heard noise coming from there a few minutes ago. Sometimes they get together and play Assassin's Creed."

"Thanks," Benjamin said.

"Anytime." Both girls lingered in their doorway, probably hoping to see something interesting since the police were there.

"You can both go back inside now," Fontaine said sternly, shooing the girls into their room before turning down the hall.

It took two solid minutes of pounding before the door to apartment number 5 finally flew open. Tucker Jackson stuck his shirtless chest out, ready to tell off whoever was making the racket. He started to retreat back inside when he saw the trooper, but Fontaine placed her hand on the door and said, "Not so fast, Mr. Jackson."

"I didn't know it was you guys," the cameraman said. He wore nothing but a loose pair of gray basketball shorts and his face was flushed as if he'd been running. It was only then that Benjamin noticed the errant flap of dark bangs that had been so bothersome the night of the bonfire was now held up high on his forehead with a bobby pin. Even in his pretrooper days, when he'd had longer hair, Sam Benjamin could honestly say he'd never worn a bobby pin.

"We need to talk to Kenny," the trooper said. He couldn't decide if the flap of hair or the new look bothered him more. There were just some people that rubbed him wrong—they had a bad smell about them. Tucker Jackson was one of those people. He might not be a killer, but he couldn't be trusted. Sam Benjamin was certain of that.

344

"He's not in his apartment?" Jackson looked down the hall.

"Well, he's not answering." Fontaine leaned sideways, trying to get a peek inside his room. Jackson pulled the door shut so only his eye and a strip of his face showed.

The deputy pressed the issue. "I hear someone else. We understand Kenny Douglas comes over to play video games once in a while."

"He does," Jackson said. "But he's not here now."

The trooper cocked his head, looking Jackson in the eye. "Has anything ever led you to think Kenny might have had a . . . more than friendly relationship with Millie Burkett?"

"What?" Jackson said. "No . . . I mean, Kenny comes on to all the girls, but . . ."

"Stop covering for him, Tucker," Fontaine said.

"I'm not covering for him."

Fontaine raised dark eyebrows. "Then who's in there with you?"

Jackson whispered, "I don't want to get anybody in trouble."

Benjamin pointed at the room with his left hand while his right drifted toward the grip of his Glock. "Kenny?" he said softly.

Tucker Jackson groaned and shook his head, opening the door.

Bright Jonas lay in a tangle of sheets on the bed at the far side of the small studio apartment. She had a knitted afghan with a weave much too large for Benjamin's tastes pulled up to her chin.

"I can't believe you," she spat, throwing Jackson a withering stare.

Fontaine gave a tired sigh. "Well, you sure made it over here quick. You must have left right after we did. It's none of my business, but I don't see how you think you'll get away with it in a town this small."

"This is a one-time thing." All the woman's earlier bravado had vanished. "It'll kill poor Fitz if he finds out."

"I'm not driving over to tell him," Benjamin said.

Bright closed her eyes. "He headed out in the boat right after you left."

The trooper stifled a gasp. "By himself?"

She nodded, the afghan moving in time with her quivering chin. "Checking the herring pens."

"I hate to break it to you, Bright," Benjamin said, "but if he braved those seas to check the herring pens when there's not a thing he can do about it if they blow away . . . I'm thinking he already knows."

Jackson pulled on a T-shirt. Fontaine looked at him and scoffed. "I'm not the morality police or anything, but have you seen the size of Fitz Jonas?"

"He's a gentle guy," Jackson said, sounding as if he genuinely liked the man. "I can't imagine him getting mad."

"Again, none of my business," Fontaine said,

"but screwing someone else's wife doesn't make a man mad. It makes him go berserk. My ex-husband suspected I was sleeping with every guy I worked with—though I never gave him cause. I'm pretty sure he'd have killed the guy if I had."

"Hey, I was thinking of a place where Kenny might be," Tucker Jackson said, eager to change the subject. He bent over the dining room table to a map on a piece of paper he ripped from a spiral notebook. "The production company rents a little house up the hill in Klawock. We use it for storage mostly. Kenny's kind of a shade tree mechanic so he keeps some tools out there as well to work on the two vans the company actually owns. I've heard him talk about taking women out there sometimes . . . for you know, privacy."

Benjamin studied the map before looking back and forth from Jackson to Bright Jonas. "You guys might try hunting a private spot yourselves next time—so I don't end up having to arrest poor Fitz for a crime of passion."

Trooper Benjamin shut the door on his way out, and then passed the hand-drawn map to Fontaine. He shot her a sideways grin before they braved the driving rain to run to his Tahoe.

"Ex-husband?"

The Polynesian woman gave him a wide grin, showing her perfect white teeth. "Hm," she said. "I never mentioned that?"

CHAPTER 40

Cutter helped January clear the soup bowls off the table, then offered to take a look at her damaged dry suit while she did the dishes. He loved to cook, but hated the cleanup—not one of his most endearing qualities, as several of his ex-wives had pointed out.

Cassandra sat across the salon at the navigation station, working contentedly on a pencil drawing of an orca. Havoc chewed a piece of rawhide at her feet.

Outside, the storm raged on with a renewed fury. Huge drops of rain, driven by gale-force winds, pounded the cabin and hissed off the surface of the protected bay in a menacing, primordial moan. The boat swung like a kite at the end of the anchor, weather-vaning to a new position with each fickle gust.

January peered out of a window above the sink. "Did you hear that?"

Havoc stood and gave a short *woof,* followed by a low growl, tawny hackles up.

Cutter cocked his head, trying to hear over the gale. "The waves slapping the hull?"

"I know that's what it is," January said. "But my overactive imagination makes me think—"

She stopped in midsentence and they both looked at Cassandra.

The girl sat poised with her pencil in the air, listening intently. After a moment, she shook her head and bent back over the drawing.

"You guys have me acting crazy." January twisted the dishrag, her cheeks flushing bright pink. "I'm usually just fine by myself."

Standing next to the dinette table, Cutter laid out the dry suit and then arched his back.

"My legs could use a stretch anyway," he said. "I'll take a walk around before I settle in for the night."

"That's just crazy talk."

"I don't mind," Cutter said.

"That wind will blow you off the deck," January said. "I'll bet it's gusting to forty knots."

"Seriously," Cutter said. "I don't mind getting wet."

"I'm not worried about *you*," January said. "I'm worried about me getting wet. If you go overboard, Cassandra and I will have to go out and save you."

Cassandra looked up from her drawing and looked at Cutter, eyebrows raised, shaking her head as if to say, *I'm not going out there.*

Cutter raised his hands in surrender and slid into the dinette seat. Havoc looked relieved he wasn't going outside as well and curled up under Cassandra's feet again.

Cross's dry suit had started life as midnight blue and charcoal, but hours of sun and salt had faded it to varying stages of gray. Heavier and more restrictive than the DUI suit he'd borrowed earlier from Benjamin, the thick neoprene operated on the same principle, keeping water out and warm air in. On this older suit, the neoprene itself acted as an insulator rather than relying on a quilted or fleece undergarment like the one under the thin DUI laminate. A long metal zipper ran in a slightly curved arc, from the left hip almost to the right shoulder. It was well waxed and appeared to function normally. A female cut, this suit was fuller in the hips with darts at the bust area. There were at least a dozen flimsy plastic grocery bags stuffed into the right cup pocket.

"I haven't gotten around to getting a swim boob," January said, giving the bags a nod. "Still coming around to the idea that some parts of me are removable—like Mrs. Potato Head."

Cutter continued his examination of the dry suit, speaking without looking up. "My wife— the good one—had this nurse who had also been through breast cancer, double mastectomy, really nasty chemo—Adriamycin, the whole deal. Anyway, she reminded my wife not to reduce her self-worth to a bag of skin with a nipple on it."

January shot a glance at Cassandra, who was looking up, suddenly interested in the adults' conversation.

"I don't think you should say 'nipple' around the girl."

Cutter gave an innocent shrug. "You just did."

"Yes," January said. "But girls can talk that way because we have nipples."

Cassandra put both hands in front of her face, peering out between her fingers, grinning.

"Well, technically, men do—"

"Anywaaaay," January said. "I'm a night owl and Cassandra must have slept half the day, so she won't want to go to sleep anytime soon. I have some new DVDs onboard. How about I make some popcorn and we have a movie night?"

Cassandra nodded quickly, dropped her pencil, and gave two thumbs up.

"I guess I could go for popcorn and a movie," Cutter said. He closed the dry suit's zipper, then grabbed the neoprene on either side and gave a healthy tug down by the waist. It held, so he moved his hands upward. At the center of the chest, the teeth on the zipper parted, and like a row of falling dominoes, the entire thing opened up.

"That would ruin your day," he said.

"It did," January said. "I probably went through a dozen very intricate yoga poses in about two seconds when that cold water hit me. Luckily, I was right below the boat so I could get in and warm up fast. It'll cost more to replace the zipper than it would to buy a new suit."

Cutter returned the wadded plastic bags and scooted out of the dinette seat. "Where would you like me to put this?"

January gave him a sheepish look. "The aft lazarette?"

"I thought you didn't want me to go outside."

"I changed my mind," she said. "This storm is really creeping me out for some reason. The lazarette's just back of the cabin, so you won't be walking up front into the wind. And besides, I'm sure you've been dying to search all the compartments on this boat since you got here."

"You'd have made a good deputy marshal," he said.

"How about *Moana*?" January said once Cutter was back inside and drying his hair with a towel she'd given him from her cabin. "It's Cassandra appropriate and a damn good movie." She held up the DVD cover. "I can't decide if your partner reminds me more of Moana or the Rock."

"Believe you should keep that to yourself," Cutter mused.

Whatever Lola Tuakana Teariki Fontaine was doing now, it was a pretty sure bet she wasn't munching popcorn and watching a Disney movie about a Polynesian girl.

The forward seats at the dinette were high backed and plenty long for the three of them to slide in. Cutter, who was rarely comfortable around anyone, watched the light from the computer screen glint off January's abalone earrings, and felt himself relax by degree in the warmth of the cabin heat.

Four hours after he'd borrowed Trooper Benjamin's pickup, Arliss Cutter found himself snuggled under a quilt around a laptop computer with January Cross and Cassandra Brown. Havoc had curled up in the cushion on the other side of the dinette. Outside, the rain still pelted the water and the little boat swung back and forth in the wind.

CHAPTER 41

Sam Benjamin pressed the phone to his ear with one hand, talking to Officer Simeon while he drove with the other—something he hated to do, especially when the roads were so bad.

"We're nearly there," he shouted. The rain hit the roof of his Tahoe with such force he may as well have been trying to talk inside a metal trash can while someone beat on it with a stick.

"I'm just coming through Klawock," the Craig officer said.

"Copy that," Benjamin said. "We're about five minutes ahead of you. I have Deputy Fontaine with me so we're going to go ahead and try the door."

He got nothing but the sound of static—which wasn't out of the ordinary on this remote rock. He took his eyes off the road for a half second and looked at the phone, just to see if he still had a signal.

"Shit!" Lola Fontaine pounded her armrest. "Look out, Sam!"

A surge of adrenaline flooded the trooper's legs when he looked up. He stood on the brakes, feeling the Tahoe hydroplane on the wet pavement. Miraculously the tires found their grip. The antilock brakes groaned and shuddered as four thousand pounds of vehicle slithered to a stop, mere feet from a half-naked woman in the middle of the road.

Soaked to the skin and wearing nothing but a pair of pink panties, she stood frozen and wide-eyed, like a startled doe in the beam of the Tahoe's headlights. It took Benjamin half a second to gather his wits after the near miss, but when he'd calmed down a notch, he recognized the rain-soaked blonde as the young woman who'd been sitting beside Kenny Douglas at the bonfire.

"I'll grab a blanket from the back," Benjamin said to Fontaine as he activated his red and blue emergency lights. "If you don't mind getting her off the road before someone comes up and rear-ends me in the mess."

Fontaine gave him a thumbs-up. She threw open her door and stepped into the rain without another word.

"He's gone crazy!" the girl said, when Benjamin met her and Fontaine on their way to the Tahoe. He draped the wool blanket around her shivering shoulders and walked her toward the backdoor.

"Who's gone crazy? Kenny?"

The girl looked at him like he'd lost his mind. "No, not Kenny. Millie's dad."

Benjamin helped Fontaine get the girl in the Tahoe, and then ran around to jump back in the front, out of the downpour.

Benjamin wiped his face with the back of his sleeve. He made sure the sliding window on his prisoner cage was open as far as possible, then turned to look at the wilted young woman. "Tell me your name again."

"Ashley," she said. "Ashley Pratt." Her teeth chattered. A string of bubbly saliva hung from the tip of her quivering chin.

"Okay, Ashley," the trooper said. "Are you hurt?"

She shook her head, lips together. Water dripped from blond bangs. Tiny ears stuck through her wet locks, elf-like. "He has a gun," she said. "It scared the shit outta me when he kicked in the door. Kenny and me were . . . you know . . . Look, I hardly know Mr. Burkett, but I've never seen him like this. He seemed to get extra mad when he came in and saw me and Kenny together."

"Did he hurt Kenny?" Fontaine said, also turned halfway around in her seat.

"Not yet," Ashley said. "Kenny's bigger, but Mr. Burkett has a gun. He pointed it at me and told me to leave. I was so scared I just ran out of there."

"Where are they now?" Benjamin said.

Ashley nodded to a gravel driveway ahead of the Tahoe and to the left. Benjamin could tell there was a house back there, but thick cedars along the road blocked much of the view.

"I think they're still in the house," Ashley said. "Mr. Burkett said he was going to 'frog march' Kenny out into the woods and teach him a lesson." She looked at Benjamin with pleading eyes, starting to sob now that she was getting warm. "I don't even know what 'frog march' means."

Benjamin grabbed the radio mic. "You stay in the car, Ashley," he said, before depressing the key. "Simeon, you there?"

"Go ahead, Sam."

"Burkett's here already. I've got Ashley Pratt in the back of my vehicle. There's a chance Burkett and Douglas will be in the woods by now."

"Ten-four," Simeon said. "Copy that, dispatch?"

"Ten-four," the Craig dispatcher said. "I'll find somebody to head your way and then I'll get in touch with Trooper Allen."

"I'm maybe three minutes out, Sam," Simeon said.

"Copy," Benjamin said as he put the Tahoe in gear. A hell of a lot could happen in three minutes.

The beam from the Tahoe's headlights bounced across rough gravel as Trooper Benjamin turned off the main road. Long shadows crawled up the clapboard house at their approach. The front door opened as they were driving up, and Kenny Douglas stumbled out, hands tied behind his back. He shrank back at the bright light, then fell

357

forward again, barely catching himself as Gerald Burkett smacked him across the back of the head with the barrel of his pistol.

"That's not good," Benjamin said.

Fontaine groaned, hand on the door. "Suicide by cop?"

"He knows we're here," the trooper said. "And he still came out into the light." He glanced over his shoulder. "Ashley, lay down in the seat. Don't get up until I tell you to."

Both Benjamin and Fontaine opened their doors and stood behind them, pistols out and trained on Burkett. Benjamin blinked, barely able to see his front sight in the downpour.

Burkett stood immediately behind Douglas, holding him by the collar, revolver at his side. Eyes swollen and bloody, the *FISHWIVES!* security man sagged.

"Gerald!" Benjamin yelled, thankful he'd taken the time to put on his Stetson. Frigid water ran down the collar of his uniform, pooling above his gun belt at the small of his back just below the coverage of his ballistic vest. His breath blossomed in front of his face in clouds of vapor. "Put down the gun and let's talk!"

"Afraid not!" Burkett yelled, his words almost lost in the wind and thrashing cedar boughs. He listed heavily to one side, crazy with rage and alcohol.

"Shoot him!" Kenny Douglas yelled, head

bowed against the rain, straining to get away from Burkett's hold on him.

"Nobody's gonna get shot," Benjamin yelled. He cast a quick look at Fontaine, who stood at her open door with her Glock braced against the post. "You got him?"

"Yep," she said, lips set in a grim line.

"I'm going to get a little closer," he said, so only the deputy could hear. "If things get crazy . . ."

"Then somebody *will* get shot," Fontaine said. "Just make sure it's not you. I'll keep him talking."

Benjamin used the cedars as cover, moving from tree to tree, relying on his headlights to effectively blind Gerald Burkett. It might work in the movies to set down your gun and walk forward to negotiate, but the trooper preferred to have three feet of timber between him and any bullets Burkett might send his way. Sorrow and anger released powerful chemicals into the brain, chemicals that were capable of making best friends murder one another. Benjamin felt certain Burkett would certainly feel sorry about it if he killed him. But sorry wouldn't make him any less dead, so he kept to the relative safety of the trees and checked Burkett's position every few steps.

Lola called out, identifying herself. "US Marshals!" She ordered him to put down the gun. Douglas hunched his shoulders against the rain and continued to scream for someone to kill his tormentor.

Burkett threw back his head and cried into the night, as if imploring God instead of the trooper. "You know what this bastard did to my little girl!"

Douglas half turned and said something unintelligible. Burkett cuffed him in the back of the head with the revolver again for his trouble.

"Will someone please kill this son of a bitch!" Douglas was crying now, slinging snot in a near mental breakdown.

Burkett swayed and began speaking to the sky again. Douglas, having had enough, threw himself backward against the other man, sending them both reeling against the door of the cabin. The revolver flew into the mud a few feet away. Douglas hit him again, this time with the point of his shoulder, slamming him against a wall.

Benjamin was still twenty feet from the two men when the gun hit the mud. He holstered his Glock and sprinted forward, floundering twice before slamming into an already stunned Burkett. Even drunk and out of his mind with sorrow, Gerald Burkett was an incredibly strong man. He'd already given up on his own life, and seemed bent on committing suicide by cop. In order to do that, he had to stay out of handcuffs— and the only way to accomplish that was to kick Sam Benjamin's ass.

Pushing one shoulder and pulling the other, the trooper spun the other man, attempting to get his hands behind him. Burkett was having none of it, and just kept spinning, giving the trooper a glancing punch in the jaw as he came around. Rather than continue to fight, Benjamin shoved Burkett away, drawing his Taser and flicking the switch with his thumb to activate it. The red laser light played across Burkett's torso and the trooper pulled the trigger. The battery released a compressed nitrogen charge, propelling twin barbed darts into Burkett's chest and left thigh, just missing his groin. Fifty thousand volts found the path of least resistance between the two darts—through the major muscle groups of Gerald Burkett's body. He dropped like a felled cedar, splashing in the muck.

From the corner of his eye, Benjamin caught sight of Douglas heading to where the gun had fallen, both hands in front of him now. Somehow, he'd slipped his bonds. An instant later there was a flash of movement in the darkness.

Lola Fontaine had just holstered her Glock when she saw Kenny Douglas slip his right hand out of the tape behind his back. He took a moment to rub his wrists and wipe the rain and tears from his eyes. Turning, he peered back at the Tahoe for a moment, using the flat of his hand to shield his eyes from the headlights. Then, coming to some decision, he dropped to his knees and began to search through the mud for Burkett's weapon.

"Step back!" Fontaine shouted, already running toward him.

He ignored her, continuing to dig through the mud for Burkett's gun, not the least bit worried about the approaching female.

That was his first mistake.

Fontaine hit him hard in a flying tackle, riding him backward into the mud. Douglas shrugged her off, elbowing her hard in the gut and knocking the wind out of her. He wasn't a tall man, but he was still a man, possessing more upper body strength than Fontaine, no matter how much time she spent in the gym. What he did not have was her guts—not by a long shot. Underestimating her a second time, he continued to grope through the dark puddles for the revolver, thinking he'd shrugged her off for good.

Fontaine fell flat on her backside, croaking as she tried to draw a breath. Freezing water rushed into her jeans, already soaked from the rain. Gathering her wits, she went against her natural instincts and exhaled forcefully, relaxing her diaphragm enough to be able to breathe again. Her hand closed around a paving stone at the same moment Douglas sat back in the mud. He tried to bring up the revolver, but Fontaine clobbered him in the side of the head with the brick.

Douglas yowled, falling sideways and clutching

his head with both hands. He'd already been bleeding from the pistol whipping Burkett had given him, and the brick seemed to undo him completely.

Fontaine confiscated the gun, tucking it into the back of her jeans. She rolled Kenny onto his stomach with a heavy grunt, not really caring that he was blowing bubbles in the rain-sodden driveway as she ratcheted on the handcuffs.

"You could've killed me!" Douglas whined. A slurry of mud and saliva dripped from his swollen lips. Blood covered the side of his face, mingling with the pouring rain.

Fontaine nodded, still trying to catch her breath.

"I could have shot your ass," she panted. "And dead is dead, by rock or bullet." She pulled Douglas to his feet.

Trooper Benjamin dragged a handcuffed Gerald Burkett over by the elbow, checking to see if Fontaine needed help. Burkett tried to break free as soon as he got close to Kenny Douglas.

Benjamin pushed him back with a flat hand to the chest. "Knock it off," he said.

"You better keep that crazy son of a bitch away from me," Douglas sneered. "Just 'cause his daughter is dead doesn't give him the right—"

"Hey," the trooper said. "You have the right to remain silent. I think you should."

Officer Simeon rolled up and bailed out of his car, sloshing through the rain.

Benjamin waved a soaking wet greeting to the slender Craig officer. "Just after the nick of time," he joked. "If you don't mind transporting Gerald, we'll take Kenny with us. And we have a girl that will need a ride back to her apartment in Craig before questioning. Put her up front with you."

"Hang on now," Douglas said. "Why are you arresting me? I'm the one that was kidnapped and pistol whipped."

"How about sex with a minor?" Fontaine said. She opened the back of the cruiser and escorted the dazed girl to Simeon's car.

Douglas stopped in his tracks, forcing the other trooper to shove him along through the muck.

"Wait a minute," he said. "Ashley said she's eighteen. Tell them, Ashley!" The girl just shuddered silently, clutching the blanket around her as she slid into Simeon's front seat.

"I'm not talking about Ashley, genius," Fontaine said as she shut the door.

Burkett screamed something as Simeon put him in the back of the Craig PD cruiser. The actual words were torn away by the wind, but the meaning was crystal clear.

Kenny Douglas turned to look over his shoulder. "That asshole over there thinks I killed his daughter."

Benjamin opened the rear door of his Tahoe. "Watch your head," he said, prodding the man inside.

Douglas bowed his body, making it impossible to stuff him into the vehicle. "Just hang on one damn minute," he said. "You don't really think I killed that girl?"

"Get in," Benjamin said.

"I didn't kill anybody." Douglas turned to Fontaine, looking for sympathy. "You gotta believe me. I'm innocent."

Lola shook her head. "You're a lot of things, Kenny," she said. "But innocent ain't one of them."

CHAPTER 42

There's something hypnotizing about the relative comfort of an anchored boat during a storm. Cassandra fell asleep first, slumping against January, who held out as long as she could, before drifting off and listing toward Cutter. He lifted his arm to readjust, and she fell against his shoulder, breathing heavily, pinning him between her neck and the back of the dinette. With Cassandra's added weight, he found himself trapped, unable, or at least unwilling, to move without disturbing them. He leaned back to watch the rest of the movie and thought idly that sitting here with this mute girl and a breast cancer survivor whom he'd briefly suspected of murder must be what it felt like to have a family.

January stirred about the time the credits rolled. She sat up with a start, looking at Cutter with crazed brown eyes in those unsteady moments between sleep and wakefulness. She calmed with a series of ever-widening blinks.

She smacked her lips. "You hear that?"

Across the table, Havoc opened an eye at the sound of his human's voice. Apparently satisfied that she was okay, he went back to sleep.

Cutter shook his head. "Hear what?"

"Exactly," January said. "The storm's blowing down. What time is it?"

"No idea," Cutter said. "You're sleeping on my watch."

"Sorry 'bout that." She leaned forward against the table enough for him to slip his arm out from behind her.

He groaned as the blood rushed back in, and then checked the time. "It is . . . not quite two in the morning," he said.

"No wonder I have to pee," she said. "That was awesome soup but it went right through me. It's probably what woke me up."

"Good thing it did," Cutter said. "Much longer and I would have come down with a bad case of Saturday night palsy."

She gave him a quizzical stare.

"You know," he said. "Where a guy falls asleep with a girl on his shoulder after a night of carousing and wakes up the next morning unable to move his arm."

"That's a thing?"

Cutter shook his dangling arm. "I'm thinking yes," he said, standing so she could get out of the dinette.

January slid out, carefully laying Cassandra down on the cushioned bench, before disappearing into the head compartment. Cutter heard the sounds one pretends not to hear in the close confines and thin walls of a boat. She stepped out a few moments later, looking much less frantic.

"Kind of amazing," she said, taking a seat at the navigation table across from him. She covered a yawn with an open hand. "A man bottling up so much anger would care about how moving his arm might wake me up."

"You think?"

January sighed. "Am I wrong?"

Cutter gave a slow nod. "Oh, I have plenty of anger," he said. "I'm just not particularly good at bottling it up."

"You were born with a temper?"

Cutter sighed, thinking, then pushing the thoughts out of his mind. "No," he said. "But I earned it, fair and square."

CHAPTER 43

Carmen Delgado lifted her head with a start, drawing in a quick breath as if she'd just surfaced from the depths of the sea. She was amazed that she'd slept at all, but the constant surge of adrenaline and the sickening ache from Luis's beating had eventually caused her body to shut down.

The rolling motion of the boat brought her instantly back to where she was.

Terror flooded her senses when she saw Garza seated across the table, eyeing her as if she were an animal in a zoo. His hair was wet and freshly combed and he wore a pressed cotton shirt. She felt sick thinking that she'd been so vulnerable and exposed, surrounded by these awful men while she slept.

"Ah," Garza said. "You are back among the living."

Carmen rubbed her neck, managing a painful nod.

It was still dark outside, but a gray horizon told her the sun would be up before too long. Luis stood in the galley, making French toast. It was almost laughable, this man who had murdered her friend, dipping pieces of bread into egg and milk.

Fausto stooped over two steel scuba tanks, affixing the regulators while he periodically checked a scuba-diving handbook.

Chago slouched in a seat beside the door, big arms folded, head against his chest. His eyes were open, but his chest rose and fell rhythmically, as if he were sleeping.

Luis threw a glance over his shoulder at Fausto. "Make sure you get those hooked up correctly," he said in Spanish. "I don't have gills, you know."

"I know how to do it," Fausto said. He turned the knob on one of the tanks. There was a hiss as the line filled with air. He checked the gauge, then depressed the front of the regulator, getting another hollow hiss. He nodded to himself and closed the book, satisfied he'd attached everything up correctly. "It's just been a while."

Luis lifted a piece of bread. "Hey, is it okay to eat and then dive?"

A glare from Garza and both men returned to their respective tasks in silence.

Garza looked back down at his phone.

Carmen studied him, wondering if there was any way out of this. On the street, she might have thought him just another man with a good haircut and nice clothes. He was a human being, just like her. He ate French toast, just like she did. There had to be some shred of reason inside him. She had a fleeting thought that she might offer him her body. She was pretty enough, and the only woman on the boat, which should count for something—but he'd shot his last mistress for no other reason but to make a point. Maybe, Carmen thought, maybe she could join him. Just say something like, "I've made a big mistake in pursuing this law-abiding life. May I please become a member of your drug cartel?"

The mind played terrible jokes when stressed past the breaking point. Carmen knew she only had one bargaining chip—the second media card. How to use it, that was something she'd yet to figure out.

The engine turned over and a few moments later she heard the clatter of anchor chain being drawn in across the bow roller. Carmen looked behind her to find Fausto back at the wheel. They were moving again. Toward what, she could only imagine.

Garza stood, and for a moment she thought he was going to go forward and talk to Fausto. Instead, he moved to her side of the dinette.

"May I?" he said, nodding to the bench seat.

She scooted toward the wall and he sat down next to her, his shoulder touching hers. For an instant she thought she might vomit, but swallowed it back and forced a smile.

Garza produced a fat cigar from the pocket of his shirt. He fished a lighter and a stainless steel cutter from his pocket. Passing the cigar under his nose, he took a long whiff, admiring the aroma before inserting the end into the circular hole in the cutter.

Finished, he clicked the blade open and shut several times. "I had a woman once," he said, his eyes half closed. "She had the most exquisite hips, and breasts . . . don't even get me started about those." He looked up. "Luis, do you remember Josephina?"

"Oh, yeah, Patrón," Luis chuckled. "Whooeee! Josephina was amazing."

Garza returned his gaze to Carmen. "She was amazing," he agreed. "In so many wondrous ways it would not be polite to mention. But the most amazing thing about her was her teeth. I have never in my life seen such straight and evenly aligned teeth. You see, Josephina could clip the end off my cigar as perfectly as this blade with a single bite." He set the razor-sharp tool on the table—as if he wasn't finished with it yet—and flicked the lighter, puffing the cigar to glowing life.

Garza continued to reminisce amid the cloud of noxious smoke that enveloped Carmen's face. She coughed, then held her sleeve to her nose, but he didn't seem to care. "Poor, poor Josephina," he continued. "My wife, Maria, she is a very open-minded woman, but she does require that my mistresses remain discreet. It is much more difficult for her if she knows who they are.

Josephina was unfortunate in that my wife happened upon us one evening while we were out dancing. Maria insisted that I have her killed."

"But . . ." Carmen heard herself say. "How could—?"

"Oh, I did not kill Josephina," Garza said. He paused, letting her think on that. "Luis volunteered to do it for me, but I had Chago do it. I knew he would be more gentle."

Carmen wanted to scream in his face but managed to speak in a controlled voice. "Gentle? It doesn't matter how gentle Chago was, he still murdered her. It wasn't her fault your wife saw her."

Garza seemed to consider this for a moment, eyes half closed. He smiled when he opened them. "Fault?" he said. "But, my dear, fault has nothing to do with it."

Striking like a snake, he grabbed Carmen's left wrist and yanked it to him. Luis had moved up from behind the dinette as if on cue and secured her right arm. The low table kept her legs pinned in place.

Garza puffed the cigar until the coal glowed bright orange, and then pressed it to the tender white skin inside her forearm. Carmen shrieked as the ember bored into her flesh, shredding her voice until nothing came out but a horrible, breathless croaking sound. She struggled to no avail. Garza held the cigar in place as if he intended to burn a hole straight through her arm. Eventually, her blood and charred skin starved the fire of oxygen, but the pain remained, nearly unbearable.

The monsters finally released her and she shrank back to the wall sobbing and clutching her injured arm. Luis returned without a word to the galley and his French toast.

Across the salon, Chago stared at the floor.

Garza put the flame of his lighter to the cigar and puffed it to life again. "Hurry up, Fausto!" he barked. "Luis is growing impatient."

Carmen breathed a sigh of relief when Garza moved back to the other side of the table.

"I imagine that such a burn is very painful," he said.

Her chest quivered with exhausted sobs.

"That is good," he said. "You see, my dear, I wish only to give you a taste—so you may see my mind. While you have been thinking that we were merely negotiating, I was imagining ways I might hurt you enough that you might have a bright understanding of what is before you. It is a skill at which I am extremely talented. My previous employer—whom I shot in the head not so very long ago—was even better at it than I, but I'm certain you will find my skills more than sufficient. We will find the body of your friend. Perhaps the storm has washed him onto the shore. If we are not so fortunate, then Fausto and Luis will dive down and retrieve the media card from his clothing."

He leaned across the table, blowing a plume of cigar smoke in her face again. "At that point, you must tell me where the second card is located."

Carmen swallowed hard. "I . . . you have to understand. . . ."

"Oh, no," he said. "That is your job. Luis has already asked me if he can help me make you understand. And though such a thing would be enjoyable for Luis, I assure you, it would be extremely unfortunate for you."

"Please . . ."

Garza raised his hand. "I told Luis that my decision all depends on you. Chago saved you before, but that will never happen again. This time, Luis will do with you what he wishes—I will give him fifteen minutes." Garza's eyes darkened and he leaned forward, the cigar between his teeth as he spoke. "When he is finished, he will take you to the shore and fill your belly with stones, just as he did your friend. I do not believe it will take very many stones before you tell me what I want to know."

Carmen gagged. There was a time such threats would have been unimaginable—but she didn't have to imagine now—she'd seen it.

Garza held the cigar out to the side, between his thumb and forefinger, giving her a lascivious up and down stare. "Or, you could cooperate and be done with—"

The satellite phone on the table gave a pulsing

ring. Garza held up his hand as if to say he would come back to the conversation in a moment, then answered the phone, situating the antenna toward the side window.

"Hello, Maria, my love," he said. "No, everything is fine. There was some nasty business with Ernesto. I'll tell you all about it when I return home. Yes . . . Very soon."

He chatted amiably for a few more minutes, asking how his daughter was doing in school and checking on some work they'd had done on their house. Carmen sat across from him, dumbfounded that he could transition so smoothly from talk of gutting her to a conversation about his daughter's homework.

Garza ended the call with a kiss, folded the antenna, and then pushed the satellite phone to the side of the table. He clapped his hands to get Fausto's attention. "How much longer?"

The *sicario* looked at the GPS beside the wheel. "Less than ninety minutes, Patrón."

"Excellent," he said, turning his attention back to Carmen. "Now, where were we . . . ? Oh, yes, your time with Luis . . ."

Carmen's mouth hung open. Her words came in rapid, breathy sobs. "How can you do this? I . . . I am someone's daughter . . . someone's sister . . ."

Manuel Garza gave a little shrug as if it all made perfect sense. "But you are not my sister or my daughter. You are only in my way."

CHAPTER 44

The dinette would have made a passably comfortable bed for someone younger than forty-two and shorter than six foot three. The cry of a seagull woke Cutter from a fitful sleep and he rose up on one elbow to peer out the window at the cool stillness of a poststorm dawn. *Tide Dancer* lay motionless on a bay of mirrored quicksilver. Clouds of fog hung among the trees along the shoreline, in a forest so thick and green it was almost black. As if on cue, a bald eagle flew overhead, chattering in a high-pitched call unique to the majestic bird.

January stuck her head up from the companionway. She wore a loose pink T-shirt and black pajama pants covered with big, red Mick Jagger lips.

"Sleep well?"

"I did," Cutter lied.

She flashed him a serene smile. "Me neither."

"You want me to put your camera back on the mount?" Cutter asked. "A short dive would be nice. I think it would help me to move around some."

"That would be most cool of you," January said. "You get the gear ready and I'll cook breakfast. I have bacon and eggs if you're hungry enough.

Though I have to say, I'm a little intimidated to cook around a marshal who keeps a recipe for cheeseburger soup in his notebook."

Cutter sat up straighter and patted his belly. It wasn't fat. Multiple divorces had proven to be an excellent diet plan. Still, it wasn't as flat as it had once been. "I'm obviously not one to push away from bacon," he said.

Havoc sat back on his haunches and licked his lips as if he felt the same way.

Forty-five minutes later, with considerable help from Cassandra, they'd eaten all the bacon and cleaned the last of the dishes. The Haida girl resumed her spot at the nav table and went back to work on her drawing. She seemed happy to be around the adults, but just as happy to ignore them.

The larger of the two neoprene dry suits was just as old and faded as the smaller one, but the zipper proved to be much more reliable. The pressure gauge on the steel tank showed it was full at 2,500 psi. The hoses and buoyancy control vest were older but serviceable, and the US Divers second-stage regulator looked to be in good repair. Cutter was pleased to find a pair of extra-large black jet fins, the same type he'd worn since Grumpy had taught him and Ethan to dive. They were heavy things and hadn't changed from when the Navy SEALs were wearing them in the seventies, but their hard rubber design allowed a variety of flutters and frog kicks that law enforcement and cave divers used because they didn't silt up the environment. Split fins just couldn't compete.

Cutter left the girls inside and went out to the aft deck to step out of his jeans and button-down shirt. His underwear and T-shirt would be plenty to keep him warm under the thick neoprene. Away from the smells of old boat and bacon, Cutter enjoyed the crisp morning air while he shrugged into the cumbersome suit. Unlike the DUI laminate, the neoprene suit had integral boots that were oversized so they'd fit most everyone who could get inside an extra-large suit—which was good, because Cutter had feet to go along with his height. Even the extra-large proved to be slightly short in the torso, threatening to have him talk an octave higher if he stood up straight.

Cutter stood on the edge of the swim step at the aft rail and watched a jellyfish the same shape and color as a fried egg undulate past the boat. He lifted the BC and scuba tank onto his back and buckled the straps between his legs and across his chest. He pressed the inflator button a couple of times to put a layer of air between him and the pinchy neoprene. Slipping the neoprene wet-suit hood over his head, he continued his predive routine, checking to make sure his weight belt was secure, and a small knife, used for cutting line instead of any commando tactics, was situated to the right of the quick-release buckle.

For January, diving was a means to an end, so she lacked some of the items he would have liked to have—like extra O-rings and a second dive light. Having just one of any piece of crucial gear was an invitation to a ruined dive. Cutter consoled himself that this swim would be short-lived. He was only going under the boat.

He liked to carry his gear in the same location each time he dove—or ran, or sailed, or shot, or fought, or rode a motorcycle, because those inevitable "oh, shit" moments were no time to be scratching your head trying to remember where you put something. He and Grumpy and Ethan had practiced the DIR "unified team" concept where every diver carried identical equipment, including lights, spare masks, and surface marker buoys, in identical places on their person—so a quick glance confirmed your dive-buddy was squared away and in compliance with rule six—looking streamlined.

January and Cassandra both came out to watch. Cutter hung Grumpy's compass rose medallion around Cassandra's neck. She'd seemed overly concerned at the notion of him going diving and he thought a good luck charm might calm her some. He was far from an expert on child psychology, but it worked on his nephews so he gave it a shot. "How about you hang on to this while I'm underwater," he said. "I don't want to lose it down there."

Overheating quickly, even in the cool of the morning, he wanted to get into water pronto. It seemed irreverent to jump in and mar the smooth surface, so he slipped in almost noiselessly from the swim step, waiting to put on the jet fins once he was in the water.

At the step, Cutter wiped the salt water out of his eyes and swished his mask around in front of him. Cassandra peered over the rail, arms crossed, frowning.

"What's eating her?"

"This is unnatural," January said. "In her mind, you're venturing into the realm of Frog, and Kushtaka, and a dozen other strange beings that do not always have the best of intentions toward man. And don't forget, I nearly contorted myself to death when my suit came open a couple of days ago. This ain't Florida, my friend. That water's a heartless bitch—around forty-eight degrees—which means you got about five millimeters of neoprene standing between you and a quick case of hypothermia. Ten minutes of exposure in this and you'd be hard-pressed to climb back up the steps."

Cutter slipped the mask over his head and adjusted it up under his nose. "I'll be fine." He took the video camera and housing and clipped it to a lanyard on his buoyancy control vest. The

381

storm had made the water more murky than usual and he didn't want to risk dropping it and having to conduct a search at seventy feet.

"And the murder weapon," January said, leaning down so Cassandra couldn't hear as she handed him the multifaceted wrench.

Cutter took the tool and affixed the idiot cord to the D-ring opposite the camera. "Speaking of that," he said, looking at his watch. "I forgot to tell you. I think I might have figured out who killed Millie Burkett."

January patted the rail impatiently.

"Who?"

"Tell you when I get back," he said, looking at his watch. "See you in fifteen."

"You bastard!" January whispered to Cutter's fins as they pushed him beneath the surface.

Cutter cleared his ears the moment his head was underwater, hearing the telltale squeal as the pressure equalized on either side of his eardrum. Diving was a familiar activity to him, almost as familiar as driving a car, and he fell quickly into the rhythm of a relaxed kick-cycle. The regulator in his mouth gave an audible click with each breath, accompanied by the burble of silver bubbles that trailed along either side of his face.

Tide Dancer had a displacement hull and sat low in the water, drawing nearly seven feet to the bottom of her deep V. January took care of her vessel but there was still enough new barnacle growth to keep Cutter swimming well away from the boat, fearful of compromising his dry suit on the tooth-like crustaceans. Caribbean pirates, and even the British navy, had keelhauled misbehaving sailors by dragging them under ships with long ropes. An unlucky sailor might be cut in half if dragged lengthwise along the keel. Cutter shuddered at the thought, and kicked deeper. He wanted to get a good look at the bottom of the boat and feel for the currents before he ventured too close.

Playing his small light in front of him in the murky water, he kicked his way down to a depth of thirty feet. Mean mug or not, he couldn't help but smile when he looked up and saw *Tide Dancer* and her accompanying skiff tied off to a stern cleat. There was something about the sight of a big boat looming overhead as if floating in midair that made him feel as though he was really diving. It was a perspective few people got to witness, and a reminder that there was a whole other world up at the surface.

Tide Dancer floated directly over a slack anchor line, which disappeared into the blackness below Cutter. There was no current to speak of, so that was good. Cutter kicked upward slowly, venting air from the BC and the suit to slow his ascent as he came up directly under the boat. There was enough light to make out the metal bracket that was affixed to the keel, the bolts of which fit into the corresponding holes in the camera housing that was now attached to his vest.

Turned on and off via an RF transmitter, the camera was fixed with the lens pointed forward so all January had to do was point the boat in the direction she wanted to film. It was a simple but effective setup, and she was out enough to get hours of footage.

Cutter wore no gloves and the cold water made threading the large nuts a little awkward, but the homemade wrench he'd suspected to be the murder weapon worked perfectly. He mulled over his theory on Millie Burkett's murder while he snugged down the camera housing. If he was right, then that still didn't explain who abducted the *FISHWIVES!* crew and why. There had to be another bad actor on the island.

The hum of an approaching boat motor drew his attention back to the present. He tightened down the last nut and vented more air from his vest, allowing him to sink a few feet so he had a better view.

It was a larger vessel, not the faster aluminum Alaska State Troopers boat he'd seen in the harbor, but another displacement hull, like a popular cruising tug. It also towed a small skiff.

Two boats sharing an anchorage was not uncommon at all, especially one as picturesque as Kaguk Cove, but this new vessel came right up on *Tide Dancer*'s starboard side, bumping her with enough force that Cutter heard fiberglass grind twenty feet below the surface. There was a plunking splash and the rattle of chain playing out over the bow roller. Cutter turned to watch a large Bruce anchor fall past, disappearing into the shadows below.

No one with good seamanship or decent intentions would anchor this close to another vessel.

Cutter surfaced quietly, careful to exhale as he rose, venting air from his expanding lungs and rising no more quickly than his bubbles. Many a diver had discovered how fragile the thin layers of lung tissue were by ascending too quickly while holding their breath. Injury to the lungs could happen in just a few feet of water. An uncontrolled ascent from deep water was almost certain to cause a ruptured lung. The bends, caused by expanding nitrogen bubbles in the blood, was an added worry.

Cutter broke the surface with little more than a ripple, keeping *Tide Dancer* between him and the new boat. He was greeted by the sound of Havoc's frenzied barks. Gruff male voices carried down from above, mingling with January's curses and the sound of someone crying.

Lapping wave action and the squeak of rubber boat fenders made it almost impossible to hear the specifics of the conversation, but he got the gist of it. These men were looking for something, and whatever it was, they were fully prepared to kill for it.

"January," the crying voice said. "I am so sorry."

"Well, Carmen Delgado," Cutter heard January say.

Carmen. She was one of the missing television crew.

The men began to laugh—Cutter counted at least three male voices, maybe four.

"We have plenty of guns, little girl," a derisive voice said in a Hispanic accent. "We need no more."

Cutter watched as Cassandra's small hand extended over the rail—holding his grandfather's Colt Python. She held it there for a long moment, and then let it splash into the sea a full twenty feet away from where Cutter floated in the shadow of the *Tide Dancer*'s hull.

Looking toward the shore, Cutter took a couple of quick references and tried to triangulate so, hopefully, he'd be able to find Grumpy's gun again. The Colt would have come in handy about now, and Cassandra's plan to drop the gun to him would have been a good one if he'd been at the right spot to catch it. The conversation topside was heating up quickly, and there was no time to go looking for it now. Cassandra had a plan, albeit a foolish one, but at least she'd done something rather than hide in the corner. Now Cutter needed a plan, and whatever it was, judging by the bloody threats being hurled around above, he needed to do it quickly.

CHAPTER 45

Two minutes earlier

January looked out the open back door of *Tide Dancer*'s cabin, a fresh cup of coffee in her hand.

"Son of a bitch," she muttered, eyes locked on the oncoming vessel. "What is this? Damn the torpedoes, full speed ahead?"

The new boat barreled in fast, chugging into Kaguk Cove like it owned the place. It was some kind of tug—Nordic or American—January couldn't tell in the low sun. She guessed it to be a fifty footer, well-appointed with a satellite dish on top of a raised pilothouse nearly as big as her entire cabin. It looked like it had a couple of staterooms, probably Corian counters, and even a washer and dryer. A boat like that was easily three-quarters of a million dollars, maybe more.

Cassandra was glued to her side, gripping the hem of her sweatshirt, giving it little concerned yanks as if January was somehow capable of stopping the oncoming craft.

Havoc scampered out and hopped up on the lazarette, barking at the intruder.

Fifty meters away, the big tug still hadn't slowed. January took her coffee outside and tried to wave them off. Two dark-haired men stood on the foredeck. One, a smiling guy with slicked black hair, waved back as if she were just saying hello instead of trying to keep them from running over her.

Finally, with just meters to go, the water behind the larger boat began to burble and froth. The guy at the wheel had reversed the prop. The boat decelerated quickly, veering as it did, to come up directly alongside.

"What the hell?" January said. She started to warn them there was a diver in the water, but saw both men wore pistols, and thought better of it. Cutter was smart enough to keep his head down when he heard the thrum of a diesel.

The larger of the two men held a line, ready to throw it across the rail. He kept his head down, a gloomy expression on his face.

January cupped a hand next to her mouth, shouting over the chugging diesel and frothing water. She addressed the guy with slick hair, who was obviously the leader—praying Cutter was somewhere down there hiding and listening. "Am I late on the boat payment or something?"

The slick guy laughed, flicking a hand over his shoulder as he did so. "You Americans," he said. "Always making jokes at the worst times."

A small man wearing a black dry suit exited the side door of the cabin and shoved Carmen Delgado out in front of him. It was startling to see her, and not just because she'd been abducted. The poor thing looked like she'd been dragged behind a train. Her face was a mass of bruises. Her hands swollen and red. She wasn't bound, but ligature marks around her wrists said she obviously had been. There was no need to tie her now. She could hardly stand up.

"January, I am so sorry," the other woman said, trying unsuccessfully to choke back a sob.

With the boat coming up alongside, the two women were less than twenty feet apart and getting closer fast.

"Carmen Delgado!" January yelled, knowing that in a few moments, anything other than a normal volume would seem like she was trying to warn someone—which is exactly what she hoped to do. It was only then that she noticed two sets of scuba gear set up on the other boat's deck, next to the transom. There was something off about them, something she couldn't quite place. She glanced at Delgado, who had tears streaming down her face. "Did these guys hurt you?"

The bow wake from the bigger boat shoved *Tide Dancer* to one side, like a cue ball hitting another billiard ball. Both boats rocked for a moment, then settled again on the calm water.

"Do not concern yourself with her," the slick guy said, drawing the pistol from his belt. "Tell your friend to come back outside."

January looked down to find Cassandra had gone back in the cabin. "Good girl," she whispered.

Her relief was short-lived. The men laughed when Cassandra came out a moment later, carrying Cutter's stainless steel revolver by the barrel. They obviously saw her as no real threat by the way she held the weapon, but trained their own pistols on her in any case.

"We have plenty of guns, little girl," the smallest man jeered. "We need no more."

Cassandra walked to the far rail, away from the tug, and peered over the side. January heard the revolver plunk as it hit the water. She wondered if Cutter had even seen it.

The big, sad one threw his line across the rail and January caught it, wrapping it loosely around a cleat. There was nothing else she could do. They had guns.

Another Hispanic man, this one older and also wearing a dry suit, came out from the wheelhouse and walked behind his boss to the bow pulpit. He pulled a pin on the roller, and then stepped on a deck control to let the anchor deploy. A good thirty feet of chain rattled off followed by the zip of the quieter nylon line behind it.

An excellent judge of character, Havoc stood on the bench over the lazarette, barking ferociously. January had to hiss at him to keep him from hopping over the rail to the other boat. The small man lifted his pistol to shoot him, but the slick one touched his arm.

"Not the little dog," Slick said. "We are not

savages." He turned to a trembling Carmen Delgado. "So, you know these people?"

She nodded, her eyes stricken when they met January's—apologizing again.

"Too bad," Slick said. "But it does give me another opportunity to demonstrate my resolve." This time it was Slick who raised his pistol—directly at Cassandra.

What sort of man was this? What could he want? January's words came all at once, trying to get the man's attention before he shot the child.

"Your dive gear is all wrong!"

Slick paused but kept his pistol aimed.

"What?"

Cassandra stood frozen.

January raised both hands, hoping to make herself more of a target than Cassandra. She nodded to the scuba tanks on the other deck. *"Air toward your hair,"* she said.

All the men looked back at the dive tanks. The older diver shook his head, then nodded as if something was finally dawning on him.

Slick frowned, cocking his head to one side. "What does this mean, 'air to the hair'?"

"Your hoses," January said. "They're hooked up backward. If your guys go down that way they'll have a big knob poking them in the back of their heads. Might even knock themselves out when they jump in the water." January doubted that was true, but it sounded good.

"You are a diver?" Slick asked.

"I am," January said. She kept her hands raised, but tipped her head toward the water. "I'm assuming there's something down there you guys need. Something you want bad enough to risk the lives of men who don't know squat about diving. What is it? Sunken treasure?"

Slick still hadn't lowered his gun. "In a manner of speaking."

"Look," January said, her voice cracking a little. She hadn't intended for it to, but it was a nice touch, and the fact that she was frightened appeared to put these bastards at ease. "You're right. I do know how to dive. I have my own gear inside. I'll help you retrieve whatever you want, just promise me you won't hurt the girl."

"Again with the bargaining," Slick said. "You Americans always think you have something to trade."

The sad-looking one leaned down, whispered something in Slick's ear.

January upped the ante. "You don't have to bother about Cassandra talking about you to anyone. She's unable to speak. To tell you the truth, she's a little handicapped—you know, not right in the head—so you don't have to worry about her."

"Oh, my dear," Slick said. "I am not worried."

The little mean one moved closer, also whispering to his boss, but he looked up and leered at Cassandra while he did. The twisted grin on his face made January shudder.

Slick finally lowered his pistol. "Very well," he said. "The girl—Cassandra, you said—she will be my guest aboard *Pilar*. You assist my men in their dive. If anything happens to them while you are below, or if you swim away and try to save yourself, please know that I will personally make the last few moments of this young one's life worse than anything you could possibly imagine."

Cassandra stood completely still. She must have been terrified, but to her credit, gave the men a wacky smile, as if to confirm January's assessment of her mental abilities.

"I won't try anything," January said. "What about after? Once you've gotten what you want?"

"I will put the girl ashore," Slick said. "I give you my word."

On the deck of the other vessel, Carmen Delgado came unhinged.

"Your word!" Eyes wild, she hissed like a cornered cat. "You lying piece of shit! Your word is nothing. Don't trust him, January. I watched him shoot his own girlfriend, then throw her in the ocean like she was garbage." She held up her arm, which was blistered and blackened with an angry burn. Chest heaving, shoulders wracked with sobs, she began to break down, even as she spoke. "He did this to me to make sure I know how cruel he is. You gotta understand . . . these people . . . they thrive on blood. I . . . I've never seen anything like it. . . ."

Slick merely sighed, then raised his pistol once again toward Cassandra.

"January . . . What an interesting name." He gave a little shrug. "Dive or do not dive. It is up to you."

January slowly raised her hands. She nodded to Slick, not wanting to antagonize or startle him since he was aimed in on Cassandra. "Of course I'll dive. It was my idea."

January shot a furtive glance at Carmen, wishing she could say something to give the poor woman even the small glimmer of hope she had. Cutter was down there, hopefully listening and coming up with some kind of plan. January had a plan of her own, but it was probably doomed to fail. He was the deputy marshal, the expert at dealing with desperadoes. Surely a guy like him went up against scuba-diving pirates every other day.

She helped Cassandra across the rail, feeling the little girl tremble in her hands. "Be brave," she whispered. Cassandra nodded, but of course, she said nothing.

Slick seemed to relax measurably when Cassandra was in his custody. And once their leader relaxed, so did the men, except for the older one who appeared flustered as he went about turning the regulators around on the two dive setups.

Slick flicked the barrel of his pistol toward *Tide Dancer*'s cabin. "Hurry and change," he said.

"None of this matters," Carmen sniffed, regaining a semblance of composure. "Don't you understand? We'll all be dead in fifteen minutes."

January kept her hands raised as she went inside, unescorted since they had Cassandra as a hostage. Maybe her plan could work after all.

A lot could happen in fifteen minutes.

CHAPTER 46

Lola Fontaine stood on top of a spruce stump as big around as her dining room table. Hundreds of identical stumps, remnants of a clear-cutting timber operation from years before, stuck up through thick underbrush on the steep incline above the road. It was no wonder there were so many deer on the island.

Less than a hundred feet from the stump forest, a yellow backhoe grumped and growled as it labored over the mountain of mud and sticks that had cut off her boss from the rest of the world—at least by road. Fontaine figured Cutter didn't really mind, since he had a warm boat to sleep on and, if his reputation as a ladies' man was to be believed, a little something extra to pass the stormy night.

The rattle and squeal of the backhoe seemed sacrilegious in the quiet wilderness. The machine was able to move massive quantities of dirt and debris, but the ground was already saturated from the melting winter snow, rendering it a slow and tedious process. Every bucketful the backhoe moved allowed space for more mud and shredded roots to slide down the fragile mountainside. Sam said they'd probably be able to squeeze by in a half hour or so. Which was good, because Fontaine was pretty certain Cutter would need a

Jiminy Cricket by now—and she couldn't do that if she was cut off from him by heaps of mud.

The trooper stood behind his Tahoe, talking to his sergeant who couldn't seem to get it through his thick head that they had done a bang-up job with little or no assistance from the brass of any agency. Gerald Burkett was drying out, and hadn't been allowed to destroy his life by killing the piece of shit, Kenny Douglas, who had been screwing around with his little girl—and probably murdered her. Douglas was also in jail. As was Hayden Starnes.

The trooper folded the antenna on his satellite phone and walked down the gravel road to the backhoe. The operator took off his hearing protection and the two men spoke briefly.

"Looks like another twenty minutes," Benjamin said, climbing up the hill to the base of Fontaine's stump. "I tried to call January's boat on the marine radio, but I'm not getting through. Hope your hotheaded boss is okay."

Fontaine motioned for the trooper to climb up with a flick of her wrist. Rolling green mountains, pockets of fog, and even a sliver of the ocean lay below her. The view was too good not to share.

"Don't worry about Cutter," she said. "I'm sure he's having the time of his life."

Cutter floated on the opposite side of *Tide Dancer* from the new vessel, his mouth just above the surface of the water. He'd slipped below for a quick moment and held his breath while he peeled off the neoprene hood so he could better hear what was going on topside. So far, at least, adrenaline kept him from noticing the cold.

January obviously had some kind of plan. He just couldn't picture one that didn't involve her ending up hypothermic—or worse. The zipper on her dry suit might hold up for a short time, if she was lucky. But the odds were, it was going to flood within moments after she hit the water.

Cutter took stock of his gear—which wasn't much. The tank had plenty of air left and he had a working dive light. The small, three-inch blade clipped to the belt of his BC was meant for cutting line. His grandfather had taught him there wouldn't be a need for any violent action underwater. *Wrong about that one, Grumpy,* he thought.

"Come outside to get dressed," a derisive male voice called out above. "I do not like to be where I cannot see what you are doing."

Cutter heard the cabin door open and January's shuffling footsteps on deck.

The same man spoke again. He had a pronounced Hispanic accent, but his English was flawless. "Do you need assistance, my dear? Certainly you do not mean to wear your clothing inside that thing."

"I do not," January said.

A derisive chuckle, and then the sound of jeans hitting the deck.

The men clapped and whistled, urging her to strip. He clenched his fists under the surface as their jeering suddenly stopped. One voice in particular, higher, and more nasal than the others, said, "Ai ai ai! Look at her. She is but half there, Patrón."

The boss's voice was quieter, but steeped in evil. "I have always wondered how such a woman would look in person."

"End of the free show, boys," January said, holding up well, considering what she was going through. Cutter wondered if he'd be so cavalier under the same circumstances.

He heard the sound of the faulty zipper as she drew it shut with a grunt. There were heavy footfalls as she trudged across the deck, no doubt lugging her scuba gear.

"What are we looking for?" she asked. "How big is it? Which part of the lagoon? Do you know how deep? On the bottom or floating in the water column?" She sounded all business as she worked on her preparations.

"This is the spot," the boss said. "Floating or on the bottom is yet to be determined. Is that correct, Luis?"

Luis nodded confidently but glanced over at the sad one, who shrugged slightly.

"My men will lead the way and retrieve what

needs to be retrieved. Your job is to make sure they come back alive." Slick rested his hand on Cassandra's shoulder as she and Carmen sat cowering, their arms around each other. It was hard to tell who was comforting whom.

"You do not put on your tank in the boat?" a new voice said—this one older, more sincere in his questions. "I have seen the Jacques Cousteau television programs. He jumps into the water backward, after donning his tank."

"That's one way," January said. "But I find it easier when I'm in the water."

There was a telltale hiss as she filled her BC with air. She dropped her rig in off the stern step, then slipped in after it.

"Remember, my dear," the one called "Patrón" said. "You know what I will do to this child, even if she does not."

The man with the nasal voice spoke next. It made Cutter's eye twitch, just listening to him speak.

"I'm watching you, bitch," the voice said, quivering a little at the prospect of the dive.

Cutter blew salt water from his lips, and listened as the men jumped off the new boat's swim platform. They winced and cursed as they hit the cold surface. Cutter put the regulator in his mouth and submerged slowly—allowing himself a rare smile, pleased that the man with the nasal voice was now with him in the water.

CHAPTER 47

Cutter leveled out ten feet down, arms relaxed at his sides as he hung motionless in the water column, parallel to the bottom. Above him and approximately twenty feet away, beyond *Tide Dancer*'s stern, three sets of legs dangled from the surface. The men were vulnerable now. They would probably both drown before they thought to get their regulators in if Cutter dragged them under. But that would leave the two other men on the surface with their prisoners.

The water was cloudy from the storm, but there was still a good thirty feet of visibility at the surface. January was easy to pick out in her faded, gray dry suit. She faced them, her legs fluttering serenely, belying her fear. She was, no doubt, briefing them on what was probably their first dry-suit dive—and likely giving Cutter time to come up with a workable plan that wouldn't get everyone killed.

The flutter kicks grew more intense, as if they were about to dive, so Cutter retreated toward *Tide Dancer*'s bow. He pushed thoughts of barnacles out of his mind and flattening himself against the hull. The boat would hide his bubbles from anyone above.

Cutter had allowed himself a short glimpse of

the one with the nasal voice. He was the smaller of the two and more tentative in the way he dove. Both January and the other man flutter-kicked their way down from the surface. The small man spun out of control, arms and legs outstretched like a starfish dropped off a pier.

Cutter submerged with them, but stayed back at first, drawing closer only when the depth gauge on his wrist indicated forty feet. Colors started to bleed away here, turning most everything gray and black. Thirty feet later, the smaller guy slammed into the bottom, throwing up a cloud of silt and further helping with Cutter's concealment. January arrested her descent, as did the larger of the two men. A few feet away, seated as if resting seventy feet below the surface, was the body of a man. His arms floated slightly in front of him, palms up as if explaining something to a crowd. Strands of long, ropy hair swayed like a kelp forest above his bowed head.

Shrimp and crab and other marine organisms had gone to work doing what they did best on any piece of flesh dropped into the ocean. Even from the shadowed distance, Cutter could tell the body was crawling with sea life.

The body was obviously the target of their search—and both men moved in immediately once they'd located it. January hung back, hovering expertly in the water column, hands folded in front of her chest as she used her fins and body position for control.

Cutter figured he had seconds rather than minutes before they located what they were after, and turned for the surface. The fact that they were side by side made it even more difficult.

It also dictated who he would attack first.

Peripheral vision is severely limited when wearing a scuba mask and Cutter intended to use that to his full advantage. He and his brother had often played a version of underwater hide-and-seek. Ethan was an expert at swimming up behind him and latching on to his tank unseen. The extra weight was hard to notice in the water and Ethan was often able to hitch a free ride, eventually turning off his younger brother's air as a joke. They never did it at depth, and though Grumpy frowned on the practice, it went a long way to teach both boys emergency out-of-air procedures.

The taller of the two divers had positioned himself slightly to the rear of Nasal Voice. Thick clouds of bubbles rose in a constant stream from both men. They were nervous and burning through a lot of air. Cutter drew the small knife from the front of his vest and moved slowly up behind the taller diver. Five feet away, he kicked toward the bottom, inserting the razor-sharp blade between the man's thighs and flicking it back and forth. He felt it drag across the dry suit, saw the blossom of blood in the water, and repeated the action again before the man even knew what was happening. The man finally gathered his wits enough to spin and face his attacker. When he did, Cutter drove upward with his fins, pushing his body directly at the other man's face and clawing away the mask. The only thing more frightening than being blind seventy feet below the surface is to be in the same predicament, bleeding and with no air. Cutter hooked his blade behind the man's air hose and upward. A hiss of bubbles erupted from the severed hose. Blood from the arteries in his legs blossomed up around him in a dark cloud. Cutter hit him with the puny knife three more times in the upper chest, prison-style, snapping the blade in the process. Panicked and weakening from loss of blood, the diver began to claw his way back to the surface.

The entire attack took less than four seconds— but that was plenty of time for Nasal Voice to wheel. And this one had thought to bring a much larger knife.

Better armed, but still terrified to find an unknown diver in the deep, Nasal Voice attempted to crawfish backward, scuttling away from danger. In doing so he ended up in Greg Conner's lap. Soapy arms wrapped around his chest, embracing him. Nasal Voice screamed into his mask, floundering now, and throwing up an underwater cyclone of silt and bits of Greg Conner.

Cutter was completely at home in the water,

but the big knife caused him to fade back. His hand swept for a pistol that wasn't there. Instead of attacking, the smaller diver held the blade in front of him and looked upward, bending his knees in preparation to spring toward the surface.

That could not happen.

Cutter shot forward now, feinting left, and then moving in to claw at the other man's mask. He missed, and narrowly avoided a gash to the torso. Breaking his momentum with his hands and the jet fins, Cutter swam in a wide arc, staying just out of reach of the slashing knife.

And then January kicked in from the shadows behind him.

Nasal Voice had either forgotten she was there, or he had severely underestimated January Cross. She clung to his back like a limpet mine. The cumbersome tank and buoyancy control vest made it impossible for him to reach her with his blade without stabbing himself or risking damage to his own equipment.

Cutter seized the opportunity, swimming in to rip Nasal Voice's mask off his face. He left the regulator in place for the moment, dodging another blind slash, before he pressed in close, reaching with both hands. His left hand flicked the quick-release buckle on the man's weight belt while his right pressed the valve on the chest of his dry suit, filling it with air.

The weight belt fell away instantly—just as it

was designed to do—and Nasal Voice rocketed toward the surface, eyes wide, gulping air. As a novice diver, he'd surely hold his breath, which was just what Cutter wanted him to do.

Above him, the taller diver rose quickly toward the light, air jetting from his severed hose. The men on the surface would know something was going on in a matter of seconds.

Cutter turned to find January kneeling on the ocean floor in a cloud of silt. Her arms were folded across the open front of her flooded dry suit. He raised a thumb signaling that they should surface, but she shook her head, shivering from the frigid water.

Beckoning him closer, she uncrossed her arms and reached inside the flooded suit. A wad of the flimsy plastic grocery bags that she'd used to stuff into the hollow opposite her surviving breast came out with her hand. Cutter caught a glimpse of the long horizontal scar inside the open zipper. He started to turn away but she grabbed his arm. Shaking her head, she held out her free hand. The flimsy bags drifted away in the tidal current to reveal the baby Glock pistol he'd left onboard the boat.

Exposing her scar while getting dressed had diverted the men's attention from the gun she had stuffed inside the breast of the suit. She pressed the Glock into his hand and then pointed toward the surface. He made a circle with his thumb and forefinger. She returned the signal, patting him on the arm with a shaking hand, as if to convince him she'd be fine. Arm in arm, they began their kick toward the surface. He made sure she was beside him, careful not to rise more quickly than their bubbles.

Thanks to January, he had a gun now. *Surprise, surprise,* he thought, and allowed himself a grim smile.

CHAPTER 48

Chago groaned at the sound of the first splash. Surely it was too soon for Luis and Fausto to be back. Things would get bloody now, and he was so very tired of all that. Perhaps it was only a whale swimming in the lagoon. He had no desire to take foolish risks going under the dark water, but he would not mind seeing a whale.

It took the big *sicario* a few seconds to realize what he was looking at—and it was no whale.

Fausto floated on his back like an oil slick, arms and legs outstretched. His mouth opened, but instead of words, he groaned the shuddering sounds peculiar to a dying man. Chago had heard these sounds before. The suit around his legs had been slashed, and blood pumped into the water. Something had gotten him. There was no way the woman could have done this. There were sharks in Alaska. Bean had said so when they'd arrived. Whatever it was, it had bitten completely through poor Fausto's air hose, which now spewed and sputtered in the water next to his face.

Garza pushed the young girl off his lap and jumped up from his deck chair at the noise, a fat cigar clenched between his teeth. Cassandra scrambled to get out of his way as he ran to the rail.

Garza made a low growling sound. Chago had

heard the noise before. The things that happened after were never pleasant.

"Miss Delgado!" Garza hissed. "What has happened to my man?"

Carmen took a tentative step, peering down at the water.

Luis rocketed to the surface before she could speak. His dry suit was full of air, swollen like a balloon ready to burst. Bubbles fizzed from the seals around his wrists. Bloody froth drooled from between clenched teeth.

Carmen's mouth fell open, her voice unsure. "You mean your *men*," she said.

Garza screamed, throwing the cigar in the water. "That bitch! Chago! Go and find her!"

"Patrón," Chago said. "I . . ."

Luis flailed toward the boat with the distended arms of his overinflated suit. He tried to speak but managed only a rasping croak.

Garza paced the rail, fuming over his dying men, but he made no move to assist them.

Chago could only stare. His grandmother had warned him that the devil lived under the sea. Looking at the film of blood on Luis's gnashing teeth, Chago was inclined to believe her. The man was surely in great agony, but had not he and Luis caused many people this same sort of agony? Murdering others side by side did not make them friends. Did it? Perhaps they were both destined to die in some terrible way.

"Chaaagoooo . . ." Luis gasped, hand out toward the boat. But Chago merely looked at Carmen and thought how much she reminded him of his sister, Lucia.

Carmen grabbed the child by the shoulder and shoved her toward the other boat.

"Go!" she whispered, before running toward *Pilar*'s bow.

"Shoot her!" Garza snapped, sweeping the muzzle of his own pistol back and forth as he scanned the surface. "I'll take care of the one in the water."

Chago drew his gun and looked to the fleeing woman.

"Carmen!" he shouted, his deep voice rolling along the deck. She stopped in her tracks, then turned. He waved toward the bank. "Run!" he said. "Take the girl in the skiff!"

Garza spun on the rail. "Chago, you gutless son of a whore!" He fired a shot at Carmen, but she'd already fled to the other side of the wheelhouse. Furious, he turned back on Chago.

The big *sicario* fired but the shot went wide, taking the top off a metal stanchion. Garza's first round caught him in the stomach. Initially, Chago wasn't certain he'd been hit. There was no pain, just a punch, like a blast of air against his belly. Gun still in his hand, the big man blinked, then looked down and saw the blood. Garza put his second round an inch or two higher. This one clipped Chago's spine, causing his legs to buckle. He fell hard, his pistol sliding across the deck and out a scupper to plop into the water.

"You think to save her?" Garza shook his head in disgust. He stepped on Chago's outstretched hand with his heel, grinding down on curled fingers, spitting in the man's face. "*Pendejo*! She has nowhere to run. You will only die with her."

Chago swallowed, images of his sister flashing through the pain that now flooded his brain. "Lucia . . ." he whispered.

Garza stood above him, pistol pointed at his face. "What?"

"The devil . . . is in the water, Patrón." Chago chuckled, tasting blood, coughing. He was so thirsty. "The devil, he has taken Fausto and Luis . . . and now he comes for you. . . ."

Garza fired again, but Chago did not feel it. He had stopped feeling many years before.

Garza turned with his pistol still raised, intent on killing again. The child stood at the rail, reaching across for Delgado. They were mere feet away from him and must have thought to sneak off the boat while he was dealing with the traitor. Both women froze, staring wide-eyed, and completely exposed. Fools! Somehow he had surrounded himself with idiots.

Carmen swung a leg over the rail of the other boat, assisted by the child, who was apparently too dense to realize Garza was about to scatter her brains on the deck. He would not even have to aim. It suddenly occurred to him that with his men all dead, he was quite alone. A hostage might come in handy, and a hostage with slow wits would prove much easier to handle.

Carmen was almost over the rail now, but Cassandra stood by to steady her. Garza leaned over and grabbed a handful of the child's hair, hauling her back aboard *Pilar*. A guttural, wordless cry escaped her throat. He struck her hard in the side of the head with his pistol, sending her sliding against the cabin wall.

Carmen screamed from the deck of the other vessel, cursing at him to stop, yelling at the girl to run, to jump in the water, anything to get away.

Garza laughed maniacally, and then aimed his pistol at the spitting woman.

"You leave her alone!" Carmen screamed, red-faced, apoplectic. She was actually foolish enough to try to climb back aboard *Pilar*. "If you hurt her, you'll never get the other disc!"

"We are beyond missing discs," Garza said. He lowered the pistol so it pointed at the knee that hung over the rail.

And then he heard a female voice from the water.

"Hey! Asshole! Over here!"

Garza spun at the sound, then went to grab a dazed but squirming Cassandra by the arm. He

413

shook her hard, barking at her to stop wiggling. He forgot Carmen Delgado. There was nowhere for her to go anyway.

He leaned over the rail to find the woman who had somehow killed both Fausto and Luis floating off the stern of the other boat. Only her face was above water, framed by the dark neoprene hood. It was now a deep blue purple, as if she were in the process of being strangled. Her teeth chattered uncontrollably.

Garza's face pulled back into a sneering grin. He raised the pistol and started to speak, but a new sound cut him off.

There were no words, more of a threatening growl, deep and angry—and very sure of itself.

Bullets slapped the side of *Pilar*'s cabin, forcing Garza to duck before he could get a shot off himself. He dragged the girl down with him, firing blindly over the rail. He cast off the two lines that connected to the two boats, then, bent at the waist, pulled the girl with him toward the pilothouse. He put another quick round over the side to keep his attacker's head down. He'd been in gunfights before, and though he hired men to kill for him now, he had plenty of experience doing it himself.

He started the engine and threw the *Pilar* into reverse. She shuddered, straining against the anchor, but did not move. He pounded the wheel.

"Idiot!"

There was movement on the other boat. Carmen Delgado was there now, looking over her shoulder as she reached down for the other woman. She spoke with someone else, someone he couldn't see—the man who had shot at him. But where had he come from?

He tapped his forehead with the back of his pistol, racking his brain for what to do next. It would take too long to bring up the anchor. Garza held the child up in front of him like a shield and peered through the wheelhouse window. Carmen was helping the woman on the boat now, assisted by the unseen man who was still in the water. Chago had urged Carmen to take the girl and flee in the skiff. Perhaps the traitor had been right after all.

Staying low, Garza dragged the girl out the starboard wheelhouse door, away from the other boat and the man with the gun. The girl gathered herself up to squeal, but he cuffed her hard with the back of his hand, dazing her, but not quite knocking her out. *Pilar*'s twelve-foot aluminum skiff was tied off the stern rail, completely blocked from view by the raised pilothouse of the big Nordic Tug. Garza shoved the girl in. She landed on her face, further dazing her, and keeping her relatively quiet while Garza jumped in beside her. He cast off the bow line and took up a seat at the rear, squeezing the bulb in the gas line a couple of times before giving the starter rope a stout tug. The motor coughed to life immediately. He wheeled the little craft in a tight arc, using *Pilar*'s hull as cover. The roar of the twenty-four-horse Honda engine growled across the still water, shattering the quiet of the glass-calm cove and covering the sound of Cassandra Brown's whimpering cries.

CHAPTER 49

Cutter had one hand on January's butt, pushing her out of the water, while he used the other hand to cover the other boat with his Glock. Carmen Delgado lay on *Tide Dancer*, her belly flat against the deck and her outstretched hands clinging to January.

Cutter looked up at Delgado. "How many bad guys onboard?" he asked.

"Only Garza," Carmen said. "You guys killed the rest. But he's got Cassandra."

The water around January agitated like a washing machine she shook so badly. Most of her blood had long since been pulled into her core in an effort to warm vital organs, leaving her lips blue, her face drawn and tight. Her words came in breathless gasps, punctuated by clicking teeth.

"Whhy ddiid hhhe sstopp sh . . . shooting?"

"Not sure," Cutter said. He felt guilty for being so warm in his own dry suit. "Could be he's trying to draw us all into the open."

"Sssooo ccold," January said to no one in particular.

"It won't do any good to haul you up if he just shoots you," Cutter said. He didn't say it, but the converse was also true. In a short time, the cold water would do Garza's work for him.

417

Carmen peered over the edge of the deck with wide eyes. "Who are you?"

"US Marshals," he said. "I was helping her work on the boat when you arrived."

"Marshals . . ." Carmen gasped. "Thank God. Garza—he's some kind of cartel boss."

"Why'd he take you?" Cutter asked.

The young woman swallowed hard, trying to catch her breath. She held the vacant look of someone who'd been beaten. When she did speak it came in an avalanche of words and tears.

"I'm not sure," she said. "Something to do with our film. His men stabbed Greg and dumped him in this cove. He shot his own girlfriend, then dumped her in the ocean tied to an anchor to make a point. She was still alive. . . . He wants the media cards from our cameras."

"I heard you mention another card," Cutter said.

"Cassandra—" Carmen stopped, rolling half up on her side, listening. "What was that?"

Cutter strained to hear anything over January's chattering teeth.

There was a metallic thud, a string of Spanish curses, and then the sound of a boat motor sputtering to life. Cutter stuffed the Glock into the pocket of his BC, relieved when he heard the distinctive *clunk* of an outboard being put in reverse. The whine of the motor began to fade as the skiff headed out of the cove.

Moving quickly now, Cutter tried to give January a boost but her grip was simply too weak from the cold to pull herself out of the water. Carmen tried to help, but the flooded dry suit acted as an anchor, ballooning out at the waist and legs and adding at least another hundred pounds to January's weight.

His own blade broken in the struggle with the other diver, Cutter searched January's BC until he found her dive knife.

He looked up at Carmen. "Hold her tight," he said. "Don't let her slip away." Then, to January: "Be as still as you can. I have to make a way for all this water to drain out when we lift you up."

January managed a palsied nod, but didn't speak.

She shook so violently now he was afraid he would cut her instead of the neoprene—which caused him to waste precious seconds as he ripped two long gashes in the suit from her hip down to her ankles.

With the threat of getting shot gone for the time being, Cutter pitched his mask up on the deck and then towed January to the small swim step at the stern. He wiped the salt water from his eyes and looked up at Carmen. "Get down on your knees and grab her vest to keep her from floating away while I climb on the boat."

Cutter jettisoned his fins and vest, clipping his BC and tank to a cleat before putting both hands flat on the platform and pressing himself up. Every second counted now, and he planted both feet against the rail as soon as he was onboard. Bending his knees, he stooped to grab January by both hands and then fell backward into a seated position. Water drained from the slashed dry suit as she sloshed onto the deck on top of him belly to belly.

Carmen rolled her into a sitting position and peeled off the neoprene hood while Cutter reached for the pistol he'd stuffed into his BC.

The skiff was almost to the mouth of the cove. Cutter had come in by truck, and though he could see green trees across the open water, had no idea if he was looking at a smaller island, or a piece of Prince of Wales. Whatever it was, it was thickly forested, and Garza would have little trouble disappearing if Cutter allowed him much of a head start.

He touched Carmen's arm to make sure he had her attention. "Do you know anything about hypothermia?"

She shook her head. "A little."

Slow is smooth and smooth is fast, Cutter said to himself, repeating the gunfighter's mantra. It would do January or Cassandra zero good if he moved forward in a panic, crashing ahead too quickly without thinking things through.

"Okay." He forced himself to take a deep breath. "We have to get her warm." He set the pistol on the deck and peeled the dry suit off January's ashen shoulders and down around her waist. The gashes he'd made in the legs made the rest easy and she was soon stripped down to nothing but her underwear. Bloodless from the cold, her flesh was a deathly blue gray.

Carmen recoiled at the mastectomy scar.

Cutter gave a slight shake of his head, signaling Carmen to get past it. He pulled January to him, chest to chest, her head resting on his shoulder. Her cheek was ice cold against his neck. He rubbed her shoulders vigorously in an effort to get the blood flowing.

January's lips fluttered against his skin. "I . . . had vvvvisions . . . of this m . . . moment b . . . bbbeing . . . d . . . different," she said, loopy from hypothermia.

"We're going to get you inside and crank up the heat." Cutter nodded to the door so Carmen would go ahead.

January attempted to get her legs under her but she seemed to be without bones. Without Cutter's assistance, even sitting up was impossible.

"C . . . Cassandra?" she said, coming out of her stupor enough to realize the girl was missing.

"Garza took her," Cutter said.

"Sh . . . shhit!" January said. "Ffforget ab . . . about m . . . me. I'm ggonna die anyway. . . ."

Carmen turned at the door. "Don't say that!"

"You're not dead until you're warm and dead,"

Cutter said. He lifted her like a child. Too cold even to hold on, her arms trailed downward. Her head lolled against the chest of his dry suit.

Cutter followed Delgado into the cabin, glancing over his shoulder as he stepped across the raised threshold. Garza and Cassandra were nearing the mouth of the cove. "What's across the narrows?" he asked, as much to keep January talking as to find out the answer. Whatever was over there, he'd find out soon enough. They walked past the salon, down the steps to the V-berth.

"Islands," January whispered as he lay her out in the blankets. "Lots . . . of islands."

Carmen looked at Cutter. "Tuxekan is north of us," she said. "Hecata Island is west. We shot some footage out on Hecata because of the caves. There are tons of them, sinkholes too, hidden in the moss and shrubs. One of our guys ended up with a compound fracture in his leg. There's a gypsum mine over there, and an airstrip."

"Got it," Cutter said, turning up the thermostat on the wall heater, then pointing at the pile of blankets in the V-berth. "You need to get in there with her," he said. "Warm her body skin to skin."

"I know," Carmen said, already peeling off her shirt.

January managed to lift her hand a few inches, summoning Cutter.

"C . . . Cassandra . . ."

"I'll bring her back," Cutter said. He leaned in

close so only Carmen could hear. "She may fight you a little, say she's starting to feel warm. Don't believe her. She's still shivering so that's good. But you need to make sure her core temperature comes back up. She can't do it without you."

"Okay." Carmen nodded. "Maybe Garza'll step into a sinkhole and break his leg. It'll make it easier for you to arrest him."

"Maybe," Cutter said, heading up the stairs without looking back. He peeled off the dry suit, slipping into his jeans and pulling a T-shirt over his head before sliding the Glock into the holster on his belt. The Xtratuf boots went on quickly.

Garza was a diminishing black dot at the mouth of the cove by the time Cutter made it out to the deck and hopped down into *Tide Dancer*'s skiff.

He'd seen the nasty burn on Delgado's arm, the hateful bruises on her body when she'd undressed to warm January. Members of a cartel did nothing without orders from their boss. His men were now dead, and that boss was hiding behind a little girl.

The outboard started on the first pull. Cutter cast off quickly, pointing the bow toward the mouth of the cove.

"No," he thought. "Broken leg or not, an arrest really isn't in your cards."

Manuel Garza sat on an overturned bucket at the back of the skiff with the throttle twisted all the way open. The little outboard caused the aluminum boat to fairly fly across the water. The girl lay curled in a ball on the floor, playing dead. He'd gone due north out of Kaguk Cove, at once astonished and elated when he saw no one following. Whoever had shot at him was apparently happy to let Garza take the girl to save his own skin.

Garza had no real idea where he was going, just away. He didn't have nearly enough fuel to take the skiff back to the mine and his aircraft, pointing it instead in the general direction of civilization. There would be other boats there, larger ones that he could commandeer and take around the bottom of the island. It would be an easy thing to slip away on his private jet before the authorities were any the wiser. If the idiot Bean was any indication as to the locals, then procuring a larger boat should not prove too difficult—especially when they saw his little girl was hurt. Thankfully, the dull child could not speak, making his job all the more easy.

Garza worked his way out of the cove and past a small bay, rounding a larger point before turning southward. Sun dazzled the choppy surface as he left the protection of the eastern mountains. He raised a hand to shield his eyes, searching for one of the many fishing boats that would be out after the storm. He'd seen dozens of them on the water when they'd flown in.

He glanced down at the child in the bottom of his boat and wished she were awake to witness the brilliance of his escape plan. There was always a chance that the people back in Kaguk Cove might call for help on their radio. Garza shrugged, consoling himself with the fact that there could not be more than one or two policemen on this little island—and they had most certainly never had to deal with anyone as committed as him. Still, it was an issue. Other boats would hear any radio broadcast—and be ready for him. Everyone in Alaska carried a gun. Perhaps a fishing boat would not be the best answer. . . .

The airplane was a little over a mile away when he saw it, coming in low and flying to the northern side of the tree-covered mountains to the west. Fausto had mentioned the existence of another mine somewhere in this vicinity.

Garza smiled. An airplane would make for a much easier escape than a boat—and it was less than two miles across the water to where the plane had disappeared over the mountains. He could easily make it with the fuel onboard.

The taste of escape sweet on his lips, Garza cranked the tiller hard over, bringing the skiff up on its side in a tight, arcing turn back to the north, partially retracing his route. The smile bled from his face when he glanced back toward the mouth of Kaguk Cove. His hand convulsed on the throttle, trying to wring more speed out of the little motor.

Across the narrows, a skiff emerged from the shadows, heading directly for him. Because he'd turned back, it was now less than half a mile away.

CHAPTER 50

Cutter proved to be more skilled than Garza on the open water, working his skiff over the swells so he kept the prop in the water and the boat on step. The cartel boss took the swells head-on, giving himself the perception of speed, but wasting valuable time as he sailed over the top and went airborne to plow into the next wave in the train. A plane passed overhead, presumably toward the landing strip Garza was aiming for.

By the time Garza drove his skiff up onto the beach, Cutter had closed the distance to less than a quarter mile—near enough he heard the scrape of gravel against aluminum and the cavitation of the prop as it kicked out of the water in the shallows. Cutter's gut seethed as Garza dragged the mute child out of the skiff like a rag doll and up the bank toward the dark line of trees.

Traveling at near fifteen knots, Cutter estimated he was two minutes out, plenty of time for Garza to hide in the edge of the forest and pick him off with his pistol before he even got out of the boat. But the odds were high that the cartel boss had spent his adult life in bars and brothels. Cutter had grown up around the water—and as such, he knew something Garza was not likely to know.

Two hundred meters out Cutter pulled the tiller

hard toward him, standing his skiff on its side and making a tight arc to the right. Garza had been heading north so Cutter assumed he would continue toward the airstrip—or whatever his previous goal had been. Running parallel to the shoreline allowed Cutter to get ahead of him. A needle of rocks and scrubby evergreens jutted from the land five hundred meters to the north. Cutter banked the skiff quickly, slowing some as he skirted the point. Out of Garza's sight for now, he reached for the anchor line and twisted it around the tiller, pulling it tight between the rotating throttle and the tiller arm itself. This jammed it open in a makeshift cruise control and allowed Cutter to keep the boat's speed where he wanted it without having to be in the boat. /

He threw the motor into neutral, slowing just enough he could jump out when he reached the shallows. The water was well over his knees and cold enough to take his breath away. Standing beside the rear of the skiff, he pointed the bow northward, and then threw the motor into gear as soon as he was sure the prop could clear gravel. Cutter watched the little boat head out, outboard droning away. Hopefully, Garza would believe it was continuing up the coastline.

Cutter had yet to spend much time in Alaska, but everywhere else he'd been in the world, animals preferred to travel in the cover of a forest. They also liked the ready source of food the water provided, making a trail inside the edge of the trees around any body of water a virtual certainty. Cutter had used these natural highways many times to great effect during his time in the military.

The Glock still in his holster, Cutter trudged up the gravel bank. Keeping his eyes peeled to the south, he took the time to sit on a recently fallen tree and drain the water from his rubber boots—more to minimize the sloshing noise than to gain any comfort. This done, he popped the magazine out of his Glock and confirmed what he already knew. So far, he'd fired six rounds. His extra magazine had fallen off his belt somewhere, likely when he'd changed into the dry suit. Including the round in the chamber, he had a grand total of four remaining shots. He replaced the magazine and slid the Glock back into the holster, getting a mental picture of Garza dragging Cassandra into the woods.

Four shots would have to do.

Cutter was on his feet again less than two minutes after he'd come ashore, crossing the braids of an ankle-deep stream a half dozen times as he worked his way up the incline between the tide line and the forest. A river of cooler air poured down along the streambed bringing with it the smells of mud and mountain. Every stitch of clothing he had on was wet due to his quick exit from the skiff. On any other day Cutter might have felt a chill, but the anger in his belly provided him with all the warmth he needed.

Just before the tree line he found a patch of skunk cabbage. Most of the broad succulent leaves had been grazed down to within a few inches from the soil. Large footprints in the mud and moss suggested more than one bear, a sow and two older cubs from the looks of the tracks. Black bears were not uncommon in the Florida swamps. He and Ethan had tracked many of them with Grumpy—who'd taught the boys not to underestimate the shy and secretive bruins, but to worry more about gators when it came to danger.

The sound of lapping waves disappeared after only a few steps inside the dense forest. Huge Sitka spruce blocked out much of the light, allowing moss and ferns to grow rampant along either side of the trail, and giving the place a timeless, prehistoric feel. The sweet smell of wet ground and decaying wood hung in an invisible cloud among the mottled shadows.

The trail was just where Cutter had expected it would be, up the gravel hill above the patch of skunk cabbage, about ten meters inside the tree line. It was wet from the recent storm, and three sets of bear tracks turned southward—ambling directly toward Garza.

Garza listened to his pursuer's boat continue north, no doubt trying to reach the airstrip and cut him off. It was probably some policeman with an overinflated sense of his own importance in the wheels of justice. Americans were like that, firm in their misguided belief that one puny effort could matter.

The sound of the motor faded, and Garza crashed into the brush, dragging the girl by the arm and cursing the watery grave of Ernesto Camacho for bringing him to Alaska in the first place. Had he been the screaming sort, he would have screamed. Handmade Brazilian loafers were not meant for salt water and mud.

The girl, who had been so docile back on the boat, had become a terror to deal with. There'd been no need to tie her at first, but now she jerked away from him, walking well ahead. He was forced to trot, which made his feet hurt worse and his head feel as though it was about to explode.

He cuffed her hard when he caught up, bringing a trickle of blood from her ear. Instead of crying, she just glared at him, making gurgling grunts and hisses like a wounded beast—and then scrambled to her feet to run down the muddy trail yet again. He would have put a bullet in her head, but the noise of the shot would have given away his location. Instead, he picked up a stone the size of a lemon and threw it, striking the girl hard between the shoulder blades. She fell face first into the trail. When she turned back to him, her face and hair were caked in thick mud. Hateful eyes looked like a demon straight from hell, but she did not cry out.

Garza strode up and hauled her to her feet by the elbow, not caring if he wrenched her small arm from its socket. "Stop running!" he hissed. Fatigue and nerves pressed at his chest, driving away his breath. "Go slowly, or I will break your foot. Do you understand?"

The girl merely blinked at him, as if he were speaking a foreign tongue.

A muffled *woof* drew his attention back to the trail. He turned to find two black bears sitting on their haunches staring at him with pig-like eyes. He had never seen a bear in person, not even in the zoo. They were frightening enough, looking at him as if he were breakfast. He'd always thought they would be larger. These were maybe two hundred pounds, like furry hogs. One of them ran a long tongue over its nose, then chomped its mouth as if tasting the scent of human on the air.

Garza pointed the pistol at this one, wondering if the nine millimeter would even faze such a beast. Perhaps they were small for bears, but they were definitely larger than him, and more heavily armed.

"Go!" he said, his voice shakier than he would have liked. He swallowed, took a deep breath, steadying his nerve. "Go, I say!"

An unearthly growl came from among the ferns to his left, deep and throaty, like a smoker clearing his throat—if that smoker had been four hundred pounds of tooth and claw. Of course, he thought, these small things were cubs. Their mother crashed through the brush and stopped at the edge of the trail. Swatting the ground with her forefeet, she loosed a terrifying roar. Her fur was long and thick, so black as to be almost blue. She *woofed,* and then rose up on her hind legs. The pistol in Garza's hand suddenly felt insignificant and puny.

"Please leave!" Garza implored. He grabbed the girl and held her in front of him like a human shield.

The mama bear barked an order that left no room for argument and the teenage cubs ambled obediently into the brush behind her. She slapped the ground again, making a hollow, otherworldly thud.

Garza stifled a scream, shoving the girl forward. Surely the bear would consider a child to be the better alternative for a quick meal.

Cassandra fell into the muck headfirst. She got to her feet and brushed the mud and sticks off the front of her fleece jacket—and then turned to face the big sow, ten feet away. The bear continued her rumbling growl, rocking back and forth, *woofing,* slapping the ground. Garza felt certain the horrible thing would charge at any moment and tear the girl to shreds. As soon as it did so, he planned to run away as fast as his handmade Brazilian loafers could carry him.

Too far gone to feel fear, the child raised her hands high above her head and clapped them three times. The sow stopped growling and sniffed the air. She turned her great head back and forth as if trying to focus. Cassandra cupped her hands and clapped again, louder this time, standing her ground.

The pig-eyed bear looked from the girl to Garza, as if deciding who it was going to eat first.

A deep voice from up the trail nearly sent Garza out of his skin. The bears were not fazed.

It was the same voice he'd heard back on the boat, the man who'd shot at him from the water.

"Hey, bear!"

The sow *woofed* again at the noise, rising again on her hind legs.

"Don't make me shoot you, bear," the voice said, deadpan. "I have nothing against you. I'm only interested in the coward who'd hide behind a child to save his own skin."

The words were surely meant to soothe the beast, but they had the opposite effect on Garza. He felt as if he might lose control of his bowels at any moment.

The sow dropped back down on all fours.

Cassandra continued to pop her hands together above her head.

"That's a good girl," the voice said, slow and steady. "You go on and take your kids outta here."

Giving one final *woof*, the bear turned and melted silently into the ferns with her cubs.

Cutter braced his shoulder against the trunk of a thick Sitka spruce and watched the bear slip away.

Garza took a half step toward Cassandra. "Come here, child," he hissed.

The front sight of Cutter's Glock was already superimposed over the man's chest. Beyond the cartel boss, he saw not Cassandra but the image of an Afghani girl of the same age.

"Don't!" he said.

Garza froze, then raised both hands, though he retained the pistol.

"Who are you? Some kind of policeman?"

"I am," Cutter said.

"Money is no object to me," Garza said. "You only need look the other way for five minutes."

Cutter didn't dignify the words with a response. He took deep breaths, trying to control his runaway heartbeat. He could see Garza clearly enough, but no matter how many times he blinked his eyes, Cassandra was an Afghan child, a child he'd been unable to save.

"Drop the gun," he said.

Garza let the pistol fall to the ground at once. "I am giving up." He took another step toward the girl.

"Don't!" Cutter barked again.

Garza turned his empty hands back and forth, more at ease now that he'd given up his pistol.

"Now look here, Mr. Policeman, I have done as you ordered. I am now unarmed. At some point you must come out of your hiding place and arrest me."

His hand began to drop slowly, almost imperceptibly. His foot inched toward Cassandra, close enough to reach her now.

Cutter blinked to clear his vision. This man would not put his hands on the girl again.

"So what do you want me to do, Mr. Policeman?" Garza said. His hand dropped even further. "Shall I come to you?"

"Don't!" Cutter said through gritted teeth, a breath before the man lunged for Cassandra.

Cutter's first shot took the cartel boss in the left shoulder, shattering his collarbone. The front sight settled into crisp focus as the trigger reset. The boom of a second and third shot shook the forest in rapid succession on the heels of the first.

Cassandra pressed her hands over her ears and looked stoically at Cutter.

The cartel boss stood teetering for a long moment, blinking, his brain trying to work out what had just happened.

His left shoulder was demolished, but he reached up with his functioning right arm, dabbing at the two holes in the center of his chest. The blood on his fingers convinced him that it was okay to collapse.

Cutter stepped out from behind the spruce and covered the dying man with the last round in his pistol.

He kicked Garza's gun away and then took Cassandra by the hand.

"Sorry you had to see that, sweetheart."

The Haida girl looked up at him and blinked her wide brown eyes. She gave an emphatic shake of her head.

"You told him *don't,*" she said.

Cutter's mouth fell open. "So you do talk."

Cassandra nodded, but she offered no more explanation.

CHAPTER 51

Cutter left Garza where he fell, wondering if the bears would come back before he could return with investigators to recover the body. He used the cartel boss's skiff to get back to *Tide Dancer* and check on January Cross. Cassandra, apparently content to speak no more than her four-word utterance, sat at the bow of the boat and stared into the distance. This was a lot to process, even for Cutter. He could only imagine what it was like for a twelve-year-old girl.

Back on the boat, Cutter panicked when he walked into what he thought was an empty wheelhouse, until he saw January at the navigation station. She had a blanket wrapped around her shoulders, a cup of coffee in one hand, and the radio in the other. Her face lit up when she saw him.

"He's safe," she said into the mic. "And he has Cassandra with him."

Lola Fontaine's voice broke squelch, chiding him for running off by himself. She and Trooper Benjamin were almost there. January had apparently given them a thumbnail sketch of what had happened, including Garza's name. Cutter told them the situation was under control and said he'd fill them in on the rest when they arrived. He had, after all, been involved in a shooting. Broadcasting the details over an open radio channel was the last thing he wanted to do.

January hung the mic back on the bulkhead and looked at him with a narrow eye.

"Garza?"

Cutter shook his head.

"Good," January said.

Cassandra scooped up Havoc and disappeared down the companionway toward the quarter berth. She was still covered in mud and bits of moss, but no one said anything.

Cutter hooked a thumb in her direction and looked at January. He whispered, "Did you know she could talk?"

"She can." January shrugged. "She just doesn't."

It was a testament to the inner workings of January's mind that she didn't ask what Cassandra had said.

"Carmen's sleeping," she said. "Poor thing's been through hell."

Cutter put the back of his hand against her forehead. "How about you?"

January leaned back in her seat and gave a long, feline stretch, her face in a twisted grimace.

"Warm and dead," she groaned, and closed her eyes.

A horn honked from the shore.

"That'll be my partner and Sam Benjamin," Cutter said.

January's eyes fluttered open. "Will you take my skiff and go get them?"

"I'll go," Cutter said, giving her a grimace of his own. "But about your skiff . . ."

Ten minutes later Cutter had retrieved the trooper and Lola Fontaine, depositing them both on *Tide Dancer*. Carmen Delgado came out with January to meet them.

"I hate to talk business," Cutter said, looking up at Carmen as he tied the skiff off a stern cleat. "But did Garza or his men ever mention Millie Burkett?"

Carmen's eyes opened wider. "You think they got her?"

"I don't know," Cutter said. "So, I'm guessing she never came up?"

Carmen shook her head. "I was so busy worrying about myself that I forgot about poor Millie. I guess I always assumed she'd just come home. You still haven't found her?"

"I'm afraid we did," the trooper said.

"I see." Carmen sounded numb, too exhausted to show much emotion.

Fontaine leaned backward against the outside wall. "Sounds like this Garza guy wasn't even here when Millie was taken."

"She's right," Benjamin said. "I had dispatch

check with the guys out at the airport. A Gulfstream overflew the island toward the Triple C Mine well after Millie disappeared. I'm betting Garza and his men were on it. I didn't get anything back on him in NCIC, but Manuel Garza works with a cartel boss named Ernesto Camacho. He's one of your Top Fifteen Most Wanted fugitives."

Lola nodded at Carmen. "Did you and your camera guy shoot any footage of Camacho?"

Carmen shook her head. "We may have. We took some of the boat when it came into the bay, but it was so far away we never would have recognized anyone. We have to blur faces out anyway if we don't get waivers."

"But Garza didn't know that," Cutter said. "It was a simple matter of you being at the wrong place at the wrong time—and Camacho wanting to silence you."

"But Garza said he killed his boss," Carmen said.

Cutter nodded. "Video of Camacho would tie the cartel to the mine. If they're using it to launder money, that's plenty enough reason to kill over."

"But that means someone else murdered Millie Burkett," January said. "And it sure as hell wasn't me."

Carmen gave her a quizzical look.

"Yeah," January said. "Turns out I was a suspect for a while."

"Then who did it?" Lola Fontaine said. "Hayden Starnes?"

"Maybe," Cutter said. "But I'm not convinced. Whoever killed Millie is proficient at knots and is probably left-handed. And he'll use a very specific kind of tool."

"Really?" January raised an eyebrow. She gave a slow nod. "I know who fits that description."

"I do too," Cutter said.

"Care to enlighten us?" Lola Fontaine said.

"First things first," Cutter said, looking at the trooper. "I'm sure you'll want my pistol for the Garza investigation."

"I've never worked an officer-involved shooting," Benjamin said. "But I'm sure you're right."

"Okay," Cutter said. "And we'll need to get another dive team in here to retrieve Greg Conner's body. But before we do anything, I need to go down one more time to find my grandpa's revolver."

The Colt Python lay on top of a flat rock in sixty-four feet of water, as if Grumpy had positioned it there to make it easier to find. It took Cutter longer to put on the dive gear than it did for him to locate the gun.

Trooper Allen came around the island in the Department of Public Safety boat and anchored in the bay to protect the crime scene and await more divers from the Alaska Bureau of Investigation out of Ketchikan.

January and Cassandra rode back to town with Cutter while Carmen Delgado went with Fontaine and the trooper. An hour and a half later, the civilians were all dropped off at the medical clinic. Officer Simeon met the three peace officers down the street from an unpainted plywood house on the outskirts of Klawock. He held a folded piece of paper in his hand.

"Any trouble getting it?" Benjamin said.

The Native officer shook his head. "Surprisingly, no," he said. "Judge Faulkner said a couple of knots and a left-handed Flemish coil was pretty thin probable cause. It was the last little bit of evidence that made him sign off."

"Mind covering the back?" Benjamin asked, looking at Simeon.

"Hell no, I don't mind," Simeon said. "They always run out the back."

"That kind of thinking could get you hired," Lola said. "I'll come with you."

The full name of the man known only as Bean around Prince of Wales Island was Bernard Everett Anthony Norton. Contrary to Officer Simeon's prediction, he didn't run out the back, but answered the front door at Trooper Benjamin's first knock.

Bean wore a pair of loose gray sweatpants and a sleeveless T-shirt, the belly of which was covered in oil and grime. His face was flushed, his wispy hair disheveled. The area around his mouth was red as if he'd just rubbed away some lipstick before coming to the door.

Trooper Benjamin handed Bean a copy of the search warrant and walked in before the man could speak.

The smell of sardines and cheap perfume made Cutter decide to leave the door open.

"You the only one in here?" Benjamin asked.

"Just me," Bean said. "What's this all about?"

"How about we make everybody a little more comfortable?" Cutter said, turning Bean around and handcuffing him behind his back. He set the man in a wooden chair in the middle of the open living room while the trooper contacted Simeon on the radio and told them it was secure and to come inside.

Cutter snapped on a pair of latex gloves and walked straight to the workbench in a small room off the kitchen. "Got it," he said, holding up a flat wrench used to build AR-15 rifles. It had the perfect number of cutouts to match the wounds in Millie Burkett's head. He passed it to Fontaine, who'd come up behind him. She held it to her nose.

"Smells like bleach," she said.

Bean's eyes flitted around the room, following the movement of the searchers. "It gets dirty," he said. "I clean it sometimes."

"With bleach?" Simeon said, rolling his eyes.

"Doesn't matter," Cutter said. "We have the tool to match to the marks left in the victim's skull."

Benjamin took custody of the murder weapon and read Bean his rights while the rest of the group continued their search.

Fontaine stepped back from a chest of drawers and held up a pair of black satin panties. She looked at Cutter and whispered, "Are you thinking what I'm thinking?"

"Hey," Cutter said. "If a guy wants to wear ladies' drawers that's his business, but people have killed to keep lesser secrets hidden."

Simeon's voice came from the bathroom. "I got a video camera!"

The writing on a piece of gaffer's tape identified the camera as belonging to the *FISHWIVES!* production company and on loan to Millie Burkett. A short review of the video revealed an almost unrecognizable image of Bernard Everett Anthony Norton cavorting around on the deck of Ernesto Camacho's boat dressed in a lady's nightgown.

"Why didn't you toss the camera?" Simeon said, shaking his head.

"I just like to watch it sometimes," Bean said, letting his chin fall to his chest.

EPILOGUE

Justified or not, Cutter's shooting had to be investigated—and being the subject of such an investigation is only slightly less excruciating than being the victim of the shooting itself. Chief Jill Phillips was unable to fly because of her advanced pregnancy, but she sent the operational supervisor to Prince of Wales Island to look out for the best interests of her deputies on the ground. The US Marshals Service General Council and Office of Professional Responsibility asked the Alaska State Troopers to do an independent review of the circumstances surrounding the deaths of Manuel Alvarez-Garza, Luis Sandoval, and Fausto Rodriquez. Investigators from Anchorage along with a blustery Sergeant Yates from Ketchikan asked Cutter to do a walk-through of the incident. They watched with keen interest as he took them through the choreography of what had happened underwater and then on Heceta Island with the bears.

Cassandra had not said anything since her four words, which only served to bolster Cutter's case since it made her look even more like she'd needed saving. January and Carmen both corroborated Cutter's timeline of the events in the water and added plenty of pathos of their own.

Three days after the shooting, the ABI investigators shook Cutter's hand. Though they didn't discuss their findings, it seemed clear that any recommendations to the prosecutor would be in his favor.

"NHI," Fontaine said, as she walked out of the trooper post with Cutter. It was almost six in the evening and the low sun stretched their shadows across the parking lot. The Polynesian woman's long, black hair had escaped its bun and hung thick around her shoulders. Somehow, she'd found a flower to stick behind her ear.

"Pardon?"

"NHI," Fontaine said. "No Humans Involved. Makes things much easier when all the bad guys are so . . . well, bad."

"Maybe a little," Cutter said, thinking she was right, and wishing she wasn't. Killing a man shouldn't ever get easier, but it did.

Gerald Burkett had been able to bond out on his own recognizance, while Kenny Douglas remained in jail. Officially in federal custody, Hayden Starnes would fly back to Anchorage the following morning with the operational supervisor and Fontaine since she hadn't been directly involved in the shooting.

Cutter looked at his watch. "I'm going to head down to the harbor for a bit and say good-bye. You can come along if you want."

Sam Benjamin was about to get off shift, so

there was not much chance of that. That also explained the new hairdo.

Fontaine shook her head. "The chief did tell me I'm supposed to keep you from throat punching anybody until we get home. But you should be good at the harbor without a Jiminy Cricket."

Cutter nodded toward the trooper post and waved at Sam Benjamin.

"Maybe I should be your conscience, Deputy Fontaine," Cutter said.

"Deputy Teariki," she corrected. "Think I'll go back to my maiden name before headquarters sends the new creds. And don't worry about me, boss. My people were known to eat our enemies until the Christian missionaries sailed in and told us we were naked heathens. Thanks to them, we got heaps of conscience."

Cutter found January in the South Harbor. Carmen Delgado was helping her carry groceries and other provisions onboard *Southern Cross*, the Westsail 32 that January had purchased the day before.

Cutter stood on the dock looking at the shippy little double-ender. It was older, built sometime in the seventies, but the furled sails looked crisp and white. The teak bowsprit and toe rails glowed in the long light with a recent coat of varnish. The cockpit was small, meant for open water cruising, so Cutter kept out of the way and handed the women canvas bags of food out of the trolley they'd rolled down from the parking lot.

He passed a cardboard flat of canned fruit salad across the lifelines to Carmen Delgado. "Are you going with her?"

"I wish," Carmen said. "I'm not as brave as she is. Anyway, I've got to stick around here until the network can send someone to take over for me."

"Take over?" Cutter said. "I thought *FISHWIVES!* was your baby."

"It is," Carmen said. "I mean, it was. I don't think I can stomach what the show's turned into. Fitz Jonas kicked his wife out and now she's living with one of my camera guys. The network says it makes for great television drama, but I just think it's sad. I still get 'created by' credit so I make money as long as the show's successful, even if I'm not the executive producer. That frees me up to explore some other ideas—maybe something about drug cartel violence." She looked over her shoulder at January. "Or badass breast cancer survivors."

Carmen's cell phone rang. She spoke for a moment, and then returned it to the pocket of her fleece jacket. "Sorry," she said to January. "Svetlana is having a fit about her wardrobe. Before *FISHWIVES!* came to this island wardrobe was whatever they put on in the morning, and now . . . Anyway, I gotta run."

She gave Cutter and January each a hug in turn,

449

promising to stop by the next morning, and then trotted up the dock toward her car.

"So," Cutter said, sitting in the cockpit of January's new purchase in his stockinged feet. It didn't matter that he'd saved her life, she wasn't about to let him on her boat wearing boots with black rubber soles. "You're really going to do this?"

January sat down beside him, groaning from a long day of double checking systems and provisioning the sailboat. She closed her eyes and leaned her head back, catching the last few rays of the sun as it set across the bay. "You've been around me for what, five days now?"

"Is that all?" Cutter mused. "Seems like longer."

"It's long enough for you to learn that I'm not much of a people person. I'm rude, and crude, and if you ask the film crew, they'll tell you I've got a flaming temper. I mean, I can get along with maybe five or six people in the entire world—and even you guys would get tired of my foul mouth and bad attitude before a week went by."

"I'm glad you included me in the list," Cutter said.

"It's a hell of a lot safer for civilization if I get away from it for a while. So, I figure I got two choices," she went on. "I can string up a blue tarp out near Blind Bob, or I can cut the dock lines and come to grips with my bitchy demons while I'm safely out at sea. I think my sailor dad would be a lot happier if I did the boat thing instead of turning hobo. I've had my eye on this beauty since the 'For Sale' sign hit it."

"You're thinking Hawaii?"

January shrugged. "I'm thinking south, then west. That's about as far as I've gotten in my planning. Cyclone season is just winding down in the Pacific. Maybe I'll island hop until I find a place I want to wait out the next season."

Cutter tried to imagine her alone on the wide open ocean. "You'll take a sat phone, right—and check in regularly with your parents?"

"Of course," she said.

"I wouldn't mind an e-mail now and again," Cutter said. "Or even a postcard from Bora Bora—so I don't worry."

"You know what I've noticed about you?"

Cutter braced himself. "What's that?"

"You seem to go for birds with broken wings."

"Maybe," he said.

"Well, I'm broken," she said. "There's no denying that. But I wonder if you'd like hanging out with me if I was just plain old January. Sometimes, well-meaning people pick up something injured and try to fix it. That might work with domestic animals—but it does more harm than good with wild things. More often than not, I think, those wild things get panicked at all the attention—and only hurt themselves worse trying to get away."

"Guilty as charged," Cutter said, feigning a tear. "They grow up so fast."

"I'd invite you to spend the night on the boat," she said. "But you seem to have some unresolved feelings for your sister-in-law."

"Sounds creepy when you say it out loud."

"But you don't deny it?"

"Well," he groaned. "I won't spend the night. Let's put it that way."

"Dammit," she said.

"I would, however, cook you dinner in your new galley."

January turned to look at him, eyes brighter. "Something from your double top secret notebook?"

"You bet." Cutter smiled.

January held out her hand, waiting for him to fish the notebook out of his pocket. "It's a good thing you're not spending the night," she said. "I'd cast off while you were sleeping and your ass would wake up in Tahiti."

Cutter was at the docks again by dawn, having spent a good deal of the night looking out across the dark harbor from the deck of his apartment not two hundred meters away from January's sailboat. Walking around the docks and looking at boats was, for him at least, far more enjoyable than just about anything else.

Seagulls squawked and squabbled, fighting

over the tiny baitfish that rose to the surface in the quiet waters of Shelter Cove. A low tide gave the air a slightly fishy smell. The snow-covered peak of Mount Sunny Hay glowed a golden orange with the coming sun.

January had said most of her good-byes the day before, so only Linda, Carmen, Cassandra, and Cutter showed up to see her off. True to her word, Carmen left her camera crews at home—though the departure of the husband-stealing siren would have surely made for some good footage.

Sailboats are inherently quiet, even when under power, and January cast off her dock lines and slipped away in relative silence, the thrum of the Westsail's little diesel engine barely audible above the cry of gulls.

Cutter's phone buzzed in his pocket and he stepped down the dock, unwilling to mar the solemnness of the departure with chatter. He frowned, grumpy that anyone would call him at this hour—until he saw it was Mim.

"Hey," he said, feeling the familiar flush that came over him when they spoke.

"I have an early shift this morning," Mim said. "Thought I'd check in. Hope I didn't wake you."

"Not at all," Cutter said. "I'm stretching my legs down at the docks, just looking at boats."

"Really?" Mim said, sounding almost giddy. "I can't think of anything much better than walking the docks and looking at boats."

ACKNOWLEDGMENTS

Years ago—almost twenty now—I went to Prince of Wales Island with members of the Alaska Fugitive Task Force to track a man suspected of murder who had fled into the woods. We eventually found our man, and I fell in love with the place despite the grisly circumstances (and boy, were they grisly). In any case, the old growth forests and incredibly interesting people made me sure I would someday set a book there.

This is it—and, as always, I had a great deal of help.

My wife, Victoria, listens, reads, plots, and generally puts up with being married to a guy who writes about murder and mayhem. My barber and unofficial publicist, Linda, let my wife and I stay in her vacation home in Florida while I researched the area where Arliss Cutter grew up. My good friend Steve Szymanski introduced me to Ben Mank, who was kind enough to answer my questions about what it's like to be an Alaska State Trooper on Prince of Wales Island.

My friends Molly Mayock, Rob Pollard, Chris Loft, and Shannon Murphy gave me valuable insight and background in the world of reality television.

My buds at Northern Knives in Anchorage, Mike, Lori, and Doug, offer me a great place to sit and talk weapons and mayhem—which I don't get to do often enough.

Though my wife and I took several trips back to Craig and Prince of Wales Island in Alaska, much of *Open Carry* was written on Rarotonga in the Cook Islands—the ancestral home of Lola Teariki Fontaine. The list of good people there is too long to include all of them, but I do want to thank my friends Bill, Mii, Tuakana, George, and Karleen—and especially Karla Eggelton and Halatoa Fua of Cook Islands Tourism, and Jean Mason of the Cook Islands Library and Museum.

The publishing world can be a rough one, but I've been fortunate to work with Robin Rue of Writers House literary agency, as well as Gary Goldstein and the rest of the folks at Kensington Publishing for the last sixteen years.

And of course, a big thanks to all my brothers and sisters with the US Marshals Service who raised me from a pup—you are, and always will be, my family.

Books are
produced in the
United States
using U.S.-based
materials

Books are printed
using a revolutionary
new process called
THINKtech™ that
lowers energy usage
by 70% and increases
overall quality

Books are
durable and
flexible
because of
Smyth-sewing

Paper is
sourced using
environmentally
responsible
foresting methods
and the
paper is acid-free

Center Point Large Print
600 Brooks Road / PO Box 1
Thorndike, ME 04986-0001 USA

(207) 568-3717

US & Canada:
1 800 929-9108
www.centerpointlargeprint.com

ML   JUL   2019